Sketch
7.
10-26-2024

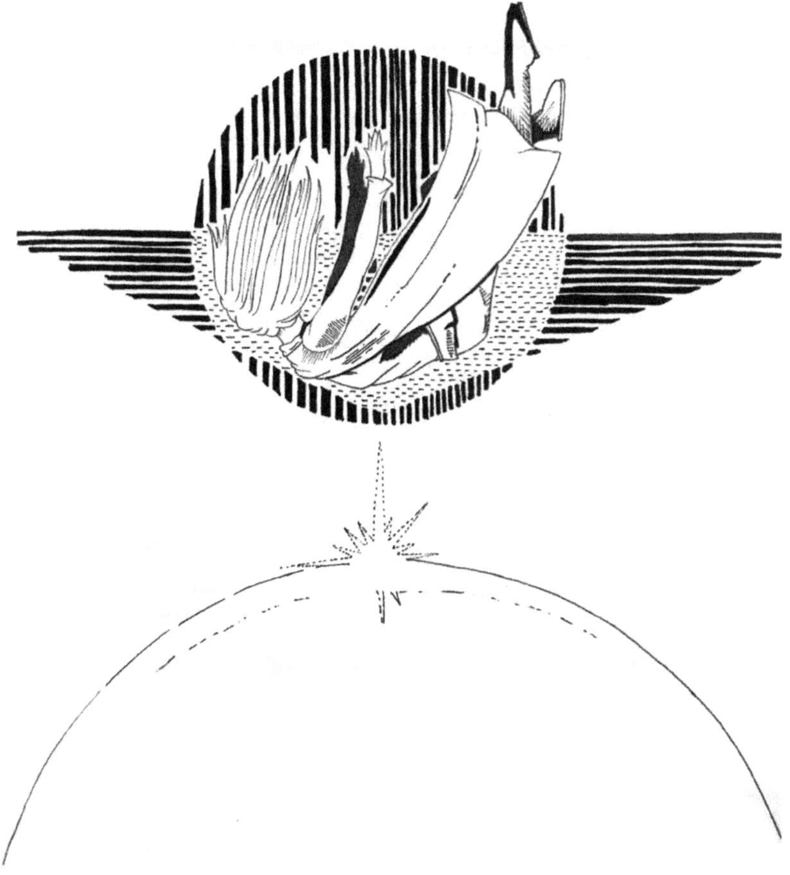

ISBN 13: 979-8-9876227-2-8

**AUTHOR’S NOTE**

***To my family and friends who have continously supported me.***

**GREAT THANKS TO STEPHEN BLACK FROM *BLACK THOUGHTS EDITORIAL* FOR EDITING MY NOVEL.**

@stephenRB4

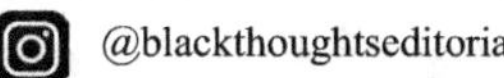

@blackthoughtseditorial

# Chapter 1

IN THE YEAR 1417, at Caen, France, victory was celebrated in a tavern barely untouched by violence and constant turmoil. The soldiers and knights joyously cheered for King Henry the V of England after just winning a battle. They had successfully captured another village and taken the majority of the population hostage as an attempt to halt any eventual uprising against them. The match had been one of many, part of an inevitable war that had started in 1337, years after the death of King Charles IV of France, who had no sons or brothers. His closest male heir had been his nephew, Edward III of England. Yet the succession has been passed to a patrilineal cousin, Philip VI of France. Humiliated and angry, Edward attacked swiftly to reassert his claim over the country, prompting a prolonged conflict that had thus far lasted seventy years. A row that passed on to the sons and other male family members. Lord Adam Bonel was one among many that felt the war was meaningless. His dolorous attitude had been brewing since his first battle.

The young Lord was more of a lad than a man by his appearance. At one and thirty, he still resembled an unseasoned boy, barely entering adulthood, and was neither spindly nor portly. He was shorter than the average Englishmen, with light brown hair cut to his shoulders and held back by a thread. His hands were proportionate to him, but there was some feminine and childish softness to them. It was astounding and entertaining to see him in practice. He moved with a dexterity and proficiency that was equivalent to an old master. Furthermore, his rationality and intellect were beyond his peers—thus, imparting with him an inability to behave like the rest. He did not approve of whoring, indulging, or inflicting suffering on others. He had a code that the other lords rarely observed. A unique quality among his people who said the words but did not follow.

Since youth, he had been taught by his many tutors the glory of dying and killing for one's sovereignty. It was an honor to kill for a king. That was not to be confirmed later. When it was his turn to fight, he had given death's kiss for the first time to another soldier on the field, and he had felt only stupor and paralyzed at how easy it had been in the end. He swore he could hear the steady drip of blood as it slipped off his blade to the muddy ground at his feet. Little by little, battle after battle, his soul changed. Every day he killed to survive and soon found death becoming his continuous companion. It was not long until he did not like who he had become as the war raged on and he suffered in silence.

While his men reveled into the night, Adam was sitting in a shadowy corner hiding with a full cup of ale on the table. He knew he was by himself in his turmoil. Unlike him, his men seemed to breathe in the death and chaos they created. They fed off the blood that was spilled and counted the bodies they had amassed, though, their true natures did not show on the outside as they danced away.
Adam looked at them with disdain. The candle on his table, radiating his features with each pass, gave him a haunted look that promised to cause harm to any that dared to come near him. His thoughts dwelled on the events that had happened earlier in the day. He couldn't help but reminisce on the faces of the tortured souls his countrymen had imprisoned.

At first, the villagers had been rounded together with false promises. Then they had been separated by needs, desire, and personal submission. The few who had a specific look were roped and taken to answer questions on the soldiers who had formerly stayed in the village. A tiny bit of themselves, the little that separated them from animals, was taken and what was left was a formless mass of an unrecognizable shape that withered on the ground after their "questioning" had reached a peak. It was them Adam pitied. They had shrieked and wept. Their eyes, that once had life, now stared at him vacantly. They might as well have died.

"Sir," a soldier called cheerily. Adam jerked back in his seat as a tankard slammed on the table he occupied, portions of its contents spilling out. He glared at the soldier who dared break his solitude. He quickly recognized him as one of the men who had laughed during the interrogations. Just before the soldier could take the empty seat across from him, Adam pulled out his dagger and skewered the table. The blade stood upright dangerously. There were seconds of silence from those who sat nearby, the dagger catching them off guard. The soldier took the hint that he was not welcomed and stumbled away. He stammered out a sort of apology as he tripped on his own feet.

Adam smirked at the clumsy, run-away figure. He then turned his eyes on the others, daring them to say anything to his face. When they had turned away, Adam pulled his dagger from the table and sheathed it. His glee of being alone for the rest of the night was short-lived.

"You look like a man who is lost and forlorn in a forest. Nonetheless, there is a fest. Why do you not participate?" a man uttered from his side. Adam spun in surprise. There had been no one leaning on the wall moments ago. Where had the newcomer appeared from? Adam was curious to know how a peasant had managed to enter the inn. He regarded the man who ventured into his space. He was a poor traveler, evident from the travel-worn cloak, tattered pants, and overused shoes that had seen better days.

The peasant was about average height, lanky, almost deathly pale, with a map of wrinkles that showed he had overcome past hardships. There was a sharpness to his cheeks, teeth, and ears that was unworldly. His hair was black, limp, and dirty. The most compelling feature Adam beheld from the man was the amber eyes that glowed like sparkling jewels, when hit by the candlelight.

"There is no pleasure in losing in oneself," Adam answered with a nod to a group of warriors falling on their feet, laughing uproariously at their irrational behavior. The peasant chortled at their antics and clapped his hands together in joy.

"Then what conviction do you have to continue living if there is no joy?"

"I do have conviction. I have the conviction that my King is the rightful ruler of France, chosen by God himself, and I am on the right path to bring his lands back to order," Adam said, repeating the words he told himself daily as means to convince himself that was the truth.

"Do you really believe that?" the peasant annoyingly inquired.

"He is my King," Adam snapped back. He stared down at the old stranger and warned him, "And if you are as wise as your age, you will be more sensible to keep your mouth shut."

"It is nice to see a young lad, as you, worry for me being."

"What do you want, beggar?"

"Not a beggar," the man corrected. "To think about it, not of your kind neither." Adam scoffed at the lunacy. "Name is Robin Goodfellow. I am an admirer of you sir, may I say."

"You may and good for you. Well, you have seen me and talked to me. Your life goals have been fulfilled as here I am, the knight you admire. Go away."

"I wish to simply ask questions."

"For what intent?"

The stranger answered slowly, "Inquisitiveness of the one they call the White Knight. Do you fear the questions I may enquire?"

Adam became fraught with outrage. Him? Afraid? He eyed the lunatic. He could kill him. Send a message to the others how serious he was to be alone. He mentally shook his senses. He couldn't. He wouldn't be like the others.

"Speak," Adam begrudgingly commanded with a light wave of

his hand.

"Honestly?"

"Aye," Adam said. "Swiftly, I demand— your questions. My bed calls."

"Hmmm. My words will be arduous to speak in this room. Outside would be an appropriate location. What say you?" Goodfellow proposed with a cheeky grin. "The sky is clear and the moon bright." Adam mulled over the move of the locale. He wasn't pleased with the continuous companionship, but if talking to Goodfellow was the only way for him to continue his brooding, there were no other options but to agree. He preferred to be surrounded by his men. If the stranger pushed his luck, Adam only had to order his dismal, and his men would pull the troublemaker outside to do with what they wished. It was a waste of their skills though. He examined the man again. If it came to blows, slaying Goodfellow and throwing him into an unmarked grave would be simple. Adam was a skilled fighter.

Resigned, Adam said, "A fantastic suggestion." The two men walked out with Adam trailing a step behind, his eyes narrowed on Goodfellow's back. He observed the elder's movement, looking for a weakness in the man's form. He concluded that Goodfellow was sprite for his age.

Outside the tavern's relative cleanness, the rest of Caen lost its beauty to the savageness from blood and destruction. The majority of the homes and merchants' quarters had been burned to cinders by the orders of England. The air was pungent with the stench of death and brimstone. The castle, Chateau de Cain, stood with its walls covered in scars. It had been stormed and sacked. Presently, it was a ghost of its former self. Its rooms were now occupied by soldiers of high rank. Due to his recognition, Adam had been invited inside the chateau but had declined. He preferred to sleep on the ground. It was his form of self-punishment— a way to cleanse his soul that blackened with each kiss of death from his blade.

Adam and Goodfellow found a spot not far from the joyous merriment but far enough from prying ears and eyes. They settled in the open with the moon illuminating brightly above them. Impatient,

Adam bitterly demanded, "Speak."

"Straight to the point. No fun. Oh, let's play a game and put a smile on that face."

"Do you determinedly seek to vex me?" Adam hotly retorted, not amused. He rethought his position on killing the fellow.

"Temper. Temper," Goodfellow tutted with that cheeky grin and eyes twinkling with mirth. "A game will make this go faster, is all. Please let us play?"

"No jest for the night," Adam warned. "My bed calls and awaits. Proceed or begone."

"Pooper," Goodfellow mumbled. "Fine. Fine. This man will move forward. Just let me gaze upon the moon for a time. The night is beautiful, and I feel it shall not be in the morrow."

Adam scoffed and watched Goodfellow indeed turn his gaze to the moon. He followed, unconsciously wondering what was terrific about the shining orb. A smile, then, graced his lips when a fable came to mind about a fox lowering himself in a well and getting trapped. The fox, stuck in a bucket, stared down to see the reflection of the moon and convinced himself that he was looking down at a piece of cheese. Imagine! Cheese hanging in the sky held by invisible strings. Or was it part of the mythical orbs that the new fringe philosophers believed?

Subsequently, a melody formed in Adam's mind. It was accompanied by a striking female voice. Curiously, the words came to him clearly, but he knew not what the words meant. Yet, they brought a familiar ache to his chest. It couldn't be that of his mother. His father had a sick delight in reminding him he had been at fault for her death as it happened during his birth.

"*Ex luna scientia*," Adam mumbled. Could the moon give him the answers he sought? It saw all, did it not? It must know the name of the woman who had cherished him as a babe. Notably, perhaps it knew why he was different from the others.

Goodfellow chuckled knowingly. "Knowledge from the moon. Peculiar choice of phrase."

"An old foolish and childish saying," Adam sadly said.

"I don't believe it to be foolish. Reminds me of magic from the world of the old," Goodfellow argued.

"Magic isn't real," Adam sorrowfully spoke. "It is a wonderful thought."

"Not even the hope of its existence."

"No."

"I know what ails you."

"You?"

"Ah, wit. Brilliant. But no. Your problem is you are blind to the other world that exists."

"There is no other, you fool!" Adam shouted. He stood and spun in a circle with his arms spread out. "Look at it, old man! This is all we have! This and nothing more! So, you better get used to it!"

"I see it. It is only broken to the individual who is also broken. Happens to many with good souls."

"I am not— "

"You are good. Humble. You have just closed yourself to protect yourself from the cruelty of the world."

"The world is cruel," Adam rasped. "Better to be used to it."

"Yet we have legends. You are a legend. You are the White Knight. You inspire men to fight. They wish to be you. You who were named by the King."

"Idiots, the lot of them," Adam mumbled in annoyance. He massaged the bridge of his nose. "Fools. Why would they wish to die?"

"Pardon?" Goodfellow asked in confusion.

"I died," Adam explained. "I no longer drew breath. I had left to fly with the angels."

"You jest?"

"The angels didn't want me. Must not have been good enough for them."

Goodfellow choked on his laughter. Adam followed not far behind.

"Probably didn't know what to do with ya."

Adam's laughter died. His eyes glazed as he couldn't help but revisit the battle that had irrevocably changed his view of the world. "I found myself on the ground, lying face forward in the mud. I had just awoken, breathing the fresh air deeply, and the world somber as bodies were being dragged away to be buried. Their swords and armor were taken to be given to the next of kin. I just stood, startling the few men nearby. They ran towards me to see if I needed aid. I, of course, brushed them away and walked from the battlefield. It was then, during my walk, I saw myself covered in blood. I did not know who it belonged to.

"The King heard the day after. I was brought forth to him. He rattled about men seeing me fall after being speared, stabbed, and skewered multiple times. I calmed his mind and confusion. Told him what was seen had been a misinterpretation of what had occurred. That I had not been killed but only knocked unconscious. The King believed me. But word had still spread of my resurrection, and thus I was named the White Knight. From then on, I was placed in front of the battalion. Many thanks to that confounded moniker, I have had an invisible mark on me. I am constantly attacked when the chance comes."

"But did you meet death?"

"They say I did," Adam laughed. He was not foolish to tell the validity of the situation. Why would he say to a stranger that it was his blood that had covered his armor and clothes? He had been killed and that the truth of it would be his execution. Better for it to be a mystery. He wished to speak of it. He wanted to inform the church. Yet, they had lied about what happened after one died. Death wasn't what he was told it was. It had been cold, dark, and empty. Then he had been pulled from its grasp. What was he to be alive once more?

"You are lying, sir," Goodfellow told him. Adam went to deny the accusation, but a raised pointed finger halted him. "Everyone has their secrets. I can see it in your eyes; you want to speak of it. But you can't. Not here. But there is a world you can escape to let your burden go."

Adam pulled away with disgust on his face, hands clenching at his knees, body tensed. "What you say is impossible and unattainable."

"What I say is not," Goodfellow hotly returned, eyes opened wide in stupefaction.

"How? Tell me then."

"Feys. They live in the world hidden from this one."

"Feys?" Adam asked dully.

"Yes!"

"No."

"Yes. Yes!"

"You are out of your mind, old man," Adam said with a dismissive wave.

"They are real. You must have heard of the stories of the great King Oberon and his wife, Queen Titania."

"Children stories," Adam snapped.

"They are not stories. Not fables. They are as real as you and I," Goodfellow tried to convince him again. Adam shook his head. He wanted to believe the fool. He wished for the existence of magic. If there was anything supernatural, there were only the angels and demons. One lived in the sky and the other deep in the ground. Due to his death, Adam had a strong feeling he was of the latter.

"What proof do you have?" Adam taunted with a smirk on his face.

"Me," Goodfellow answered with a mischievous smile. Adam's smile waned as the man in front of him transformed. His eyes enlarged and the pupils glowed a warm ember color. The tip of his ears sharpened into points, his face smoothed slightly, and his skin became translucent. Then a shimmer to his form and an aura emerged that warned Adam that Goodfellow had power beyond his capabilities. What was this man— this thing? "I am Puck."

#  CHAPTER 2 

ADAM JUMPED AWAY and pulled out his dagger to point it at the thing in front of him. "What is your game? What trickery and ruse have you pulled over my own eyes?"

"Seriously," Puck responded. He sat magically on an invisible chair with one leg crossed over the other. He looked as innocent as he could with wide doe-like eyes. His lips quirked up slightly, showing he was in a merry mood.

"What poison have you given me, demon?" Adam demanded to know, his voice rising in pitch. He rubbed both his eyes to confirm what he saw was true. But there it still was. Like many others, he had read of Puck; if true, here the fable was, out from the books of tales, sitting and lacking any signs of current unease or worriment. The same could not be said of him; he was agitated and confounded. Adam pinched his cheeks, slapped his face, and looked for others in hopes of finding the evidence of a jest being played upon him. He could find none.

"Sit down," Puck ordered with annoyance. He had tired of watching the knight pace back and forth. If he had reacted like a lunatic with this news, Puck could only imagine how the other tidbit he learned would be taken. "It isn't a big deal, you know. You act like an evil calamity has struck you down and that the havoc and annihilation of the world are here and now. Calm down, you fool. Get a hold of yourself."

"He tells me to calm down," Adam mumbled to himself, covering his face with both his hands. He stopped his to and fro movement to point at Puck, "This is real?"

"Yes! You have it!"

"It can't be real."

"— and you just lost it," Puck pouted in disbelief. "See me! I am here. I am showing you that my existence is true! How can you not think it is real? That I am false?"

"I died," Adam said to himself with several nods of his head. He lifted a finger as if he had solved a puzzle. "I died. This is hell."

"Honestly?" Puck questioned in wonderment. "You must be joshing?"

Adam ignored Puck. "Yes! I am finally dead! And hell is an endless torment of what-ifs. I am trapped in this dreamworld of war for eternity. Punishment for the lives I have taken. Befitting for a soul like mine."

Puck's mouth gaped open in bewilderment. He closed it and rubbed his chin, looking for the words that would persuade Adam that he wasn't deceased— or in hell. He ran various scenarios in his head; none of them better than the other. To convince a man he isn't dead, one must know death. Puck had never died.

"Is it really that hard to believe who I am?" Puck asked angrily with arms crossed over his chest. He was affronted that a mere mortal didn't believe in him. Didn't accept magic. He needed to find a way to motivate Adam, engage him, and have him help him. He wished not to trap the man to do his deeds, but he could do little. He had traveled the world for a century looking for the right individual to help him. Then he had heard the legend of the saint warrior: The White Knight. The mortal in front of him was a disappointment, but Puck was desperate. One more attempt, then he wouldn't have a choice but to use what he knew. "Why can you not believe?"

"Believe? You wish me to believe in this world? You tell me you are real. If so, where were you then when I needed your kind the most? Where were you when my father berated and beat me for never acting appropriately?" Adam angrily asked. "I called for beings— from any world— and none came to my aid. Fairies don't exist. So, fairy— "

"Fey," Puck corrected. Of course, the knight would jump to fairies. They always were recognized. Yet, there was little acknowledgment to the fey. "What I am. I never mentioned fairies?"

"You sure?"

"Yes! For reasons beyond my own, those pesky little miscreants are widely known and written about. They bite and yet it is them— THEM that is talked about," Puck gabbed. "There is a difference between feys and fairies. Feys are taller. Witter. Cleverer. Craftier. Stunning. Fetching. Suave— "

"I understand," Adam cut in.

"Then you have realized that you are not dead?"

"No. I am dead."

"Agh! You cannot be this bloody stubborn?! What words will it take to get the notion out of your head that you are not part of the living? You are not departed or deceased. You are alive!

"Additionally, I am not a fairy. I am fey. I do come from another world hidden but among this one. One I wish to go back to and only in which you can help me with. I ask, need, for you to take a quest of a lifetime and one that will bring you glory.

"Help this Puck, and off you shall be to the great and magnificent Avalon seen by few mortals. I cannot accompany you, as I have been banished and exiled. For I to go home, an item is needed. During my immediate departure, a key of mine was lost in the chaos. Word came to me that Oberon has it and keeps it in one of his many treasury rooms. It is a family heirloom, a dagger made real, but not seen by eyes if only by light. Just whistle once you are in possession of such fortune, and Puck will hear and bring you back he will," Puck requisitioned with a deranged glint in his eyes and a large smile plastered on his face.

"You are insane, and nothing you say will change my mind. I. Am. Dead."

Puck growled. He had no choice. He had to say the one word that would be his death or his savior. The word that was a secret, a name hidden in the past. A name that told of Adam's true being. "Eve."

Adam's laughter slowed to a halt with wide-open eyes of distress. A pain formed at his— her temple as worry flooded his— her body. He, she, had not seen herself as Eve for so long. A name her father had banned from being spoken until she was at the peak for breeding to another. Luckily, her father had died before he could sell her off.

"Astounding that here one can be executed for acting, or impersonating a man," Puck commented.

"How? How did you know?" Adam, nay Eve, asked with the pitch of her voice becoming to its natural level, feminine. She knew— wait, no— her father had informed her that those that had known her sex were killed by his hands. It was only he and herself that knew what she was.

Eve Ronan Bonel was the only heir and child to the great Lord Henry of the Bonel family. Her mother had died giving birth to her and her father was never able to remarry. Women were wary of him, which grew more when those present for her birth suddenly died in tragic accidents coordinated by her father. The rest of the household, that had not been there to witness her birth, were told lies. As Eve became older, her father hid her womanly figure under tight bandages daily, and she was ordered to always lower the pitch of her voice. Those who questioned her appearance were answered that God had blessed her with an extended youth. It explained the lack of facial hair and rounded face.

Eve had managed to be Adam for years— until now— and she was not pleased as she ran to Puck. She grabbed him by his tunic in blind fury. She showed an unnatural strength that surpassed even the strongest mortal as she easily rose him above her height.

"All who know are dead," Eve growled. "Tell me how you

know, and I promise a quick one." Eve's eyes began to glow eerily in the darkness of the night.

"It can't be?" Puck breathed out.

Centuries ago, there had been children of magic, born of a mortal and a mythical being. Due to their mixed blood, the children had grown to be unstable and dangerous. After so many deaths caused by the hybrids, Oberon had them hunted and killed. He then forevermore made a ruling banning any being from his world from having a relationship with a mortal. Puck wondered who or which being dared to break the rule for Eve to exist.

"What cannot be? What do you know?!" Eve ordered with tears in her eyes that never fell. Her grip tightened furthermore that the tunic started to tear under her hold. She was oblivious to her strength as she internally panicked.

Puck didn't answer. He was in awe. It had been so long since he had laid eyes on a hybrid. He watched the glowing ember turn into a bright red, then tensed as the skin around her eyes darkened. She was dangerous. He stuttered, "Your eyes."

"What?" she asked in confusion. She shook her head and then glared at Puck. "You are trying to distract me. Answer my questions!"

"No, your eyes. Look," said Puck, pointing to a hanging mirror outside of the tavern. Eve released him, and he fell to the ground haphazardly.

She ran to the mirror, and a gasp sprung from between her lips. She prodded her face. Her eyes widened in fear. A cry of relief escaped her as her eyes slowly became ordinary. She thanked the Lord and afterward, her thoughts spun to Puck. Her eyes had never changed before until presently. She could only conclude the fault lay upon Puck.

"You," Eve growled as she faced Puck. She quickly approached him. "What have you done to me?"

"Nothing, Puck swears," Puck answered fearfully. "But...but, if you do as I bid, perhaps on the journey, would you then receive the answers you seek. Puck has heard stories, more like whispers spoken possibly of creatures like you. And— "

*He lies,* Eve's voice hissed at her. Yes, he was lying to her. *Kill him. Consume his magic. We need it.* Eve's eyes began to glow anew, her inner voices urging her to attack.

"And— if you do this for Puck, Puck won't voice to any your secret. Accept the quest for not only Puck's sake but your own," he expertly finished with a flourished and exaggerated bow.

"My sake? Mine! You lie. Your death draws near. What reason is there left for me not to end you now?"

"Yes! Yours! You died. Yes! You did! That is what started it all."

"No," Eve denied fervently. "It is false. I am here. I never died."

Puck continued. "I wager you have gotten stronger. Faster even. You are part of my kind. Part of my world."

Eve continued to deny his words. It wasn't true. Yes, there were times— rarely— where things did not go the way she had wished them. She had swung once, taking out more than one man and throwing them to the ground. She did not tire easily under her armor as she had before and when attacked, her opponent's movements were slower. Yes, she was different, changed. Though that did not mean she was otherworldly. That she was from his world.

*He lies.*

"You lie."

"I can prove it. All you need to do is agree with me...say yes to my quest. If nothing happens, you can kill me. I won't even defend myself."

"Prove it then. I will be your thief," Eve commanded with finality and coldness in her eyes. She knew he was a liar. Once the farce was over, she just needed to pull out her dagger and kill him. She wished there was a way she could leave him alive, but that was not to be. He knew her secret, and she couldn't allow that. She needed to be Adam again the following day.

"Get ready," said Puck smiling. He snapped his fingers, a black hole opened in the ground underneath Eve, and swallowed her up. She screamed, and it was silenced quickly as the hole disappeared. Puck looked around and was glad to see no witnesses. "I hope she likes her look. She did call herself a thief."

# CHAPTER 3

A HOLE OPENED HIGH in the sky with no sound nor fanfare. It was just a dark tunnel that came from the world above. From within it, a woman's body was flung out with the gateway closing right after. She was unconscious and falling to the ground quickly. Her form was surrounded by a black, billowing cloak that covered her body thoroughly to keep her warm from the cold air. Beneath her was a forest. Miraculously, her body not once impacted a tree, and the closer the ground came, her body started to slow down. It slowed enough that, instead of hitting the land, she was gently deposited on the grassy floor.

Eve's eyes were closed as she lay with her limbs sprawled out. There was a noticeable difference in her appearance and state of dress. Her hair had grown longer and been placed in a simple bun held by a leather string. On her face, she wore a mask, dark as night and covering the upper portion of her face. Her tunic had stayed, but her trousers had changed. They were no longer tight or snug. They now hung loosely on her legs, with multiple belts that had individual purposes. Her hands were covered in leather gloves. At her feet, she wore black, cavalier boots that were brand new and unblemished.

At her sides, were two long swords and at her feet a dagger, all three sheathed.

Abruptly, her body came alive. Her eyes opened wide, and she stared into a void that no one but only she could see. Her chest then heaved as she took deep, long breaths. Her body jolted as it rushed to determine what injuries she may have received. She then panicked as her mind worked to remember what had occurred. She only knew she was alive, but she was still disoriented. Still trying to piece where she was and who she was.

She flipped onto her hands and knees as the coughing worsened. An object of unknown properties rose from her stomach to her throat, making it difficult for her to breathe. Tremors wracked her body violently. Not long after, she expelled the food she had previously eaten. Afterward, there was only bile left to spew that turned into empty gags. With nothing left, she fell to her side. She felt weak and tired. It was as if she hadn't slept for many moons.

She mentally massaged her eyes as pain bloomed at her temples. She remembered the sounds of cheering, drunken idiots, talking to a villager, and a hole opening underneath her. Then, nothing else. Wait, the villager. *He was a silly-looking fellow... What was his name again? Goode? No! Good...fellow...*

*PUCK!*

Puck was fey. He had spoken truthfully. He had just snapped his fingers, and now she was— *Where am I? Is this his world?*

A groan escaped her lips. "Bloody hell," she rasped in annoyance. She relaxed and closed her eyes to just listen to the world. The forest seemed to be nothing different. Same sounds, she thought happily as she slowly became drowsy. Her peacefulness was broken as something poked at her nose. She opened her eyes, disgruntled as it continued. At first, there was nothing to see. Then, there was for a fleeting moment she noticed quick blinking and fluttering illuminated living beings.

"What is that?" She squinted her eyes on the tiny thing. It was like nothing she had seen before. Her eyes widened as one of the creatures flew down and landed on her nose. She found it weighed almost nothing.

The creature was a tiny, glowing person with translucent, butterfly-looking wings. Its clothes were made from foliage and flowers. When she noticed its hair, Eve couldn't help but grin at its turbulent state. She guessed it was not pleased with her actions because the little thing started to make faces at her, showing off its sharp, little teeth. Eve blew air at it mischievously, which caused the tiny thing to lift away. It shook its fists angrily at her. She swore it was calling her all sorts of names that were not kind, but its squeaky voice just made it adorable. As its tirade continued, Eve started to laugh. It narrowed its eyes and swopped down. The bugger decided to latch on to the tip of her nose, biting.

"Yeouch!" Eve cried. She was surprised to find the creature had formidable teeth and swung at the beast with her right arm, forcing it off her nose. It didn't fly that far away. She rubbed her injured appendage to soothe the pain. Then, a gasp escaped her as the creature came back in a flurry. It attacked her with its little hands, scratching. Tired of its game, the blasted thing pointed its little finger at her mockingly, laughing. Soon it was joined by others. Not finished with their antics, they pelted Eve with pebbles before finally flying away into the forest. She wondered if those evil, winged creatures were the fairies Puck had angrily spoken of. If they were, he had been right about them. They liked to bite.

Eve once more tentatively touched her nose. It still throbbed. If she saw another fairy, she was going to kill it. Before she could act on such a thought, she needed to move. With little grace, she sat up with a loud groan. Her bones creaked and cracked in protest as if they had been overused. She rubbed her eyes. It was then she noticed the difference in her state of dress. The bandages and wraps that she wore to hide her womanly figure were no longer present. Instead, there was a lace-decorated garment that now supported her breasts. Her tunic had been fitted to her size and customed to her body. It was even slightly open to show her cleavage. She attempted to close the blouse more but was unsuccessful. She felt her new wear was inappropriate and one she would have never dared display in public. For this,

Puck was added to her death list with the fairies for giving her such a new outfit. The rest of her dressing, Eve did not mind. Her primary issue— other than the tunic that belonged on a harlot— was the mask.

This was the first time for her to wear a mask which outraged her sensibility. Only those with villainous hearts wore such articles of clothing. She was not a villain. She was a knight. She lived by a code, old as it was. She was determined not to wear this mask any longer, even though her purpose in this world was to be Puck's thief. Her fingers eagerly searched for the edges of the disguise to find that nothing held it in place. No buckle, no strap, nothing. So, she pulled on just the borders themselves, but the mask did not budge. She cried in frustration startling the animals nearby as she attempted to pull the guise off repeatedly. Each attempt was unsuccessful. Exhausted, she gave up, scratching the mask in self-loathing at her weakness.

She took a deep breath, needing to calm herself. Her first steps in this world would be determined by a plan that she had yet to make. *What do I know? What do I do?*

Eve began to pace, worrying her bottom lip as she contemplated the past events. It amazed her how much had happened in a short amount of time. Yes, it started when she died, and if Puck had spoken truthfully, she had been changing since then. Yet, it was him that had brought up her secret in an attempt to blackmail her into doing his deeds. She was going to kill him but at the time, feeling there was nothing to lose, had given him a chance to prove himself of his existence— the existence of feys. She was positive that nothing was going to happen, but then he had snapped his fingers, and the ground had opened underneath her feet. She fell, became unconscious, and woke up in a world that was allegedly not hers. She was also dressed as a thief— which she admitted she technically was— and left in the middle of nowhere with no map to assist her. She was pleased to find Puck had at least gifted her with weapons. Weapons that weighed less than her own. She strapped them on appropriately, in case she was attacked, and started to search for a way to find where she was and if she was in another world.

She looked around. The forest was familiar, but at the same

time, not at all. It looked like every other forest she had traveled. The only way she could confirm her location was to walk in a single direction and hopefully find a village. The village would prove if she had been poisoned and moved or was in a new world filled with magic. She was not pleased with the unknown distance she was to travel, but that was the only way she would determine her location. She would have to keep her eyes open for water and food to survive, wherever she was heading.

As she walked, she realized there was a calm beauty and mystique to the forest that she had not paid attention to while traveling with company. Now, with time on her hands, she was able to take in all of its mysteries and wonders. She had forgotten there was a harmonization to the creatures. Also, the silence in the forest allowed her to think about her life and the future. She knew that once she was done with the quest, Puck would send her back home. All she could look forward to were more deaths, either hers or ones she inflicted on others. Then, if she survived the war, she only had to once more worry about her secret and her extended family finding out. She doubted she would be asked to stay in the magical world she was supposedly in, as she would be stealing from a well-known magical king. She could make a plea, but again, she was Puck's thief. Or, if she was lucky, she would be killed by the said king. Then she would just be another missing soldier. She shook her head. *Pity. It isn't me to run with my tail between my legs,* she thought to herself glumly as she continued hiking through the forest.

She stopped walking. Once she reached any civilization, she would need to put more thought into her actions. She would also need to find assistance to get back home or directions to Oberon. But before she could, a single question presented itself to her: When did the forest become silent?

She had been so deep in thought she had not realized how much time had gone by. The sun had been hidden slightly by the trees, when her adventure had started. Now, it was overhead. How she had not noticed the changes and the gutted deathly silence worried her. She needed to get out of her head and quickly. The forest now gave off waves of foreboding. It was so eerie that it sent shivers up her spine, which raised the tiny hairs at the back of her neck to attention. Additionally, she was uncomfortable that her breathing was the only sound. Worse, it was unnaturally loud.

In an instant, the stillness was broken. The pebbles vibrated and jumped from the ground. From the tress came many frightened animals. Even the predators were stampeding. They all ran past her with looks of fear on their furry faces. The last creature flew past and, once more, there was quiet. It was short-lived. The ground once more shook vehemently, and soon her body moved with the trembling as she worked to keep herself in a standing position. She was overcome with the urge to run away; the primitive instinct hidden deep inside instead caused her to be in a paralyzed state, leaving her mind to rampant with chaotic fear at the unknown that was progressively coming closer.

Further out in the distance, where the forest ended, Eve witnessed a storm of dust peeking through the foliage. The storm did not settle when it hit the tree line. Instead, it became stronger. The trees, roots and all, rose up in the air and dropped one by one to the ground. They crashed with a symphony and resounding thud that rang and reverberated. Her heart jumped in sync with the impacts. As they quickened, so did the knowledge that her end was finally near if she didn't hide.

After her death, she had rushed to meet Saint Gabriel. She ached for the end of her life with her arms wide open like a fool and ringing a bell. It was her attempt to prove there was nothing wrong with her, but not this way. Not where she did nothing or could do nothing. It was pitiful and despicable to die without fighting back. She was suicidal, not idiotic.

"Come on, move you fool," she mumbled harshly to herself. "This is not how we die." She gave one last mental shove and managed to stumble away to hide behind a tree. Her movement was just in time as ugly, ghastly beasts emerged. They swung their wooden clubs with iron spikes. On them, and hanging from the tips, was torn flesh or skin. Eve could not be certain from a distance she was at. Disgusted, a gasp flew from her mouth, and to muffle the sound, she clapped her hands on top.

The creatures stood still and what she saw was astonishing. A wonder. And...

Bloodcurdling.

She counted seven filthy, large, and imposing monsters that reeked of something fierce. The stench of them towered above the smell of her own men who had walked through wet and humid lands, wearing their equipment and weapons. Her men were roses compared to these brutes. She wondered if any of these mythical savages ever became sick from their lack of hygiene.

The monsters stood almost as tall as the trees that they had not yet destroyed. If Eve had to guess, they were about the height of the pilaster buttress that supported the castle walls of Dover. Their skin was a dry green with patches of muck and grime that covered the bulk of their frame and the little clothing they were clad in. Each of them wore a leather vest that varied in design but stretched tightly over their chest. Kilts hanging from their bulging hips were held by vast belts. Their feet were protected scarcely by meager, thin, and small sandals.

"I smell somethin'," growled the only monster, with a cone-shaped helmet that lay heavily over his eyes, as he sniffed the air. His head swiveled in her hidden direction. He must have been the leader. Instead of looking for an escape, Eve was surprised by a single fact she did not think was possible: *I...I can understand them.*

#  Chapter 4 

EVE HAD SURVIVED longer than most would in her world from the problems she had that had been passed down to her by her father's greed. She had managed this feat by the knowledge she had accumulated from reading, observations, and words from the mouths of others. She made sure she never entered a situation without knowing some information about the land, the people, or the enemies. Knowing at least one of those kept her and her men alive. The situation she was now in was not to be the case.

She wished she could push the lack of information she currently had onto Puck's shoulders. It was partly her fault. Yet, who could blame her for not believing that magical beings existed? Believing in the Almighty was difficult enough as she was surrounded by greed, corruption, and death daily. Her belief in Him was kept in place by the need to keep herself grounded and help her have a sense of a goal of being a good person as best she could. Without Him, she would have gone insane so long ago. She also accepted that sometimes you had to have something to believe in during the dark moments.

Her lack of knowledge now left her with the biggest unanswered question; well, one of many questions, how could she understand these beings. At least at home, the languages she knew she had studied. She doubted her linguistic education had included these monsters. However, poor and weak, a single reason could explain the ability to understand beings she had never met. Puck had mentioned the possibility that a part of her was from his realm. Perhaps, her blood stored the languages— a laughable postulate.

Momentarily, a crazy idea blinked into existence. Mayhap Eve should walk up to the monsters and ask them the questions she had. One specific question nagged at the back of her mind: if they had witnessed her form of arrival. They had come to her location rapidly. She doubted that was a coincidence. At the rate the forest animals had sprinted away from danger, the monsters had been nearby. The problem she was viewing was that they looked more ready to eat her than kindly tell her any information. She could tell they were hungry by the drool leaking from the tips of their protruding fangs. They must have been hunting when she had arrived and saw a tasty morsel that differed from what they usually ate.

Eve narrowed her eyes. They didn't look that intelligent, honestly. She could take them or trick them into letting her go. They had the look of one who was happy with the simplest of goals. All they needed was to eat, fight, and sleep. That was their purpose of living. She could be wrong. It would be safer to sneak away, which in itself was going to be difficult. They could smell her.

Their excellent sense of smell had her groaning on the inside as helmet-head sniffed the air again. "I know this smell. It has been years. It was when I started to learn how to kill. But I know it."

"What is it?" the others asked.

"A mortal."

"They are not real," one scoffed.

"A story," another one spoke out.

"No," the leader corrected. "They exist. And tasty. It is young. Female."

"Female!" the rest, but one, groaned with long and exaggerated misery.

The one who had not joined his brothers scratched the little of his hair. "You sure it is female? Are not the mortals all the same?"

"You dunderhead! Females have breasts," the widest of the group explained.

"But you have breasts."

"I do not!"

"What do you call those then?" the dimwitted one asked, pointing at the other's chest.

The fat monster's mouth opened and closed, speechless. Instead of replying, the brute decided not to defend himself with words and bellowed a war cry. Then, he rose his club over his head and started to swing it in circles. He took significant steps to the idiot and attacked. A chortle almost escaped Eve's lips in amusement as the one attacked screeched in fear. He clumsily lumbered away, tripping on his feet but not falling. The others laughed and decided to interfere with the fight. They pitied the smaller one, so they held back the larger one who cursed at them for being in his way.

"Stop it! The lot of you! We have not had a proper morsel for years. Mortals are a delicacy," the leader said, licking his over-large lips, his eyes glazed in bliss as he recalled the last mortal he had eaten.

Another monster with a haphazard goatee said, "But to eat a lowly female. The ones here rarely have any meat on them."

"They are different," the leader insisted. "More tenderized meat on their bones."

"But how many will this *female* feed?" the smallest, and youngest, of the group asked. An awkward silence followed the question as they all looked at each other in confusion. Then, they started to argue about who deserved to eat the mortal. Eve blocked their loud voices and the repetitive arguments happening between them.

She was curious about what the leader had said. He— and possibly others— had been to her world, or people from her world had been to this one. When had this occurred? His words explained the folklore and stories that the generations in her world had passed on. At one time in history, these creatures had existed with her people. Still existed and how much and in what manner was evident by

Puck's presence. How many like Puck had been punished and banned from their world? What even had occurred that had separated her world from this one? And why had these monsters been forgotten in the stories of old?

Eve needed to know and started to listen once more to the quarrels of the monsters. They had unintentionally given her the information she had not had before and more questions. There was a chance the monsters could share more knowledge. Though it was not going to happen anytime soon as the dimwitted one shouted, "Then he is a female!"

"I am going to kill him. Don't halt me. It is the last time he says I have breasts!"

"We all have breasts," a short one angrily spoke, and he looked to Dimwit, "but it is different for women. And they do not have our great manhoods."

"My sister does," Dimwit informed him seriously and quickly.

It was over. A massive and unrestrained snort of laughter slipped past Eve's lips. Her mind ran rampant with imagining on what kind of "sister" this creature had. It was these images that had her breaking her silence. Her hands were too late to obscure and hush them.

The tree she had been hiding behind was pulled out of the ground and thrown at an unknown distance. The bushes were swung away by the large hands— the rest of the foliage torn away to make a circular clearing around her.

Her laughter decreased to giggles and then silence as she found herself surrounded. A dark, creeping fear filled her being as her eyes jumped from one monster to the next trying to find a weakness in them. That fear was short-lived. She received a proper glimpse of the fat monster's torso. She laughed. Dimwit had been correct. The fat one's breasts were pretty big, covered from full view by a small vest that pushed them together and made them more prominent. Her laughter grew at the thought that women in her world would kill to have such assets.

The fat one was not amused. "You wench!" he snarled, raising a foot.

Eve, still laughing, looked and watched as it came down upon her. She lowered into a crouch, before his foot could crush her, and rolled out of the way. It was not graceful as she had planned. Instead of immediately getting up on her feet, she fell on her rear. She rolled her eyes, annoyed with herself that she had destroyed her image of not being weak. Not even the large-breasted monster's jiggling body would distract the others from her sloppy movement.

"Clumsy bitch," the fat one growled. She glared at him and threw the closest rock, aiming for his head but missing. "I believe she can understand us, boys."

The leader laughed," Can't be. Mortals are savages— animals. They have no respect for nature."

Eve grabbed another rock and this was time successful in her aim, hitting the leader on the head. "Compared to you, we are roses." His eyes opened wide comically at her defense. He lowered his face to her level and sniffed, pulling back with apparent disgust on his face.

"She is touched, she is." The others proceeded to mumble hateful words at her, taking steps away as if she was tainted and afflicted with a deathly illness.

Eve stood and pulled her sword out. She pointed it at the leader, eyes narrowed. He could smell the difference in her heritage. How did it smell? What did he mean when he said she was "touched"? *I need to know, and I will beat it out of them if I have to. It might cost me my life, but I am tired of being in the dark.* "Tell me! What does it mean? How am I— touched?!"

"You don't know," sneered the leader laughing. The others followed, laughing with him. Then, helmet-head rose a hand. There was silence. "I would tell you, but what is the point? You will never find out. Kill her." His order was straightforward and gleefully obeyed.

Eve was not going to back down. She would kill them all except for the leader and then make him talk. She knew the task ahead was impossible, but it was too late to stop. Her blood was pumping in preparation for the fight that was about to start, her mind focused on killing her enemies.

One of the monsters lumbered forward, and Eve went for her secondary sword. Just as she touched the hilt with her fingertips, another opponent grabbed her from behind. His hand enclosed the bulk of her body, her sword arm trapped in his grasp close to her side. He brought her close to his face, the stench of him solid and nauseating. She struggled, squirmed, and twisted to get loose from his hold. It was futile. He tightened his fist, which slowly started to cut her airway. She snarled and reluctantly opened her mouth, biting into the troll's flesh. He howled in pain. His fist opened, and he threw Eve away as he overlooked his injured hand.

Eve gritted her teeth and kept a hold on her sword as her body flew through the air. The wind passed through her hair, sounding loud in her ears, and it felt as if she had been flying forever. It had only been seconds before her back impacted the tree's trunk, which knocked the air out of her. She fell onto the grass with a groan but picked herself up as quickly as she could, dizzy from the pain and ill-prepared for another fight.

Eve went to lift her sword and go into a position that didn't leave her helpless. Before she could, a large hand smacked her. Up she went again, flying into the same trunk. Back on the ground, the monsters chortled above her. She dug her sword into the dirt and used it to push herself up to an almost standing position. She stayed there, weak and not able to hold herself up. She could feel her body crying at her to just lay down from the pain that wracked through her. She wanted to show a more extensive front, but she could hardly even pull her sword out or grab the other one. If she tried, they would eventually fall from her hold, and her soon afterward. Her fight was indeed impossible. She managed a small laugh at her foolishness and ended up coughing up some blood onto the ground, her lips staining red.

"Is that all you have you revolting, repellent, nauseating pieces of waste?" Eve sneered at them mockingly.

One of them took the bait and swung his club at her. With the last bit of strength in her, she dodged it, rolling away. The force of his strike caused his weapon to dig into the soil. He grappled and twisted, attempting to loosen it from the ground.

Eve saw an opening and took it. She threateningly growled as she ran up the arm of the monster and ducked under his hand as he attempted to pull her off. Once safe, she continued her journey upward. She had a disadvantage due to his height. Being almost at his level would give her a chance to hit his most vulnerable parts: his face and neck. His fingers brushed her legs. She attached herself to his back to keep away from his reach. Eve managed to hold on to his vest with one arm. She reached for her dagger with her other arm and found it through a combination of concentration and luck. The monster spun furiously. To not fall, Eve dug her blade into his back. He cried in pain, his arms waving wildly at his side.

Eve's legs swung at his movement. If she stayed where she was, she would, in time, lose her ability to hold on and lose the chance she had to take this creature down. She gritted her teeth and, with the dagger, climbed higher up again until she was up to his shoulders. He snarled as his hand came swinging down at her. She jumped out of the way and grabbed his nose. Her foot hit his lip and kicked off it, putting herself at his eye level. She then brought her dagger down on him and started to stab him continuously, blinding him. He wailed in agony, and his hand clawed at his face. Before he could touch her, Eve pushed off his face and rolled to the ground onto one knee, in a crouched position.

Eve watched the monster fall to the ground, his hands feeling his face covered by his blood. Eve panted and smiled. She had one down and many others to follow. She looked up to his friends and beamed. They were stupefied.

"This is just the beginning," she teased as she walked to her sword and leaned on it again for the support. She gave an air of superiority and elation. "Who is next? Come on boys, don't be shy. I won't kill. Just a little pain here and there."

Eve hoped they didn't see through her lie. She was thoroughly exhausted from that one battle. Fighting the others would be even more difficult, given her physical status. She would be unconscious halfway through the second fight at her current pace. Then, it was bye-bye her— the end of her existence.

#  Chapter 5 

"*VENI, VIDI, VICAM,*" Eve mumbled to herself. *I came, I saw, I will conquer.* She had to conquer. It was her life that was on the line. In the back of her mind, she knew it was futile. Yet, she had to try. She would not go down like a coward.

Eve warily watched the brutes break into two units. One group flanked her right and the other her left. If they attacked in a united front, with a single large charge, it was going to be the end of her life. It was the most brilliant move they could make if they decided to. It would end any chances of her incapacitating them one by one.

Though what was the point? She was dirt tired. There was little time for her to rejuvenate, and she doubted they would allow her a reprieve. She would need to stall any future advancements they might launch. Perhaps, a little time would be enough to take another down. She had a theory how to temporarily halt them, but were they dense enough for it to work?

Eve knew she had to say the right words, or they would be her last if spoken incorrectly. Though not raised to play the fool, she entered the mummer's game today. She put herself into what she believed was a relaxed, non-threatening posture, then took a plunge into danger and asked, "What are you?"

"What?" The leader was taken by surprise at her question. She made an exaggerated sigh and then asked the question again slowly.

"Is this a game?" the leader checked with his eyebrows shooting up and narrowing in suspension.

"No. I do not dare trick you as you will grasp the deception easily, oh great one. I have never been here," Eve informed him. "My world has stories, but I don't believe I have heard about your kind."

"Then why do you have the smell of taint?" the dimwit snarled, interrogating her. Eve saw his attempt to catch her in the lie but had prepared for that question.

"Didn't you hear?" She tilted her head in the direction of the leader, saying, "Your leader realized I didn't know." Eve turned back to face the leader. "But at least tell me what you are."

"Why is it important for you to know? Your death is soon. How will knowing what or who we are aide you?" the leader growled.

Eve thoughtfully answered his probe. She had to make them believe her words. "In my world, there is a tradition as warriors we follow. It is necessary to know who and what had defeated us for our deaths. As my life dwindles into the unknown fog of death, I say the name of the one who ended it in honor."

The leader scrunched up his nose in disbelief. "You positive there are no stories of us? No tales of monsters so great that the Gods swore on their prowess. Swore on them being such formidable warriors that they used them for the greatest battles in history."

"None at all," Eve answered, placing a hand over her heart. At least in this, she was truthful.

The leader eyed her suspiciously. "When you stare at Death, you will say our names in honor?" Eve nodded in affirmation. The leader rubbed his prickly jaw. "If that is the tradition...then that custom shall be followed. I like that you honor those who defeat you until your last dying breath. I am the Elder of the Jotul, of the tribe Jotun."

Eve nodded in understanding. She remembered that *jotul* was the word for trolls from the Kingdom of Norway. The woman shifted on her feet and pulled out her secondary sword, attached to her back, while still in thought. She could be wrong, and there was a chance her next words would start the battle she had been pushing back. "So, you are trolls?"

"Such a dirty term for us great giants, but yes, we are *trolls*," the leader said, affronted by her question.

"I apologize if I insulted you. I did not do it to harm your pride," Eve said as she grabbed her other sword from the ground. "It is just that trolls, in my world, is a denotation used for men— mortals— who are large, hairy, aggressive, and brainless. It is used as an insult to my kind, when one cannot follow a simple command."

"Us grand beings have lessened to an insult," the leader said to himself incredulously. His face contorted in anger, and his mouth turned into a snarl. He bent forward, his head almost touching Eve's. "You lie."

The Elder pulled away, allowing Eve to take a deep breath. There was nothing she could now say to push the fight further. Her hiatus was over. She could no longer keep the conversation going. If she had known that the word "troll" was a derogatory term to them, she never would have said it. Well, what was done was done. She was ready to bow to fate and seal the deal instead of prolonging the inevitable fight. "Never a liar. You can't blame us, mortals. You are like the description of our version of trolls, just with the addition of being ugly as sin."

Eve smirked as her words did as she expected. The Elder went from anger to rage. Thus, instead of being attacked by many, she only had to deal with one rampaging troll as he charged her shouting. "I will kill you, wench."

She sprinted under one of his incoming arms and ran past until she reached the edge of the circle that the trolls had created. She skidded to a halt facing the Elder again. He turned to her and again headed her way. She dropped her arms to the side and charged at him with her swords dragging behind her. Both of them slowed as they neared each other.

Eve's eyes narrowed on the club in her enemy's hand. It rose over his head. She also brought up her swords in defense. Just as he swung it down, she crossed her swords together in the nick of time as the weapons struck together. Eve's swords almost left her firm hold as she was forced down to one knee from the impact. She gritted her teeth and pushed back at the club, managing to move it enough to step out from underneath it. She went into a defensive stance, putting one sword up ahead and moving the other behind. Elder grinned at her with a wide smile, but she answered it with her own.

Eve then took the initiative to attack before he could again. She quickly thrust her sword forward and then followed this with a step in the same direction. She slashed with her other blade at his leg to slice into his flesh. Both her attacks were useless. Her first thrust fell short of his knee. The slash was not strong enough to cut into his skin as she had hoped. Elder sniggered at her weak attempts to injure him and backhanded her. His hand hit her left shoulder, dislocating it and making her left arm useless. She pinched her lips and held back from whimpering in pain. She became angry with herself. She could have moved away from his attack, but instead, she had stayed still. She needed to do better. She wasn't going to die making mistakes.

*We can help you kill them. Let us out!* Loud voices, eerily familiar voices, echoed in her mind. Their volume caused her to drop her weapons and let them fall. She placed her hands to the side of her head. *Let us out. Let us out! LET US OUT!*

The voices grew louder, their anger causing her pain. Eve fell to her knees from their cacophony and attempted to drown out the voices of the dead. It was the laughter from the trolls surrounding her that silenced them. Yet, with the voices gone, the pain was still there as an aching throb at both her temples.

The leader spoke in a cocky tone. "Pitiful creature, how dare you think you can harm me." He chuckled darkly. "I can't wait to tear you apart."

Eve shook her head in an endeavor to clear her mind and was partially successful. She stood up shakily on her legs and picked up her swords. Doing some odd movements that pushed her body's flexibility, she was able to pick one up with her left hand. Though, when she tightened the grip on the sword's hilt, a wave of pain went from her fingertips to the injured shoulder. She grimaced but kept her hold. She couldn't drop her weapon again. "Really? How will you do that after I kill you?"

Helmet-head growled. "I will tear you apart while your heart still beats," he said, licking his lips. "Then, I will enjoy eating and tasting your flesh."

"You can try."

The fight between the two began. It was a spectacle. Eve had found her rhythm, and the battle now was equal in skill. The exchange between them was swift and precise. Sword and club rang and banged, hitting and cutting into metal, armor, and flesh. Blows exchanged between the two combatants decorated the field with blood, one red and the other grey. Unfortunately, red was the prominent color on the green foliage.

Eve was barely hanging on to life, and she was becoming tired. Each move, hit, and slash took a lot of effort out of her. She was putting a lot of force into her attacks, but what she saw was not promising when she glimpsed the ground around her. She was pushing beyond her physical limits. When she had increased her aggression, it had increased the throbbing pain at her temples. The pain made it difficult for her to pay attention to her surroundings. She was so focused on her opponent that she missed the simple hand movement he gave to his men. Her one-on-one skirmish was no more as the others surrounded her.

The situation was once more becoming dire. Eve was worried, as there had already been many times she had been close to being defeated. Now any chance she had to kill another troll was far in the past. She blocked, dodged, and swung her sword at her adversaries as they came at her. Then a kick came from the left. Her body rolled on the ground, and she could not protect her face as she kept a hold on her swords. Her body skidded to a halt face down on the floor with her arms sprawled awkwardly out. Her body was on fire from her accumulated injuries.

"Move," she demanded of herself. She couldn't die like this. She didn't want to die lying on the ground immovable. "Move."

*Let us help. Let us out. Let us kill them.*

"No," Eve grunted.

The shadow of a troll fell upon her limp form. The dimwit picked her up and tossed her back into the center of the fray. Eve cried when the troll jolted her body. She kept a hold on her weapons with a locked grasp, landed on her side ungracefully, and her head bounced on a half-buried rock with a loud thump. There was a bright flash of light. The world spun around her, and she could hear her heartbeat. It was a loud, constant, pounding thud with a high pitch tone that never ended. Then there was an urge to vomit as nausea filled her being. Instinctively, she went to her hands and knees, spewing out blood onto the grass.

Breathing hard, under the watchful gaze of the trolls, she noticed the blood covering the side of her head. She fell to the side again, shivering as her body became cold. The open wound on her temple continued to bleed profusely. It continued to accumulate underneath her head, making her hair wet and sticky. It wasn't long before she was lying in her pool of blood. The smell of iron overwhelmed her senses. Her sight became blurry. Her throat tightened and her eyes started to burn from the unshed tears hidden partially by her mask. *I don't want to die.*

"You foolish shit. Thinking you can kill me," Elder growled. He pushed Eve on her back, bringing his club close to her face. "Let us end this."

Eve watched the club rise, thinking, *this isn't the right time.* She didn't want to die here. *I don't want to die.*

The Elder never brought the club down. He watched as the girl's eyes became a bright red. The skin of her face started to pale as her veins became more prominent. He had to kill her, or it would be his death soon. Just as he began to drop his club, a horn rang out. The sound scared the birds into the air.

The horn cried, grabbing the attention of the trolls. Their

heads all turned in that direction, their faces one of alarm. They frantically started to shout at each other in utter panic as Eve's facial skin tone and eyes became normal.

Dimwit dropped unexpectedly in front of Eve close to her face. His tongue lolled out onto the ground. His neck had been pierced by an arrow, his warm blood flowing out from the open wound and spreading out around him as it slowly started to mix with Eve's shed blood, making the lifeforce on the ground a dark maroon. The flies began to make a permanent home on, and in, his flesh.

Eve wanted to move away from him and the stench. Unluckily, the wracking pain that filled her being, and the damage to the side of her head, kept her paralyzed. She could only watch and listen, although her view was slowly dimming into nothing. She slowly plunged into a deep black ocean with no floor to stand on. She could only rely on her hearing to know what was happening, piecing the information together in her mind.

A stampede of hooves came from animals that sounded like horses. Yells and orders were coming from many different men. The ground shook underneath her as the trolls tried to escape. The unknown warriors quickly blocked their way and the trolls were rounded up. The group then yelled and was killed, their blood hitting the floor with a loud splash. It was then Eve lost the ability to breathe. She started to cough and hack in an attempt to breathe in more air.

"Captain! The fallen female is alive! She wears a mask."

"We take her with us. You grab her and go ahead. The rest of us will ensure the vermin are dead and burn their bodies."

Eve felt herself being grabbed and lifted to sit on top of a horse. Arms circled her waist to keep her from falling. Through the narrow slit of her vision, she believed she saw pointed ears. She rasped out before darkness took her, "Puck?"

#  CHAPTER 6 

EVE FOUND HERSELF in a dark, bare, and forsaken abyss. Her mind was empty. It was devoid and free of thoughts. There were no more concerns or distress. She had no more responsibilities or engagements of any sort. She was just there, existing and extant. Time had no meaning in the place she found herself. Time was infinite. There was only serenity and tranquility.

She felt doors open underneath in the dark, and Eve fell through them. They were doors into her mind. Echoes of her life streaked back to her broken, incomplete, and sporadically. It jumped from the war to her childhood, interplaying between the present and the past. She would find herself fighting enemies, then being surrounded by children as they tormented and ridiculed her for having no mother. As one of the children punched her face, it morphed to her father slapping her after she had asked for a single story about her mother wanting to know the woman she had never met. Later, she found herself looking, out of a window, as the man she loved rode away, called to the war before her. He had been her first friend, and she had gotten to know him but could never tell him the truth. She had sworn to herself that she would share her secret when she met him again. It was months later she had received news of his death from his mother. She never had the chance to cry.

The mixed memory nightmares continued. Eve found herself in her childhood room. It then transformed into a dungeon, and she became surrounded by the faces of those that her men and herself had killed and tortured. In addition, there was the horde of prisoners she had last seen. They all shouted at her in their native tongues. Taunting. Angry. Hateful. Their hands scratched and tore at her clothing. They grabbed and pulled her to the floor, their hands never once letting her up even as she pushed against them. She tried to talk to them, but they thirsted for her blood, misery, and pain. It was a thirst that they could never quench. Eve screamed out her anguish and fear, but it was deaf to their ears and did not rise above their wailings.

"Little shit. Weak as ever," a man's voice boomed. The crowd pulled away, and she stood to face her enemy coming face to face with her dead father, his body covered in gashes and blood running down his face contrasting with his pale skin. His eyes were piercing and soulless. "Why God couldn't give me a male heir, I will never understand. Instead, he left me with a pitiful, disgusting, sniveling worm who breaks under pressure. Worthless shit."

"Father," Eve mumbled weakly, face covered in perspiration, feeling dread and failure in her stomach.

"You want to die?! You want to give up?!" his voice boomed. He pulled out his sword from his waist and threw it at her feet. "Pick it up! End it! Do the living a favor."

Eve stared at it. Her hand moved slowly to take it from the ground and follow her father's advice, sobbing all the while. She paused, hand hovering over the hilt, closing then opening, tightening and relaxing. Her hand wavered as she started to move it forward and then back repeatedly. She was indecisive.

"Take it!" he commanded. His order echoed in Eve's mind persistently. There was an urge to follow his demands, but in the end, she couldn't.

Her consciousness went to her first death that had changed her life. The blades from the opposing knights had come at her during the battle. She had found herself lying on the ground on the open field. Her mind had not been thinking about the coldness that was creeping through her limbs. She hadn't thought of the man she had lost. Nay. Inside her mind was a dormant spark that told her she needed to live. Why? She didn't know. She knew her soul was doomed to the fiery pits of hell. A deserved punishment for the torture of the poor innocents, she had been an accomplice in that had led to their deaths. She just knew it wasn't her time. "I do not die here!" she shouted to her father, hoping that would make him go away.

There was silence. Then, Eve's father laughed at her. He taunted her, his words hitting the furthest part of her spirit. When he had been alive, he had reminded her of her worth and all that she owned. That he had molded who she was. Even now, in death, he wouldn't let her forget his importance in her existence. He spat his cruel words at her. The others joined, congratulating her on becoming the monster her father had made her. She denied it, but her father called to mind her lessons in war. Exhausted by the voices of the past, Eve sat and tucked her knees to her chest, building an internal wall. She rocked back and forth...back and forth to keep a pattern that helped her keep it up. Soon after, the calls were followed by violence. Now, as they shouted out her weaknesses and uselessness, it was accompanied by a punch or a kick. Inside, her being was being killed and taken apart; her body taking the abuse she couldn't help but think she deserved. Her walls started to crack as, little by little, she agreed with them.

"You need to move," a child's voice spoke. "You can't let them know how much they can hurt us."

"I can't," Eve whined. A small hand touched her head, and she followed it to look upon the face of her younger self. The younger version of her was smiling, eyes glowing with hope that then broke into the despair she felt.

"You can," was whispered to her. "It is time to stop hiding." Eve took the hand of her younger self and rose. The cries of hatred died, and Eve turned her eyes to her dead father. She would not take his abuse. He was dead, and the dead couldn't hurt her.

"What am I?" she asked him.

"A demon," he snarled.

"Then a demon you will get," Eve told him. She looked to the child at her side, who smiled at her. She watched the girl disappear into dust. Eve then ran to her father with clenched fists. She pulled her arm back, but before she could deliver a fatal blow, another arm came from the shadows to hold her back. She could not see the face of the person who dared interfere.

"He is your father," the person behind, a woman, berated. "You never use them against the family."

"Use what?" Eve seethed as she struggled to get loose from the firm grip.

"Your gifts," was the simple answer. Eve narrowed her eyes in frustration. She had no idea what gifts the woman was speaking about. The only gifts she knew were the facial change from annoyance and that she could take beatings that would have killed others. Goodness sake, she could be dead now.

"Just going to knock some sense into him," Eve swore.

"Your anger can do more damage than you realize. Your father is dead. The dead can't hurt you," the woman said. "You must let him go."

"This I cannot allow. Father must pay for the harm he has done to me. Perhaps then, when his soul is at its end, he will give me the answers I seek."

"Then get them," the woman said. "But it is not with him. He does not have the knowledge you seek. It is on this path you must go!" Eve was forcibly turned to the right and pushed into a large, open hole. She twisted her body midair to get a glimpse of the woman who had held her back from attacking. As she continued to fall further, she stared up into glowing ember eyes and a sinister smile that belonged...to her. She looked up at her face and watched the duplicate wave goodbye in bewilderment. Eve thrust an arm out to grab her counterpart, but she was too far. The entrance of the hole closed, and her surroundings buzzed to life. A bright light grew in intensity behind her until she was enveloped by it. This warmth started at the tips of her fingertips and continued to fill her, tingling her body into awareness.

She woke with a start, mask still on, her back arching off the cot. Her heart was beating at a rapid pace as she took deep breaths.

#  CHAPTER 7 

IN A VILLAGE, not far from where the trolls lay in pieces, was a small cottage occupied by soldiers with pointy ears that looked to be of Puck's kind. They all wore uniforms of dark but different colors. The uniform consisted of a vest with many belts that crossed the torso. Over the vest, they wore coats with long tails. On their arms was armor that extended a little over their hands. Hanging at their hips were curved swords with guards to protect the back of their sword hands. Fey healers were at the other side of the cottage, outside with them. They had light hooded tunics with long tails and green blouses underneath, and their hands were covered with long gloves that left their fingers naked, so that they might handle their items with care. A satchel hung at their hips over their brown trousers, finished with dark brown boots and a strapped dagger. Unlike their companions, they oozed kindness and compassion. They walked as if they were flying on air, smooth and graceful.

The cottage was not large or luxurious. It was small and simple, consisting of just a single room. There were two tables in one half of the room and many shelves lined the walls with books, plants, baskets of herbs, and a mixture of vials. Across the shelves and tables was a single cot where lay Eve, who had been unconscious until not long ago.

Eve's awakening was dreadful. Physically, she ached all over. It was worse than being stabbed or standing after her death. At least then, it was only her wounds that hurt. Now, she felt a hot and cold that randomly came to her in different areas of her body. Looking on the positive side, she could move. Though, she might as well not be. Her body felt stiff and uncomfortably itchy. It was driving her insane.

Furthermore, the longer she stayed in bed, the more she found herself gasping for breath. She just couldn't get enough air. She felt that she was suffocating even though she was only under a thin, simple linen draped over her. With a lot of effort and pain, she pushed herself into a sitting position. She dragged herself back until she leaned heavily on the wooden wall behind her. The blanket fell to her waist to show that she was bandaged from the neck down.

In fear of what other possible injuries she could have sustained, Eve kicked the rest of the blanket off. It slipped to the wooden floor, disturbing the dust. She then found her legs also bandaged. Her pants had been cut to her thighs to keep her modesty. She breathed out heavily as her eyes burned with shed tears. Were her injuries that damaging they had to wrap her up like someone who had boils? Did she have blemishes? Not knowing had Eve panicking. She wanted to scratch away her coverings to see what she could not.

Unknown to her, an elderly female healer had noticed that she had awoken from one of the windows. The woman's mouth opened in shock when she saw Eve start pulling at her bandages. The healer ordered some of the soldiers into the room as she noticed blood starting to appear in the area of Eve's ribs.

Eve, herself, didn't feel any wounds reopen through the increasing of her heart rate, the tensing of her muscles, and her mind focused solely on the task of taking off the tight wraps. She needed to know how badly she was injured. She never received the chance to see as four soldiers ran inside and pulled her back down onto the cot. They held her legs and arms down. She cursed at them and struggled to get out of their hold, kicking and shaking her limbs. As her agitation grew, her eyes progressively glowed disconcertingly.

She freed one arm from a soldier and punched another's face with newfound strength. When she repeated her actions, the soldier captured her arm again. Eve gritted her teeth and pulled her arm, adding a twist. She broke the soldier's arm in the process, who cried for help.

The elder healer, Aine, had followed the soldiers in and had watched the events from a corner. She was a tall woman, still in her prime, she believed, with shining brown eyes and short, wild, white hair. She had an inner beauty that leaked out an infinite quantity of compassion, strength, and love. When she heard the soldier's bone crack, she moved into action, coming closer to the group.

"Keep her still as best you can," Aine commanded. "Something is not correct." She lifted her hands and ran them inches over Eve's body. They started to glow slightly, and she closed her eyes, concentrating on finding why the remedy she had given the mortal did not keep her asleep. She warily looked into the girl's glowing stare. Had the mortal been cursed?

Aine groaned, pulled her hands away, and ruffled her hair. She would have to call to the Elements to assist her in determining why the young woman was not healing or acting appropriately. She closed her eyes once more, brought her hands into a prayer, and made motions with her fingers. When the God of Fire called, she answered. When the Goddess of Earth cried for attention, she gave it. Then, Water came and cooled her feverish mind. Air followed by lifting her soul and uniting her with the others. The soldiers were caught off guard by her skin illuminating. They turned their heads away, closing their eyes tightly. Eve didn't.

Aine walked toward Eve slowly. She then placed her hands on Eve's head. Aine's head snapped back at the contact, and her energy flowed from her to the mortal. She assisted her patient and mentally touched Eve's mind with her own. Aine found herself thrown out and shocked by this action. Somehow, Eve had lifted a barrier and blocked Aine from reading any ailments that could have occurred in her mind. Aine decided to read the young girl's life source. What she found made her gasp. She pulled away.

"No. You can't exist," Aine said. She put a hand to her mouth, shook her head, and her skin no longer glowed. The others turned to her, curious about what could have caused such a reaction into this woman who had lived thousands of years and who had seen more than they had. They watched the elder run to a shelf and grabbed a vial. She came back. "Open her mouth and close her nose," she said to one of the soldiers. He did as ordered, letting go of the arm he held until another took it. Once Eve's mouth opened in distress, Aine tipped half the contents of the potion into it. Eve quickly calmed and then entered a deep slumber. The feys in the room breathed out a sigh of relief.

"What did you give her?" the soldier who had assisted the healer asked. Aine did not hear him.

"Call for Captain Aelfdene and stay out of this room." Aine turned away from them to stare at Eve.

"Are you sure, ma'am?" Aine nodded, and the soldiers started to protest. She silenced them with a glare. One by one, they walked out. None looked back. They left with a huff, feet stomping, and acting like children. Once the men finally cleared the room, Aine went to Eve and moved the young woman's hair from her face. "There is much for you to learn, but it must wait until you wake."

Hours went by until the arrival of Captain Aelfdene. He walked into the room with a jump to his steps. If Aine had been younger, she would have swooned at the young captain's feet, yet his personality was not one would find attractive. Presently, wiser due to her age, she discovered his handsomeness disgustingly nauseating. He was tall, taller than her. He had piercing blue eyes with elegant eyelashes that curved up perfectly. His high cheekbones and a lower plump lip made him the most wanted and chased bachelor with the high society single women. He ran his hand through his dark, curly hair like he often did after an entrance.

"Aine, what have you found?" He walked past her to Eve, leaning over the sleeping mortal. "Pretty," he mumbled. He went to touch the skin of sleeping beauty but thought it better not to. At least, not with a witness. He coughed and pulled away, putting his hands behind his back.

"I can't tell you." He narrowed his eyes. "I will only inform the king and queen. Privately."

"They are distances away."

"Precisely why I called for you. I want her moved to Avalon."

"She is just a mortal," Aelfdene scoffed. "And you know the laws that a mortal is healed, memory wiped, and sent back."

"I can't allow that."

"You have no say. It is the law." Aelfdene looked to the floor and back, rubbing his chin thoughtfully. "If you tell me what makes this one so important, I can help you."

"I will tell. But only when we get to Avalon and not earlier."

"Or, I could walk away and order my men to take her home."

"You wouldn't dare. You are ruled by your curiosity." She watched the younger man pull at his hair in frustration. She had him. A blessing, as Aine had already plans set. She would have her guards watch over the girl. She didn't trust the captain's proclivity with the opposite sex. Then, before the journey began, send a hawk to her sister. Her sibling had to convince the court to allow her to speak for the woman in her care. She knew once Aelfdene knew who the woman was, he would kill, or use, her without any thought. He was a manipulative bastard when it came to power. She couldn't let that happen. She needed to outthink him and move steps ahead of the ones he would take.

"Deal."

# CHAPTER 8

DAYS PASSED UNBEKNOWNST to Eve, who lay on a luxurious bed inside the majestic palace of Avalon. The city had a surrounding forest. Beyond was the unknowns and villages that were further out. Inside its walls, a town of those who worked with the royals and soldiers surrounded the castle. The castle itself had five towers, three floors, and an underground labyrinth that contained cells for the worst, a treasury, and the potion masters. There were three open yards in the castle's center with different gardens. At the side were the training ground, stables, and the armory. Citizens of the underworld lined and practiced daily for a future of war they had not seen for many years. Only a few of them had been born after the great battle and doubted they would see any.

At Eve's arrival, she had sent the state of the court of the magical world into chaos. As promised, Aine did inform Aelfdene on the uniqueness of the mortal. Just as she had expected, the captain had jumped in eagerness to enact an old law that would have put the young girl under his thumb. Aine's quick thinking to send a message to her sister saved the mortal from being Aelfdene's plaything but had focused the young fey's sight on the mortal more.

Aine's sister had gone beyond the letter and had taken it upon herself to talk to the court before the group's arrival. She had stood in front of the council and convinced them of the importance of Eve's presence. The committee had then permitted the healer to settle the mortal into a medic ward with trustworthy guards. This decision proved well because when the captain later realized he had lost his new toy, he had attempted to kill the girl. The guards had dragged him out before he had completed the deed.

The young captain insisted on the punishment of execution to the mortal. If not, his complaints would go to the king or queen, his parents. Distressed, Aine sent a message to the royal couple's youngest son. Caoimhghin was the royal's family black sheep. He was young, arrogant, and mischievous with a deeply hidden kind heart. He already ruled a land at the outlands of his family's kingdom over creatures that many said were untamable. He saw them as his friends.

Caoimhghin came to Aine's aid. With a quick hug and kiss on her cheeks, he promised the woman to talk to his parents to make Eve a new resident of the Underground. He did it post haste, taking time off his duties. His brother was not pleased and loudly showed his disagreement about keeping their enemy so close.

The rescuers took Eve to recover in the Healing Ward located on the first floor near the east tower. The ward had many rooms, some larger than others. The use of which room depended on the healers' need. Eve was in one of the smaller ones with a large, open window that faced the direction the sun rose. It was during this time, a week later, that Eve awoke in a groggy state to find herself in a new room. Her first thought she could string together was that she was tired of seeing herself somewhere she did not remember being. She attempted to lift her arm and hissed at the ache she found. *Indeed, not a dream I have been.*

"Well," Eve mumbled to herself in resignation of her situation. "What shall I do now?" She huffed in a quick-approaching feeling of boredom. She eyed herself as best as she could in her pitiful state. Her head lifted slightly to see she was not bandaged as heavily as before and wore a comfortable, white robe. She then assessed what she could of her new quarters. She was in a comfy, mid-size bed that gave her space to move about, and it was extraordinarily soft. She might as well be lying on clouds. She saw a chamber pot in one corner, three chests of drawers, a single dresser, and a shelf filled with medical knick-knacks; she could recognize some of them but many others she did not know.

Eve kept looking around when a slender, young woman with long silver hair, silver eyes, pointy ears, and a long neck, dressed as a healer, walked into the room and past the guards. The newcomer's eyes never wavered to the bed, so she did not know of the spectator. The healer moved past Eve to one of the chests of drawers. She started to pull out, and lay down, new bandages and other objects on the surface. She was in the midst of preparing her routine chore when she finally looked upon Eve. She jumped from startlement and knocked into the dresser behind her. "Pardon me. I didn't realize— "

"Fey." The word had come to Eve as she looked at the stranger.

"Excuse me."

Eve sluggishly pointed to the woman's ears. "Fey?"

The woman blanched and angrily placed her hands on her hips. "I am an elf."

"The most stunning elf would be more accurate, love," a man spoke smoothly. The elf turned to the doorway, her cheeks flushed with a deep blush showing how she viewed the stranger.

Eve rotated her head to look upon what many would consider handsome. For her, he was cocky, arrogant, and pretentious; evident by how he strutted like a peacock wearing his spotless and pristine uniform. Eve was thankful to see two guards stepping forward to block the pompous soldier's advance into the room. The guards were obstructing him for a reason, and she hoped it was for good intentions. Noticing she was watching him, he gave her a wink and a suggestive smile. Eve eyed him distrustfully, raising an eyebrow and slightly scrunching up her nose in disgust. His eyes flashed with displeasure at her attitude.

"Captain Aelfdene," the healer said, and she started to walk toward the man, her hips swaying side-to-side sensually. The guards watched with their mouths gaping open, swords lowering, as their attention became preoccupied with the sultry female. Aelfdene weaved between them and entered the room. The guards were not reacting to him. They mysteriously had been placed into a hypnotized state.

Eve narrowed her eyes, biting the inside of her cheek, as she watched events unfold. The elf was more dangerous than she had initially anticipated, which caused Eve to become warier of the captain. What powers did the elf have to make men into a living stone? Eve could only determine that the elf was like a succubus or Medusa herself, but she had no snakes in her hair. So, the purpose of the woman's powers was to trap weak-minded prey but not kill. Captain Aelfdene, it would seem, was immune to her charm. This could not be said of the woman enraptured by the captain's beauty. The woman's goal was to take Aelfdene to bed, which blinded her to the fact that he was using her, or she just didn't care.

"Luthien. I missed you at the morning meal," the captain flirted.

"Aine had listed a plethora of chores for me to do. I missed even my mid-meal the day before." Luthien reached the captain, placing her dainty hand on his chest gracefully, lightly touching, her finger playing with the buttons on his vest. "However, I do believe she is jealous. She doesn't appreciate the way we connect on a spiritual level. Something I doubt the old bat has felt and won't before being called into Elysium."

"There might be truth to your words, Luthien, but *this old* bat is wiser when it comes to men and their ability to play even the most arrogant woman like a fiddle," an older female voice, Aine, from the doorway, interrupted. Aine touched the guards with glowing hands, pulling them out from the veil that had placed them into a stupor. "Get out and never return. You will do well to find another mentor, for I will not complete your education. Go. Rush. Before I spread the word of your unique and questionable gifts."

The tips of Luthien's pointy ears reddened as the rest of her paled from embarrassment at being caught. She rapidly nodded her head and kept it down as she picked up her things to flee the room, leaving in a hurry. The guards went to Aine, informing her that they had been caught in the elf's magic but would take the punishment for allowing the captain to enter the room. Aine patted their heads understandably. She proceeded to wave them away, ensuring that there would be no consequences to their actions, as it wasn't their fault. The guards, glad not to be punished, returned to their station.

"Captain Aelfdene. Good day. It is a surprise to see you. I believed I had been clear that this room was off-limits. I thought my guards dragging you out would have given you the message." Aine smiled at Eve kindly and walked to the table, standing where Luthien had been moments ago. She picked up some of the materials and started to organize them. In a bowl, she began to mix different items. "What do you want?"

"A talk...with our guest," Aelfdene smiled charmingly. Aine turned with a well-placed twist and a forced smile that never truly reached her eyes.

"No," she replied. "But thank you for visiting. You may leave."

"I am a captain and a representative— "

"Oh, shove it." Aine scooped the contents of the bowl in a vial, the liquid a light blue. It was the daily medication needed to rejuvenate the girl. "This should help you, little one. You will be up and standing, jiggling and jumping around for two days. Your healing so far has been beyond any expectations I had."

"Aine. I will talk to her," the captain said.

"No. Talking isn't what you wish to happen. You wish to kill the poor, injured girl."

Eve swerved her head to look at the captain. Did they know why she was here and had talked in her sleep? If not, as far as she knew, she had not committed any crimes. Eve sat up, and her body became wracked with erratic shivers from her limbs because she had been prone for so long. "Kill me?" she rasped out. "Why?"

"None of your concerns," Aelfdene snapped.

"It is of her concern," Aine defended Eve.

"Then you tell her?" Aelfdene challenged.

Aine looked at Eve sorrowfully. "Nay. My findings must be confirmed by the king and queen first. Their skills and reads are better than my own."

Eve's eyes widened. It wasn't because the older woman was not telling her the secretive information that she and the captain knew. No. It was the mention of the king and the queen that she would be stealing from if she wished to return home. The other problem was her mask. She hadn't checked, but she knew in her heart the blasted cloth was still attached to her. Just with that accessory, her life was indeed forfeit. They would just take one look at her, and poof, it was the end of poor Eve Bonel.

Eve opened her mouth to ask for more details, but a coughing fit interrupted her communication. She scrambled back and pushed herself into a sitting position. Aine aiding her as Aelfdene smirked at her pain from the side. It took a while before the burning in her chest stopped.

"I apologize. There are side effects to the potion, due to your physiology. I have done my best to adapt them to you. The medicine works perfectly while you are sleeping, though. Awake, your body tries to fight it," Aine explained. She grabbed a jug nearby and poured water into a wooden cup, handing it to Eve.

Aelfdene chortled. "Pitiful weakling. Let her choke to death. She's just a useless bitch."

Tension in the room rose to an oppressive state because of Eve's temper. She was not a weakling. She had traveled between worlds, almost been killed by trolls— and not to forget the biting fairies. Her grip on the cup tightened from boiling fury. This captain knew nothing of her, and she would prove to him her strength. Eve's eyes flickered in and out of a glowing red.

"How dare you!" Aine's voice echoed. "You have reached the limit of my patience, boy." Quicker than Eve's eyes could observe, Aine stood before the captain looking like a woman possessed with clenched hands glowing, her stance ready to lash out at the one who offended her.

"You can't harm me," Aelfdene laughed. "They will kill you."

"You may be their son, but by the laws, what you said can be viewed as a threat to one under my care. Remember, words have power."

"And, what's said is said you have taught me," a smooth, silky voice broke into the room, all occupants looking at the new arrival.

Eve forgot about her anger. Instead, her mouth dropped open, and her face flushed. She had seen and been surrounded by many men before. Yet, she had never swooned for them. This fey was like no other. His presence had her lifting her cover to her chin. He had sun-flower-kissed hair pulled behind with a ribbon that stood out widely. There was a toothy grin showing off his canine teeth, which, extraordinarily, exuded mischievousness and sensuality. One of his eyes was a shining blue, the other a gleaming ember. His outfit glittered and was simultaneously sinful. His blouse was open to show a chiseled chest. Then, there were the exceedingly tight leather pants with dark leather boots.

"Prince Caoimhghin," one of the guards mumbled before both bowed to the man. Aine followed suit.

"Brother," Aelfdene snarled. Caoimhghin continued to smile sweetly at his sibling.

"Prince Brother to you," Caoimhghin joked. "I see I have missed the fun. What did you do to get the hag riled up?" Eve expected Aine to correct and scold the prince, but she didn't. She smiled with affection at him instead. It must be a nickname of sort that the prince had given as a sign of their friendship. "Well? Is anybody going to answer?"

"He threatened the girl," Aine answered, once more glaring at the captain.

Caoimhghin tutted, walked to his brother, and slapped him hard on his back. "Brother, this woman raised and cared for us. How could you think threatening one under her care would work in your favor?"

"She isn't letting me do my duty. As Captain of— "

"A rank only given because of father and mother," Caoimhghin pointedly told him. "That doesn't give you a right to forget your manners."

"I am Captain because our brothers— "

"And sisters. Don't forget them— "

"— are Generals and in the line for the throne which father should give to me as I am here and they are not."

"Jealousy doesn't look well on you. You should leave before you put your head up your arse."

"I am older than you— "

"Yet, out of the two of us, I was given the responsibility to rule a kingdom," Caoimhghin snapped. He then pointed to the door. "Go. Don't make things worse." Aelfdene straightened his uniform and stomped out of the room. Caoimhghin clapped his hands. "Well, now that evil incarnate is gone, how are we all doing?"

Pardon?" Eve asked, not expecting a question about her well-doing. She couldn't understand what was going on. Her mind was befuddled by this man who had the presence of a prince but did not act like one. She had a mind to add more words to her "pardon," but no others could she form. Yet, that single word she uttered was enough to bring attention upon herself, earning her an alluring smile from Caoimhghin.

"Oh. So, this is the girl who had angered my brother so," he spoke as he approached Eve. He started to lean forward, entering Eve's space, and she fell back onto the bed, pushing herself further into the bedding. She was glad he came no closer. "Pretty and with a fiery spirit just waiting to be let out. Are you single, lovely girl?"

"Pardon?" Eve squeaked out. She was unprepared by the look and actions directed upon her.

"You look beautiful when you are confused," he stated, his gloved hand touching her cheek lightly, caressing it. He pulled it away quickly with an endearing pout. "But...you are not my mate or my soul. We could have had some fun. Pity."

"Pardon?!" Eve shrieked. Just hearing the words "mate" or "soul" scared her. They played over and over again in her mind. Feys' behaviors were undoubtedly confusing, and Eve was unclear about reciprocating. But she had to speak. She had to find the words to know what her present situation was. "Excuse me? As flattered as I am by your proposition, may I at least know the dealings that involve me? Someone, tell me something."

"You have really nice eyes," Caoimhghin flirted. Eve rose an eyebrow. She had expected more to come from his lips.

"Can you please remove yourself from my being?"

"I can hear your heart. You like how close I am." Caoimhghin winked at her, and Eve's face became red in...well, she couldn't tell what in. She was irate at his playfulness and concurrently thrilled to be admired but a man such as he. She didn't like having any words, and at the moment, that was where she was. She had never been in this circumstance where a man gave her his undivided attention. Neither had a man declared things about her with such passion and easiness.

"Caoimhghin, stop scaring the girl," Aine berated. "Can't you tell she isn't used to your charm?"

"That is what makes it more fun," he said. "Her discomfort and embarrassment taste so delicious in the air that I wish to drown in it. It has been years since I met a woman self-conscious of herself." He paused and shrugged his shoulder. "But we have other matters at hand to speak of. I have good news to tell. Excellent news, really."

"You managed it? It's done?"

Caoimhghin laughed at the joy in Aine's tone. "Yes. Yes. I have managed to grab the ears of father and mother. In three days' time, the council will bring you to court. I must warn you if your findings are true...they may not allow you to defend the girl. You will have to act— " He lowered his voice and pulled Aine closer to whisper into her ear.

Eve was glad that Caoimhghin no longer was near her. His closeness flustered her to no ends and made it difficult to think. Now that he was far away, her mind was more straightforward. Yet, watching him whisper to Aine was not agreeable. If the conversation was about her, she should be part of what was said. She needed to demand to know what they were hiding from her. Yet how to approach this subject without alienating the two who had recently protected her?

Since her arrival, though, Eve no longer knew how many days had passed since she had been rescued and healed by feys and elves. As she had witnessed so far, elves could seduce and turn others into living stones. Captain Aelfdene, who was a prince, wanted her dead. He also had a younger brother, Caoimhghin, who was already a king of an unknown land but had no military rankings of any sort. Lastly, Aine was her guardian and one you did not cross.

Lost, and contemplating her limited information, Eve did not notice that Caoimhghin had joined her again. "Your eyebrows scrunch adorably when lost in thought." Eve jolted and saw that he was lying next to her on his side. He was holding his head up by his hand. Aine was no longer in the room, and it was only the two of them with the door of her room closed. The blush she had finally gotten rid of came back with a vengeance, and a sound of surprise left her lips as she hurried further to her side of the bed. Eve almost fell to the floor when she reached the edge of the mattress. "What took your mind so far away? Were you thinking of a man left behind? Oh, is there a man? You never answered my question about being single."

Eve sucked in her lip and pulled further away. She impossibly became redder than she already was at the impropriety of being left alone with a flirtatious man who was an enigma. It was uncomfortable not to read his actions or know his next move. His thinking jumped from one subject to the next and back.

"Hmmm. Beautiful and silent. Deadly combination. I hope my soulmate has these qualities. It would make our relationship ever so easy," the prince mussed as he moved to sit. "But knowing my luck, she will have the beauty but not the silence. It would depressingly prove my father right like he usually is. He believes a strong-willed woman is the only kind that can tame me."

"Your father?

"Yes, King Oberon. The high king of all."

"He is never wrong?"

"Ah, she is interested," he editorialized with a sly grin. "There are times, a trickle, when father is wrong but again, rarely. It is his gift, you could say. He can look at a person, stare deeply in their eyes— " and he, in turn, stared at her intensely. "— Then, with just that look, your whole life is his. Everything you have done or said, he will know."

Eve became lost in his eyes. "Truly?"

"No," he deadpanned and looked away with a laugh, a transparent sphere popping in mid-air that he played with, rolling it from one hand to the next. "Of course not. That is preposterous. Nobody can do that, and even if we could, we wouldn't do it without permission. That is just rude." He caught Eve's glare, throwing his orb for her to catch. Just as her fingertips touched it, it burst into bubbles floating up into the air.

"You are a cad." Eve crossed her arms over her chest, turning her head away from him with a huff. It wasn't long before she felt a poke at her side and watched as the prince lay his head on her lap. She looked down, and another unladylike sound came out of her lips.

"Don't be mad, love, as sexy as it is," he pouted at her. "Smile. And if you do it well enough, I can tell you about my parents. Maybe you can use it to keep this lovely face alive to find your answers. For why else would a mortal cross-boundary but to find answers? Or dare challenge Puck?"

"How?" Eve felt all the blood rush to her fingers and her head swim. Shock kept her from pushing him away.

"I am the master of dreams," he answered. "And even awake, yours had called to me. I could swear I wasn't being rude. They were odd and frightful at first. I am surprised Puck had lived for so long. I, like many, believed he would have died existing in your gray, dull, and barbaric world. A life without magic, just imagine the horror."

Caoimhghin sat at her side. "For us fey, we live for our magic. We can't picture never using it, even for the simplest tasks. But we'll talk about this later. So, what do you wish to know?"

"Why are you helping me?" Eve couldn't help but be suspicious of his motives. She hoped he wouldn't disregard the question or go around it. What did he gain from allying with her, and would he betray her?

"I like the fun and to create chaos. Also, it would be nice to see an inferior being stick it to my father. Get him off his high horse."

"Stick it?"

"Hmmm. You lot are still behind. Don't worry. You will get there. Now, foremost, a little history will do you good."

#  Chapter 9 

EVE WAS STUCK on bed rest for the following days by Aine's strict order. She had a new nurse who was also an elf but kinder and playful. The nurse helped the time pass, but the rest of Eve's days became filled with extended visits by Prince Caoimhghin. He thought it best that she learn the management of the underground. As an ally, he saw it as his duty to make sure her quest went well and to keep her from dying. Though Eve thought there was another reason he was aiding her and wasn't telling the whole truth of his motives. It wasn't only him. Eve had a feeling Aine was hiding something also. Aine joined them daily, but mostly, they were left alone. It did not take long to conclude that the two acted like siblings and that there was no fear of love happening between the two. Caoimhghin was the mischievous one of the two, so if there was any wrongdoing, it was apparent he would be the ringleader.

Eve pouted one day and fell back down onto the bed, saying, "This is boring."

"You need to learn or off with your head," Caoimhghin commented as he flicked her nose. Eve glared at him. He moved to flick her nose again, and she attempted to block it, missing his arm. His next flick tickled her nose. He laughed at her facial reaction of annoyance. He then purposely moved slower to flick her once more, but this time teasingly. She pushed his arm away with a mocking glare.

"Well?" she said impatiently, imitating the young prince's arm gestures and unique accent. He grinned at her with cockiness. "Continue then." Caoimhghin did as Eve implored, and she listened as intently as one could when boredom threatened to pull them into a deep sleep.

"Oberon and his kind had traveled to a new world. Where they came from was forbidden to acknowledge by a mutual agreement of the elder council that contained representatives of many different species. Their arrival had changed everything and started a sequence of events they hadn't foreseen. At first, the feys and others needed to bond with the world's inner core to exist in unity with it. The reformation then led to new, unparalleled mythical beasts born from the elements and animals in the present ecosystem. Afterward, the council decided it was time to choose a ruler. Being one of the strongest and part of the ruling assembly, Oberon became king of their new home by anonymous voting. Titania, not long after, became his wife after years of tumultuous courtship. She was equal in powers to her husband and more lethal due to her blood. The couple's combined force assured that the other magical creatures couldn't harm themselves or others—the others who were the non-magical original inhabitants of their habitation, the mortals. The mortals were primitive due to having a diminutive form of communication that caused them to have a low survival rate. Oberon and his people assisted the mortals. They taught them to survive, create tools, and work together to achieve their goals. Oberon's people and the mortals became close, and not long after, they joined intimately with one another. King Oberon and his wife saw this unity as a chance for a new beginning. Disappointingly, that was not to happen."

"Why? I would gather children— "

"That was what my parents hoped would occur. But they overlooked an issue."

"And what could that be?"

"That those involved were individuals. That they had their own opinions and could not expect them to take on a great responsibility they did not wish for.

"Magical and mortals joined together because of their intense love for one another. They didn't do it or care for children. They just wanted to be together but that didn't mean they didn't try to procreate. Truthfully, both groups were skeptical about the possibility of having children. Eventually, it did happen. The halflings were adored, treasured, and worshiped when it did occur. Society willingly gave a majority of the children all they asked. They lived their life without wanting or worrying about poverty. Yet, to every happiness, a problem arose.

"The halflings were born without magic and showed no signs of developing them. This was then proven wrong. One of the halflings went out of control after reaching the age of six and ten. Others followed not long after. With no training in their newfound gifts, the halflings with the most destructive powers accidentally killed others when they lost control of their emotions. Those who ruled did not punish them.

"For this reason, a few of the halflings continued their murdering streak, randomly here and there, and still there were no consequences. Their actions were swept away and hidden. Thereupon, the halflings united after they noticed that their powers were superior to their magical parents. So, they went to Oberon and demanded that they lead the world, not him. King Oberon shook his head and scolded them. He believed them to be too young and worried over their inexperience with their powers. In retaliation, most of the halflings went on a murderous rampage to prove that they were unstoppable.

"The rampage turned into a big war. Many died from both sides. The warring halflings were superior but still outnumbered by those against them. Soon, only a few of them were left. For a few, their parents hid them away in isolated areas. King Oberon hoped that the many deaths were enough to satisfy all the people. It was not. The masses were terrified of the few existing half breeds. So, with a heavy heart, after advice from his council, he ordered the extermination of the halflings. His direction included the deaths of traitors and the parents of the hybrids. A group of superior soldiers hunted the half-breeds and the others whose names were on a list. Then, with all in agreement, Oberon created a law after the bloodshed:

*If any magical beings fall in love or breed with a mortal,*
*they shall be killed and hung with their partners for all to see.*
*A warning to those who dare break the peace.*

"The deaths didn't end with the destruction of the halflings. There were movements from rogue groups determined to divide the population. A majority came from the tribes of the mortals. The more the mortals learned and became educated about the world, the more they became aware of their low and vulnerable place. They realized that one day, one of their magical companions could decide to use their powers to dominate them. Having no gifts of their own, the mortals were no match. They did not have the appropriate defense or strength to rise victorious over such powerful beings. Furthermore, they did not believe that Oberon could protect them all."

"Worry grew into fear, and fear became paranoia," Eve mumbled knowingly. She had seen it many times. When new advancements surfaced, the church would terrify the population away from it— shouting out the evil it could bring. Unknowingly, the church only made the people more curious.

"Correct," Caoimhghin voiced.

The mortals had concluded correctly that their disadvantages made them weak. Unfortunately, a radical group saw this weakness as the end of the existence of their kind. They were determined to act because of this knowledge. They believed they could solve their problems with violence and intimidation. First, they recruited others to their cause by exaggerating their fears. Fights broke out throughout the land. Sides chosen. One was not allowed to be in the middle of the dispute. Thus, the world plummeted into unending battles. Many lives were lost, and their blood seeped into the lands, creating shadowy creatures of untold horrors.

Tired of the deaths, and fearful of the shadows, Oberon

reached an agreement with the mortals. He would take his people to the world below— including the shades that fed on the turmoil of death. The longer the monsters stayed above, the stronger they would become by eating the hatred. Though disappointed with the mortals' fear of him, Oberon saw them as his children who still needed his protection. So, the magic disappeared to the Underground, where another war of a different kind occurred. When that war ended, Oberon and his queen established more rules to oversee who could cross between the dimensions of the now two worlds."

"But how do you have a sky? Animals? Clouds? Light?"

"We are not literally below your world, just in an extension of it."

"I still don't understand."

"I could explain the science of it, but the information is beyond your knowledge."

"Science?"

"Magic. Alchemy. Witchcraft. Medicine. *Philosophica.*"

"*Philosophica.* That word I know. Continue though, as I wonder how did us mortals forget about the existence of magic if it is so grand and magnificent?"

"That is where you are wrong. Mortals never really forgot," Caoimhghin replied. He continued to tell her the history of her ancestors that she had not known. The mortals did not ignore magic or its impact. The leaders of the many tribes of the mortals agreed to make laws to destroy the knowledge of magic. An impossible task as one could not destroy what was already known. So, instead of destroying the notion, it was banned from being spoken aloud. If one dared to break the order, it was a death given to them. Then, Oberon and his people became stories and nothing more as time passed.

As thrilling as the information was, Eve did fall into a deep sleep as the prince continued to talk. He stopped when a soft snore came from her and chuckled. The young mortal was still innocent, which Coaimhghin could see on her face— or the parts of it in view. He wondered what she looked like underneath her mask. He had attempted to remove the disguise with his abilities. Nothing had happened other than Eve had become irritated because he had made her sparkly.

Absent-minded, Caoimhghin created another sphere and looked at the sleeping girl. He had a childish urge to cover her once more with glitter. She would be angry when she awoke. Though, he would not be present when that happened. He wavered the globe over Eve, but before he could enact his spell, a guard burst into the room.

"Sire!" the guard shouted.

The orb burst as Eve awoke from the guard's entrance. Eve did not become covered in glitter as the prince had hoped. Her hands flayed out, and her legs kicked up in perturbation. Unluckily, her legs went up to the side and down upon the prince's royal jewels. He eeped, a single tear left his eye, and he cradled his damaged and throbbing organs.

Eve heard his cry and twisted around to see where she had injured him. However, she accidentally tangled her feet in the blankets due to her tired eyes and fell off the bed. In her attempt to stay on it, she grabbed one of the bedposts, which came down with her. Caoimhghin looked up helplessly as the bed's clothed canopy fell on top of him, hiding him from the eyes in the room.

The guard and Eve did not speak or move. Both were still processing the activity that had occurred. No movement or sound came from the bed. Eve shakily stood to check on the prince. Due to her long bed rest, her legs were not that strong, so she fumbled on her feet and ended up falling multiple times, wincing in pain. The guard who had rushed in came to her aid after her fourth fall. She glared at him as he approached but was happy to stand finally. With the guard's assistance, the two effectively reached the bed's edge. They leaned forward and then pulled the canopy off. It fluttered up and away to the side. The prince had wide-open unblinking eyes, and was still cupping his manhood. There was no visible deathly injury.

"Prince?" Eve called out. Caoimhghin's eyes met hers after hearing his title. Neither said anything to the other. They just continuously stared at each other. All three individuals in the room were in various states of shock, so none had an idea what to do or say.

Eve felt a need to speak or assist the prince in making the situation less tense. Or was it to make it less awkward? How? Well, she didn't know. Should she ask him if he was in an acceptable form? The more she thought about it, that seemed rhetorical. Obviously, she had kicked and wounded him in a susceptible area. Should she order the guard to help him sit up? Not possible as the guard was the only thing helping her stand. Eve luckily didn't have to voice or take action in the end. The prince inexplicably burst into a peal of bellowing laughter with tears forming in his eyes.

Outside the chamber, Aine was doing her routine walks around the ward when she heard a crack and a burst of laughter. She rushed to the sound and found herself in front of an open door. She wondered what had happened to the guard who was supposed to be standing outside it. She walked in hurriedly. The scene she came to was difficult to believe. The bed was in disarray and broken. Instead of Eve occupying it, it was the prince manically laughing. She eyed him, curious why his hands were cupping the front of his groin. Her eyes then moved to the two individuals standing nearby. They both looked like children doing something naughty and had been caught in the act by a parent or guardian. What irked Aine was that Eve was standing and not resting. The girl was perspiring on a cool day which meant she had not yet recovered.

Aine placed her hands on her hips and demanded, "What is amiss?" The laughing prince continued to guffaw. She narrowed her eyes on him, but it did naught. She then turned her glare to Eve, who gulped. The guard next to Eve looked down at the ground like it had a fascinating floor. "Well? Speak!"

"Well—," Eve started to explain. Incoherent sounds, that should have been words, followed. In Eve's mind, she knew what she was saying, yet her mouth wasn't working proficiently. The look of the old "hag," as Caoimhghin lovingly called her, had set Eve's nerves afire. For that reason, Eve added gestures and movements, hoping that maybe that would give the woman an idea of the situation and her words. It didn't. Aine looked at her like she had gone insane. At her failure of communication, Eve dropped her hands and stopped her attempt to speak the English language. Her nose scrunched as she eternally winced in humiliation, fiddling nervously with her fingers.

Aine took a deep breath. She could feel an annoying throb forming at the left temple of her head. "Child," Aine spoke calmly, "tell me what occurred. Slowly." Eve did, and by the end of it, Aine was close to laughing. She coughed to hide it, but the girl's embarrassed face shattered her will to remain serene. Laughter burst forth from her lips. Incidents of the nature she just heard were rare in the world of magic, where a flick of a hand kept it from ever happening. So, when it did occur, well, one could not help but react.

Eve and the guard looked at each other with open mouths and large wide eyes, dismayed at the elder's reaction. Eve couldn't determine if Aine's response was typical for the feys. She wanted to ask but didn't have the strength to shout over the rumbustious laughter that took seconds to become annoying. If the two laughing took as long as the drunkard jackals from her world, she might as well make herself comfortable and wait for it to end. Eve pulled away from the guard and leaned on the closest wall. She then eyed the laughing idiots, slightly jealous they could find humor, and she could not. She had just injured one of her few allies' precious jewels, and he was laughing like it was nothing.

It took longer than Eve had wished, but the mirth did eventually die down. Aine looked to the guard who stood off to the side, unsure. "No harm was done. You may leave." The guard nodded fervently and, with down-casted eyes, fled the room, never looking back. The predicament had visibly shaken him. His reaction amused Aine, but she couldn't blame him. The guard had worked his whole life near and at the palace; the royals were well known for their fast and sporadic tempers.

The bed creaked, driving Eve to observe Caoimhghin blankly. He was crudely attempting to get off it. His foot was tangling with the fallen canopy, making him fall back onto the bed repeatedly, laughing once more. For the life of her, she didn't know why he kept one hand protectively over his manhood. It would be simpler if he used both hands to escape his confinement. It would make it easier for him to remove his legs from the tangled sheets. Her gaze then turned to the elder, who was smiling and giggling at the prince's antics.

"Oi! Hag! Help me!" he demanded between his chortles. His eyes shone with happiness.

"You seem to be having so much fun, and I dare not stop it," Aine said. Caoimhghin flashed her a toothy grin and splayed his arms out. He turned his gaze to the ceiling, breathing hard and content.

"Fun, I say not. Humorous though, yes."

Eve pushed herself off the wall and approached the prince. She silently gave him her arm for assistance that he grabbed on to gladly. He impishly pulled her to the bed. Eve barely missed impacting his groin and apologized profusely. He placed his hand on her head gently, whispering to her that she need not apologize.

"It is all fun and games until someone gets hurt," he commented and then admitted that, before the unannounced shout, he had been close to covering her in glitter. Eve glared. The prince was lucky she did not have a blade on her. Thus, she had to find another means to punish him and what more than to punch him. Not hard, just enough to send a message that she was not amused. He caught her fist.

"Why the violence? I did not get to exact my fun."

"You still thought of it."

"No love to the man who may not be able to have children in the future." The two broke out into laughter.

Aine was pleased with how the prince and mortal communicated. If she hadn't known them better, she would have thought them to be siblings by how they acted together. It was obvious to tell how comfortable the two were with each other's presence. There was mutual respect between the two. Aine wondered how such understanding came to be. Was it a quiet knowledge they had easily shared? Or a feeling of just knowing one another? Either way, it had happened. Importantly though, she wished to see the mortal's feelings of her time in a world that was not her own. "Alas, how do you fare? What are your thoughts so far of our lives or our world?"

Eve narrowed her eyes in thought. She had expected the question yet had not thought of an answer. She only knew the basics of the history the prince had told her and her short experience. At her arrival, she could conclude that fairies were annoying little buggers. Trolls were violent giants who liked the flavor of mortals. The fey had the good and evil of beings like her own kind. Lastly, elves had a shimmering and eerie beauty that women in her world would kill to own. Though, as Eve so far had observed, the female mind was still easily enchanted by that one male who knew how to manipulate it. As she could tell, the parties here were similar to those in her world—but with magic. Though, she doubted the rulers she knew would have bowed down to any evil and given up their land for the good of all.

"If our worlds were to merge, would the creatures ever leave the shadows? Would there be peace?" Eve questioned, looking deeply into Aine's eyes.

"Pardon?" Caoimhghin broke in.

Eve turned to the young prince. "My people view magic to belong to those from the evil realm. Then, others see magic belonging only to the many named gods. Do you believe there will be no fear, no hiding, or destruction if our kinds meet?"

"When the time becomes right, I believe there will be an almost peace. It will take time for it to happen, though," Caoimhghin answered. "But at this present, it is not one of them."

Aine added after his comment, "You are an example of what the mortals could be, could reach. The problem is you are just one single female. One mortal from a vast population. Your people still fear others. They still fight for land. For greed. They don't understand the concept of acceptance and compromise, an issue we too face but have managed to dispel to a minimum with our best efforts."

"How can this be achieved? Perhaps I can show my people, nay, push them to understand that there is a better way to live."

"Tis not that simple," Aine said with a shake of her head and great sorrow in her eyes. Aine knew how much Caoimhghin had told the girl due to the strict instructions she had given him. The knowledge she had allowed was just a straw in a large bundle of hay. Just as well, as even if the young mortal received an answer from them, it would be difficult for her to understand.

"Tell me. We can do it," Eve pleaded.

"No, you can't," Caoimhghin said coldly. His eyes were ice sharp. He gave off an aura that warned Eve not to continue on her path. Eve was blind to his tone and uncomprehending of his body's action. She wanted to learn how the ruler here kept control of so many.

"Please," she continued, her eyes moving between the two feys. "I do not know how much longer the wars in my home can continue until there is none of us left alive."

"Cease your inquiry," Caoimghin ordered. "You are young. Your people are young. There are times when one can only persevere, survive, and be patient. Not all can happen quickly and immediately. Mistakes must be made for others to learn." Eve eyed him distrustfully, but then she saw it. In his eyes, there were years of sadness weighing heavily on his shoulders. But not only on him. Eve looked at the elder and thought, but Aine also. It was in their eyes that persuaded her not to continue the subject.

"I apologize," she told them. "I am just tired of war. Of death. Of killing. It tears me apart and leaves a gaping hole in my soul. I want it to end."

"And it will," Aine stated. "But I can't tell you when. Just know, there is hope. Be happy with that. There will be a future."

"You give us mortals more praise than is deserving." Their hope— their praise was not worthy to any of her kind— that included her. She was here to steal from them, that was if she lived long enough to do the deed. Caoimhghin knew she was not there for good. Yet, still, they made her seem to be better than she was. If she told them her true purpose, every sin she had committed, and the history of her kind— What then would they think of her?

#  CHAPTER 10 

EVE'S FOLLOWING DAYS did not continue as they previously had been. Not long after, a messenger walked into the room. He spoke not, but pulled out a scroll from the satchel at his side and gave it to Aine. Eve stared at him, her head tilting to the side. He appeared— normal. When his eyes swerved to hers, she saw his brilliant oddity. He had shining light blue eyes that could only belong to the sky. They were entrancing. His eyes almost assisted her in ignoring the toga he wore. He held a staff adorned with two serpents entwined together at the top. He said nothing to her. He just stared at her with a piercing gaze. Then, as quickly as he had arrived, he left.

The scroll that the messenger gave to the healer was from the court. It contained information about a future summons. However, there was no date or time specified. For this reason, Eve's thoughts tormented her at her unknown fate that lay in the hands of King Oberon and Queen Titania.

The same day, Eve was deemed healthy enough to be moved out of the medical ward. The castle's helpers gave her items of necessity, including a new wardrobe, accessories to bathe, and the little that came with her— except her weapons. The court did not trust her enough to hold on to them. The location of her new chambers was not far from her previous room. Her new space was smaller but simple and contained all she needed: a bed, a chest, a table with a chair, and a single drawer. She still had guards outside her door. Aine still came by for her daily checks but, Coaimhghin did not stay. He had to take care of his responsibilities in his small kingdom.

Eve kept a tense silence around Aine. She had no one to talk to about her temporary new place of work. It was Aine who would always start the conversation. There was one that left an impact on Eve. Aine had walked in and casually said, "You are healing exceedingly well. Good. You might have a chance then to get that damnable dagger."

"How? Who told?!"

"Caoimhghin appraised me. I'm astonished you had let yourself become read so easily. Fortunately, I am in thought with him. It would be nice to see the palace overturned and shaken. We haven't had the pleasure of any original distractions here for years. I would like to know more as I saved your life and wish it would not end soon. Think on it." Aine left the room. Eve's mouth gapped open. Out in the hall, Aine allowed herself a small smile.

Feys were wild creatures. Woefully, Eve needed their aid. The next day, Eve informed Aine of her quest in more detail. Aine's best plan was to strategize their next moves after her summons. There was no point wasting time and energy if there was a possibility of Eve's execution.

"Any advice you may give to survive that coming day? I wish not to enter the halls blind."

"Mortals are considered stupid and inferior by all that live here. Use it."

Aine was forthcoming with her knowledge of the underground. Oberon was a man set on traditions--but only when they worked. After all, he was a leader and knew that even though the outdated path had been successful before, there wasn't a certainty it would continue to function as it did. There were times a new approach was necessary.

Queen Tatiana was moderately different. Unlike her husband,

she scoffed and sneered at the laws but followed them regardless. The Queen showed her displeasure with the rules by running and hiding in the world above. She stayed there for a certain amount of time to spite her husband. During those intervals, there were affairs with many mortal men to make her husband jealous. There were no children in those unions, and she ran back to Oberon consistently. The Queen loved her husband deeply. Even when she was with another, Oberon was always first over any others.

Eve followed a routine in a feeble attempt to get her mind off her problems. She was dissatisfied with not having a plan to get her back home. Hence, Eve woke at the crow's call and hesitantly tested the limits of her body by stretching out her muscles. Following her conditioning, she did a rudimentary sword-work instilled in her since she could walk. At first, her muscles were tense from being unused. They quickly and slowly strengthened to the form she had been before and perhaps, better. The rate she healed was extraordinary. It was unnatural— another thing, another problem, another difference that made her more aberrational than she already was.

Eve was not alone in thought about her abnormal rate of healing. Though not frightened as the mortal, Aine was impressed by the speed the young woman had recovered. It was marvelous. If the girl had died, Aine would have concluded it was due to her extreme injuries. That did not occur.

A messenger had called Aine and her field team after the soldiers had killed the trolls. She was mystified immediately by the who that had survived their brutality. There was doubt the girl would survive the night. She was proven wrong. The young woman endured many nights in fever and pain. Then, Eve had awoken. Aine's first speculation was that the girl was not just a mortal but something more. She wondered if the girl had always been able to heal or was it a reaction to the magic in the air. There was a test in mind that would clarify her hypothesis. An assessment all the children had to participate in when the time came.

Though it rarely occurred, not all of the children born in the world of magic had the ability. There were two groups of species in the underground: the lesser intelligent ones and those with higher understanding. The majority of the imbecilic species had natural chaotic magic in their veins. Overall, it was harmless and weak. Their magic allowed them to take several beatings and harm that others couldn't. For those of higher intellect, most of the children's magic didn't appear until adulthood. The age varied. Like most lower species, their powers were passed down from family to family. It was rare when a child received gifts of their own that an ancestor previously contained or was new to the family.

The test Aine wished to use on Eve was not complicated or dangerous. It helped determine the element— and sometimes, elements— of the individual's magic. If Aine could ascertain Eve's power, she perhaps could narrow the species that the mortal was. Once completed, she could have an idea of Eve's gifts and use a secondary evaluation test to show their benefits to the council. Hopefully, that would increase the hybrid's life. If the King and Queen wished to end the girl, they wouldn't be able to by the people's choice. To a certain extent, the royal couple still followed the will of their people. If they did not, they would be in danger of having a rebellion on their hands.

Aine created a list of the needed items for the test and slipped them into Eve's room, dismissing the guard for the day. The day before, she had brought in a small round table, telling the guard, who was there at the time, that she needed extra space for the medicines. There, she placed a bowl of water with a single floating leaf that contained magical properties. Eve watched her movements curiously.

Caoimghin had spoken in length to Eve of a test that identified the status of a magical being. Eve had chortled at him when he explained how the test worked and its materials. She couldn't understand how a leaf floating in water could demonstrate magic. It was just a floating leaf. Eve was disappointed to be left in the shadows by the prince as she became perplexed at the two chairs Aine had dragged to the table. They were positioned opposite and facing each other.

"Sit, please," Aine said, sitting down and waving to the only other available seat. Eve approached carefully, sitting on the chair warily. The two sat in silence, staring at each other. Neither of them moved as both waited for the other to stir or speak first. The only sounds perpetrating the silent room were those from the outside. Eve became anxious and unconsciously was the first to shift. Her leg started to twitch and then moved in a rhythmic up and down pattern.

"Agh," sighed Eve, "a bowl with water. Fascinating." She waited for Aine to reply, but the other woman remained silent, staring at her with her unwavering gaze. Eve laid a single hand on the table, began to tap her fingers, and let out a single, long yawn. The awkwardness turned into boredom. Perchance, this would persuade Aine to speak to her finally. It didn't. Aine kept looking at her. The constant stare created an unknown tension in her body that she released with a quick tilt of her head, the bones in her neck cracking loudly. "You wish for me to wash my hands?" she joked.

Aine's determined silence almost cracked at the childish personality Eve showed. Her silence was a necessary evil. The more passionate Eve's emotions became, the easier it was to evaluate if the girl had magic or not. Regrettably, Aine's quick peek at the bowl welled feelings of worry. She bit the inside of her lip. She was not seeing what she wished. There was no shifting of the liquid or destruction of the leaf.

Eve's jaw tightened in frustration. Under her mask, she felt the side of her temple throb in agitation. "I am tired of whatever game you have brought for us to play. Why do you stare at me so? Have I done you wrong?"

Aine didn't answer. She wondered that, since Eve was older than the children, perhaps the girl's magic came if only placed in danger, or did she have some limited control upon it? Aine eyed the mask on the girl's face. That specific article of cloth was intriguing since the first day she had tried to pull it off. The energy surrounding it gave her a feeling of old and new magic. She swore it felt like fey and something unique. When she touched the mask a second time, she realized that the mask was not a mask. It was a touchable illusion that could only be created by the strongest of magic. She had watched Eve attempt to take it off relentlessly without success in secret, which was odd as it was strictly part of Eve. Aine decided to try another way to show the magic and ordered, "Place your hands over the bowl, hands open flat, palms facing down. I want them low enough that nature can feel you but high enough that you are not touching the dish."

"Why?" the question came out from Eve.

"Just do it, you child," Aine snapped. She watched with exasperation as Eve defiantly crossed her arms in front of her chest, a pout on her face. If her work didn't press her for time, she would have laughed and cajoled the girl into doing what she had directed.

"No harm will come to you," Aine informed.

"Truly?"

"I promise."

"You sure..."

"Fer the love of Oberon, get to it, girl!"

"But I don't love Oberon," Eve replied with a large grin. She was enjoying her childish insolence in riling up the older woman.

"Ugh!"

"Fine. Fine...fine." Eve gave in to Aine's demand as she saw the woman puff up her cheeks. If Aine inflated anymore, there was a danger she could erupt. That would be sad and comical but one she wished not to see. Her imagination could significantly differ from reality. Therefore, she moved her hands warily over the bowl as the fey had instructed and waited...and waited...and waited some more. Nothing happened.

The water didn't overspill, transfigure, create an object, or act as a weapon. It stayed undisturbed. Feelings of anger and disappointment welled in Aine. With it, her patience was running thin. She urged Eve to keep her hands hovering over the water. The girl undoubtedly wanted to speak. *Come on. Do something. Overflow. Shift. Move. Just react,* Aine thought.

"Aine?"

Aine didn't heed Eve initially. She was oblivious and focused solely on her thoughts. Oberon was not a fiend, but without any merits or valuable skills that Eve could contribute— he would have no choice but to execute the girl. Aine couldn't allow that to pass. She had to demonstrate and document the importance of the mortal.

"Healer!" Eve shouted, finally gaining Aine's attention. "Do you fair well?"

"Indeed," Aine croaked. "Do not worry."

"I was informed this test was to transpire some results. Perhaps the water is not feeling like itself today," Eve quipped. Aine stayed silent, still lost in her mind and staring at the bowl. Eve decided to rest her hands on the table. "Water is special at my home."

Aine looked at Eve, who took it as a sign to continue to talk, "There was this woman. She was an older friend of mine. Even without knowing who I was, she treated me with a kindness that I had never received. She lived out in the wilderness, on the outskirts of my family's lands. She had a small cabin where people would come to her with ailments the church could not heal. She followed the old ways the villagers would call it.

"The fateful day came when a boy died under her care. Wolves had attacked him, and there was nothing anyone could do as his injuries were significant, but the people did not see it. The villagers proclaimed that she was a witch, a follower of Satan. They told the church that she followed the pagan gods of her family that had come from Leinster.

"As the lord of the small farming land, my father's duty was to charge and prove her guilt. A priest came to oversee the series of tests. The first consisted of the woman being stripped naked. My father, his men, the priest, and the monks diligently viewed her body. They looked for a mark upon her body and found one positioned high upon her inner thigh. The priest then loudly shouted that she did have the brand of evil for those to hear outside. The church's procedure was to have the discoloration burned away. His shout fueled the crowd into a frenzy, and they called for blood. They threw her outside for all to see her taint of sin. The blacksmith walked out. In his hand was a heated prong that had the shape of a crudely made cross at its end. The crowd watched as the men held her down and the metal pressed onto her skin. She screamed with anguish. I remember the smell of burnt flesh filling the air. I hoped that would end the inquisition— but it was not to be.

"The second test was to cleanse her soul thoroughly from Satan's hold. She was walked out of the village to the nearest lake, wearing only a dirty rag to keep a portion of her body from lustful eyes. The people threw rotten food at her, yelling and shouting until they all reached the body of water to continue the ritual. The priest prayed for the woman as the men tied her hands and legs with a rope. At her feet, they attached a sizeable heavy stone. They carried her to the water and threw her in. The men gave no second glances, and the world became silent other than from the priest's mumblings. If she floated, she would be tied and burned to a stake. If she sunk, the priest had cleansed her soul. Either way, she died. Her body, to this day, is still in the waters.

"I wonder if the same is done here to those who do not reform to those in power," Eve said. She sighed and spoke sadly, "I failed your test, have I not? Am I to see my death soon?"

"It was just a test," Aine answered somewhat hopefully. "It doesn't prove anything." Eve looked at the woman with blank eyes.

"A test. A test that I failed," Eve blankly said though inside, something dark and ancient brewed. It fed off and amplified her despair and anger. Just as her father had predicted, she was worthless— nothing.

Aine narrowed her eyes in confusion as the room became polluted with darkness. She saw it seep out of Eve. Was the key to Eve's power negative emotions? Seelie's magic did not work as such. Unless ... "No— "

"Puck fooled me. He played me like one would play the harp. He sang enchanting words, weaving hope that the answers that I needed had been at my fingertips. And I, like a simpleton, fell for it." Eve clenched her fist, her nails lengthening and digging into her palm. She felt no pain; there was only a flame roaring to life in her.

No. That is not right. Eve knew she was in this world because she had taunted Puck and was his involuntary thief. The temper and waves of anger clashing and disordering her thoughts, were illogical. Her skin burned and itched, and tears flowed down her face, adding to the chaotic symphony in her. Her wrath was solely on ending Puck's life. Further, there was a constant and unending pounding in her head. Voices, not her own, shouted, urging her to kill Puck. Nay, to kill anyone in her vicinity. She covered her ears to block them out, but it made them only louder until the voices merged and became indistinguishable. "Quiet. Quiet. Quiet— ," she repeatedly said.

"Child?" Aine questioned worriedly. Eve wanted to ask her for help but could not as the vileness pulled her into a blackness that was not hers. There was only a notion in her mind— to destroy and leave no one alive.

Aine watched Eve become deathly silent, the girl's head dropping to her chest. The change in the young woman was quick and disturbing. Then, the girl pushed from the table and eerily stood up, her hands dropping to her side. There was something malicious about the mortal that made Aine slowly stand up herself. She crept away from any obstacles that could impede her path if the mortal decided to attack her. She eyed Eve more intently and watched in sick captivation as smoke started to escape from the edges of Eve's closed eyes. The effect from the brume of it made the mask the girl wore more haunting.

The magic Aine sensed, at the surface, was evil. She had witnessed it once a long time ago. The dark magic had belonged to the brother of the Queen. At the end of his life, his unnatural powers possessed his being. He had turned against his own and perished under his abilities soon after. His soul was gone, and only a husk filled with cruelty was left. Since he had no children, there was no worry that any would inherit his powers. Yet, somehow, it did. It now resided inside the mortal. Mortals did not have the capability to reign the powers of seelies. *Damn him. Damn Puck. His proximity must have acted as a catalyst,* Aine reflected.

The bowl on the table started to tap-dance in spot, slowly becoming more erratic in its movements— the water inside boiling and spilling out. Visibly underneath the bowl were scorched marks on the table's surface. Aine stared at it in shock. It confirmed the girl's power was that of an unseelie, just like the Queen's brother. She needed to wake up Eve from the trance she was in, or the girl was doomed to the same fate as the fey who previously had the same magic.

"Eve," Aine called. The rest of the words she wanted to speak choked in her throat. Eve's head snapped up. Her eyes opened to show illuminating red pupils. Underneath their power, the old healer became paralyzed on the spot. She felt as if her soul was being torn apart, analyzed, and then reformed into something that wasn't her. Aine couldn't look away. Near her, the bowl exploded, throwing shards in all directions. One flew and sliced her cheek, sending her into action. Hoping they were nearby, she shouted, "Guards!"

Two elf guards making their rounds burst into the room with their swords at hand. They saw the panicked healer and rushed to her. Unexpectedly they were halted by an invisible pressure. They turned to where it was coming from and looked at their "prisoner" to see one of her arms lifted, palm facing them. Their eyes widened in shock. The elders or the royal family usually emanated such strength. To see it come from a mortal was frightening, but they pushed through their fear--they had to. When her eyes snapped to them, they involuntarily took a step back. Only such eyes could belong to the darkness they had spent years training to fight. Such evil could not exist. The guards' eyes shined a bright blue as they activated their gifts to make them faster and fiercer. Soon afterward, they channeled their energy into their swords, flaring them to life in blue flames. They attacked and shortly after died, their fight was short-lived.

Eve avoided their attacks with ease. She danced between the two, reading their body language to determine their subsequent movements. Even as they sped their assaults, the young lady continued to keep clear of them and, evidentially, tire them. She opened her right hand and pulled their swords from them across the room. With a graceful turn of her body and using her other hand in a swatting motion, she hurled the two guards against the wall. Upon impact, they became unconscious.

"I see assistance is needed," a man spoke. Aine looked around the room to find the mysterious rescuer. She saw only herself and Eve. "Psh. I am here."

Aine and Eve searched the small space with their eyes, looking in different directions. Aine was the first to spot a smirking Caoimhghin waving at her enthusiastically from the mirror attached to the dresser. Aine was relieved at his perfect timing to visit the girl. There was little she could do to stop the mortal. She was a healer, not a warrior. Her training was to medically help her people and research new ways to aid others. The field of battle was not, or had ever been, for her.

"Yes. I welcome the assistance," Aine said. Her voice had Eve following her gaze to Caoimhghin's location. A deep threatening growl escaped the girl's lips.

Unbeknownst to the mortal and others, Caoimhghin had deviously linked Eve's mirror to his magical orbs. When he wasn't busy, he would take peeks and check on Eve. He had his sentient hairy-calling rock guards, the *petra trog,* watch over the girl in scheduled sessions when he couldn't. It was lady luck that they had seen Eve change during their watch. One had come running to him with gurgled and broken words, hands gesturing radically to emphasize the importance of the occurring event. He had called up one of his seer's globes to himself and watched as Eve injured the guards.

Aine's acceptance of Caoimhghin's help allowed his orb to transform into an almost duplicate of the mirror on the other side. It hovered slightly on top of the ground. It was sturdy enough that the prince was not worried about climbing through the portal to the other side. When his body fully emerged into Eve's room, darkness surrounded him. He could see its mist seep out of Eve. It slowly floated to him and caressed his skin, asking permission to merge with the malevolence he had buried deep in his core. It was darkness he had inherited from his mother, Queen Titania, who was half-unseelie herself. He was her only child to be a quarter unseelie while his siblings were like his father, pure seelies. He gritted his teeth and fought away the calling. "Eve, awake child!"

Inside herself, a roaring ocean kept her lost. Her body thrummed with the rhythm of her rapidly beating heart. When she tried to clear her mind, the pain was her reward. She was becoming tired from fighting. It would be easier to drown in the rage and be free of her humanity. Her darkness was intense, and it wanted her to submit to its incredible powers.

It was odd that she felt that there were two of herself. One was her innocence. The other was an evil taint growing with each cruelty she did or allowed. That taint wanted to dominate her. It gnawed at the edges of the defense that protected her consciousness. It kept her mind in a chaotic state.

Caoimhghin watched Eve's head move snake-like to his direction, a low growl coming from her. He was confident the girl was an unseelie hybrid with a single look and a powerful one. Her darkness gained strength as the white of her eyes filled with black. It then spread out like veins down her cheeks. Her skin swiftly paled so that it came to the point that she was almost translucent. Yes, she was an unseelie. Though, how was that possible?

Full-bred unseelies were the ultimate evil of the world below and were constantly kept in check. They were watched and guarded by the best warriors. A hybrid of unseelie blood was destructive and evil incarnate. Their actions created stories that shook the bones of all living beings. They left nightmares in their wake so horrendous that it was difficult to believe they had occurred.

Luckily, Eve was not at this stage...yet. She has not fully transformed into a daemon. Internally, she had to fight it to keep the transformation process from completing, or so Caoimhghin hoped. If true, it meant not all was lost. There was a chance to bring her back. First and foremost, he needed to calm Eve down so she could gain control of herself. Afterward, he would have to teach her to bury the darkness and never use it again, even accidentally.

"Aine, listen, darling," Caoimhghin called to the healer while he faced Eve. He rose his arms to show he was not dangerous to the girl. As he looked calmly at Eve, he said to Aine, "Your lovely calmness is needed. When I get to Eve, I shall grab hold of her and keep her as still as possible. You shall come upon her and touch her mind. Give our mortal a reprieve from what holds her from retaining her humanity. That will bring her back to us."

"When?"

"You will know." The young royal smiled at Eve and lowered himself in height to look weaker. He steadily took steps forward to the berserker. If he rushed at her, he took a significant risk of possibly being killed. Eve owned him a favor once this day was over. "How are you doing? If your memory stays intact of these events, I apologize for any injuries that might happen to you. I promise I will not hurt you much as I can. The same you cannot say or promise to me in your state. If little of you is left, do not hurt me badly."

Caoimhghin ran to Eve, became close enough to catch her off guard. He grabbed her at her waist, lifted her from her feet, and pushed her to the ground. He proceeded to pin her down, using his weight and strength to keep her movements to a minimum. He took hold of her wrists as she struggled underneath him. He watched Aine approach and felt triumph that his plan was going as intended. Like his life, his win did not last long. A knee to his precious jewels loosened his grip on her. She then punched his face. He rolled away from her as a red ball of energy formed from the girl's hand. She threw it at him, and he ducked underneath it. Caoimhghin followed her action by throwing a defensive orb at her. It exploded into a brilliant bright light, blinding her momentarily. His second globe hit Eve directly. It surrounded the mortal with smoke to disorient her. Then, he moved behind the young woman and pulled her into his chest. He tried to soothe her with sounds and words as she struggled in his grasp. He used one foot to spread her legs further apart so that she could not kick him. "Eve. Love. It is okay. Nobody is going to harm you here or now. Let the pain and worries you feel go."

Aine moved forward and placed her hands upon Eve's temples. Soon afterward, the mortal's erratic movements stopped. Despite that, her breathing was harsh, loud, and labored. Eve's head rolled back so that she was looking up at Caoimhghin. The transitional stages of her face bewitched him. The evil fell from her form. She was back to her vulnerable mortal self. He noticed there was awareness and tears in the girl's eyes. She turned around and cried in his arms, burying her face into his shirt as she sobbed heartily.

"I am sorry," she cried.

*She remembers,* the prince thought. "You are indeed a hybrid. A dangerous one. How did this come to be? A girl born half-mortal and half unseelie. You poor child."

# CHAPTER 11

EVE LOOKED UP to the ceiling. The young woman detached from the world around her and contemplated the events that had transpired yesterday and during the early morning. Caoimhghin had held onto her as she had dissolved into tears. He didn't mind, but she couldn't help but continuously apologize for her inability to control her actions. He shushed her gently. He aided her to her bed and under the blankets. He joined her, lying on top of the blankets instead. He didn't hold her, but he stayed at her side through the rest of the day and night. Many times, Eve would fall asleep and then be awakened by nightmares. Every nightmare ended with her murdering her allies. Furthermore, the voices in her head wouldn't leave her alone. Luckily, neither did her face transform from the erratic feelings she had.

Aine left and returned to the room. The first time she came back, she came with help. The guards and healers she brought walked into the room right after she did. Their fellow warriors carried them out with the healers stuck at their sides. The injured guards were taken away on a cot laid upon a wicker frame.

Aine left again to bring the cleaners. The cleaners were brownies that stood in height about three feet at most. The creatures were thin, and their appearance slightly distasteful. They were brown-toned like the earth and had a wizened-shaggy look. They were dressed in rags, barefoot, and had a childlike mannerism as they diligently did their duty to make the room pristine. Aine had tried to help them clean, but they had glared and kicked her out of the room. She did not come back. Then, after the laborers had done their job, they left not long after, leaving just Eve and the prince.

There finally came a time when Eve could no longer cry. The need for sleep was non-existent. Caoimhghin randomly broke the silence in the room. He summarized and disclosed very little about the shades known as the unseelies.

He didn't explain the origin of the unseelies. Common knowledge was that they were old and ancient as magic itself. They once had a kingdom located next to his parents. Together, they had helped humanity flourish from outside the caves. Instead of possessing light magic, they were darkness and desperation embodied in many different creatures. Lastly, unseelies were possible to exterminate, but it came at many costs his parents had discovered.

Disappointedly, Caoimhghin did not divulge any more information. His tone did confirm to Eve that unseelies were evil incarnate. She couldn't help but hate the life force that flowed in her blood. Why would God allow her to be born if she was some sort of a demon?

Quickly and unexpectedly, the sun rose. The night had gone by fast, with Eve and the prince falling asleep. They woke up in a jolt from a series of knocks. Eve opened the door to see a familiar guard. He smiled at her hair and curtly notified her that her time to be heard had finally happened. The guard added that she had to look respectable for the King and Queen. He then handed her a basket with clothes almost identical to the ones Puck had dressed her in when he had flicked his fingers together. The prince's eyes widened in surprise as he heard the news that his parents would be talking to the mortal. Usually, such talks were the council's job. He knew his brother had a hand in this recent development. So, with a quick farewell, Caoimhghin disappeared in a scattering of glitter.

Eve was left alone in her thoughts. All she could think of was that today was her last— as far as she knew. The young knight doubted that the King or Queen would allow her to live if they did know what kind of creature lay hidden inside her. She had angered Prince Aelfdene, who she knew was determined to see her dead. He probably had run to his parents excitedly when he figured out what she was. It was daunting, terrifying, and soul crushing to know that perhaps this was her end. She was not to die in battle, or as a hero, as she had hoped.

For all these years, Eve had fooled those in her world. Yet, she was not or could ever be a master deceiver. It wasn't part of her nature. Every lie she had done— told— had been for survival. The unsavory acts she participated in and the outward attitude she had shown were to keep up her family's legacy. A legacy that still sat heavily on her shoulders, more so now that she was not on her lands to protect her people. She did not know how time worked in this world or if it was faster or slower than was average, but she needed to go home. If she didn't, her cousin would immediately rise in status. It would be a significant loss if that came to be as it would end in heartbreak and possibly the end of her family land to another lord that could play her cousin for a fool. Then, her people on her land would have no protection from the evil of greed. They would be vulnerable to many other Lords' insidious demands.

On the other hand, perhaps it was better that she never went home. Eve was something dark. She was an *unseelie*, a monster in the world of monsters.

"Only to me should this happen. Always on the wrong side of the river full of brimstone and flames," Eve bemoaned. "And I can't get this buggering mask off my face." She hit the cot in anger and once more tugged at her mask. She wanted it off. Not only that, she wanted her sword, so next time she saw Puck, she could impale him with it for coming to her at the cavern. Unfortunately, neither of her wants were available. "Remember the words. I must keep to faith. Persevere not in wrath."

*Knock. Knock.* The door reverberated from whoever had come

to visit. Eve looked at the door in confusion. She wondered if the guard who had come in the morning had returned, bringing more news. It was not yet late in the evening and rarely did someone ask permission to advance into the room.

Eve jumped to her feet, pulling a blanket over her form when she felt an unexplained chill. She then rushed to the door and opened it. When she placed her hand on the knob, the darkness came to her in a startling rush. Its strength almost blackened her vision. She quelled it quickly back. The evil's odd arrival put Eve on alert as she moved her attention back to receive her guest. She opened the door, and standing there was the other prince Eve wished never to see again. She narrowed her eyes at his smug face. She peeked out of her room to see the hall empty and void of all. There were no guards or nurses. There was no one. Slight panic entered her chest as she realized she was alone with the prince.

"I see you have not properly dressed for the day," Prince Aelfdene commented with a sly and pervy twist on his lips as his eyes raked over her form. Taken off guard and feeling unsure of what was happening, she tightened the blanket around her in an attempt to cover her body more. She was casually dressed but not to take visitors. Her clothes at the moment were loose, ragged, and comfortable. Yet, it didn't stop his eyes from their roaming. Instead, it seemed as if they had become fiercer. Revulsion and humiliation rolled over her, her skin coming alive at her feelings.

"Where are the guards?" Eve asked, blocking the entrance to her room, taking a step forward. Aelfdene answered her action with his own, one of his hands hovering to touch her shoulder. There was a sick glint in his eyes.

"Nowhere and everywhere," he mysteriously stated as he started to touch the ends of her hair, causing a shiver to go up and down her spine. He didn't notice her discomfort as she kept her face empty of any other emotion except annoyance. She held herself back from attacking him. It would do her no good to injure the prince. His parents might end up hanging her for hurting their son.

If Aelfdene went further than was appropriate, Eve wouldn't

be able to keep herself from subduing him. If that didn't work, well, damn to Caoimhghin and his warning. She would give Aelfdene a taste of her darkness. It was begging for her to kill him. Giving into it to put the arrogant prince in his place presently was worth losing a part, even just a hint, of her soul.

"If your purpose here is to irritate me, I give you leave," Eve said, raising her head to look taller than her short stature. Aelfdene walked closer, and Eve stood her ground. His hand wandered down her back. He jerked the blanket off her, and it dropped to the floor. Next, he moved to touch her again. Eve allowed a little of her *powers* out as she swatted his hand away. His eyes flashed in surprise at her increased strength and speed. The prince then took a step back, confused and angry. Afterward, he pushed past her and into the room. Eve was not pleased to have her sanctuary taken over by the one person she, at the moment, intensely disliked. She clenched her fist as the darkness chewed at the edges of her mind, incessantly whispering that she should listen to them. No, she must hold it back. Caoimhghin had predicted that the pull of her evil would become more intense. She did not know how much longer she could stay away from its temptation. But first— "I wish you to leave now! You have no right to be in this room."

"I am a royal! I can go wherever I wish, you filthy mortal!" Aelfdene spat. Eve moved away as she watched his personality switch rapidly, his face twisting in what he must have assumed was a perfectly charming smile. "There was a rumor of an incident? I wish to know more and demand you tell me," he ordered as he turned in place at the center of the room, his eyes brightening in the morning light.

"It would be a pity to break such demand, but as there was no incident, there is nothing to tell," Eve lightly answered as she pushed past him, hitting him with her shoulder and sauntering to a drawer to pull out clothes. "Thus, with the lack of news I have for you, why don't you sod off." Before she knew what had happened, Aelfdene was behind her, holding her tightly to himself, pushing her into the drawer so her hips dug and pressed uncomfortably against the surface. She struggled in his grasp, panic constricting her throat. She wiggled in his hold and took deep breaths as her vile nature rose to the surface once more.

"You will tell me."

"Nothing happened, you dimwitted oaf, so there is nothing I can tell!"

"Yes, there is," he whispered harshly into her ear. "You think I don't know. I have my spies tittering here and there. They told me that your past guards left with extreme injuries. Then, there is the unexpected arrival of my dear brother. So...tell me, and I won't hurt you— much."

Eve was already determined to give him nothing. She calmed herself by breathing in a repetitive pattern. Many thoughts rolled in her mind about her newfound friends. As few as she had, she would not place them in harm. "No," she growled.

"It would do well to inform you that I take pleasure in getting the information I want when done forcefully," he crooned evilly as one hand went down her back and touched her bottom lightly, pulling her waist to his own. A cry of distaste escaped her lips with the addition of a snarl. She knew what he wanted, the sick bastard. She could feel his arousal. With little choice, she let loose her animal. She would no longer allow him to continue his caress as if her body was his own to take.

Damn Caoimhghin's words! She would take hell over her soul to end this man who dishonestly dared to handle her. She would kill this one man. She was willing to give Satan her soul to ensure Aelfdene would harm no one else for whatever sinister plans his mind had concocted. An ice-cold feeling trickled from her head to her toes, her heart rapidly beating loudly in her ears. "Oh. You want to play. I can feel your want. Your heart aches for me," Aelfdene moaned in her ear.

"Do not TOUCH ME!" Eve turned around and brought her hands to his chest. She pushed him with half of her strength. She watched with satisfaction as his body flew across the room and hit the wall. His eyes never once strayed from her own. He had an understanding expression and a sick knowing grin on his face. *What have I done?*

The voices in her mind answered her question. They were adamant she hadn't done anything but hurt a scum who should not be alive. They ordered her to finish the deed, to kill the prince where he lay, helpless and vulnerable. *No,* she internally screamed. She fought against the change she felt overcome her, the feeling of cold and hot waging war inside her. She would not harm a man on the ground with no weapons to protect himself. Tears dripped down her face from frustration. The cold she felt didn't want to recede and was winning over the warmth that was her.

In the background, there was a voice. It was familiar and warm. It was Aine. It sounded as if it was far away but getting closer, worry in its tone. Eve's name was shouted, pulling her from the trappings of her mind. "Eve— ." Eve opened her eyes to look at the older woman, closing them quickly again as half her vision was red. The old healer hugged and started to soothe her. Once Eve was calm, Aine directed her words to the man on the ground. "You fool."

Seconds after, they were joined by another. "Aine, where is your lovely— AELFDENE!" Caoimhghin's voice boomed. Eve rose her head and watched the younger prince, her friend, enter the room. He stomped in his brother's direction. Once close enough to his older brother, he grabbed him by his collar, pushing him to the wall with cold, emotionless eyes. Around her friend was a dark aura that was almost like her own. Her inner wickedness answered the call of his evil. She gritted her teeth against it. "What have you done, dear brother?"

"I know now. I saw," Aelfdene laughed, blood seeping from the corner of his lip. His nose was broken and bleeding. "I saw! And everybody will know of the unseelie bitch in our midst. When our father finds out, she will be dead before the trial starts." Aelfdene twisted his gaze onto her. "Evil mistress, take this day for it is your last."

"If I could— " Caiomhghin started to threaten.

"What would you do, brother? Tear me limb from limb? Play puzzles? Duel? What? Tell me, brother," Aelfdene taunted. "Let me go before you make it worse for yourself. You know how mother is when 'her boys' fight."

Caoimhghin threw Aefldene out of the room, slamming the door behind him. His brother let out a burst of booming laughter. "Why father gave him power, I will never know," Caoimhghin said more to himself than the women in the room. "He has no control of his actions or feelings. He shouldn't be in charge of others."

Eve nodded in agreement and leaned her head down to Aine's shoulder. The woman patted her gently behind the head. Eve knew that what had happened had been her fault. She should have asked who had been at the door before opening the blasted thing. She had let her guard down, thinking she had been safe. Eve had forgotten momentarily that this world was not her own. That there were dangers that lurked in the places she did not know.

"Aine, where are your guards?" Caoimhghin questioned urgently.

"I do not know, and my lack of knowledge of their unknown location worries me," the woman answered. Aine again patted Eve's head and guided the girl back onto the bed, giving the young woman time to sit down. "Watch over the girl while I grab a servant to look for my men. I fear your brother has done something afoul to them."

"Go," the young prince permitted. Aine left the room at a rapid pace. Caoimhghin crossed his arms over his chest, and he walked to Eve. She did not look up at his approaching figure as her eyes were on her entwined fingers on her lap. "Eve, I apologize for my brother."

"No apology is needed from you. I must hear it from the Captain. I do not see that happening in the foreseeable future. Your brother looks to be a man rarely acquainted with punishment when he does wrong," Eve flung herself onto her bed, her head hitting the cot. She faced the young King. "I swear to that of my God that next time he will not live if he dares touch or comes near me again without permission." Caoimhghin nodded in understanding. She could see in his eyes he was not pleased with her definitive statement. He knew no word he could say would change her mind, and he could not fault her for her feelings. She was a warrior.

Eve turned away from the prince. She was angry with herself and not pleased with how she had reacted. The young knight should have done more against her assailant. She could never have anticipated a man would ever dare assault her as Prince Aelfdene had. She knew it happened to women in her world but seeing it differed from being part of such atrocities. If the situation ever arose again, she would not let her attacker live. They would not go unpunished, armed or not.

"I apologize, either way. Father will hear of this. But it will do little good, as you are correct in assessing my brother's personality. The love of his children blinds our father. My brother has been disciplined for past transgressions, still never to an extreme that taught him any humility. Then, there is what is in your blood. Unseelies of your magnitude are not a good omen, especially since you are still in a physical form. With the knowledge we have amassed over the years, the history of the things those monsters did is unbelievable. The fear of these creatures is still present in this world."

"It is rare to dispel old fears," Eve mumbled, thinking of home. Her world was somewhat similar. The people lived by either following the church, and then their sovereign not because of loyalty but fear. Rebelling against either was death. Eve had seen many hung in the name of God because an individual or a family followed a different ancient religion that the priest taught belonged to Satan. If the offense was extreme, the people or persons did not have the mercy of a quick death. Oh no, they were tortured and burned alive with loved ones left to watch while the rest of the population cheered for the punishment to continue. It wasn't difficult, nor was it a choice, but to follow the word of the man who said he represented God or the ruler born to rule because God demanded it. Eve knew when to nod and what to utter at the right moment to these men. "Away we should move from the topic and what we could have done. Tell me more. You said you would. What is there to know of the unseelies?"

"At the beginning of magic, unseelies had existed together with us seelies. They did have a physical body like all living beings. My mother and her brother were the first hybrids of light and dark. They would also be the last. Instead of their birth uniting the seelies and unseelies closer, it pushed them further apart. My mother's father did not wish to continue following the unseelies path into darkness. He saw the future of his people losing themselves, and he wanted no part of the direction they were taking. His people killed him not long after expressing his views, in the hopes of stopping his kind from making a huge mistake."

"I am concluding that the unseelies' path was dangerous."

"It was. You see, the unseelies feared death. It was inevitable for all things living. We are born, we age, and we all die. Their fear became forever trapped in their minds. It grew into paranoia, and the need to be immortal was all they could think of. Even though they had as long a life-span as the fey, it was not enough for them. Their fear drew them to become immersed in their dark magic. Soon, they dived into unnatural powers that went against the natural order of life. It transformed them from the inside and drove them into an evil hole they couldn't escape.

"The forbidden power drew others, human and seelies alike. They became tempted by the idea of living forever— to be like the Gods they saw and the greed for more power. My father couldn't allow this idea to flourish more and ordered the death of all unseelies, which included the children. The soldiers completed the orders successfully with few causalities. My uncle died during this crusade. It would not be until the war with the mortals that my father realized that the essence of the unseelies had lived deep in the ground," the prince informed.

"The shadows your father feared you mentioned."

Caoimhghin nodded. "Bloodshed fed the unseelies. Death made them stronger. Yet, with all the energy they had consumed, it wasn't enough for them to regain their physical bodies fully. Before that became a possibility, my father submitted to the mortals. He brought all with magic down to the underground. Later, another battle occurred that has not ended even now."

"They are alive?" Eve asked in shock.

"Yes. We keep the monsters at the border of our kingdom in

a manageable population," Caoimhghin said. "We are losing against them slowly. Destroying them costs lives, and our magic has a price. Our magic keeps us living longer than normal— slow aging. It is a trade to keep our benefits of longevity. We cannot have children as easily as the mortals. Soon, there will not be enough of us to keep them in a small number or at bay. They are invincible in that they do not have fear. They will never give up."

Eve worried her lip at the new information. "How can they be killed?"

"With great difficulty and sacrifice. Soldiers must place themselves before evil and be close enough to magic their powers into an item. We weaken them, and they cannot keep themselves together or alive. We then melt the item, destroying the shadows forever. The soldier mostly likely dies or becomes infected as we capture their energy. If we notice the infection, we have no choice but to eliminate the soldier before we lose control of them. If we don't, the soldier is unconsciously drawn to the border and becomes one with the shadows."

"Will that happen to me? Will I become one of them? Will they call for me?"

"Possibly. Do you hear their voices?"

"I hear me."

# CHAPTER 12

THE FOLLOWING DAY came quickly, and like the one before, Eve was once more looking up at the ceiling. This time though, she had a throbbing pain behind her eyes, an unknown sickness in her stomach, and her legs and arms were unnaturally tense. This morning, the young woman had awoken to frayed nerves. She surmised it was because of the little sleep, due to the many different thoughts circling incessantly and maddeningly in her head.

Eve swore she closed her eyes with an empty mind as the moon had waned slowly. When she opened them as the first rays of light rose on the horizon, they beamed unnaturally bright through her window. The streak of the sunlight hit her eyes, creating untold infuriating chaos and pain in her head. She was at present not in the best of attitude, which was unfortunate as today needed her to be calm and kind. Knowing herself, she would be short-tempered, which would likely result in her answering in short and tense wordage to the couple who had her life in their hands. An approach that would not do her well if she wanted to see another day. Presently, a part of her didn't care what the royals thought.

"Good day, me lady," an unknown voice uttered in a feminine, low-pitched rasp.

*When had the bloody door opened?* Eve threw her arm over her eyes, groaning airily. Had her head flown so far that she had been oblivious to her surroundings? She should have known better after her interactions with Aelfdene. Her eyes should have been watching all that went around her. Regardless, she didn't want to get up from the bed. Caoimhghin had told her that her chances of survival were low, and she doubted it had gotten any better now that Captain Aelfdene had witnessed her unseelie nature. Why shouldn't she spend her last moments in her room— her cell?

"Me lady?" the same unfamiliar voice called out shyly. Eve groaned and lifted her head to see an exceedingly pale curly-haired brunette woman with yellow-reddish eyes. Eve pulled in her lower lip and scrutinized the newcomer. She felt worried about how thin the woman was but was in awe of the unnatural being's hourglass shape figure. Then, Eve's eyes moved to the odd, peculiar sackcloth and ashes garb the woman wore that contrasted with her skin tone. It was a high-quality two-piece black outfit with a long overcoat and skirt. The coat had a high collar with a military-accented ruffled edging, half-lined, a button-up bodice with lacing in the back, cuffed sleeves; the outfit reached down behind the newcomer's knees. Unlike the elf that shone brightly and gave out an aura of hope, this woman had a sinister, but cautious, atmosphere. Eve knew it would be better to have this maiden as a friend than an enemy.

"Uh, and you are?" Eve croaked out. The pale woman grinned, and it caused a shiver of alarm to go down Eve's spine. The woman did not have what Eve would call conventional teeth. They were unexpectedly razored and highly serrated.

"I am your personal attendant, me lady," the woman answered. "I am to assist you in dressing for the day. Afterward, I am to adjust your clothing if necessary."

Eve bit her lower lip in thought, "Adjustments?" She then watched in horror as the nails on her attendant's hand grew to an unimaginable length. "No."

"Adjustments are necessary," her assistant assured. "Your new clothing was based on an estimate of your physical form and your previous outfit. Do not worry; it will be a quick fix. My nails have never failed me before."

"No!" Eve shouted, jumping into a sitting position. She quickly calmed herself when she saw the puzzled look from the other woman. "No, all is fine. Mm...my clothes have been made properly and in the right size. Also, I have dressed myself for years. No assistance is needed. Thank you— though."

"Are you sure, me lady?" her attendant asked. Eve winced a little and nodded her head in affirmation.

The door opened to her room again, and a very familiar Aine questioned loudly," Is she present?" Eve fell back on her bed, groaned, and swung one of her arms over her face. "I see that you are not even up for visitors?"

"Good morning Aine," Eve spoke, her voice muffled. "Is it already that time?"

"You are in bed!"

"I see your eyes are astute as ever. Where else should I be?"

"You dare mock? Today? When your life hangs in the balance?"

"I do not dare mock, and today is like any other day. I have spent my life toying between meeting the angel of death and seeing the sun. In my personal conclusion, this day will be my last, and I shall spend it here, in bed, in peace. I wish to meet my maker with little disturbance to my form or mind." Eve was tired. For the past few days, her back had been taking the brunt of the many secrets she kept.

Since her birth, Eve's life has been a series of unfortunate events. She had never known a day of peace. She spent days and nights struggling to survive. Every moment of her being, she wished for another existence. Or, many times, her wishes went down a darker path of hoping to end her life ultimately. A fleeting, but daily, reflection.

She had no siblings, nor a mother to guide her when she first bled. Furthermore, instead of having a loving father, her father did not hide his contempt for her being. He eagerly told her of his plans for her maidenhead. When she had exhibited her disgust, he had gifted her with endless beatings. Most days, he made it known that she could never have love or friends. She would never have a chance at a family from a man of her choosing. Then, she had to be Lord over the many that despised her family, and under her father's watch, she was able to show little kindness and only to her servants. When he left, her duties became more arduous as her extended family decided to visit, which were, in reality, many attempts to end her life. Then, without little choice or say, after her father's death, her aunt and cousin, as next of kin, took her place as master and Lord and she left to fight. Luckily, as long as she lived, her *family* had limited power. Her steward kept her updated with letters on the comings and goings. Now, that was impossible.

Her misfortunes didn't end there. No. She had died in battle and come back alive, death casting her out from an endless blissful sleep. It was at that moment she knew she was different. A difference that Puck had proved and then been confirmed by Aine. She was a creature of nightmares, and the possibility she would see home again was slowly decreasing. Yes. Her life was full of trials, and she wanted them over. She was tired. Exhausted. And alone. She knew it was alone that she would die in this strange world she found herself in.

Aine continued to berate her, emphasizing the day's importance as if Eve didn't already comprehend what was happening. She did understand the magnitude of the problem she had found herself in and, thus far, had not seen a real solution. Additionally, what could Aine do to her? She was younger than the old wom—

"Ah!" Eve squeaked in unladylike fashion.

Eve's undignified yelp came as she had been unceremoniously pushed off the bed by a heel— a very sharp heel attached to her attendant's boots, who had moved quicker than Eve could see. Her blankets did not fall with her. Aine had grabbed them at the last moment to keep them on the cot. Eve found herself on the ground with arms and legs flayed in different directions and her hair tousled. Her confused eyes stared out from her half mask. She rose onto her knees and glared at the other two women.

"I beg for pardon, me lady. Lady Aine, the day before, had ordered that by any means necessary, we are to have you out and ready. Due to the importance of this meeting, it is best to have you dressed and in court before our King and Queen's arrival," the pale woman explained, Aine nodding her head to confirm the woman's words. Eve watched her attendant move her foot slowly and gracefully off the cot in awe and envy. Her movement was fluid and smoother than any dancer Eve had seen.

Now, Eve knew the body worked to a set limit. She was a prime example of using brains over physical force. Her intelligence had kept her alive— to a certain point. She did, after all, die and had multiple chances of being close to death. With this knowledge, her attendant's movement should have been impossible. So, what being was this woman? She was not an elf nor a fey. Eve's companion was deathly pale, had long sharp nails, and red eyes with yellow pupils. She had an inkling what her assistant was, but— "You are not burning," Eve dumbly spoke out loud and then showed her teeth. "You have razor-sharp teeth. *Vampyr?*"

Eve cringed into herself as her assistant glared at her with sharp lighted eyes. "Yay or nay is all I...I...I am asking," she sputtered.

"Vampires do not burn or turn to ash in the sunlight if that is your speculation," the attendant said.

Eve jumped to her feet and tried many ways to apologize. unsuccessful as she stuttered through her defense. "No. No! NO!" Eve hastily started. "I am probably incorrect. Mmm...maybe your kind— used to burn?" The other woman shook her head. "Oh— never burned— then. Tha...that means the information in my world is not right, and if I ever go back, I will inform the Masters of their errors. My people— "

"Girl, stay silent," Aine ordered.

"*Meep,*" Eve said, and she clapped her hands over her mouth, mortified at the sound that she had made. With her mouth inaccessible at the moment due to her worries about saying other gibberish nonsense, Eve's head tilted, and her eyes narrowed as she finally properly viewed Aine. It wasn't because of the woman but more what the woman was wearing. It was indeed so unique and shocking that Eve had no words. She had never seen such atrocious garments in her life. "Don't you look *extraordinary* today?"

Aine was not a severe person, but today was not a day for play or fun. She wasn't in the mood for jokes. She knew her outfit was not appealing, and she didn't need a reminder of how horrendous it was. Due to her role today of being an advocate for the mortal, her clothes were the required *traditional* garbs to wear in court. Her clothing was loose black dress robes that lightly kissed the floor. Around her neck was a silver chain necklace with a simple ornated selenite crystal that signified her position and occupation in the kingdom. Then, there was a heavy chain at her waist with small bells attached to remind her of her responsibility as the representative for the mortal whose life depended on her actions.

"Get ready. I will wait for you outside," Aine commanded with a stern look, walking out and slamming the door behind her.

Eve's eyebrows rose in shock. She was surprised by the anger— or was it disappointment— that Aine showed. Whichever the feeling, it was strong enough for the older woman to slam the door shut as she left. Eve hoped the emotion Aine was feeling was fury. The thought of the latter hurt her heart.

The young woman sucked in her lower lip as she felt her stomach drop. Perhaps, she had gone too far with her comment about the Fey's clothes. Her jest had not meant to offend or harm Aine. Eve had only been attempting to lighten the stress she felt of her foreseen death sentence— for that was what her fate was going to be at the end of the day. Her reasoning process was that if she was to attend court, she wished at most to be completely distracted from her demise. Thus, it did not matter to her what the distraction was, be it a stain on the ground or just an odd outfit.

"You should not make fun. Lady Aine loses much by being your advocate," her handmaiden chastised as she fixed the bed.

"I know of her position; she stands for me. Yet, what does her outfit matter in those dealings?"

"I was not born when my people lived in your world, so I do not know how your kind act in court. Here, we do not hide our thoughts. During a tribulation, our stance and ranks are shown by our clothes for all to see. If those we stand by are not accepted, we lose our reputation and place in this world," the woman explained. "Lady Aine is honorable for what she does and probably dislikes the outfit but wears it for you."

Eve let out a sigh. "She does have honor. I will apologize as soon as possible. Let us ready me for my death. If I am to die, I shall look exquisite while it happens."

"Yes, me lady."

Eve watched the vampire lay her clothes on the bed and accessories of paint for her face. The little her handmaiden had informed her put her deep in thought. Guilt pooled in her stomach, which grew stronger as time passed so that even breathing became difficult. She bit her lip when she felt she was about to cry. Why hadn't Aine and Caoimhghin told her the consequences that came to them if she was not favored? If she had known, she would have demanded they abandon her immediately. She wouldn't have allowed them to risk their position in society for her. If her punishment were death, she would take it gladly for them. Now it seemed past the point for her friends to leave, and it looked like they wouldn't even abandon her if it had been a choice. They had attached themselves to her, even knowing she was a thief. What would that mean for Caoimhghin? He was a King. Would he lose his ruling? Was there nothing she could do to help them or scare them away from her before it was too late?

Eve turned to her companion. Maybe the vampire had a solution that she could not think of. Then, Eve realized she had not once asked for her handmaiden's name. The young woman reprimanded herself for forgetting her manners. "What is your name?"

"Greema, me lady. Greema of Nightfall."

"Greema?"

"Yes, me lady. Given to me by me master, the dog that had bitten me."

"Master? Dog? Pardon me," Eve squeaked. She flitted through

her maze of memories created just that morning. The short conversations with Greema had contained nothing of being a slave or having a master. Eve could swear the woman had mentioned being born, but as she knew personally, being born did not mean another did not enslave one. Greema had said *her people*— Eve was utterly confused and close to massaging the bridge of her nose.

"It was a jest, me lady. I was born a vampire, as I have informed." Greema smiled and laughed a little.

*Well, that little sneak*, Eve thought in astonishment. The pain at her temples that had been about to form vanished at the indignation she felt. The despair that had been building inside from the stress left as she laughed. Greema had managed what Eve had not been able to: her assistant had allowed Eve to forget her worries momentarily.

"Thank you. I am grateful for the jape," Eve said after her laughter died, leaving her in a sort-of blissful state. All worries and problems that she had contained had not evaporated, but they no longer laid heavy upon her head or shoulders. The load had constantly showered her with a non-ending gloom. With the burden gone, she looked at the clothes on the bed. They were normal. Bland. Boring. She wasn't going to walk into court and look insignificant. She needed to make a grand entrance— like Caoimhghin. "Greema, I thank you, but perhaps you can help me find an outfit that will be awe-shocking."

"You are due to court soon," Greema reminded. Eve gave an unladylike snort and a languid wave. What was court to her if she did not go to it her own way? She needed to shock and amaze. If, in the end, her sentence was death, the populace would at least remember her. She wished not to be like those before her. Nothing. Not even worth a memory.

"Yes, I know this," Eve started as a manic grin formed. "I do not wish to wear the clothes given to me."

"They replicate the ones you arrived with, or so the witnesses told me."

"This is true. Despite that, my outfit is not shocking to the crowd. I ask for new wear and do not worry about the probability of being punished. The royals will place no blame on you. I will take full responsibility for my new appearance."

"My lady. I must persist— "

"No," Eve interrupted. "I have decided I must have another outfit. I wish to shake the ground under their feet with my appearance if I am to perish. They will remember the day a mortal walked to them with their head high and wearing the most shocking attire they have ever seen. An attire that will make women swoon in envy and men shudder in orgasmic delight. They will not forget me."

Greema replied in resignation, "What may I do for you, me lady?"

"I believe Prince Caoimhghin— "

"High Prince, me lady."

Eve rolled her eyes to hide her surprise at hearing what could only be the proper title of her friend. "Indeed. High Prince Caoimhghin, I believe, had snapped his fingers together and brought a chest into existence. You know where it could be?"

"I remember seeing such an item in the closest." Greema walked to the storage room and pulled out the chest, dragging it along the floor near Eve.

"Fantastic." Eve rubbed her hands together as she approached the chest. She slowly flicked the clasps, and the chest lid opened. Inside she saw a variety of clothing, from leather to linen materials. There were also accessories of a different kind that Eve had never seen before. "Can you assist me in unloading the wares onto the bed?"

Together, the two women emptied the contents from the chest. They searched, shuffled, and pulled out clothing they approved. The outfit had her pray for her soul because of the sinful image she now showed. Nerves crawled up and down her arm. Before Eve could doubt continuing her insane plan, she ordered her handmaiden to dress her. Once Greema begrudgingly deemed her ready, Eve took a deep breath and walked to the door. She waited with an anticipated breath of what reactions she would receive at her boldness.

She didn't have to wait long to see what others thought about her new choice of fashion. The door opened, and she came face to face with Aine and two minotaur guards. Aine's eyes widened in surprise and alarm as she fully regarded Eve. The guards leered at her that brought shivers down her back but nothing more.

"You foolish girl." Aine looked up and spoke to the heavens, "May Gaia protect me and let Oberon be kind." She proceeded to bless herself before bringing her eyes back to Eve. The young mortal was not wearing the prepared outfit that had been laid out for the day. Instead, the girl's clothes looked suspiciously elvish and came from the minor kingdom neighboring Caoimhghin's because of their dark coloring.

Eve had dressed in a way that would make her the center of attention. Her clothing was as such, starting from the head and down—

Greema had pulled Eve's hair back into a bun with little tendrils and bangs surrounding her face. Wrapped around her head was a black head scarf. Her cheeks were slightly pink from either paint or embarrassment. Aine could not tell. The girl's deep, dark, blood-red lips could be considered noir in the dark. She wore a gold necklace with a miniature duplication of one of her swords at her neck. A black tunic and tight corset pushed her bosom in plain view. A sight many lustful men Aine knew wouldn't mind. At Eve's waist, a belt hung at her hip. Finger-tipless gloves that extended a little below the elbows completed the upper portion of her body. Lastly and simple were her leggings that flared out over her boots with a slight heel, making her taller.

"Why?" Aine gestured at the outfit.

"Why not?" was the short reply, which earned choked snorts of laughter from the guards.

Aine shook her head in annoyance. She bit the inside of her mouth to keep herself from reprimanding the girl on her latest form of expression. There were other vital matters Aine had to impart. "There is no time to make any changes with the little we have. I will proceed toward court without further ado. I anticipate meeting High Prince Caoimhghin already present to stand as your secondary advocate. Then, these guards will escort you to the hall. Do not let your eyesight wander as the guards take you down. Look only forward."

"What do I do if one of your citizens throws an object at me? Should I not choose to look at it to have the appropriate time to avoid its impact?"

"You will look straight, walk the directed path, no deviation, no faltering, and do not once let your gaze wander."

"Thus, do nothing in defense?"

"Yes. When you reach the court's doors, another guard will halt your progress. He will ensure you have no weapons to harm our leaders. Once that safeguard is confirmed, the same guard will bring you into the room where you will be placed at a certain distance to bend your knee to High King Oberon and High Queen Titania. Oberon will thereafter signal the guard to have you stand. Afterward, the guard will bring you to Caoimhghin's and my side. You are not to speak. Understand?"

"What if someone slights me?"

Once more, and with fire in her tone, Aine strictly commanded with narrowed eyes, "Do not speak."

Eve placed one foot back, leaning upon it. She lifted her hands with a flash of fear and anxiety in her eyes, which she quickly hid. She nodded in agreement fervently, saying, "I shall not say a single word. Not one. Or God smites me down."

Aine blared another warning look at the young mortal. She then felt satisfaction that Eve had received her message by the look of fear on the young woman's face. Then, she seemingly floated out of the room, her robes dragging behind her. The door then closed with a slam. Its boom reverberated throughout the room. Eve, Greema, and the two guards looked at the shut door in surprise. It was followed by them looking at each other afterward. In their own ways, the four individuals shrugged the moment away.

Eve stood for an unknown amount of time between her escorts. She tried not to stare at the minotaurs, but it was futile as she studied their appearance. They were as the stories of old told. They were half-man and half-bull. They had the face of the animal while the rest was ostensively mortal like Eve. Otherwise, their skin was the color of ash and leathered. She wondered if the monster's origin was from Pasiphae, wife of King Minos, and that of a white bull was authentic. Did that mean Poseidon himself existed? Eve wished to ask them but thought it better not to. Their intimidating height and Aine's order kept her from seeking answers.

Finally, and at last, Greema gave a light nod to the minotaurs. The one on the right of Eve placed his hand on her shoulder. The other opened the door and waited for her to enter the world that hated her kind. The minotaur on her side didn't guide or push her out. Like his partner, he waited for her to move. It was left to her to decide to step out and Eve was grateful they allowed her at least this. She closed her eyes, heart thudding, body shaking, and stepped out of the room calmly.

She found herself stopping in the middle of the hallway. For the first time, she had a better view of the ward she had been staying. The hall was long, with many identical doors that led to the room that possibly was externally similar to her own. Each entry had sculpted arches with golden carved veins that interlaced and spread from one door to the next. Though the doors appeared indistinguishable, some had a subtle bluish light glow like the one she had stepped out from.

"Why do some of the entrances glow?" Eve asked no one in particular.

One of the guard's interests peaked. "You can see it?" Eve nodded absently. "Very few can see what you can see. I, myself, cannot or have the ability to view such magic. What you are glimpsing are protection and barrier spells. Though they do not work well on superior beings, they protect you from the lesser curses."

"So, this is not a common healing ward."

"They are, but the rooms are substitute dungeons for prisoners of great fascination to our ruler."

A bell then rang, which caused the walls to tremble all around.

# CHAPTER 13

BELLS HAD GREAT importance to Eve. As a Lord, she had helped oversee— more bowed to the wishes of the priest in charge— the workings of the church's bell. Her duty was to ensure a man constantly rang the bell when needed. Usually, that man was from a family approved by the church. The bell's typical use was for Sunday functions, celebrations, the death of a prominent village member, and marking specific hours of the day.

The sound of bells— or bell, in this case— generally eased Eve's mind due to its routine usage. Presently, its sound made her feel the opposite of what it usually did. She was paralyzed with fear, anxiety, and nausea. All the possibilities of how her future ended flew through her mind, each horrible or worse than the other that had come to her mind previously. It took a nudge at her back from one of the minotaurs to jolt her into moving forward.

The hall was longer than she had anticipated as her steps echoed loudly over those of her guards. To her, the walk took forever before they entered a large and spacious rotunda with a high dome made of glass panels. The overall structure was held up with Doric columns. Spread out evenly along the walls were half circular tables filled with familiar objects encased in glass. The rest of the room had short rudimentary Roman columns with other items hanging upon them, also encased. There were benches present for one to sit and enjoy the artifacts. As Eve looked at old swords, pieces of wood, and other unique effects, she remembered the dagger. She glanced around inconspicuously, but there was no sign of her booty.

Passing the rotunda, the doors opened with no assistance. Eve was immediately blinded momentarily by the natural light. The guards, thankfully, gave her eyes time to adjust to the new environment she found herself in. Not long after, Eve saw they were in an open room, a garden...and it wasn't empty. Many different creatures she knew by stories and others she didn't were in attendance. They all stared at her, and the young woman did the same to them. As she walked, they parted for her, creating a path to a set of large doors, where two minotaurs stood as guards.

If the time and purpose of Eve's visit to the world had been different, she would have halted in the middle of the grandeur garden and cherished the view. Currently, she could only glimpse such wonder at a passing. As much as she wanted to stop moving forward, Eve believed the action was inappropriate as she knew she was being paraded and doing a walk of judgment. There was a childish, rebellious urge to anger those around her. The tension in the open space was already palpable. She was reminded of Aine's order of not speaking or staring. Now surrounded by the populace, the orders given made more sense.

Look straight, walk forward, and don't falter to look anywhere else, Eve repeated.

She was surrounded by the dregs of society, and there was nothing she could do about it. All she could do was tread past them, even as their whispers grew louder. Her body unconsciously tensed uncomfortably as she followed her plan. Eve fought the urge to bounce on her heels and rush forward. She doubted she would be able to hold herself back if someone attacked. If one of the creatures neared, she was going to punch it. Luckily, as the tension grew around her, she reached the doors that loomed over her.

One of the minotaurs approached and started to search Eve. He grinned sickeningly at her as he let one of his hands touch her bosom longer than was necessary for a need to humiliate her. Eve huffed and bit her lip, but nothing more. She was glad when her escorts growled at their comrade, who rushed his quest to find weapons of any kind on the mortal.

The minotaur stood and gruffly pronounced," I will take her inside."

Eve felt one side of her cheek twitch in wariness and anger. Her body jolted as her harasser placed his hand on her shoulder and stood at her side. He waved his hand at his companion, who turned to open the great doors. As he pushed at them, they creaked under their weights. Eve's mouth slightly opened as she finally laid her eyes on the throne room.

The throne room was filled to the brim with citizens. The floor to the second balcony, even to the third, was packed with many bodies. Further on, at the end of the room in the center, sitting upon the dais under a large stained-glass window, was the royal couple—High King Oberon and High Queen Titania.

The loud chattering of the population assaulted Eve's ears as she took her first steps into the room. As she passed the upper doors, the talks slowly diminished into silent gossip and a buzzing rhetoric of hatred. It wasn't long before all turned to look at Eve with awe or distaste at her being.

King Oberon was a tall fey with a brooding and gaunt face. He was visibly lanky with pale skin and ashy short brown hair. His ears slightly protruded from the frame of his face, his nose belonged to the Romans, and his light hazel eyes glowed like smoking embers. He wore a long white leather coat with buckles crossing his chest and a black linen tunic peeking underneath. On the lower portion of his body, he had on black leggings with long, high boots.

Then there was Oberon's wife, Queen Titania. There was a unique beauty to her. She was as sullen as her husband, but her shining green eyes showed something darker. She was slightly smaller with ghastly white skin compared to her husband. Titania had high cheekbones and full lips. The bright red coloring of her lips contrasted with her bright blonde hair. The queen was fitted in a long, white dress that flowed down to her ankles. It had front and back lace-ups, shoulder ties, and long sleeves.

Both majestic and frightening monarch had capes pinned with a half-sphere brooch. Their eyes were cold and unforgiving. They did nothing but look at Eve sternly. When Eve's eyes met theirs, a shiver went down her back, and her skin prickled uneasily.

Halfway through the room, a fully armored guard blocked Eve's movement forward. She was grateful to no longer be under the scrutiny of the king and queen. On the other hand, she could see her reflection on the armor. She was not pleased with what she viewed. Her skin was shiny from perspiration with a sickly complexion. Her uneasiness was obviously showing. Eve took a deep breath and looked at the new guard, who put his arm out for her to grab. Her minotaur companion tightened his grip on her shoulder and reluctantly let her go. She took the arm in front of her happily. The guard escorted her the rest of the way and brought her in front of the king and queen. Eve kneeled, making sure she did not look up.

She didn't like kneeling as the position made her vulnerable. Always alert, her other senses took charge. She noticed there was this new suffocating pressure in her head that was causing her mouth to become dry. She felt chilly tendrils touch and slither into her mind. Eve couldn't tell where they came from and started to fight the feelings they caused as the memories she wished not to think of were at the forefront of her mind. The inner skirmish produced an ache behind her eyes, followed by a painful trickle down her back. Shortly after, the tendrils pulled away, leaving so quickly it was if they had not existed. And perhaps, they hadn't. Perhaps, it had all been a dream.

After the supposedly 'mysterious' presence, Eve realized that her tunic was now clinging to her back. She was also freezing and trembling heavily. Perhaps, the feeling of an unknown being assaulting her mind had not been false. Unfortunately, now was not the time to think about it. With relief, Eve's armored escort touched her elbow. She stood up, head down, still shaking. Up ahead, King Oberon stood with a solemn face. Eve's face was gently nudged so she could look at him, their eyes meeting each other.

"Do you know who I am?" Oberon asked, his voice booming in the room, arms relaxed at his sides, hands in a fist. Eve nodded, giving him a look of defiance to mask the churning in her stomach at the strange play. "Why are— "

*Boom!* The doors burst open, slamming against the walls, groaning under their weight. All turned to face the intruder to see who dared break protocol. A man in a billowing cape, wearing the robes of an advocate, his hair untamed, a devilish smirk on his face with canine teeth gleaming unnaturally, rushed in. "I apologize for my lateness. My subjects thought having their chickens lay their eggs in my boots was hilarious. A feat I never thought possible until now." Eve relaxed and smiled brightly at the voice of Caoimhghin. She looked between the king and his son, content that any attention had moved away from her. Her friend was happy to have said attention. He was delighted to be the main event, temporary though it was. "What have I missed?"

"It seems you have left your manners at the door," Oberon growled. "I didn't believe you would show?"

"And miss this?" Caoimhghin covered his mouth in mock injury. "Oh, father..."

"Your majesty, boy!"

"Last I knew of our family status, you are my father and shall always be. Unless a change of status has occurred that I was not made aware of."

"Why are you really here?"

Caoimhghin pointed at Eve confidentiality, striding to her side with his cloak swishing on the floor behind him. Eve smiled weakly, though it was more of a half-grimace, as she was depressingly once more the center of attention. She had an urge to wave at the viewers to break the renewed palpable tension in the room, which rose higher when Caoimhghin linked his arm with hers. He then graced her with a wink that promised trouble. For who? By Oberon's face— for her. The king wouldn't harm his son; he was an important figure. She, on the other hand, was a nobody. A nothing. An aberration.

Eve now knew how those of lower rank felt at her home. It was not a pleasing yet somehow familiar feeling. She felt as if she was trapped and was nothing but a pawn between two egotistical maniacs. At least as a man, she had some power and freedom, as little as it was if she went against some rules. Eve wished she could promise herself that when she returned home, she would help the lower class in every way possible, but that would be false. More guilt added to the large one she already carried inside. A soldier's duty was to stand and allow people to be caught in the games of those of higher status only because they wanted to stroke their ego. Eve was a farce to the words she had sworn to uphold. She was an untrue knight.

A gloved finger tipped Eve's head up so that she looked into worried mixed-colored eyes. Eve had been wrong in her first quick assessment. She was trapped in a game of power, but only one of the players sought her harm. There was a friend for her that was present. "Milady, let us take our place and gain your freedom."
Caoimhghin escorted Eve to the right where Aine stood. She felt safe standing between her two advocates. Oberon watched with a mistrustful intensity and, eventually, sat back down on his chair with one leg stretched out. "Let us continue then," he said.

Aine stepped forward, hands entwined inside her sleeves, face stoic, and bowed. "Your majesty, I stand— "

"Stop. Due to the rarity of this event, I wish for the mortal to advance. There are questions that must be asked. Her mind told me little," Oberon announced.

Aine's mouth opened in astonishment. After the shock wore off, she reminded Oberon of her position as an advocate and that her central role was to be the speaker for the individual in the trial. She then listed the laws that stated firmly that non-members of the community had no right to speak. Her attempt to take control and keep Eve out of the proceedings was feeble. Oberon knew it as he waved her excuses away with a simple gesture, silencing her. The old woman could only lower her head in defeat.

The inhabitants gasped and lapped up the turn the proceedings had taken. They whispered to each other. Many were hoping to see an execution in the end. They then hushed as Eve took a step forward. Just as she moved further away from her friends, Aine grabbed her elbow lightly. Eve turned to see the worry in the old woman's eyes. She gave the elder a smile in the reassurance that she was well. Aine nodded grudgingly and let the mortal go. Eve took three more steps forward and looked at Oberon with calm eyes.

"Your name."

Eve didn't answer. It hadn't been a question.

"Speak!"

Eve felt a huff of cold air hit her back and then a kick behind her knees. She fell onto her hands. Another hand roughly pulled her hair back, her scalp burning, and her throat stretched for viewing. A hot breath blew behind her ear, a smell of rancid stench coming from her unknown attacker. She at first struggled in her assailant's hold, but when she felt the excitement her actions brought him, stopped moving. Her breathing was loud from exertion.

The court came alive, flooding her senses. Using her peripheral view, she saw the populace urging her attacker to make her suffer more. Behind Eve, Caoimhghin was holding Aine back. Both were angry and had an urge to rescue Eve. The young woman postulated that they shouldn't, or they could lose their position in being her champions of a sort. Eve was staggered. The High King and Queen were not stopping this travesty. Did they have little to no care at all at how barbaric their people were acting?

"Answer my father, you filth," a voice loudly projected. Of course, Captain Aelfdene would be present and interject himself into the trial. Had he always been present? She had not seen him standing in front of his parents or the other guards, nor in the crowd. Had he magically appeared inside the room?

"I can't wait for them to give you to me. Just the thought that I will get to taste you before your death makes me shiver in joy," Eve's assailant hissed in her ear, accompanied by a nibble of her lobe.

Eve felt her body boil internally. Her outrage was tipping past her control. She couldn't let her adversaries know their words affected her. The demon inside cared not. Its only thought was on maiming the creature who dared touch her. Being in a position of vulnerability had the demon clawing its cage. It wasn't long until a blanket fell over Eve's mind. Her inside was turning, twisting, and flipping in random directions. Her world then steadily turned into a red haze. The young knight shut her eyes tightly in a futile effort to halt her unseelie transition. She focused on her quickening heartbeat as it pounded painfully against her breast. With her thumb and fourth digit of her right hand, she tapped them together to her heart's beat, matching its rhythm, waiting— and waiting. The tap gave her an outlet for her growing anger. Her father first came to mind when her heartbeat slowed, and her logic returned. His presence was significant, looming, and ashamed of her. He was berating her, calling her weak. For this reason, as her heart slowed, she ceased all struggles.

"My name is Eve!" she shouted. Her eyes snapped open with a rebellious twinkle. Her voice boomed and bounced off the walls. The local resident became silent, and Eve continued to speak while looking straight into the king's eyes. "I am Eve Bonel. Head, Lord, and Lady of the Bonel household. Soldier and the White Knight, under King Henry the Fifth, my king," she emphasized. "And, if you do not let me go, I will tell you here and now, any future actions I may take, I shall not apologize for."

There was a moment of silence before King Oberon tipped his head back. He laughed heartily with his citizens following suit. The royal couple was underestimating Eve. They believed her to be weak. Well— she would have to show them the change the mortals had developed away from their tutelage. How Eve would demonstrate this development came when Captain Aelfdene took her unknown combatant's place behind her.

Eve knew she could get out of her helpless state now that she had a weaker opponent, so she widened her stance to take the next step of disarming the captain. She had to move, at the right opportunity, when the captain's defense was at its weakest point. He also had to be sufficiently distracted. When Aelfdene joined his father in laughter as Eve had expected, she inconspicuously slid one of her feet back. She fortified her back by slightly tensing it and snapped her head back, impacting the captain's face. A crunching sound told her she had hit her mark: his nose. Aelfdene's grip loosened. Eve swiftly elbowed his stomach, twisted around, and promptly grabbed his sword. She took a few steps back and pointed his own weapon at his throat. The point of the blade kissed the young prince's neck. Aelfdene moved to the side in a flash to grab his sword back. Eve anticipated his movement, and she tutted and then gave him a small nick to show him the error of his ways. A single dab of blood dripped down his neck and onto the collar of his uniform. Her eyes spoke of retribution and that she wouldn't hesitate to kill him— given reason.

Aelfdene snarled that he understood, then raised his arms partially in surrender. Anger grew behind his eyes, with a promise of endless torture for Eve. She knew he wouldn't forget this slight and public humiliation. If Eve did live tomorrow and the days following, she would have to watch herself and those around her. Aelfdene would not let this confrontation be the end.

A shout from Oberon broke their stares. "Useless. Absolutely useless you are. My own flesh and blood," the king said, enraged with his son. "How could you lose to this chit?" he gestured to Eve.

Eve felt forlorn, awkward, and unsure between father and son. She couldn't think of what actions she should take and so looked to Caoimhghin for guidance. The young prince subtly motioned for her to kneel. Using the weapon as a crutch, Eve turned and kneeled before Oberon cautiously. She didn't realize that Oberon had not once looked at her moving form.

King Oberon's eyes, in fact, had never left his son's. Once Eve had kneeled, the royal stood up angrily. "Guards! Do what my son couldn't. Keep the girl in place. If one of you let her go, I warn you now, you will have forfeited your life. Furthermore, take that weapon out of her hands, you fools. She is our prisoner, not our guest."

"Father— "

"Oh, silence your words, boy!" Oberon angrily commanded, and Aelfdene shrunk under his father's gaze. "Guards? Guards! Do as I say forthwith! I will not repeat myself again."

Oberon's anger startled the masses. Most of his guards looked at each other, wondering who would risk taking a step forward. Most of them were afraid of receiving their king's attention. Two guards on the far right left their post striding towards Eve. They roughly grabbed her arms. Eve went to pull away from them, but their grip tightened. Not long after, the young mortal noticed a horrid stench coming from her new jailers. Their smell was sickly bitter and nauseating— it was the smell of death.

Eve's eyes narrowed at the two, and she was close to berating them, but a chill went down her spine as her eyes met theirs. She noticed their translucent skin and red eyes that smoked at the edges. The two guards shared similarities, almost precisely like her handmaiden. Yet, they had a menacing presence that informed Eve it wouldn't do well to antagonize the two at her side. It wouldn't end well for her if she did.

She relaxed, hoping her two companions would see she wasn't a threat. Instead, her arms were pulled forcefully behind her, causing a small yelp to escape her lips. Then, a shout followed as her overseers kicked the soft spot behind her knees, forcing the young woman to the ground on her knees. A scream came out next as a crack filled the room from one of her shoulders. It was dislocated from the uncomfortable position Eve had been placed in. Anger and pain filled the warrior's body.

"As today is not on the captain, the day must go on as scheduled." Oberon brought his gaze to Eve and said, "Let us continue... Lady Bonel." If this was his way of grabbing a person's attention, perhaps the stories of his cruelty were true. Eve was disappointed to find he was indeed like many sovereigns she knew. Without an open mind and no say from herself, Oberon had deemed her guilty without thought. Her trial was just an interrogation. Eve could only wonder now if the queen had already condemned her.

Queen Titania was emotionless with blank eyes. The woman was a statue, completely still and silent. Unforgiving and cold. Through pain-filled eyes, Eve couldn't determine if the queen even took a breath. Or was the woman just an illusion and had been a puppet under Oberon's magic all along. Was that even possible?

"Our world has been closed off between ourselves for years to protect not only my people but yours as well from annihilating each other. How did you, a mortal, cross between the veils created by the strongest of magic we have available?"

Bugger, Eve thought. Her eyes widened as she contemplated what her answer would be to his royal highness. Obviously, the young woman couldn't admit to Oberon about Puck's quest that she had foolishly been tricked into participating. As happy as it would make Eve to see Puck punished, she was still his personal thief. In the king's eye, that would be singing a confession of guilt if she told the truth. What could Eve do? From the little stories she remembered, being a puzzle to those of magic kept the mortals alive longer— usually. It would be better not to say anything at all. She would be the puzzle for the king to solve. Then, God willing, she could complete Puck's quest and find more information on her origins. Perhaps, even find the knowledge of what kind of being her mother came from.

Eve's momentary silence was noticed by Oberon, so he asked," Do you lack the understanding of elementary speech?" Eve tightened her lips. "Fine! Fine. How are you here?" Still, Eve did not speak and felt a growing satisfaction watching the king become impatient and frustrated. "I have ways to extract information. And I can assure you, they are not pleasant. So, girl, give me the answers I need. Save yourself some pain. What is your purpose? How did you get to this world, and who had helped you?"

Did he just call me 'girl'? Eve bristled a little at the epithet. She hadn't been a girl for years. Not since her father had forced her to conform and accept her duties as a Lord. Her past experiences had forced her to grow.

"Answer me!" Oberon thundered.

"No," Eve growled. She needed to show him that she wasn't

one to be easily intimidated. "You can place your inquiry in your royal arse— yer majesty." She blanched. There were times her mouth would run afoot, ahead of her mind. The words she had been thinking before her addition after 'no,' had been less insulting. She had been about to repeat her rank and position. Which would have been followed, perhaps, by something witty. That, of course— had failed in a grand proportion, and the words she had spoken instead couldn't be taken back. If there had been a sword nearby, the young knight would have thrown herself— more flung upon it because of her outburst. Bullocks.

Eve watched Oberon grit his teeth and stand in front of her at an astonishing speed. From Eve's perspective, it was like Oberon had disappeared and rematerialized from the air. One hand glowed, ready to attack. Using his other hand, he wrenched Eve's head back. He brought his face closer to hers, teeth gnashing. "Insolent child. You dare insult me?" he started, his eyes blackening into an empty dark endless pool. "If you will not answer, then deal with the consequences. Pity, you could have spared yourself from this coming agony."

The court was deadly silent with a cough randomly breaking the apprehension of Oberon's threat. The king's movement was slow as he brought his glowing open hand crashing onto the side of Eve's head, his fingers digging painfully into her scalp and touching portions of the skin on her face. Nothing happened, and Eve became confused. She wondered if the king was playing her a fool and trying to trick her into giving information. Then, behind her eyes, forcing itself into her soul with a single goal to corrupt her mind, came thrumming pain. It wormed into Eve's head and slowly broke down the barriers she had built to stabilize her mind and soul. The harder she fought against the invisible force, the worse the pain became, increasing to one she had never felt before, not even when she had died. She couldn't see the world and tell what was up or down. Her surroundings were a blur. So, the young woman focused solely on the invisible snake continuously attacking her mind, which brought forth an unholy scream.

One of Eve's mental walls broke, and memories spilled out from the cracked dam. Images over images of memories piled on top of each other. Conversations lost or forgotten, found in frightening clarity. Dreams that had been destroyed from reality came in a disorganized jumble. Somehow, Eve knew all of this was being seen by another that wasn't her. All the private experiences that made her... her were being taken.

Oberon was cruel. He dared enter her essence, and Eve was determined to stop him. She didn't know how to achieve this. Could she push another out of her mind? It is an excellent time to try, she thought.

The knight hoped that the most potent emotion given by the God Almighty would assist her in getting rid of the parasite: rage. She pulled on that emotion from her memories; then, let it swell and build deep in her. When it grew, passing her body's limit, she released the pent-up feeling. Her eyes closed, and a ripple of air rushed out from her in a sizeable, explosive gust. The energy from her power pushed the citizens to the ground and forced the king to let her go. He didn't fall and simply slid away. In her haste, Eve released her unseelie aura for all to notice.

"You shouldn't exist," Oberon croaked. He went to the dais and stopped to look at Eve with one foot on a step. "An unseelie, at that. The boy had spoken true. I had believed he had exaggerated. You are an abomination!" shouted the king, pointing his finger at Eve accusingly as if she had a choice on who, and what, she was. Eve stood up straight and stiff. The king's insult was well deserved and rang true in her soul. Yet, she shook her head in denial as she was not yet entirely a monster. She still had a choice to take the path of honor and righteousness. Until her heart and mind blackened and became sin itself, her life was still her own to rule— to decide on future actions.

King Oberon moved to insult the hybrid again, when he was stopped by a single touch from the queen, who quieted her agitated husband. His body relaxed, and he looked at his wife lovingly. It was a fantastic transformation to watch. The royals stared at each other and let their eyes communicate. Words were not needed between the bonded couple. Their love was beyond anything Eve had seen and one she wished she could have. The king and queen had an understanding, a passion that Eve would hold, and knowing it broke her heart.

Queen Titania coldly looked down on Eve, while King Oberon sat back in his seat. He welcomed his wife's contribution to the trial. Afterward, the enchanting queen walked down the dais but moved no further to Eve. The queen interlaced her fingers in front of her abdomen calmly. "Do you know what a halfling is?"

Eve cocked her head to the side, giving herself the face of ignorance. Caoimhghin had informed her about the terminology, but what did it mean to the queen of the Underground? For those present?

The queen started to say, "The primary definition of a halfling is a child born from two worlds. A child created for the union from an unmagical and magical being, seelie or— and rarely— unseelie. When our worlds coexisted, these children were a happy and welcoming gift. They were the middle ground to bring the worlds together. It was not to be. Time passed. Fear increased. Not just on us but on the halflings. The fear was understandable. There were unforeseen consequences to the children born. A majority of them became insane and unstable. Most took their lives. Others burned from the inside from their insanity and killed many with no regrets. Procreation between our people was, and still is, banned. The halflings were exterminated. That is why we are surprised as you stand here before us. To see one so young as you...it should not be."

The queen paused before talking again. "How old are you, girl? Older than you look? I wager you can lift more than possible and have noticed shadows where none should be...." Titania continued. "Did you feel the powers of the unseelie on the ten and eight of your years? Or was it death that started the transformation?"

"I had hoped, prayed even, that it was all in my mind," Eve said more to herself than to the queen. "Perhaps my father had seen the difference before me."

"And your mother, what of her?" Queen Titania asked.

#  Chapter 14 

QUEEN TITANIA HAD watched the proceedings with interest. Like many others in the room, she was looking forward to an execution. As the trial progressed, she had confusingly felt there was a familiarity with the young woman. She didn't understand how that could be possible. She took the chance to take over the interrogation as her husband became frustrated with the hybrid. When Titania explained to the young woman the rarity of her existence, she listened as the girl spoke of a father, but nothing of the mother. Titania needed to know why and asked, "And of your mother, what of her?"

Eve didn't answer. Instead, her jaw clenched. It wasn't like she had much to speak of to her royal highness. She had never met her mother, so she knew very little of the woman they were asking about during her questioning. Even now, as Queen Titania gave her the coldest dead eyes with a look that intimidated the mortal, Eve didn't— couldn't answer. What help would there be if she told the truth?

Eve's silence was long, and Queen Titania became impatient. She was not one to wait for others, so she used her powers to compel the young woman to speak. The queen was shocked to see her aura blocked by the warrior. The girl glared at her with gritted teeth as she fought powers beyond her own— or so she believed. The queen had seen this deterrence once before by her older brother after he betrayed their ideology, and she had to kill him. The type of defense mechanism confirmed absolutely that the girl was an unseelie hybrid and sturdier than should be possible.

Shock and panic filled Titania at the power this mortal contained inside her weak frame. Unseelie, when they had physical forms, were unstable beings. She had firsthand knowledge of this instability because of the inner demon that lived in the darkness deep in her core. Queen Titania was the last of her kind of dark Feys. There was a danger, even to herself, when using her gifts. During any battles, there was always a chance she could lose herself in the feeling of the destruction she created. Seeing those fall called to her darkness, and there were times she almost swam to the calling that promised her that she would see her enemies worshiping her as they bowed at her feet. That tempting, sweet call destroyed her people because they wanted more and pulled her brother to betray those he called his family.

Being an unseelie did not make one susceptible to the urge to want more power, to the point of corruption. Sometimes, even a seelie fell to the darkness, but it was rare. Some seelie hybrids were born with gifts they could not physically or mentally handle, making it easier for them to fall into temptation. The queen could only imagine the excruciating pull an unseelie hybrid felt.

Yet, it wasn't that the girl was an unseelie that made this trial crucial; it was because she existed. After the war against the hybrids, to ensure the mixed breed were all destroyed, Watchers had been left behind in the other realm to assassinate stragglers. A hundred years after the destruction of all the crossbreeds, there had been a confirmation report that must have been incorrect because here stood a mongrel. Perhaps, the Watcher had overlooked a halfling because it had no power. It passed its blood to the populace, thinking nothing of it. If true, why were there not others like the young woman? The link to the answer had to be the mother that girl did not want to speak of.

"Please. Tell me about your mother. Who was she?" Titania softly asked as she retracted her gifts.

"My mother— ," Eve croaked. "My mother was a nobody," Eve said while holding constant eye contact with the queen.

"And— " The queen knew there had to be more to the story the young woman was not saying.

"And nothing. What more do you want of me? The woman is dead. She was a filthy orphan who opened her legs for a monster," the mortal spat with venom. A part of the queen died hearing such words come out of the girl's mouth. She didn't understand why, as the direction of anger was not at her.

"How dare you speak as such in this court!" Oberon spat.

"You bloody asked, you shit," Eve retorted unconsciously and rapidly. Her comment was not in spite; it had come from annoyance.

A gasp resonated in the room at Eve's audacity to be impertinent to their mighty leader. A banshee shrieked that there should be a punishment for the girl, and the rest followed. The chant grew in sync, reverberating against the stone walls. Eve shivered as she eyed the chanting people with disgust. They had no shame in their antics, which should not have surprised the young woman. Perhaps, today was the day she was going to die.

Queen Titania watched her husband stand from his seat. She knew he was going to give into the mob's cries. She couldn't allow that. The young mortal could be helpful to them. So, Titania raised her hand, halting Oberon. He sat back down and left his wife to do as she pleased.

The mob's chanting grew bolder and louder. Titania knew she would, nay, COULD NOT kill the girl. Yet, her people would not stop their chants until appeasing their outrage with some show of violence. With a loud sigh, and an elegant hand flourish, the queen lifted Eve into the air. The girl cried out in startlement as her face paled in fear. Titania opened her hand and then started to squeeze at an invisible enemy, watching as the mortal's body compressed into itself. Eve gasped and screamed out from the pain. Through her torture, the young woman wouldn't ask for mercy, even as her skin started to turn into a sickly purple hue.

Prince Caoimhghin went to intervene. His mother stopped him using her free hand, paralyzing him on the spot. He glared at her as he struggled in her invisible hold. After court, Titania knew she had to talk to him about befriending criminals and showing emotional attachments. Though her son was only a minor king, he was still a king. No fault of his good nature, others would see his actions as a weakness. Be it a friend or an enemy, someone would use that shortcoming as a viable reason to usurp his powers.

"Stop," Aine's voice cried above Eve's cries of pain. Titania arched an eyebrow and dropped the girl, letting her crumple to the floor harshly. Eve took large gulps of air, the color of her skin returning. Once able, the young woman stood and glared up at the queen. Her eyes flared for want of retribution. In the background, there was cheering at the torture witnessed.

Their shouts, laughter, and taunts aimed at Eve brought forth a strong feeling of loathing inside of her. They were animals. Her darkness rose to the surface, lapping the horde's hatred and evil. The realization that her demon was gaining strength worried Eve. She realized there was a possibility her evil was an entirely separate entity from her own. Why hadn't she been warned, or was this entity, this thing, in her a rarity on its own? No. She couldn't allow herself to believe that it was the end of her soul. Because it meant that who she was could be taken away and destroyed at any moment. She didn't want to think that her body would no longer be hers to control in the future. She had reasoned there would be a merging of sorts. She had not anticipated that she could be a prisoner in her own body.

If Eve survived this day, she urgently needed to create a contingency plan when the time came that she would fall into her darkness. She would rather have a friend give her the mercy of death than find out what actual entrapment meant. That was to say, once more, if Eve survived the day. Then she could move forward to instill plans of her absolute demise before she became evil incarnate. Yet— she didn't know how to achieve this feat in what looked to be an extremely short and bleak existence.

"An opportunity," Eve softly spoke to herself, the words spilling out unconsciously from her lips.

"Did you say something, dear?" the queen asked.

Eve stood with a straighter back, a hiss of pain escaping her lips, and her eyes swept around the room. She was thinking about her studies as she looked around. She remembered that how the mortals survived without the aid of power was enchanting to the immortals in old stories. For those with long life, it was interesting for them to wonder how those with short lives lived off dreams, hopes, and gods. What did they think of Eve? She was a hybrid who survived when that should not have been possible. She knew she was feared, hated, but still, she caught the curiosity— the attention— of those with her unnatural gifts that went against the laws of nature.

To live, Eve had to play on their curiosity about her being. "Give me a chance. Only one. One chance to prove my loyalty to this world and you." The words she spewed tasted disgusting in her mouth as she continued, "I wish I could tell you all that I know, but alas, this world is new to me and will take time to understand."

"Since I have arrived, I have been enchanted, frightened, and lost in the unknown. I know my blood links me to monsters. I carry the demons I had always believed were only in stories told to discipline children. Here and right now, I am not a monster. I am not the shadow that hides in a dark realm to take one's soul. I am not the black ink that sends shivers down a spine, that gives nightmares— not yet.

"I ask not to be treated as your enemy because of what may and will come of me." Eve kneeled in false resignation and gave the best sorrowful eyes she could. "But, if only to quench your thirst for blood and take away your fear, I will forfeit my life."

"No, you fool," hissed Caoimhghin at her side. His voice was drowned by the crowd's cheering, who waited with bated breath for the slaughter they knew would come.

"You will give us your life?" Oberon questioned with insincere confusion. Eve knew he was waiting for her to show her true feelings. She was never one to give a sovereign such complete satisfaction.

"Yes, if I must. I ask, though, a brief time— I am told it will be— to see the wonders of your world. I wish to meet the beings I have only read about. After, when I am no longer myself, you may make away with me. I will give you no fault nor blame. My life is in your hands. You know better of my situation than I do, so I am left with nothing but to have trust in your judgment when my end comes."

"No," Aine croaked, fearing the worst.

Eve heard her allies and friends despair. Her heart clenched agonizingly from being insensitive to their emotions. Regardless, the game of life she played had to be won. There was a strong desire to walk to them so that she could reassure them that she knew what she was doing. She didn't want to hurt them any more than she was, as the two had already placed themselves in danger for hiding her true purpose. All the same, as long as she kept them in the dark about her plan, the safer they were. It was a horrible necessity she didn't feel cozy with. Their fear was cracking the innocent and ignorant wall of the façade she was keeping up.

Queen Titania hurried to Oberon's side, taking her place next to her husband. The couple started to whisper to each other fervently. Eve was disappointed that neither of their faces showed any hints of their discussion's direction. She was displeased that she had no read on their emotions, not one bit. Not knowing what was going to occur was killing her from the anticipation.

"Captain Aelfdene. Counselor Avo," Oberon called.

*Sard. Who from Satan's hellish nightmare was Counselor Avo?* Eve thought as she tensed. Her neck tightened uncomfortable, making it harder to breathe. Her nose burned. Her cheeks flushed in frustration. She knew she had set the pieces of manipulation accordingly...she believed. Her most significant problem lay with Captain Aelfdene. He had a snake's tongue and effortlessly whispered words of harm to those of influential ears. She doubted he would speak words of kindness. The man hated her— exceedingly— with all his soul— a hatred that spanned to the stars and beyond.

Counselor Avo was the royal's advisor. He stood to the side before leaving his spot to answer the king's call. He was a short, stout, balding fey in large brown robes that dragged on the floor, the garb frayed at the ends. Large and bulky chains hung from his neck with various charms that symbolized his studies and expertise. In his hands was a large book with a thick leather covering that he cradled with reverence and devotion. The book contained the rules of the Underground. Avo knew the laws from front to back and back to front. He was the one the royals went to when they had to make a serious decision that bordered the rules they had created.

Eve subtly smirked as she watched anger grow on the captain's face. She wondered if the book did have the answers that were being sought. Was there a rule for her and their plight?

"What prospects do we have that do not break our sacred code?" Oberon snapped with impatience and ire. His wife touched his arm to keep him from shouting.

"Freely and openly, sire, I wouldn't be able to tell you," Avo replied. "We have not dealt with this exact situation that I am aware of. I warn you, what you do this day will follow for days to come if and when it comes upon us again."

Aelfdene grimaced and gritted his teeth in anger. His parents were considering keeping the filthy, hybrid bitch alive. When he had told them what she was, the mortal's survival did not decrease as he had hoped for. He wished for Eve to be humiliated, then executed as a show of intimidation and power. His parents didn't want the same. They were foolish and had become soft through the centuries.

Aelfdene's parents wanted to try to bring the girl into their world as a test to see if the time had come to rejoin those above. The young mortal would assuredly be placed under the guidance of his soft-hearted fool of a brother. His brother would be in charge of teaching her magic. Then, after trust has been obtained, she would be honorably gifted with a position. Aelfdene could not let that happen. He was going to take advantage of any chances to sabotage his parents' plans. Then, convince them to once more join the world above to be rulers overall. They were superior to the mortals. It was their duty, their place, to rule over the weak shits.

The three elders started to agree on keeping the hybrid alive.

Aelfdene was no longer able to keep his mouth shut. "No," he hissed at his parents and advisor in disbelief. He needed to dissuade them. "You know *King* Caoimhghin would take her as his whore and later make her his queen to rule over his...subjects. We must kill her, or a mortal will gain the power of an important kingdom. There will be war."

"Do not speak of your brother as such," Titania admonished. "He would do no such thing, and even if the thought came to him, we wouldn't allow it. The girl is destined to die— in the end. There is nothing he can do for her, even if he wanted to."

"Then you do remember," Aelfdene started, "what happens to a halfling unseelie when left unchecked. As far as I can remember and have studied, there has not been a case of an unseelie hybrid lasting against their nature. Let us just end her now. Put her out of her misery."

"It is not that simple," Titania growled, her eyes illuminating red. Memories of her brother flooded her mind and, with the recollections, returned the sweet sadness of his death. His eyes had starred at her not in hatred but in happiness. In his last moments, he had regained a part of himself. Titania had proceeded to drop to his side onto her knees, sobbing at the loss of her sibling. The unseelie part of her increased her anguish at her brother's death.

"I am just reminding you, mother. No need to lose that pretty head of yours. Please, tell us. Give us a history lesson so we may take the matter at hand with *more* deliberation." Titania narrowed her eyes at his bravado to speak as such to her. Despite the ferocity of her stare, Aelfdene did not squirm underneath his mother's intimidating gaze. He was no longer that little boy who lowered his head in submission or cowered away from his parents' ire. He was a man grown.

The queen closed her eyes. She took deep, calming breaths. Then she looked to the advisor before saying, "It may be true that the temptation to give into the unseelie's call is strong. The girl is different. We had no notice of her. Our spies in the other realm had no news of her. She had survived with the unseelie blood without transforming until recently. We need to know how that was possible."

"You are unwise to think we will find such information," Aefldene commented with a roll of his eyes.

"She is older than the previous hybrids to show magical abilities. She had suppressed her powers longer than has ever been recorded. Perchance, for future reference, we can use how she did this feat for others after her," Avo logically argued.

"She didn't suppress her powers from free will. She didn't know she had them, you fool," Aelfdene informed.

"Then we must know what brought upon this change," Avo bit back.

"To know this, we must gain the young woman's trust. We can also learn the changes that have occurred in the world above from her lips and not from one of our scouts. With the knowledge attained, we can open our borders," the queen spoke.

"Thank you, mother, for your enthusiastic, yet naïve plan," Aelfdene said condescendingly. The captain turned to his father, "Now, father, what do you see in the mortal's heart?"

Oberon sighed profoundly and answered solemnly, "She is of pure of light, but at the frays, a stink holds, its grip tightening little by little."

"Then, shouldn't we save her from a life of misery? Save her soul from corrupting? Free her with a kiss of mercy? If we explain the pain and hardship, she will readily agree to a quick and painless execution," Aelfdene conveniently proposed with an ostensible kindness.

"You ignorant boy. You talk on the assumption that she doesn't know. Can't you feel it?" Oberon said, placing his hand over his heart. "Her soul is only pure as it is because she holds the darkness at bay. Someone has already told her about her battle. She fights even now."

"In spite of that, she can't hold it back fully. We should end her life now instead of later," Aelfdene pleaded.

Titania stared intently at her son. Her heart broke when she found no genuine empathy. His pleading was an illusion. She could see the hints of deception at the corner of his mouth that was tilted up with glee. His fists were clenched tight with not anger but anticipation. The slight crinkle of the outer edge of his eyes was of amusement, and his sight shone with joy. His true intentions were meticulously hidden from any who did not know him well. Unlike them, Titania had the practice of recognizing her son's recent number of deceits. His body was a traitor to her masterful eyes. This wasn't the boy she had raised— or had she not been there enough for her son when he had needed her the most?

Captain Aelfdene's words were that of compassion and worry. Beneath them was revenge. He was thinking only of himself. His thoughts focused on his humiliation in front of the people he was to lead. His past and current indiscretions had piled to the point that he could no longer hide his disdain at the unfairness of his life.

"Hold your tongue," admonished Oberon. "Your arrogance and self-worth blind you." Aelfdene looked aghast to be talked to as such.

"Father..."

"You overstep your station, son," Titania spoke softly, becoming the new recipient of her son's wrathful gaze. Oberon appreciated her interference, his own patience running thin, nerves fraying at his son's impertinence.

"How can one overstep one's duty? What I do, I do as one who is next in line. I am the protector of my people," Aelfdene haughtily asserted. "My thoughts and actions are to help guide us on the right path so that we may not be inert in time."

"Your people?" Oberon probed.

Aelfdene laughed nervously. "*Our* people. I meant...our people, father."

"I doubt the honesty of your correction. You must not forget I am king, and they are *my people*. Your words send worry to my mind and cause me to rethink your position in this family," Oberon grievously whispered. He paused, and in a surer tone, he commanded, "Your mother and I shall judge the mortal. After court, with a heavy heart, I behest you to join me in the master's chamber. I need to speak with you, my son."

"Of what?" hissed Aelfdene.

"Away, boy, before further words of hurt are spoken," Oberon directed.

Before the young fey could express his dissent, Titania chirped, "I thank you for the advice you have graced us with, my son. Please, take your place with the others." Her son fixed her with another glare. He corrected the collar of his uniform and strode off with a sneer.

"The boy has not yet learned," Oberon said to his wife in defeat.

"He is of high opinion of himself. A quality, I fear, we passed on to him."

"A quality that surpasses even our own, my love. He must learn some humility."

"Then you will speak to him about what we had discussed privately?"

"It is time, and he has shown no growth in character. In fact, it has been the opposite I had hoped for," Oberon sighed. He then looked to Avo, who shifted uncomfortably for being privy to the short conservation about the young captain. Oberon smiled mischievously to the man. "You are still present, my dear man?"

"My love," Titania chided playfully with a twinkling giggle, "Do not irritate the poor man." The queen saw the counselor was not amused by the king's teasing due to the seriousness of the trial.

Avo wasn't a fey who, per se, enjoyed life to the fullest. His happiness lay in his immense, but crowded, chambers filled with books and scrolls he had borrowed from the majestic and grand library east of the kingdom that was attached to the Academy of Alchemy and Orders. It took tooth and nail, perhaps even a limb, for a messenger to pull Avo from his intense studies. His life consisted only of learning, and he was grateful for a position that allowed him the time. He disliked communicating with those of the living. He saw them as obnoxious twits who couldn't just get right to the point.

Oberon tried to apologize, but each word that came out didn't emerge properly. The king coughed and awkwardly dismissed his friend and subject, who stomped away with his head held high, joining the other counselors. Titania hid a grin behind her hand as her husband pulled himself together, putting on a cold face. He could see Avo's face turning red, cheeks puffed, hand tightened, posture rigid, and a vein at his temple slowly bulging and throbbing from irritation.

"I have a reasonable judgment in mind, but to ensure it is conclusive, all inquiries must be completed. My wife, are there any questions you wish to ask before this court's conclusion and judgment is bestowed on the mortal?" Oberon asked, turning to Titania. She answered with a nod and intertwined her fingers together, laying her hands on the top of her lap.

"Why do you not remove your mask? How can we be merciful to one that doesn't show their face? Only a coward hides behind such blackness of a rag."

Eve smiled unevenly and croaked. She was afraid and unsure. How could she explain with flourish and sophistication that she had been unsuccessful in removing a piece of hardened fabric? It was humiliating that a simple object caused issues that lasted further than the distance of her known world. Maybe the royal couple could help her with her dilemma. They were the High King and High Queen. From Caoimhghin's knowledge and experience, his parents were the strongest beings in the Underground.

Another problem to worry about was their view on a person's value. They might find Eve to be inadequate and kill her. *Do they take people's heads off here?*

"I can't," Eve rasped, taking a chance that admitting her lack of control over her magic would give the high court a reason to aid her in removing the guise.

"You can't what, my dear?" Titania prodded. Eve babbled her retort; her words were jumbled and incoherent. "Are all mortals incapable of proper communication?"

Eve cleared her throat with ill-timed coughs and calmed her fast-beating heart before acting in response. "This mask is not who I am but has, since my opportune arrival, been a foul stain on my person. Attempts of removal have been futile. An unknown magical factor keeps it attached."

"Why magical?"

"Why not? It doesn't take an idiot to pull off a mask, and this one," Eve pointed at the offending item, "doesn't come off."

"Have you tried?" Eve looked at the queen with disbelief and decided to evade the absurd question. Of course, she had tried pulling off the mask. Even Caoimhghin and Aine had used their abilities in an attempt to remove the loathsome material, getting the same results as her. "Have you tried using your magic?"

"And go up the river and become bloody mad?" Eve threw back. "I wish to stay sane as long as possible, thank you very much."

"Hmmm...your words are true. Another way, perhaps...if you live, which will be determined by this final and last inquisition?"

"I will respond to the best of my knowledge."

"Is your life so miserable that you ache for death? Why else would you be foolish enough to come to this realm."

The world around Eve disappeared, and all she could hear was dead silence. There was nothing beyond her own being; there was only herself. Did she crave death? After her resurrection, she had thrown herself into battle after battle. Found she could still feel pain but healed unnaturally— or could she still consider it such? Perhaps the healing was natural to her unseelie nature. Then, there was the queen's reasoning on why Eve had entered the Underground. It was not her fault. Sure, Eve had taunted a magical being thinking all Puck said was a play— a ploy. She doubted that meant she had jumped to take the manipulator's quest. She had expected nothing to happen from her mocking.

Yet, she had mocked Puck. She had seen his magic, and perhaps, unconsciously, there had been hopes he had killed her. Her life had never been a calm pond. It was a destructive flood where one false move could have her drowning in the water. Eve thought over the question given to her once more and replied honestly, "I do not know."

"Then, I shall leave the finale of this trial to my love," Titania said as she roamed her gaze over the court. She looked at the groups of citizens, telling them with her eyes that what would be decided would be the end of the matter.

Titania sat as Oberon stood, taking over. "You have been brought to the front of this world for us to judge you on crimes committed. Your first crime is entering this realm. The second crime is being an unseelie. Having said that, the crimes you committed differ from why the laws were created. Your existence is not your fault. Also, how you had not transformed or given into your darkness intrigues us. Perhaps it has been destiny's hand that has0 brought you to us. We will never know. So, in light that many facts have not been answered...the ruling I give today is not set in stone. Though, it will be remembered for future reference and so forth."

Oberon looked intently upon Eve and continued to speak. "Until we find the origin of your powers and who had brought you here, there are two routes available I have seen. You have the honor to decide your own fate from those two only."

Eve's eyes squinted in annoyance. Internally, she was feeling troubled. It was only when Oberon explained the two options that she felt fear. Nay, it was more than fear; it was terror. The feeling created a dread that hurt. Her stomach felt as if it had dropped sickeningly, and she was on the brink of sobbing. The air in her throat was stuck, and her mind raced back and forth between panic and agitation.

Oberon's options were bleak, and Eve won in none of them. The first choice was simple. She was allowed to go home— just not alive. She would be returned fallen, viewed as a casualty of war with a mangled body and mutilated beyond recognition. Her body would have a necklace that contained the crest of her family insignia. This would make it easier for others to know who she was in life. Eve did not like this proposition because she had no yearning to see or join her father in hell. She knew she had committed sins under her king's name, no matter what the church preached about God forgiving them for their transgressions.

The second option Eve despised. Oberon explained it in many words but overall, the plan was a temporary stay of execution.

Though there was a slim chance of a forever, the choice allowed her to live a bit longer, but she would never return home— never again. The extent of it required her to behave, followed around by others until she was deemed trustworthy, and ensured Eve didn't transform into an unseelie during the time she was going to be observed. During this period, the court would investigate the origins of her gift and how she had come to their world using means they had no eyes on. Eve would be assigned a tutor to help control and stifle her powers to keep her occupied. Additionally, there would be history lessons and a minor training position in the royal military. Ultimately, and after being considered trustworthy, Eve would be given a low citizen's designation and placed in a position or rank they believed would fit her best.

Eve stood in thought, contemplating the choices given; knowing herself, she had to choose between immediate death or— death. She doubted they would find information on her mother. Her abrupt entrance into the realm would be an issue as the problem was Puck. It wouldn't take long for them to find out what she was working, non-voluntarily, with the banished fey. Eve had found out from Caoimhghin that all magical beings felt differently from each other because they had their own unique signature. To the young woman's shock, the kingdom had phantom black dogs with psyche masters who could recognize the individual's magic. It wouldn't be hard to track the location she had landed from her battle with the trolls.

"These are your only options. You must choose wisely. You have til' the next day to decide your future," Oberon stated. The king and queen stood, went arm in arm lovingly, and Oberon dismissed the court with a final saying. "*Lady* Eve Bonel makes her decision. Citizens, let it be known that this is the end. An announcement of her pick will be proclaimed by the crier in all villages and towns."

The royal couple vanished into the air. In their place was a scattering of twinkling dust. Sound returned to the large chamber as the denizens dispersed, grumbling and chattering about the lack of disciplinary actions. They were not pleased with the conclusion of the trial. Many whispered hopefully that the mortal would go home so that they could view her demise. It took a while for the room to empty, leaving Caoimhghin, Aine, and Eve with only a few guards. The young prince quietly spoke to the men, and they nodded to him. Loud enough for Eve to hear, he thanked them and rejoined Aine. The two approached the young woman.

Aine enquired with tight lips, "What will you choose?"

"And what can we do?" Caoimhghin posed, placing a hand on Eve's shoulder.

"I will be fine. For my selection, I will do what I must do. This will not be the end of me." Eve would agree to the infinitesimal stay. She would not beg, nor look at the ground, or show any other signs of weakness. She would, though, inquire if she may join, if she could, to investigate her origin with the others sent. Mayhap, ask in-place for good behavior, a reprieve from her babysitters. Even if they said no, she would find a way to lose them, then scout and survey the palace for the item Puck wanted: a dagger that could not be seen without the help of light.

# Chapter 15

EVE'S GUEST HOSPITALITY has ended— obviously. Just after the trial, she was now uncomfortably lounging in the dungeons lying on top of a dirty, overused cot that had seen better days. Eve had expected to be returned to the room she had previously occupied. Still, as she was healed, the room was no longer necessary.

Her cell was located away from the rest of the populace. She was so far from the moan and groans of the others that she could easily believe they did not exist. Perhaps their voices were muted not only by the distance but also by the cold, damp room and the thick, locked door that kept her as a prisoner. The door was not made from simple bars. It was a large piece of wood heavy from the metallic stripped beams and a nailed-in border. The door was an art of beauty in Eve's eyes and experience.

The magnificence of the entrance clashed with the room. All four walls were covered in moss from the little water source continuously dripping down from the ceiling. Attached to the wall opposite the entry hung chains covered with a feeling of death. On top of her environment, her nose was assaulted with the stench of rotten flesh and feces. The smell of excrement was strong in the corner coming from a wooden bucket that flies buzzed above and around.

Oberon had given her a day to dwell on the choices. If placing her in a cell was a way to inspire her to choose in a particular direction, she didn't know which one he wanted. With her new treatment, she might as well be dead now. The guards gave her no food. They had taken to beating her periodically. One had even attempted to assault her sexually, earning a kick to his privates. Eve had laughed at his wail, her lip broken and bleeding. She was rewarded with a beating that placed her in an unconscious state. She was left alone afterward as she was no longer entertaining her torturers.

Outside, a rooster crowed in the sky hours later as the first rays of light emerged on the horizon. In the dungeon, the beaten woman slept, and many voices whispered her name. Their voices carried into her unconscious state so much that it woke Eve up. Her head jerked, and she looked around the room with her one good eye. The other one was swollen shut and red, turning purple.

"Who is here?" Eve whispered with a rasp. No one replied back.

The young woman dropped her head back to the dirty ground and groaned. Her body ached all over, and her head was pounding. There was a fire clawing in her guts to be released, but she squashed that feeling down. She recognized the flaming presence as her magic wanting to heal her, and she had to practice controlling her gifts despite the pain she was in. Might as well do it in her present weak state. Also, she hoped that perhaps her condition would keep her enemies away and give her time to heal as she slept. Eve should have known better by now to wish for such a relief because it seemed that every time she dreamt of what she wanted, the opposite occurred.

The first visitor for the day was in the form of Captain Aelfdene, who loudly asked, "How was your night?" He then proceeded to slam the cell door, causing an ache behind Eve's eyes.

"My night was brilliant and peaceful. I had the best sleep ever. Can you thank your guards for punching my face?" Eve struggled into a sitting position and was relatively successful. "Though, one hit would have sufficed."

"Still an insolent bitch. You have ruined my life, and it is all your fault," fumed Aelfdene down at her. Eve smirked in return for his comment. "My kingdom was taken from me yesterday. Given away to my whore of a sister."

"Maybe you should take a lesson from her on how to appease your parents," rasped Eve, a laugh gurgling from her throat. "I wish I could assist in that class, but I failed in it epically." Inside, her unseelie clawed and shook the bars of its cage. She held it from escaping.

Aelfdene swiftly moved to Eve. His hands shot out to grasp and squeeze her neck. His fingers dug and cut into her skin. He shouted and spat that he wanted to hear her scream, but she didn't. Even if there were guards nearby to listen to her call for help, they would likely not come to her aid. From Aelfdene's cocky entrance, it had to have been him who ordered her thrashing by men loyal to him. Eve's breathing stopped, and she let herself relax into oblivion.

Then a hand slapped her face, and she gasped for the limited air, her throat still squeezed but not entirely. "I wish I could kill you."

"Then, do it," Eve pushed with a croak.

"Oh, I would, but then there will be questions. Most of them would be directed to me and cause more trouble than what it is worth. I am not done here, and I doubt you will tell because if you do, I will kill all who have become so close to you. Make them look like accidents."

"You wouldn't kill your own brother."

"I have little love for the flamboyant bastard."

Captain Alefdene threw Eve to the ground. Her body bounced. Her face scraped on dust and stone, cutting into her skin. Eve took deep gulps of air, filling her lungs with life. Life and dirt. Her mind felt heavy, and she heard the captain walk away without closing the door through the fogginess. He was accompanied by many more footsteps. They had taken off hurriedly.

Not long after and close by, there was the clash of metal. Men shouted at each other as they fought against one another. The bangs echoed around Eve's brain at the loud clanking the swords produced. The voice became louder, followed by footsteps running in her direction. Eve didn't see who entered and closed her eyes as a hand unexpectedly touched her face. She didn't notice the touch was gentle as she tensed in fear. Her fear fed to her monster that was rising to the surface.

"Your majesty, let the prisoner go," a man spoke in a warning tone. "She is transforming."

"Don't worry. My luck will change— once she awakens from her torment," Caoimhghin believed. To Eve he said, "Come on. Let this not be my last regret, girl. This isn't my time to die, nor the way I should die. Someone waits for me."

*Girl? I am not a girl, you pompous—* "basket-cockle," Eve managed to utter throatily as she reined in her fear, pushing the dark back in its cage.

"There she is."

"Thou are an arse-breath'd flax-wench," Eve muttered as she was helped from the ground. A bulk of her weight was placed on Prince Caoimhghin. He held on to her leaning form with an arm around her waist. Her pain increased tenfold in her new position. She gritted against the wave of hurt. Her hands tensed, wanting to hold on to something tightly between her grips. She waited to get used to the injuries, and when there was a dull throb, she asked, "What time of the day is it? If you have yet to notice, I have no windows."

"Next time we know your next destination is the dungeons, I will make sure there is a view for you. For your information, it is the early morning of the new day. With Aine's aide, we shall get you healed and back to your best to perhaps visit my father," Caoimhghin comforted weakly.

Eve was half-dragged upstairs and back to the healing ward again. She was stripped and laid partially bare on a bed so soft that it felt like she was in the air. People shouted around her as her eyes slowly closed. Trays and bowls of water were brought in and out in a frenzy. Her body was prodded, strung together, and wrapped multiple times in layers of dressings. She howled when a splint was applied to her arm. Eve hadn't realized it had been broken. She had felt no pain when she had moved it around. She couldn't even remember when she had received it.

"Who has done this?" Aine asked.

"Some of our castle's guards loyal to the family did this," Caoimhghin answered.

"Did they say why?"

"The ones that survived the fight took their lives before we could stop them. There is no one to question," Caoimhghin angrily informed her.

"Your father beckons the girl," Aine's voice rang out after a bit of silence. "The message had come before she had arrived here." Eve watched tiredly from the bed as the old woman washed her hands, cleansing off the blood that had turned the water a pinkish red. "We tell him the truth on how extensive her injuries are. She needs rest. The girl is already on her way to Morpheus."

"Her injuries are extreme, but that will not stop him from bringing Eve to him."

"We have the bodies of the traitors! We can tell him about them and plead for time."

"He would think we were lying. Without any of those guards alive, he will presume that we had possibly injured the girl to give her more time and that we had magicked false bodies."

Caoimhghin growled. He knew Aine was correct. High King Oberon's life depended on being cautious, seeing each shadow as a possible enemy or an assassin waiting in the corner. Yet couldn't he delay for a few moments? Couldn't he trust the words of those closest to him that, so far as he knew, had done him no harm?

Caoimhghin was aware once his father saw Eve's wounds, he would question her fervently about them. He doubted Eve would be able to answer as she could barely stand. Even with Aine's abilities in medicine, the mortal would not heal enough to be slightly presentable. By sending her to his father so soon, they would leave her vulnerable to attacks. The young minor kind knew that the only way the girl could stand on her own was to siphon her unseelie abilities to heal herself. That would mean taking a step closer to losing her essence.

Thoroughly exhausted, Eve listened from the bed as Aine and Caoimhghin thought of ways to allow her some peace. That wasn't going to happen. Captain Aelfdene's threat still rang in her ears, and he was vindictive enough to follow through on them, she now believed. King Oberon had given her today to decide, and she had made it just as the court had ended the day before. Hopefully, he would take her choice and not ask about the damages inflicted upon her.

"I will go," Eve called from the bed achingly. Her friend's conversation ended mid-way. They turned, stunned to see her awake. "I have been called by a king— your king. He had already ruled on my choices and how long I must decide on one of them. I have been taught to never ignore the one who is superior to myself if I ever want to continue my existence."

"You can't be serious?" Aine asked. "Look at you."

"Give me a mirror, and I will," Eve retorted with a winced smile. She wiggled to the edge of the bed and swung her legs to the side. The injured woman then pushed her torso up, her arms shaking as they held her weight. Excruciating pain went down her spine, causing her hands to squeeze the soft blanket she was on top of. The world spun rampant as she finally sat, and Eve placed a hand on her forehead. The simple touch set fire to a part of her face. Underneath her fingertips, she felt a large protruding bump with a gash in the middle.

"You are mad," Caoimhghin told her. "You need to stay in bed. I will deal with my father."

Eve rubbed her eyes. "You know I must see him and the consequences if I do not." She turned to the two, looking at them through the puffiness of her eyes. She expected to see worry, but there was only surprise. Did she look as horrible as she felt? She was alive, so it couldn't be that bad or worse as their shock made it seem. The two even had their heads tilted to the side.

"Does my look offend you so?" Eve asked the two fey, who didn't answer or move. They were still as statues, staring at her intently, which slowly aggravated Eve. She could hardly believe her current image could cause her friends to become speechless.

She shrugged her annoyance away from their stares. She decided her first priority was to herself by inspecting her malleability. She ignored her friends' gawking and started to stretch her limbs, neck, and back. Her body was mainly stiff due to the excellent healing from Aine, with most of the lacerations cleaned. Nevertheless, a few extreme afflictions were still present that sent shocks through Eve's body at the simplest movements. She bit her lip from the stabs. "Could be worse, and if I take it slow, I shall be fine."

Eve saw that the feys were still ogling her and demanded, "Pray tell me why your eyes have not moved from my face?"

"Wonder at the beauty we had not seen until now. The flesh around your eyes shows such weariness and hardship. Yet, there is a softness of one who has carried hope," Caoimhghin rapidly responded with awe.

*Had the young prince been hit in the head also,* Eve wondered. She doubted she was beautiful with all the bruises she now had— and her thoughts stopped. The prince had mentioned flesh around her eyes. How could he know unless— could it be? The mask! Eve hesitantly touched her face. She started at her chin and moved up to caress her cheek, where she felt a slash and large bruise. Further on, she felt— no mask. Her eyes widened, and a small laugh escaped her lips. "How can this be?"

"I have a thought," Caoimhghin exclaimed, clearly proud of himself for identifying how her mask worked. Eve giggled as the old woman at his side jumped at his outcry. The giggle transformed into a laugh when Aine smacked the prince's chest and then ruined his unruly wild hair. He fussed over, what he believed, his perfect locks. After he was satisfied that his hair was adequately corrected, he opened his mouth to tell his findings, only to be interrupted by the door opening. A royal guard stepped in with a solemn face.

The newcomer was a female vampire with long hair that flowed down her hips. Stoically, she said, "The king's calls have not been answered. We are here to accompany the mortal to his study chamber."

Before anyone could speak, more guards came in, and Eve was roughly dressed in an oversized tunic bigger than her frame. Aine shouted at them to be careful, but it was ignored when a guard pressed upon Eve's ribs. Later, the young woman was pulled out of her room and marched away. A few steps ahead, she was blindfolded and sputtered roughly at the indignation of her treatment. She became quiet when her complaints were rewarded with a blow to the back, of her head, causing her to trip over her feet.

The group stopped, and Eve was led into a room where the blindfold was taken off, eyes squinting. The chamber had books and papers lined and stacked at the walls, placed haphazardly on bookshelves. A long table was at the center of another wall, close to the vast empty hole considered a window. At the table, Oberon sat between a young fey woman and Avo. The advisor had a journal open with a writing tool in hand. A little jar of black ink was not far from his reach. Eve noted that his face was as grim as ever.

Eve's attention was focused on the fresh face in the room. The newcomer was a young female fey that shined from an inner radiance. The woman's aura made Eve feel inadequate. The fey had the same eyes as Oberon. Her hair was dirty blonde, similar to Caoimhghin, and she wore a silky long-sleeved dress with a large silver medallion on her chest. She had low shoes and donned a wolf pelt on her shoulders. The energy around the fey was familiar. Eve could not understand why. This newcomer could be another ally, yet there was an edge of danger Eve felt could be the end of her.

Eve was shoved forward, her feet scraping and pounding loudly on the ground from a misstep. She turned and glared at the guards quickly. She then faced the king, who had papers in his hands, writing notes here and there in the margins. Eve's hands twitched in impatience as she waited to be spoken to by the majesty. It wasn't until one of the guards coughed that Oberon gave her his attention.

"Ah. Welcome," Oberon spoke.

"Your majesty," Eve politely greeted, bowing low sloppily. He looked at her curiously. His eyes moved back and forth to her face and the injuries. He shrugged and gently placed his pen down.

"She didn't lie, did she? What did you say to get beaten?" Oberon mussed. He then smiled, saying, "Nice, though, to see you indeed have a proper face. The mask did you no justice," he flirted, giving her a wink.

Eve flushed. After years spent pretending and being treated as a male, she hadn't yet fully come to terms with her femininity being acknowledged. She wasn't comfortable with others teasing her. She was used to being a warrior, taking orders from her superiors and giving them to those of lower ranking. She understood the opposite sex better when fighting or training with them. Eve couldn't lie that there were times a man had flirted with her, when she had been Adam. During those moments, fear had crawled up her back at the leering looks they had given her. She had been afraid of what they could do if she said 'no' and what they would find when they assaulted her.

"Father," the young fey at his side warned and looked at him expectantly with mirth. Eve was thankful to the girl for the interruption. Oberon grinned and reintroduced Avo. He next presented the girl as his daughter, Queen Petal of the Wolves. He explained her presence. She was with him and would be until she learned the running and routine of being the future High Queen. Eve nodded and remembered Aelfdene talking about his "whore of a sister". She hoped the girl was a better fey than her brother. So far, Petal was attentive. While Oberon talked, the woman seemed to listen without the contempt or smugness her brother had shown.

"Your answer, girl," Oberon demanded, getting to the point. "What will be your path?"

"I will stay."

"To another business in hand, though, I doubt you will give me an answer, but it must be questioned: Which of my guards did this to you,

and if you perchance know by whose orders?"

Eve bit her lip and looked down. Oberon sighed unhappily. He ordered his men to move Eve into a better room with two guards outside her door. They would watch and follow her at all times. A written routine would be set the following day to determine when she would be tutored about the history and control of her magic. She would also be given a chance to train with his guards. Later, if good news came that she was trustworthy, he would have her placed as one of his closest royal commanders and a leader for his soldiers.

# Chapter 16

SEVEN DAYS— seven long grueling nettling days was the length of time Eve had been a resident in the castle. Nay, if she was being honest with herself, she was a prisoner of the Underground with strictly limited rights. Oberon had done as promised and arranged for her a routine that echoed daily, never changing. Additionally, she was given four escorts— guards— and her friends were ordered to stay away, leaving her alone. The king had knowingly cut and isolated Eve from those she trusted. She had been thrown to the lions, per se, without a sword or shield to defend herself and found herself spending her days surrounded by those who loathed her with Satan's fire. This feeling extended to her own guards. They looked the other way when a random inhabitant tripped her in the hallway. Magically, the guards were never near when unknown assailants threw spoiled food in her direction.

In the mornings, Eve was pressed awake and pushed into the training yard with Oberon's personal family guards. A majority of them were fey, a few elves, and the rest were minotaurs. All of them were giants in height compared to her. On the first day of practice, she had been displaced to the side to watch the others work on their drills with practice swords and staff. Their swords were similar to the ones from home. Some weapons were broader, and others were made to stab with little surface to use for blocking. The staves were brilliantly designed and built with what looked like lightweight bronze metal. Well, it was heavy in her hands but light in theirs. She was impressed by their agility and speed as she watched and learned from their conditioning. These men and women could take down Eve's men with little effort and movement if the time ever came for them to meet in battle.

On the second day of training, Eve was handed a sword with a blade that had blunt edges and was a bit shorter than she was used to. One of the men scoffed and pointed out that her sword was for children. She ignored him and proceeded to test the weapon. The grip lay nicely in her palm, and the hilt the correct length. She performed some basic slashes and thrust movements, checking the blade's balance and weight. It was satisfactory, and she adapted to her new weapon quickly.

Before joining in the first drill, Eve was informed that she was banned from using magic due to personal circumstances by order of High King Oberon and Queen Titania. That was understandable. Yet, her voice spoke before her mind could take appropriate action. Sarcastically, she had enlightened the surly fast-tempered minotaur sword master that she couldn't acquiesce to the order. She had no control over the darkly terrible powers that had been dormant until recently.

That day ended for Eve right after practice. She was carried to her room due to a large gash at the side of her lower torso. The injury was from a broad and sharp horn that could only belong to a minotaur. An elf healer dark of skin had, unkindly and harshly, scolded and bandaged her. He then commanded her guards that she could not leave her room. Before the healer's departure, he gave her a vile concoction that she had to drink every time she awoke during the day and throughout the night. The rest of her waking hours mainly were spent sleeping; by the coming morning, the area of her injury was tender and no longer bleeding. All that was left of her serious puncture was a circular scar.

Eve solemnly joined the men in line at the yard. She mainly kept silent unless spoken to and listened to every command. Subsequently, the young mortal had fewer problems with the commander. The same could not be said for the men she was training with. Their dislike was shown by the bruises, muscle aches, and occasional cuts given to her by "accident". During the little breaks given between practice, she tended to her scrapes herself. After drills, she ate with the others reluctantly. They left a wide berth between themselves and her. Eve didn't mind as she went to her quarter afterward to clean up before meeting the grouchy healer who had seen and attended her impaling the night before. The elf healer, as mentioned earlier, had been given the task of being her personal doctor. Eve did not know that he was also to keep a journal of her comings and goings to be handed to Queen Titania monthly.

The healer was not pleased with his new position and less delighted that he was to be an informer. He was an Asclepiad. His job was to help others, not spy on them. Unknowingly, he placed his aggravation upon Eve when she didn't react to the seriousness of her injuries that he had pointed out. The everyday traumas the mortal seemed to amass were fractured ribs and a few twisted joints. He knew that the more critical injuries he found had been caused with intent. Caicey, the healer, asked who had harmed her, but the girl said nothing. When she did answer, she swore it was her fault.

Upon the next full moon, Eve's routine changed. The last few hours of the day were no longer going to be time for her to contemplate and plan for her next moves. Instead, she was guided to a cottage outside the castle, at the edge of the nearby village. It was a short horse ride away and left little time for Eve and her protection to talk. The tiny home was owned by a very old, grumpy— *vampyre*. The night creature appeared to be extraordinarily ancient. The man was shaking while holding on to a cane, back bent forward. Eve feared that he would fall from a slight breeze at any moment.

"Lord Melchior, your new student," Eve's guard said as a way of introduction with a small respectful bow to the elder. The old man nodded and waved the guards away. They hastily left, and soon it was just Eve and Melchior standing in awkward silence.

Previously, on the ride to Melchior's home before Eve knew his name, she was informed by the guards of his position and importance in the Underground. The old man had formerly been Oberon's advisor before Avo. He had a reputation for being an expert on the Underground's world before its separation from the above and before Oberon was named High King. Many with money came to him to teach their children. Eve would be counted among the privileged, and she was warned not to show him any disrespect.

Lord Melchior, stooped down, was at a height with Eve. They were able to see eye to eye. Well, that was partially true. The man had wrinkles over wrinkles that made his eyes barely visible under his bushy, furrowed eyebrows. Eve observed a few strands of hair peeking from his almost entirely bald head. He was dressed in a black monk-like robe with long sleeves that reached just below his wrist but did not impede his ability to hold on to his cane.

Without a preamble and only a simple nod of a head, Melchior walked further into the cottage. Eve followed. Quickly, she found that the old man would not be teaching her magic or control of her unseelie gifts. Neither would she be taught the knowledge of the fey before their interaction with the mortals. She was not *pure* or *deserving* to know it, Melchior notified her as he pointed at a desk for Eve to sit. From her new teacher's summary, her education contained more details about the little Caoimhghin had already informed her of. Those little details were more than she cared to memorize by the time the first lesson had ended.

With each session, the tutelage was dull. Eve could admit she had some blame for the boredom she felt. It had been a while since she was forced to sit and listen to a tutor. She couldn't focus as she once did when younger. Yet, her lack of concentration was not all on her. Melchior's voice was soothing— but bland. The elder stretched each word out, giving each syllable a sort of reverence or praise. Then, he would pause between phrases making the lesson longer and slower than it should be. It was distressing. Eve had done all she could think of to stay awake and alert. She was convinced her teacher's ungodly gift was using his voice to lull creatures to their deaths by way of sleep. She would even swear that a spider had curled up to nap during her third lesson, only to die before her eyes grew heavy as she entered Morpheus's realm.

Unluckily, her visit to the celestial and calming kingdom of blissful nothingness was often disrupted rudely and viciously by the old vampire. She was either awoken by a harsh and well-placed flick at the back of her head or her tutor slammed heavy bound books not far from her face. She understood, she really did that all that was being taught was important, but she just couldn't stay awake and away from the nice mist of haze that called out her name in a siren's song. It didn't help that, once alert, Melchior would continue with the same droning voice that would restart her cycle of going in and out of awareness.

For two moon cycles, Eve's life was eating, drills, being checked for injuries, and her studies. She had little breaks and was seldomly left alone at night. There were minor changes in her itinerary that allowed her to sneak away and continue the quest for Puck. At night, when she was posed to be relaxed and asleep, Eve rubbed her eyes in frustration. It was evident that the ruling party wished and was intent on keeping a tight grip on her as she was constantly watched. She just needed that one chance of a bit of freedom to look around without her attached guards.

Eve had attempted to escape multiple times in different ways. Her first endeavor occurred during the early meals. She had snuck away when all were busy and the room chaotic. Eve took the distraction as an opportunity but found her path, without fail, blocked by one of her guards, who smirked at her guilty face. They kindly said nothing and escorted her back to eat with her rations cut in half. On her second attempt, she used her blankets to make a crude rope to climb out her window at night. Peeking outside, she found a griffin, alert and deadly. On her last effort, she had gone to the privacy, the most sacred of all places, where her sentries had no choice but to leave her alone. Unfortunately, Eve found all her possible exits covered by Aelfdene's men and left before they saw her. The captain seemed to be also eyeing her. She knew it was to find an excuse to have her killed.

Eve swore at her foolishness for forgetting her problems with the knotty-pated captain. She had been so focused on slipping away to look for Puck's item that the fey she had to worry about had been out of her mind. That could not happen again. She needed to move Captain Aelfdene's attention away from herself. With his eyes always upon her, she had fewer chances to move about. At least her guard let her be when she was in the lavatory. They knew the importance of personal space. That sort of manner, it seemed, had not been taught to Aelfdene or those under his employment.

The young woman groused about how to lose the captain's attention or have him distracted by other matters. Yet, who would listen to a stranger? Who would hear the mortal whose kind had pushed these magnificent beings to a realm that existed under the ground? Eve was no one special in the Underground. Captain Aelfdene, on the other hand, was born in this magical world. He had a charm that Eve knew hid the blackness of his heart. Under his façade, he was a traitor willing to plot a coup to overthrow his own family from power. If Eve whispered this knowledge to someone respected, she perhaps would gain a little favor and find the dagger to go home. So far, her secondary personal quest was failing to discover who her mother was. Eve was giving up on that and, at the moment, just wanted to see home once more. But who to tell about Captain Aelfdene's actions for that to happen?

It then came to Eve that the one person to whom she could probably whisper her knowledge of Aelfdene was Melchior. The elder knew the comings and goings of the castle. He knew the right people to keep an eye on the young prince. If Eve was to use the right words, Aelfdene would no longer be an issue. His eyes would no longer follow her. Instead, someone would be watching him.

Now that the young woman had an idea who to talk to about the young petulant prince, Eve had to decide when to speak to Melchior. Her words had to be given to the old man without him wondering about her real reason for what she gained in return. Logically, he would surmise that Eve wanted to achieve the royal family's trust. That was the only suspicion she could afford the old man to have.

The time came when Eve gained the courage to speak to Melchior. She anxiously waited to approach him after her lesson, hurriedly putting her notes away. She then closed her books and walked toward the old man, clearing her throat to gain his attention. He looked at her warily before he let out a huff, signaling she had his ears.

Eve opened her mouth, but a terrible pain in her mind suddenly clouded any thoughts she had. That pang turned into a cacophony of voices shouting a warning to keep her mouth sealed. She would have gone against the alarm if it had not been for the heavy, dark feeling of dread welling inside her. So— at the last minute, she decided to not speak to Melchior about Aelfdene.

"I apologize," Eve mumbled. "I had an inquiry, but it left my mind."

"You look pale, child," Melchior croaked. "You sure you have forgotten?"

"I can't remember. I believe I ate a fruit that did not settle well," Eve explained. The tutor scrutinized Eve's form, and she gave him a small smile in return. He must have seen nothing suspicious because he turned away from her, giving Eve his back. She recognized the dismissal and rode to the castle to sleep and wake up to the coming new day.

Eve attempted to sleep, yet it was far from her grasp. So, she lit a few candles and pulled out a book to study from her satchel. All she managed to do was stare at the pages. She was utterly uneased by the warning her demons had conveyed. They usually wanted to attack and tear a living creature apart. Eve had never experienced such foreboding. Not even with Captain Aelfdene had her darkness reacted in fear.

*Tap. Tap.*

Before Eve could think further on the matter, her eyebrows

knitted in confusion. She looked around the room to see if her abode had been compromised. She waited to hear the knock she'd heard not long ago but was only rewarded with silence. Eve shook her head and concluded it was all in her mind.

*Tap. Tap. Tap.*

She pushed her chair back and jumped to her feet, then walked around her chambers and started to look around the room. She searched for the sound but was unsuccessful in finding where it had originated. She mussed her hair in frustration. The first knocking, had been easy for Eve to believe it was all in her mind. The second time, it had been surer and a bit louder. The sound could no longer be blamed on tiredness or paranoia.

*TAP. TAP. TAP!*

*The window*, Eve recognized. She ran toward the racket but paused halfway through her dash. Outside that opening, a monster should be sleeping. What kind of man, creature, or thing could bypass such horror? Eve's eyes narrowed in caution. She quietly tip-toed to her door and opened it, grimacing as it creaked loudly. She shook her head and went to whisper to the guards, only to find them unconscious on the floor. They did not look injured or hurt, only asleep.

"Bullocks," Eve hissed.

*TAP! TAP! TAP! TAP!*

"Hold your bloody balls," she groaned to herself. She rubbed her forehead and bounced lightly on her heels. Once more, the knight looked again at her useless guards and mentally cursed their incompetency. Now, she could shout for aid and hope others would hear before she was attacked or her assailant escaped. Yet, that option irked Eve. Her curiosity demanded to know if it was Aelfdene making another attempt on her life or if there was someone new she had dismissed?

She knew she was boil-brained for not asking for help since she was weaponless. She could use her books or the candlesticks for defense but knew it would be insufficient protection. In this world, she doubted her improvised weapons would damage the beings beyond anything she had to deal with, proven by how many times she kept getting injured by them.

The knight moved to the window, calling herself all sorts of names for walking straight toward danger empty-handed. There was an urge to grab her reading material, but what was the point of looking silly? She knew she wasn't an ordinary mortal; if Eve had to defend herself, she just needed to unleash her gifts. A prospect that she was not pleased to utilize.

Reaching the window, she opened it cautiously, jumping back and tripping on her feet as she was startled by red glowing eyes. Her heartbeat increased, and she had to place her hand over her chest to calm herself down. The movement did nothing, and as the eyes became closer, the beats became faster, causing a pain Eve needed to be gone. The candlelight hit her attacker's face just as the pain became unbearable.

Eve's panic stopped immediately as she looked at her assailant in confusion, who stayed just at the opening of her window. "Melchior?"

"I apologize for reaching you so late at night. I noticed you appeared distressed," he said. "I couldn't help but worry about your state of mind that I needed to visit you."

"I am not distressed," Eve told him.

"Yes, you are."

"No, I am not."

"YES. You are distressed," Melchior pushed. His words repeatedly echoed in Eve's head, louder than the warning from her monster and demons. His eyes called to her, and Eve tried to turn her gaze away from him but found she couldn't. She was locked in his stare and had no power to stop that from happening. "You wish to allow me entrance."

The young woman glared at her soon-to-be ex-instructor. She gritted her teeth, shook her head, and said, "No. Perchance we discuss any business you wish later in the day after the lesson." A lesson that Eve would not be attending now, of course.

"No! This must happen now! Invite me in," Melchior commanded sternly. "There is nothing to fear. All will be alright. You are safe with me."

*Sard,* Eve cursed. She could feel she was losing control of herself. Not her mind, but her body. She fought against Melchior's order, holding the muscles back from doing what he wished. No matter how much she fought, it was a losing battle. Her mouth opened, and she regretfully said, "Come in."

That simple phrase, those two words, and Eve's demons started clawing inside her to escape. They were not attempting to control her; they wanted out of her body to force her to run away. They were afraid. She held them back easily as their panic state made them vulnerable to her control— and in return, made Eve gullible to Melchior's power.

Melchior stepped into the room with an unsettling youthfulness. His hand lifted, and Eve felt a pressure surround her body, partially paralyzing her. She squirmed on the spot, eyes wide. The old man grinned, his stride extending. In a single step, he was in front of Eve with a tight grip on her throat. She wanted to scratch or punch his smug face, but her body did not want to comply, as she was held still by an invisible force.

"I am sorry— but your darkness calls to be possessed by one stronger," Melchior moaned lovingly. He brought Eve closer to him and sniffed her neck. "I never had an unseelie who was in a physical form. I wonder how you taste. I need your energy, or I will grow weak without consuming such power. Don't worry. I will make sure you dream sweet dreams while I feast on your soul little by little. Nobody will miss you. No one will care about your death."

Eve was frightened out of her mind. She couldn't believe how blind she had been to the danger that was so nearby. From years of experience, she should have known better. She hated this world, her unknown mother, and her life— but she would not lose her miserable existence to this old man. She dug deep inside herself and grabbed onto the darkness with a tight and steady grip. It was hers to use, not the other way around. The monster would listen to her.

Calling to her demons, Eve grabbed their strength with an iron fist. The invisible force weakened its hold upon her body as her energy flared against it. She kicked at Melchior, releasing herself from his hold. She then magicked her mask on, eyes a glowing blood red though not as bright as the vampire in front of her, rimmed by a bright yellow. The skin around her eyes darkened, spreading into multitudes of cracks down her face. The darkness continued past her neck, disappearing underneath her blouse.

The vampire lashed out, swiping his hand at her like a bear, fingers curled with long claws. Eve used her arm to stall it and barred her teeth when his nails gouged into her skin, tearing strips of flesh away. Blood flowed freely out, running down her arm to the center of her palms, hardening and crystalizing into a solid shape, forming a translucent red longsword. With a simple shrug, she looked upon it with a quick wonder and started to attack, catching Melchior by surprise. He jumped away but not fast enough. Her slash hit his arm, cutting away into his skin, but not as deep as she had hoped. Afterward, Melchior flashed-stepped behind her, but Eve matched his speed, turning to face him, sword in the air, coming down over her head. He stopped the incoming blade with one hand at its down-arc, the sharp edges cutting into his grip, black blood dripping onto the floor.

The two combatants struggled for dominance over the weapon. Their strength was equal. Both gave and took the ground as they fought for an advantage over one another. Tired of continuing this tug of war, Eve growled and crouched down. She used her weight to pull the sword from Melchior's hold, rolling away to the side. She then leaped forward with a thrust aimed at his midsection. He flipped over her head, landing with one knee touching the ground, hissing, saliva escaping at the edges of his mouth.

The battle was fierce and quick. The two hurt each other with each strike they wielded. As they started to tire, Eve faked a move, but Melchior anticipated her action. Both arms out, he went to tackle her. She side stepped and, with a yell, swung her sword in a long circular curve, finally decapitating the old man.

The room became deadly silent. The sword in Eve's grip liquified and splashed out onto the floor, spraying in every direction and covering the furniture and walls in her blood. Wincing, she grabbed her bleeding arm using her hand to staunch the wound, hissing at the burn she felt when she put pressure on it. She twitched in shock when she heard gurgling laughter come from the head. The vampire was still alive! Eve fell on her behind in shock and crawled away from the corpse. Away from the maniac eyes.

"It is so beautiful," cackled Melchior, black blood spewing from cracked lips. "Your darkness. I can't wait for it to consume you. Such royal darkness. It will rule over everyone." With those last words, his eyes shut, and he took a final breath. He was finally no more— hopefully. His body greyed and hardened into stone, sections crumbling off until the vampire was only dust.

Eve's door burst open, and she screamed. One of her elf guards stumbled into the room on unsteady feet. His sword dragged on the ground as he surveyed the area with eyes blinking blearily, waking from his deep sleep. He saw Melchior's head and shouted. He revived the whole castle, and his cry was followed by many more. Others ran into the room, joining the guard. A nurse caught sight of Eve bleeding profusely and ran to the young woman. The newly arrived elves and fey rushed to Eve. Her eyes started to droop as wariness caught up with her. As they enquired what had happened, Eve could not hear the words coming out of their mouths. She could only hear her heart beating. Her head tilted to the side, her darkness and mask vanished, and the world blackened into nothing. Just as her body was about to impact the ground, she was caught. Eve smiled lightly at the warmth that surrounded her.

#  Chapter 17 

A GATE CLOSED noisily at an unknown distance. Footsteps stomped away on a stoned floor. Iron keys clanged against each other. Voices wailed in a familiar racket. A horrid smell hung in the humid air, provoking Eve to crinkle her nose as she lay unconscious atop a stone slab. Her arm was bandaged, clothes unchanged, and hands cuffed by two attached wide bracelets with etched fey symbols.

She was in a restless state of sleep, the aroma of the cell adding to the nightmare she was caught in. Her body jerked, and her legs kicked at an unseen enemy. Her hands clenched on top of her lap. Moans of distress escaped her lips as she envisioned being stabbed by a myriad of invisible spears. She turned over and fell from her cold, unfeeling berth, shocked awake by the contact with the floor. Eyes looked out at the world unobservant as she was still caught in a trance until she became aware of the real world. She breathed in and out heavily, body shaking, her surroundings sluggishly coming into focus. She went on her knees, swerving and turning her head this way and that, getting her bearings, her last memory recovering.

It took a little time for her to realize she wasn't on a battlefield as she had been dreaming about only moments ago. She hadn't been killed— again. Additionally, she wasn't covered in blood. Neither had she been buried alive underneath cold, unforgiving dirt. Her heart was still beating a vigorously constant frequency that, if she wanted, she could dance to. The throbbing in her arm confirmed that she was awake and had killed old Melchior, her teacher, who had gone completely insane. She wouldn't lie that there had been times she had wanted to strangle her previous instructors. Still, it wasn't like she would ever actually do it, and none of them had tried eating her in return.

Now that she was appropriately awoken, she saw that she was in another cage that was not in the dungeons, which was a blessing in itself. Birds sang happily outside as it became morning, and Eve listened to them with a small smile. She wondered what they saw and if the world looked more beautiful in the air. Did they see the corruption? The horror? The deaths? Or were they oblivious to all the evil? They did have the freedom to travel and see the world, to be away from all the mindless greed and battles of being alive. Eve wished she could take flight and just see the world like them.

Alas, she had been born in God's image, which came with living through the good and the bad. So, without further ado, she checked on her physicality. As she could remember, her fight had been rapid. Through the quick movements, Eve knew that she had been hurt by Melchior. She was happy to see that they had bandaged those wounds. She was unsatisfied, however, that they had left her in her old clothes. They still stank of iron that had come from her lifeblood. The healers had even torn them in some sections when they had dressed the torn skin.

On top of everything else, Eve now had manacles. She pulled and twisted them in annoyance. Each wriggle chafed the skin at her wrist, gritting her teeth as she added more force in her attempt at instinctive escape. A scream of frustration burst from her lips. She stood up and kicked a wall. She then pounded her 'bed' with her fist, bruising them, cracking the skin open, and covering the surface with her blood. Animal-like screams and shouts tore from her throat, her hair wild and tousled. It took time for her to realize her situation's futility. She stopped her berserk actions as pain laced from her bandaged wound, bringing her to a somewhat calmer state.

Confused about why she was in a cell, Eve began to brush out her frazzled hair with her fingers. She took in the room, unhappy to see no other furniture but her 'bed.' She got up from the stone slab she had been placed upon and walked to the only single port window. Her hands held on to the bars that kept her from escaping. No point because from the little she saw, she was up in a tower, levels too high to even want to jump. Eve looked down and watched the mist slowly dissipate to reveal the courtyard below, bustling with citizens already hard at work.

Somewhere nearby, a door banged, echoing through the tower. Rushed footsteps climbed stairs and became louder as they headed toward Eve's direction. The young woman smirked as she heard curses from a familiar voice. She sat back upon her rock slab and watched the door open to show wild hair. She smiled at Prince Caoimhghin as he entered her "home," but he was not elated to see her.

"You killed your tutor," Caoimhghin said with outrage. Eve shrugged and looked down at her bare feet. "Why? Melchior was old. Harmless. Annoying and well-known. Well respected. He had support even from those who, if they wanted, could bring the war to the underground...to my father."

"He was going to kill me!" she countered, her face flushed with anger. "He said...he said...he wanted my darkness. That he needed to own it."

"Those were his words?"

"They were a lot stronger, but yes," she answered with an affirmative nod.

Caoimhghin shook his head and ruffled up his hair, sweeping it back. "I will tell my father. If what you say is true, that...that Melchior had wanted to fest on one of unseelie...tis a taboo act." He moved closer and sniffed the air. "You need a bath."

Eve stuck out her tongue, then said, "If I wasn't imprisoned, I would wallop you." Caoimhghin laughed and walked away with a promise she would be out soon.

Unfortunately, the young woman wasn't released until the following day. Neither was she given a chance to take care of her hygiene. Eve was marched out of her cell. She found herself in another section of the castle and was then taken up a set of stairs. Her escorts informed her that she was being taken to the royal's family study chamber. Prince Caoimhghin, halfway toward her destination, decided to accompany them but only spoke to the guards. He seemed to be ignoring Eve in favor of joking around with her escorts, who did not react to his horrible humor. They didn't even speak back to him when he asked a question.

"Oh, I wish to halt here. Father won't mind," Caoimhghin declared cheerfully, shocking all in the group as he suddenly stopped in front of a closed room. The guards looked at him quizzically. Eve was confused as she watched Caoimhghin dance around, exclaiming happily about a room he had to show her. Before the guards could say something, the prince was already dragging her away. Eve stumbled, trying not to fall over her feet, as she was unexpectedly pulled into a room with more glass cases. The prince continued talking loudly about the obscure items, but she didn't know why. Then his subjects would change from food to (if Eve heard correctly from his quick words) a woman who had flirted with him shamelessly. Said woman had walked away as he had professed his love to her. Eve still didn't know what was going on. She just dumbly followed him around until she was rudely pushed toward a case near the wall.

"What is going on?" Eve finally inquired. Caoimhghin didn't answer but smiled smugly at her. He raised his hand and pointed to the case at her side. Eve saw nothing of interest, and shook her head, still confused. "Can you just tell me why we are here?"

Caoimhghin waved his hand at the case again. She rubbed her eyes and decided to comply and look at whatever he was showing. The casing was empty, or so she believed at first glance. As she studied it more, she noticed it had many locks, more than were required. Such action was either to keep something or somebody in or out. Eve slowly walked to the case, and an outline of a weapon appeared. There, in front of her, was the dagger that couldn't be seen. She looked up at her friend and smiled. She owed the young royal a favor for being her savior. Her chance to go home was closer than she had hoped.

"What room is this?" Eve whispered.

"The trophy room," Caoimhghin answered. "This room is where Father keeps his most precious personal treasures of those he has punished or killed."

"Pretty morbid, is it not?"

Caoimhghin laughed and gave more information about the space. "As you see, this area also contains forbidden and dangerous artifacts that must be kept away from the populace. Only those of royalty and their guest are allowed in here." The prince walked to the dagger, tapping its encased glass. "The original purpose of this item was to open a portal to your realm. Now, it bars others from entering this world by taking the essence of their magic, keeping those with that signature away and exiled. The only way those individuals can be allowed to return is to have their essence returned or for the dagger to be destroyed."

The guards outside finally ran into the trophy room. "Prince, we have discussed this situation and have concluded that the king will not be pleased she is here. We must leave this area now."

"My apologies," Caoimhghin feigned and then looked out of one of the windows with a pout. "Oh, look at the time. We must hurry. Father deplores to be kept waiting." With that statement, the group left and soon found themselves where they were posed to go.

#  CHAPTER 18 

EVE'S HEAD LIFTED, and she became paralyzed at the door from a stupor. Expecting to see King Oberon, the group was met instead by his wife and Princess Petal. Both women were dressed comfortably in long-crossed tunics and leather leggings. Their feet were protected by scaled reptilian boots. Two swords leaned nearby at the edge of a small, round table. Both their faces were flushed with giant smiles. Eve surmised the two must have been practicing against each other or their men not that long ago.

Prince Caoimhghin skipped first to his mother with a wide grin. Titania giggled and patted her son's cheeks affectionately. He then went to his sister, who budged him away in annoyance. He laughed and tried again, but his efforts were in vain.

"Now, Petal, don't be like that," Caoimhghin childishly sulked with an almost mischievous grin.

"You can persist, but I shall not allow not even a handshake," Petal growled and waved him away. Caoimhghin boyishly stomped to Eve's side, taking a pompous stand with his hands at his waist and chest puffed out— and *why were his eyes sparkling?*

"Where is father? His jubilant face is missing. I do wish to see it before my departure," Caoimhghin enquired.

"He was called to the borders of the Southern kingdoms," Titania answered with worry.

"Problems?"

Titania glanced at Eve and back to her son. "Not an appropriate conversation with the present company. Later, we shall talk." To Eve, Titania said, "I hear you have murdered one of our prestigious tutors. The guard at your door swears you struck him down unconscious as he was on duty."

Eve's mouth gaped open in shock and anger. "That is incorrect. The guard was asleep. He was dormant outside my door when Melchior *visited*."

"Why did he come to you so late? Why allow him access to your domain? Were you surprised by his appearance?"

Eve fiddled with her fingers nervously. "Curiosity took my mind before logic could rear its head. Though I checked to see if any of my guards could aid me, they were useless lumps outside my door."

Titania squinted her eyes in suspicion. "Yet, why allow Melchior in?"

"I did not at first, but he must have placed a spell upon me. Words escaped my lips, giving him permission to walk into my abode. Once I gained control of myself, and my life was in danger, a fight ensued."

"You— a mortal, were able to escape his hypnotizing. How?"

"I...reined in my demons and broke from his pull. And...and a sword formed in my hand, made of my life. I do not know how it came to be other than my need to defend myself."

"I have heard by those that defend you that Melchior must have been determined to kill you for you to extinguish his life. Why? For what purpose? Did he tell you?"

"He wished to feast on me. He wanted to own my darkness," Eve replied with a faraway look, voice deep and frightened, dragging out the word 'own'. Gasps of surprise came from the guards, the queen was noticeably angry, and the princess appeared shocked and horrified. Eve expected their reaction. She logically doubted it was a regular occurrence for one to eat another. It must be taboo as it was at her home.

"That cannot be true," Petal commented, shaking her head in shock. "For a vampire to consume such darkness...it creates a monster that fuels nightmares of all still in the light. Consuming others changes one. It soils one's soul. It becomes a horrid addiction that tempts one to become part of the shadows— an unseelie."

"He didn't look like a monster— he felt like one withal," Eve mused, speaking loudly. "Though such feeling only occurred once previously before his wicked attention came to fruition upon my person."

"And you said nothing? Told no one?" Titania questioned.

"How? I am a newcomer. Would you have really believed me?" Eve asked.

"I wish I could say if you had brought your concerns forthwith, we would have acted on your information. But that would be a lie. I am impressed, nonetheless, with the control you have over your evil. I must inform you, though, those demons are just your darkness. Why it had manifested as many, I do not know. Yet, I am not pleased you let your malevolence out. We need to teach you to bury it deep inside, so you are not tempted by its presence," Titania informed. She then gestured to the princess. "Princess Petal, will you give this lesson? With your talent, it shan't take long to grasp this skill."

Eve took a step back into one of the guards reflexively as she glanced at Petal, who, for some odd reason, was giving her a hungry gaze. The princess's eyes roamed over her form, licking her lips simultaneously. Eve watched as Petal smirked at her obvious discomfort at being assigned to spend time with her. The young woman doubted she would survive and smiled weakly as Petal waved at her with a saucy grin.

Eve was not fully blind to the world she lived in. She knew that women had relations with other women. They were usually called bonded companions and were carried out in great secrecy. If the women were caught together, they were taken to the church. The priest usually ordered those women to be tortured and then publicly executed.

Eve's eyes met Petal's awkwardly, who kissed the air and blew her affection in her direction. Eve shivered. By Petal's blatant flirtatious show, it must be a norm for women with women...perhaps even men with men. Eve was astounded by their openness to relationships— but it wasn't for her. She might fight and pretend to be a man, but her heart was on the opposite sex. Though, it was forbidden for Eve to show her appreciation of the male body as the patriarch of her family.

"Is that necessary?" she complained with a tight smile. Caoimhghin chortled and covered it immediately with a cough. "I mean, mayhap there is a charm I can simply wear to dull my unnatural gifts? That would be preferable— for me— please. I was never one for study."

"Oh, that is excellent. I do not use books," Petal commented. With a suggestive look, she added, "I am very...hands...on."

"Bloody hell," Eve mumbled to herself in fear. Caoimhghin shook at her side from barely concealed laughter.

"Then it is settled," the queen chirped. She clapped her hands twice afterward, the guards becoming alert. "Your lesson will be after drills when my daughter has time. You shall also be escorted from now on by a single guard. Additionally, there will be no punishment for Melchior's death. What he did is forbidden, and I will let the news out to my people to ensure nobody attacks you in retaliation." Eve nodded numbly in dejected acceptance and readily followed the guards out of the room, becoming lost in a haze of uncertainty.

While waiting for the call from the princess, she imagined scenarios of her lesson. Each one was as frightening as the others. The abridgment of her nightmares started with her being pushed roughly into a mysterious room with no windows. In this room was a single bed in the middle. No other pieces of furniture were in sight. The door she had come through was slammed behind her, the sound echoing off the stone walls. Eve turned to escape but found another wall. The door was gone, and she was trapped. Princess Petal would suddenly appear with a predatory, hungry look. The look would change to something more sinister, and the princess would suddenly attack, the fear Eve felt ending the dream.

Eve later told Caoimhghin about her recurring nightmares. His eyes widened in surprise, then he burst out laughing. She smacked his arm and told him her fear was a serious matter. Through his laughter, he told her his sister would do nothing to her. Apparently, Petal loved and lived to make non-family members uncomfortable. It meant that she had no ill feelings toward that person. Caoimhghin had been correct. When the call came that it was time for her lesson with the royal family member, nothing happened as she had envisioned.

Eve's new constant escort that took her to the meeting with the princess was a minotaur. He was shy and a gentleman. He gently guided Eve into the room, staying behind in the hall. Eve was pleased not to see a bed anywhere and curtain-drawn windows dimming the room's lighting. Instead, over-large cushions were on top of a rug that covered most of the space. On the left and right wall were two long tables with candles and incense on top of them. Petal stood in the center of the room dressed in a loose tunic and comfortable pants, her feet bare. Her face had no worries as her eyes were closed and her head tilted to the ceiling. She was utterly serene. Eve doubted she ever had a moment to be in such a state of bliss.

"Jacen, can you please light the candles and incense for me," Petal spoke dulcetly with eyes still closed.

*So, that is his name.* Eve watched in amusement as the minotaur behind her walked awkwardly and as quietly as he could inside. She knew he was trying to be soft on his feet, but it came out more as a loud shuffle. His hands fumbled with the tinderbox and fire steel. They were tiny in his hands. Surprisingly, it didn't take him long. The room brightened significantly in an orange glow, and the area slowly filled with the smell of lavender and myrrh. With his task achieved, Jacen walked out, closing the door behind him gently—with an accidental slam.

"Please, join me," Petal gestured to Eve. "Before we fortify your control, we must relax our form to start a basis. We need a foundation to ensure you don't fail." Petal opened her eyes when she didn't hear Eve move. She smirked knowingly, saying, "Don't worry. Caoimhghin had me promise not to make you uncomfortable, and a fey heeds their word. Once a deal is struck, we are unable to break it."

*Promise or deal? Which is it?* Eve knew the importance of words, including those two. A promise was a contract on one's soul. It could not be broken without asking for ruin from the Almighty. Additionally, a broken promise was the disintegration of one's honor, credibility, and dignity. On the other hand, a deal was a promise of a different sort. A deal asked for something in return. Eve had to know which one had happened. "Which was it? A promise? Or, a deal?"

"If you come closer, I will answer," Petal proposed.

Eve mulled the proposition, worrying her bottom lip. "As long as you do not give me that look."

"What look?"

"You know which one I speak of."

"Fine." Eve nodded hesitantly. Slowly, she moved forward without taking her eyes off the princess.

"What do you know of deals?" Petal inquired as she sat comfortably on one of the cushions, legs crossed in front of her.

"Then you admit to a deal," Eve said, glaring down at the princess. "What did your brother give you in return? What price did he pay? What part of my soul do I need to give to help him?"

"Obviously, his loyalty was what I asked for and gained. No part of you is needed, as you have little to give. A war is on the horizon, and sides must be chosen. Dear Brother wanted to stay out of the inevitable, and I took advantage of his weakness for you to make him take a stand. He does love and is loyal to the outcasts. He would soon learn to regret his soft heart for them."

"You self-righteous— "

"Hold that tongue. I am a princess. You are only a dim-witted, useless sack of fragile flesh, mortal."

Petal's true self leaked, and it was repulsive. The royal was a two-faced snake-like Lucifer himself. She looked at, and found others, weaknesses and used them for her own. Petal's personality was one of a person who used another's good nature against them. Then, that weakness was turned into a lesson to tear their naivety away, show them the horror of the world, and dim the hope that existed. The concern that had yet to be answered was whether Petal was like Aelfdene. Eve would have to wait to see if the princess showed the same sadistic hunger as her older brother. Which of the two siblings was the less of two evils? Though, personally, evil was evil in Eve's opinion.

The knight hated manipulators. They ruled and sullied the world. Fey may be unable to tell lies, but they could still twist their words and hide them underneath the dust. Caoimhghin once commented that a closed mouth and silent indifference were his preference when dealing with issues. He was a man who liked the world to be black and white. Yet, if the time came and he had no choice but to speak, he would twist the words and circumvent to another topic. If that didn't work, he had to play the game that his people did. Caoimhghin hated himself when he acted like the others. His most significant rule was that the action was for the greater good.

"I can see your disgust. Trust me, I wished not to have done wrong to my brother's kindness, but I must prepare. You have met my elder, the captain. He will do all he can to rule. To take power. He cares for nobody but himself."

"I see no difference between you," Eve spat. "You hide under smiles and beauty. Show only what you want to show."

"I bid you quiet! Your ignorance of my world is palpable. With the few words you speak, your feelings are known. It is obvious you see me as a monster. You don't know what a monster is; you can't imagine— "

"I can envisage plenty," Eve piped angrily.

"No, this I doubt. I can educate you on the matter. It would be easy. I just need to dangle you as a juicy prey at the edge of the border where the unseelie lie. Then, with your eyes, you will see the true horror. The true monsters."

"Not all monsters are as unsightly as their souls."

"That is indeed a fact," Petal agreed. "But, not always true."

The princess crossed her arms to show there would be a finality to the issue. "I care for the kingdom. I admit some actions are for my survival, but that is minimal. My life is insignificant to my loyalty to my people and keeping order stable in this world. In addition, without us, there is no wall to protect you, mortals, from being conquered and enslaved. Your people will not be able to defeat them."

"That is not true. We are stronger, smarter, resilient— "

"You naïve fool. Your people have not grown enough. You are primitive and use the old world as stories to scare your children to obey."

Eve bit her lip, holding back a defensive retort. The logical part of her knew that Petal was correct. If her people saw any of the creatures of the Underground, there would be hell on earth. The simple mortal had no chance to win against the magical beings.

Then, there was the matter with Caoimhghin. He was trapped in a deal he should not have taken, and it was Eve's fault. She had to try to lessen the consequences that could harm her friend. "You are correct. My people are not ready. Your actions may aid us, but that doesn't make you a saint. You exploited your brother's weakness. So, I have a proposition for you." Eve looked at Petal intensely. "When the time comes, and all hope is lost to your— goal, I will come and lay my life at your feet for you to use. Even if it means my death and giving into my darkness."

"And in return, what do you ask for?"

Eve hesitated before saying, "Prince Caoimhghin be excluded from any future plans that will tarnish his soul."

Petal contemplated the offering. With a smirk, she said, "Deal."

"Do we need to shake hands or write it on paper to finalize this arrangement?"

"No, our ways are a bit more unique. It will take a little while until you can feel our deal take effect. It does leave a lasting impression."

*Feel?* A pressure surrounded Eve's beating heart. The tips of her fingers tingled uncomfortably. She started to panic. The last time her fingers had prickled, she had been holding a training sword for the first time. Her instructor had trained her roughly until her arms felt heavy, and she couldn't feel her hands. Now, Eve did not like being uninformed of what was happening to her. She was about to ask Petal if what she was feeling was expected when the pressure left. It was followed by a burning feeling on her forearm. The burn felt similar to when a hot dagger was pressed to flesh to close a deep wound. Eve was sure she had not hurt herself and hastily raised her sleeve. She flinched at the sight of her skin. There, she saw branded on her flesh an image of an owl with horns sticking out of its head.

"Only those of magical abilities will see that. I advise that you bandage and hide the mark away. Trust no one."

Eve nodded. "I shall do that." She covered up the mark and said, "I suppose before the day ends, you can teach me the skill the queen has ordered."

Princess Petal proceeded to the main reason Eve was in her company. The fey instructed Eve to enter a sitting form with her legs crossed. The young woman recognized the position the monks took when they entered *meditari.* She then grimaced as Petal told her to close her eyes and slowly count to ten, breathing in and out. Eve listened as the princess encouraged her to find her darkness and take hold of the abomination. She was to feel for the evil's boundaries and then push it into an imaginary cage.

The knight could not complete the task given to her. Every time Eve went to her darkness, she became tired. It was as if she was pushing through a dense murk, and the effort to do so exhausted her. When this occurred, she was brought to awareness unfailingly by a bucket of freezing water being poured over her head. By the time dinner came, she was drenched and shivering. Petal angrily ordered her to clean up and said more lessons were needed.

The next day, Petal took another approach to Eve's education. The princess had easily ascertained that Eve's patience was nonexistent. The mortal's character was one who reacted first before thinking. Petal still needed to learn if the personality was of nature or a recent occurrence. Either way, the royal had to work with what she had. So, she planned to make the lesson intriguing to one who became bored effortlessly. The princess understood mortals were competitive and acted like peacocks in front of those they were attracted to. Petal smirked as a plan formed. It would either fail or succeed.

She invited a male off-duty elf guard for the second lesson to join Eve and her. Though the man was at height with Eve, he was absolutely breathtaking, with his shirt open, showing a chiseled chest. She watched, amused, as Eve's mouth dropped open. The mortal's cheeks flamed at the gorgeous specimen that sat at her side.
Eve internally cried. Today would be an utter failure if she was required to focus. She did not pay attention very well with stunning men like the elf in front of her. Even his hair looked softer than her own. She wondered how it would feel between her fingers— and oh, he smelled delicious. Unknowingly Eve was gradually leaning toward the newcomer. The elf was smugly eying the mortal back. He seemed to like the attention she gave him and was willing to take it further.

Petal snapped her fingers in front of the woman's face, startling the mortal from her constant gaze on the elf, who now had a giant smirk on his flawless face. Eve's profile reddened brightly. She stuttered out an unintelligible apology for her lapse of concentration. The young woman couldn't believe how lacking her social etiquette presently was. Petal and the elf snickered. Eve was not amused and could only glower at the two, insistent that the lesson should commence. Unluckily, her embarrassment continued. She was ordered to hold hands with the elf. She did so with a tremble, her hands becoming sweaty and pale from her nerves. Then, she was tasked to mingle her aura with his magic without killing him.

"Kill?"

"Magic is unstable. To mix with one that is not controlled kills the balanced one. It is a shock to their system. If you do not control the flow, your darkness will eat up his light, and death is imminent. Now— begin."

Eve apologized fervently that she was unable to do as was instructed. Her words stumbled out, and she fidgeted profusely from her nerves. Petal assured her that all would be well— or so she hoped.

The princess started to instruct Eve step-by-step on how to complete the goal she had given her. The young knight had to carefully take hold of her evil, pull a section of it, and bring it up inside herself to her fingers. Then, Eve was to grab the elf's hand, allowing her power to touch his skin. If Eve didn't control her energy, she would kill her partner.

Eve proceeded with the lesson, when the princess gave her a gentle push and more assurance that all would be well. Over and over again, Eve tried doing as instructed and frustration grew at each failed attempt. Each time she touched the elf and injured him, she wilted inside little by little. He didn't seem to mind. He gave Eve a soft smile, but that could not stop her from hating herself. She couldn't control her gifts. When she saw the elf waver in his spot, she angrily swore to herself that she was the master of her own body. Eve felt a light connection inside of her. Finally, after being tired of hurting the guard too many times, she successfully stabilized her magic. It was only for a moment, but just that moment exhausted her. Her body swayed as she smiled and pulled her hands away onto her lap. She felt herself become lax and fall sideways. Her practicing companion quickly caught and sat her up, placing himself behind her as a crutch.

Petal handed her a cup of an unknown light beige liquid with a leaf of mint floating on its surface. Eve drank it gratefully. "What happened to me? I feel weak as a young fowl that had barely been born. I have used my gifts before yet controlling it has exhausted me with such ferocity that I feel only when I go berserk."

Petal explained nonchalantly, "In this world, our children's magic arrives to them as a slow cooling stream. Yours is more of a forceful ocean. For this reason, your magic is either fully released as a flood wiping out crops. Or, it is nonexistent as the sand that dries and cracks from thirst, suffering under a blazing sun, waiting to unleash its underground springs. You had no middle ground to stand on strongly from the onslaught of your sorcery."

"I handled myself well against Melchior."

"You became unconscious not long after." Eve pursed her lips so she wouldn't reply as a petulant child. "The meditations are the foundations of a dam to control how much of your gifts you can discharge without hurting and inevitably killing yourself."

"Was it not requested that my magic be banned from ever being used?"

"Exceptions have been made with my father's permission and without my mother's knowledge. Trouble comes to you like a flock of birds. It isn't your fault. Your unseelie calls out to its family. Also, you have more worth as you are, and it would be a pity to kill you so soon."

Melchior had mentioned the same as Petal. Eve's darkness had called out to him as a bright beacon in a dark unseeing night. "What is next?" Eve's eyes met Petal's with a determination she had not felt for a long time. "What more do I have to do to control what lies inside me?"

"We start again tomorrow. You need rest."

"No! We continue until I can last longer than a few minutes."

Petal was impressed by the mortal. The young woman showed characteristics she had not seen for a while. The girl's talent increased as the days came and went. She picked up magic quicker than the children who had years to learn. Petal was amazed to see what magic the girl harnessed but was shocked by the physical change Eve went to when the limit was reached. Petal was reminded of her uncle, who had died from giving into his unseelie's demand. The mortal's magic was eerily similar to his. It was worrying and arresting. Petal couldn't wait to see the girl's future unfold. Which path would the mortal take when all hope was lost? Would she follow Petal's uncle to a dark grave or die, never giving into the darkness?

"I can't wait to see how your life ends," Petal mumbled as she watched Eve block a thrown fireball with an electric field.

#  CHAPTER 19 

EVE STRODE DOWN a hallway with her new black robes billowing behind her rushed steps. She dodged between and past the moving, bustling bodies, almost stumbling in her new outfit, apologizing here and there to every person she bumped. Once she reached the center of the courtyard, her pace decreased significantly when a group of giggling idiots— women peacocks— ambled in front of her, gossiping all the while. They had no care for those around them as they took up the walkway.

Eve growled in irritation, and with a short impatient hand wave, forcibly split the group in two with her magic. She jogged through her opening with a grin. Many of the tittering fools started to send hexes at her. Because many disliked her, Eve had learned and mastered a protected shield spell, which she kept activated when out of her room. Thus, the hexes bounced off her hurried form and rebounded to their original owners, whose cries of dismay echoed behind her. Their cries were shortly followed by laughter from those who had been watching.

Eve had nimbly become a part of the castle's household in less than two moon cycles. At first, Oberon and Titania were displeased when they found out about the lessons Petal was giving her. They had witnessed Eve stop a falling brownie from dying by slowing down their descent to the ground. A trick she shouldn't have known. Petal made a logical argument on behalf of Eve on the importance of control. The princess pointed out that burying Eve's gifts might one day boil over into an uncontrollable storm that could be the end of all in the vicinity. Wary, but trusting their daughter, they allowed the continued lessons. Eve's escort was pulled; she had free rein in the castle except for the guarded corridors and was given the position of a mage-in-training.

Eve's days were mostly the same. The morning training was followed by magic lessons with Petal or visiting Caoimhghin. Then, she was off to the library to study or work. Mercifully, Eve had no more tutors. None of the available scholars were willing to take her as a student. They feared she would kill them as she had Melchior. It was challenging to study by herself, but she did learn better alone.

Work came after her chores, and it was luckily where Eve studied. The library had two floors above. The second floor had books and manuscripts that needed translating. The third floor was filled with extraordinary objects, journals, and books left by the last mage— Merlinus, or as Eve knew him, the great Merlin. The young woman had skipped at the realization that a wizard, a great wizard, had existed.

Merlin had been a seelie-hybrid fey. As a child, he had been cursed by blindness; and without magic, it couldn't be broken. His mother had been a witch named Mab, Queen of the Dark Witches, who lived in a mountain far north with caves made of crystal and ice. The cave was not only home to witches but to pixies and annoyingly evil biting fairies. Queen Mab was also a child of Oberon and an unknown banshee.

When Merlin grew into a young adult, and his magic emerged, Mab brought him to the Underground. His sight returned from the magical atmosphere. Mab taught Merlin magic, nature, and the ruling system of order. She wanted Merlin to bring back the fey world so that magic could rule again over those she believed needed guidance.

With the help of a boy who did not become king of all England, though he was king of a small isle, he brought knowledge when there had been little to none. After causing chaos, Queen Mab was pushed back to the Underground by King Arthur, who sacrificed himself, joining her in the other world. Arthur was to forever sleep in a tomb whose location was only known by Oberon and the Lady of the Lake, Mab's twin.

Eve had been excited to hear that the stories told were close to being true but saddened by Merlin's design. Merlin's fate was different from the young boy he had cared for. He had been cursed again, but this time by his mother before her unwanted departure. He had the ability to have children but would watch them grow old, and he didn't. He was cursed as a helpless spectator as the world changed around him. Only to be forgotten not long after.

"Has his story finally ended?" Eve asked Caoimhghin when he visited.

"I believe Merlinus' story has yet to end. Destiny has not finished with him," Caoimhghin answered cryptically as they walked to whatever benign chore his mother had sent them on. During their mindless adventure, Caoimhghin decided to test Eve on the ruling status of his world so that she might compare them to the ones she knew from hers. They were similar. The only difference she found was that a single High King ruled over smaller kingdoms. In her world, there were many selfish, greedy cockles of kings trying to conquer each other. Though, once in many years, a good king would come by. They usually died at a young age and were remembered as a fool in the history told by the victors.

As the days came and went, Eve, started to miss her world more. Reading about the Underground, learning about it was intriguing. There was always something exciting and new she would come upon. Yet, when it was night, her worries would emerge. She still hadn't stolen the dagger. Eve knew where it was, but how to get it was another matter. It wasn't like she could go in disguise. Everyone in the castle knew how she looked now without it. Oddly, walking around without her facial cloth had the populace staring at her more.

Besides that, most of those working in the castle or land knew Eve and her routine. Having a schedule should have made it easier for her to scurry about unseen into the trophy room. That was not true. It only took a short notice for her day to be changed. Eve was worried that her planning would be broken by a messenger calling for her to do chores for some royal family member. Then, if it wasn't a messenger, Aelfdene's informants were causing her problems. Some of them had already tried to attack her, eager to prove their worth to the captain. Eve managed to disarm them before knocking them unconscious with the hilt of her sword. Afterward, she walked away. She couldn't draw attention to herself, which meant none of the men who harmed her could be punished.

Today was one of those days that would not be dull. A royal guard had burst into her study room. He bid her to hurry to the king, who needed her immediately. Eve found herself jogging through the castle to meet his highness. The last the woman had heard of him, the king had once again ridden back to the southern borders. At least from his second departure, she had learned more of the problem he was trying to end. There were still unseelies alive, a throng of disorganized beings attempting to take charge of the Underground. The whispers from the soldiers who returned with the king were that there were more evil creatures than had ever been before. Eve wondered what use she could be against this evil. From Merlin's journal, being an unseelie, or even part of one made it easier to fall into the temptation to join the darkness. It would be dangerous for Eve to go near such beings.

She reached the king's private study room. His doors were open, with two guards standing rigidly outside. Eve skidded to a halt as she heard a loud argument between many individuals, each person attempting to be louder than the other. The guards gave her a look of pity, not wanting to be her. She took a deep breath and rushed in. The shouting stopped and Eve closed her eyes. She could feel many eyes upon her and the tension in the room. She was just waiting for a spark to start a fire between them all. Getting her nerves in order, Eve opened her eyes hesitantly to take in the horror she was about to face.

Avo stood dumbly near the doors, off to the side, fidgeting and unsure. Aelfdene smugly stood near a shelf full of books with Caoimhghin by him, who had his fist at his side, ready to attack. Petal and Oberon stood together away from the two, faces red and brows furrowed. Eve wished she had not hurried to the king. The mortal really did not want to be in the room. Perhaps there was a chance she could turn around, and all present could go back to their argument..30265

"Please, come in," Avo calmly said once he saw Eve.

Eve glared at the man but did as he commanded. It was then she smelled burnt flesh. She followed the smell to the middle of the room, where the charred, grotesque body of an unknown creature lay on a table. The young woman unintentionally moved closer and fought the urge to cover her nose and mouth. With a better view, she saw the corpse was mangled and mutilated. It had the head of a goat with sheared horns and its eyes open were wide with fear. The knight gulped.

"How may I help you, your Highness?" Eve asked in a disciplined manner, turning away from the unfortunate dead soul.

"Ah, the wench! You may leave. We have no need for your expertise," Aelfdene hurled. Eve paid him no heed, keeping her eyes on Oberon. "Didn't you hear me, you little shit?"

"Enough!" Oberon's voice boomed, his very presence filling the room. "It has been years, and we need another perspective on our problems. I will not see us enter a war. We can't afford it."

"W...wa...war, you say?" Eve squeaked.

"Yes. One that you can stop," Oberon said, "based on the knowledge you can supply."

Eve winced. She didn't have the faintest inkling of what guidance she could impart that could stop a war. She would have to politely remind the king of her place. If he still insisted on hearing her words, she had to be blunt about her inability to stop any war. "Your highness— King Oberon— I am only a guest who has become a lowly servant for you to use. I am new to the politics of your world and doubt I can shed any light on your worries."

"You see, she is useless," commented Aelfdene righteously with a dismissive wave, giving her his back. He continued to talk, insulting her with every breath he took. A movement near the captain brought her sight to Caoimhghin, who was taking steps toward his brother, his face familiar with one who wanted retribution. Eve would not have him fight for her.

She walked over to him, putting a hand on his chest, halting his movement. He glared down at her, and she shook her head. His eyes begged to understand why and, again, she gestured no. He swiftly turned and walked away with a growl. Eve coughed and pulled her sword from inside her robes, pointing it at the captain. He didn't notice it until he faced her, his tirade stopping midway. Eve moved closer to him until the blade touched his throat, kissing his skin with no blood being drawn. She wanted him to feel the icy cold of its edge.

"I am here by the beck and call of your father. If you cannot hold your tongue, I will have no problems removing it. Stand and be silent good sir, like the spider you are." Eve returned her sword to its sheath and she backed away, her eyes on the captain. When Eve was far enough from the blabbering idiot, her eyes flicked to Oberon, giving him her utmost attention. "Tell me, your Majesty, all I need to know to assist you on a path of peace. I will try my best but make no promises my aid will be useful."

Oberon started to explain what had happened. "There was news of the unseelie crossing into our lands. Nothing new. I took my men to the border where a village lay, and to my horror did I see no living souls. Nor shelter standing. There was no life at all. There was just blackened ground made of cracked, waterless dirt."

"I continued forward, my men at my heels. I had hoped that my eyes were deceiving me. Hope that my people lived. Closer to the border we went, and there I felt it. There was a deep chill that penetrated deeply into my bones. What is more, there was this silence. A horrible silence I had witnessed long ago. One so old, I had almost—almost forgotten it. An absence of sound from a dead war when this world was anew."

"Then it came. The laughs and chuckles of the damned. I

realized the unseelie were no longer afraid of us. They no longer ran away at the sight of us. Nay, they rose out from the black ground, taking on their past corporeal form. A form not seen for centuries. Suddenly, their laughter died, and all they did was stare at us with their dead eyes. To my shock, tendrils of black ink swirled toward my people and me, never touching us. Then together, they snapped. A body emerged from their hold, thrown at the ground in front of us."

"I saw my citizen's face, and there was such agony. In anger, I charged the unseelie. As my men and I neared, we hit a barrier protecting the evil horde. Then, their tendrils attacked our horses, tearing them apart. We grabbed the dead faun— for it could be nothing else— and retreated. Using my torment of knowing my people were gone, I threw a ball of flames their way. It passed their barrier, disappointingly setting only a single evil creature aflame, and its cries shook the ground. The unseelies took a step toward us as one, and their darkness spread, killing the grass under our feet. One of their kind stepped forward. His face was covered by a hood, and they followed him. We left, seeing as we were outnumbered," Oberon ended. "You are here because these things do not act logically. They act as mortals. Primitive. Only you may have the sight of their possible future movements."

Eve didn't know whether to be insulted or flattered. Either way, she would do as he asked to the best of her abilities. "I need a map." They all looked at her. "I need to know your lands and theirs, before and after the unseelies movements. I wish to see all changes that have happened. I need to know if anything odd has occurred, such as the difference between your meetings with them. Do not leave anything out, small as it may be. We can't leave anything unchecked by my own eyes if you wish to have the value of my expertise."

"A bitch like you is undeserving of that knowledge," Aelfdene spat.

"You. Out," Oberon commanded, pointing his finger at his unruly son, disdain, and anger dripping from his eyes. "Have your mother bring me my papers, you know which, and away with you, boy."

Aelfdene tipped his chin up haughtily and stared at his father emotionless, eyes cold as ice. The two faced each other, neither moving, each in their own way trying to subtly intimidate the other. Giving in, Aelfdene gave a tense nod before stomping out of the room. Eve narrowed her eyes at him suspiciously. The captain was not acting like himself. She had thought he would have spoken back against his father. When he didn't, it worried her. He had to be planning an uprising or a trap.

"I see the fool has finally grown," Petal commented. "He no longer tempers and speaks in return as a petulant child. It seems he has learned his place now that the kingdom's future has been taken from his greedy grasp."

Oberon snapped at his daughter. He would not have his children insult each other to a degree. "If you continue to speak as such, I will also pull you from the line of succession."

"Nay!" shouted Caoimhghin, scaring Eve that she jumped. He was absolutely petrified. *Why?* "I don't want it. I like my child— subjects. The fey here put my insanity to shame." Eve chuckled. Only Caoimhghin wouldn't want to become High King.

"I will do as I please if you two continue on," Oberon threatened, putting his children in place. Eve watched, amused at the familial squabble.

Queen Titania arrived with some men following behind her. In their arms were rolled scrolls which they piled on the long table. Oberon opened them one by one, placing them into groups. Maps were placed in one corner, notes of occurring problems in another. Then, on a third, journals were stacked open and flat.

The king waved his hand over the papers saying, "This is the information I have on the unseelies recent movement for the past fifty years."

Eve grimaced. It was not because of the work before her but the language in which it was written. She recognized the basic fey symbols with some elvish notes here and there. She was not yet fluent in the Underground's languages. "This may take a while," she admitted to Oberon.

"I have an item that will aid you," Oberon said. From the pocket of his tunic, he pulled out a pair of thinly framed spectacles. "Put these on, and you can read any language. Please be careful. It takes time to create this."

Eve looked at the spectacles before taking them gently from Oberon's fingers. She put them on and watched as the symbols became words. Her mouth opened in shock before gratefully saying to the king, "This will do nicely. Thank you."

Oberon and the rest of the occupants left the room as Eve enthusiastically went to work. She picked up the scroll closest to her and started to read. It took some days and sleeping upon blankets on the floor before the young woman created piles of her own. Eve had a gift she rarely utilized, and through her current task, this skill was tested to the maximum extent possible. She looked for patterns based on movement, deaths, battles, and unexplained disappearances. Afterward, she was summoning scrolls to her hands and tossing others away from her as connections were made from the unseelies' actions.

Unseelie did not have the capability to lead. Each was selfish with their own goal. There were moments when a strong unseelie attempted to rise above others. This was met with annihilation from its own kind. It was for this reason their population was low. But now— the counts showed they were gaining strength by numbers. Eve magically called for a map to show the southern border, which flew into her hold. She knocked the papers she had been working on to the ground, grabbed an ink bottle and quill, and wrote notes and dates onto different locations. Her eyebrows furrowed as she saw a problem she doubted the royal family had seen. The young mortal noted that their arrogance was going to be their downfall.

She stared at the locations she had marked intently. She tapped the quill on the table, letting out a single yawn. She could see a trap but knew more was missing from it. She marked X's on the villages where the people had disappeared. What was the catch? Why attack some areas to gain attention and, in others, take the people away silently as a passing breeze picking up leaves? The movements they made had a purpose. Half the actions were a distraction, the others...recruitment? That could account for the growing numbers of the unseelie population. Yet, there was something more.

"Eve!"

Eve shrieked and stabbed the map with her quill, creating a nasty blot to ruin her written notes. She groaned and cried, mumbling "no" repeatedly as she used the sleeves of her robe to clean up the mess. Instead, her plight became grandeur. The ink bottle tipped, knocked to the side by her elbow. More ink flowed out, ruining her work.

"Caoimhghin, how may I help you? What reason do you have so great that you had to shout my name out so?" Eve angrily questioned. She slammed her hand on the table, and it squelched as it landed in the toppled ink. She cried out in dismay as ink sprayed upon her. Caoimhghin laughed from the doorway. Eve glared at him, feeling the ink dry on her skin.

"I apologize, dear girl," said Caoimhghin, bowing lowly. Eve would have believed that his apology had been sincere if not for the cheery tone in his voice.

"I doubt you are truly sorry," Eve said to her friend. She grabbed a cloth and started to clean her hands. Instead, she was spreading the ink more on her clothes. "What do you need, Caoimhghin?"

The prince's face became serious. "It is time."

"Time for what exactly?" Eve questioned as she raised an eyebrow.

Caoimhghin chuckled. "It is very late. Very few guards roaming around. Perfect time to steal from my father. Unless you wish to stay here, I do not mind."

"You insane? We have no plan to act on. We can't just— "

"Aine and I took care of the planning."

"Without me?!" Eve asked incredulously. "How am I to know my part in this play you have concocted?"

"I thought it had been established you are the thief."

"I should smack you."

"For stating a fact?"

"For scaring me. Planning my quest behind my back, and yes,

stating a fact but in that tone of yours."

"It is called sarcasm, love."

"Sarcasm?"

"It means I am being rhetorical."

"Well, stop it. Also, it will be difficult to walk around with ink spots on my person. Prey tell how I am to sneak around? We may have to do this thievery for another day."

The prince smirked, and a crystal orb popped into his hand. He held it with the tips of his fingers. "That...I can fix my dear."

Eve grimaced, and her throat tightened involuntarily as she watched Caoimhghin eye her impishly. An undignified squeak escaped her tight lips at his unending stare. She cringed when the young prince threw the orb at her. She closed her eyes, fearful of the worst. The man was a well-established prankster. Before its impact, the globe shattered, covering her in a sparkling bright smoke. When it disappeared, Eve wore the outfit she had arrived in. All her weapons were strapped comfortably upon her form, and her hair was combed into a bun. The ink from her hands was gone. Eve smiled, impressed. She looked at her ruined parchment and pointed at it with her thumb. "Can you restore my work to its proper and original condition?"

Of course, love," Caoimhghin smugly answered. Another orb appeared in his hand with a flourish, and he threw it up into the air. Just as it came down, he produced another globe. With one hand, he juggled his spheres with a magnificent ease that would make a jester proud. Eve laughed at his antics. Her friend was a born entertainer. Whoever married this man would need to have the patience of a saint or be crazy as him, with a strong will that was equal to or possibly greater than his own.

"You going to restore my work or not?" she managed to say through her laughter.

"I already have," Caoimhghin answered. Eve looked at her work. Her notes were pristine, and the table and the rest of the scrolls were also clean. Her tipped-over ink bottle was nowhere to be seen.

"*Un grand merci* once more good sir," she hailed.

"Now that mess is gone and done, Aine is near the medical ward. She is waiting for the right to create the perfect distraction and that we will know what it is."

Eve asked in confusion, "What precisely is this distraction?"

"Do not worry that pretty little head of yours. Nobody shall be getting hurt."

"But she is close by the...," but an explosion interrupted, rocking the castle. There was a shudder underneath their feet, and the floors creaked. Eve watched in distress at the plume of smoke rising. It came from the part of the castle where she knew, not far away, lay those who had been injured from an unseen accident just the morning before. Subjects ran across the courtyard, calling all to assist and check for any who had been hurt.

"Father is not going to be pleased with the old woman. It seems that another one of her experiments has failed and ruined the castle again," Caoimhghin commented with amusement. Eve shot him a glare and feverously prayed that the prince was correct that nobody had been injured. Another explosion, albeit smaller, occurred. She materialized her mask with a shake of her head at the damage happening because of her.

Eve and the prince then turned to look at the closed door, hearing running footsteps coming their way. "There might be a problem."

As far as the young women knew, the guards for the day had left to do their other duties hours ago. The last time she had seen a guard was when dinner had been brought to her— which she had not eaten. Her stomach grumbled in despair at her lack of nutrition.

"Why are they coming here?" Caoimhghin asked.

Eve shrugged. She doubted the newcomers were coming to her for the good of their hearts to see if she was well. She could only deduce that those coming could only be part of Aelfdene's followers. The distraction worked perfectly in their favor as it did for her. It was a pity they couldn't let her be. Well, before they arrived, she needed the prince gone. It wouldn't do well for them to see him with her.

"It is time to disappear, my majesty," Eve told Caoimghin. She pulled out her swords, spinning and moving the hilts to comfortably lay in her hands. The prince started to shake his head and demand to stay, but one look from her had him huffing away in glitter. At his departure, he tossed his orbs to the ground. In the last second of his disappearance, he tidied the rest of the room. Concurrently, the door was kicked open. At the first shout, Eve ran. Her instincts were still faithful as she heard curses being called out. She never had a chance to see who her attackers were but concluded by the magic thrown, that they were elves and feys.

She managed to get behind a low shelf, wincing as each spell cast destroyed the furniture around her. Pieces of wood and stone flew in the air. Then, dead silence ensued. Eve kept still and in place, breathing slowly and lowly. She didn't dare peek at those attacking her. She knew if she waited long enough, her enemies would come to her. So, the woman prepared herself for the incoming battle. It wasn't long before she heard their footsteps walk further into the room. A man called her name and then mocked her. Still, Eve did not move. Her body tensed when a being covered in black clothing from head to bottom passed her hiding place. She moved behind them and, when they turned, punched them in the face. They fell but not unconscious, and she jumped over their bodies. Then, throwing herself into a roll, she placed herself in the middle of her opponents. They looked at her, startled at her form of emergence.

Using the shock, Eve ran onward to the furthest cloaked figure. Her swords dragged behind her as she rapidly gained ground on her opponent. She then raised her weapons over her head and slashed in a broad, downward arc when she got closer to her enemy. Her opponent's hood fell as they moved back to avoid the attack. In the low light, Eve saw that it was a female elf. The woman didn't have a chance to defend herself as Eve attacked again with another swing, this time lethal. The blades cut into the hidden armor and sliced through the muscles and bones of the chest area. The elf fell, blood gushing from deep wounds. With a better view of her attacker's face, Eve recognized the figure. It was the first assistant of Aine that Eve had met. The elf must have been so enamored with Aelfdene; she had gone from healer to warrior. The change of occupation had become her death.

Eve's momentary distraction allowed her enemies to counterattack. Their swords swung as one down upon her. She quickly kneeled, and the blades clashed around her, none hurting her. Eve concentrated on all the candles in the room. Using her magic, she blew out their flames, darkening the room. The only source of light now came from outside, and it barely penetrated the room. Instead, the little lighting brought on an eerie gloom and unending shadows. Eve's eyes started to glow a blood red, shining brightly in the almost black room.

The unseelie hybrid roared and attacked. The altercation that followed was fierce and brutal, testing Eve's stamina and her skills in welding two swords. She dodged, blocked, slashed, punched, and kicked at her attackers. It took time and some maneuvering before she had her opponents separated enough for her to fight them one by one. She continued to slash down on the sword of one of the fighters persistently until it fell from his grasp. With no defense, Eve stabbed him. Another assailant attacked shortly after. The strike forced Eve to take a *backsteppe*, followed by a down stroke. The fey blocked her hit and thrust his empty hand out. Eve was violently pushed into a wall. She cried at the impact of stone, winded.

She looked to see a female elf at her left run in her direction. The elf had a long spear in her hand. It was raised over her head, ready to be flung. Eve pushed herself from the wall and ran at the elf. The elf grinned evilly as she lowered her weapon and anticipated feeling her tip thrust into the belly of a disgusting mortal. Right when the spear was thrust at Eve, the young knight blocked the attack with a sweep of her blade. The sharp edges of Eve's weapons dragged from the tip of the spear to the elf's hand. With a sidestep, Eve pulled away, and without hesitation, swung her sword, cutting off her enemy's head.

The rest of the fighters looked at their dead on the ground, then up to Eve. She grimaced, having an inkling what their next move would be. Barely noticeable, she shook her head as her enemies attacked together. Eve blocked each of their hits. When she viewed an opening between them, she ran through, reaching the other side of the room. With the appropriate spacing, Eve retaliated, surprising them at her lack of exhaustion, which was a façade. She was dead tired, and her strength was weakening. Yet, the mortal couldn't lose. She pushed herself harder and unknowingly opened herself to the darkness. The fight became a blur. After getting herself in control, Eve found she had massacred her opponents. Parts of their body surrounded her in a circle. The smell of their blood permeated the air. She looked at what was left of their faces, remembering the look of horror upon each individual. This was her self-punishment for taking their lives.

Eve dragged herself to a chair and sat down. Solemnly, she wiped her swords clean with the edges of her tunic, the blade shaking unsteadily in her hands. She blinked away the tears that threatened to fall that always came after the quiet of a battle. Guilt gnawed inside her at the unfairness of the world that required death for one to live. Eve silently prayed for the souls she had extinguished. Outside, the young knight listened to the chaos. The other denizens were oblivious to the fight.

Eve put her swords back in place and stood up. She then moved her head from side to side, loosening the muscles in her neck before rushing as quietly as she could outside the workroom. The corridor was gratefully empty, and Eve cautiously made her way to the trophy room. Sometimes she had to stop and hide when she heard others coming her way. Once they were far from her position, she continued to her goal. It was in the last hall that Eve needed to cross where she encountered more problems. She wondered what God had against her for him to place obstacles that stopped her from getting a dagger.

At her first step, the knight heard a sniff and growl. She pulled her foot back and quickly flattened herself on the wall, hoping she had not been seen. Not hearing whatever unknown creature move, Eve quietly edged to the corner of the hall and popped her head out for a quick peek. A squeak almost escaped her lips when her eyes viewed the monster standing guard outside the trophy room. The creature was slightly shorter than a minotaur with cropped grey fur. The top half of its body was in the form of a boar. It had long, sharp tusks made for goring and, in its hands, an axe.

Eve went back to hiding and grabbed her swords. Before she could turn into the hall to face the monster, a hand gripped the neck of her shirt. She was pulled from the shadows and out into the open. The young woman came face to face with the monster she had just been preparing to go against. Her nose scrunched at its smell. The creature cackled, and Eve noticed its vocals had two tones, one low and the other high.

"You stupid wench," it insulted her, its voice sending shivers down her spine. Eve was spun and thrown. Her body rolled to a stop at the other end of the hall. The monster came at her, axe in the air. At the last second, Eve managed to go onto a knee and block the downward swing with her swords. Her teeth gritted at the vibrations going down her arm. She stuck a foot out, kicking the monster and forcing him to back away.

Eve stood and quickly went onto the defense. The boar-man attacked her relentlessly. Each hit tired the young woman, and she knew that at the rate she was being attacked, the fight would end with her death. She watched the boar's movements and noticed there were times it left its neck open. When that opening came, just as Eve had predicted, she dropped and, using all her weight, hacked. The blade sliced into the thick, course skin, but it wasn't enough to deliver the killing blow. She pushed the edge harder, but the sword wouldn't go further. The creature dropped its weapon. With one hand, it then grabbed the young knight by the head, its other hand holding one of her arms.

Eve's finger scrambled to loosen the pudgy digits holding her. Her feet flailed and kicked. The hand holding her head tightened when she hit the monster's stomach. Eve screamed in pain. She gave up on moving the fingers and dug her nails into the back of the hand holding her head. When she finally broke into its skin, the boar-man dropped her.

Blindly, her head ringing and in pain, Eve grappled for the dagger she had tucked down the back of her pants. She thrust the blade at the brute, but it was blocked by its vambrace. Then it charged her, the tusk catching her arm. Eve pulled back with a short cry but kept a hold of her weapon. The fight continued, but with her small blade, Eve took the brunt of the injuries until she was bent over and barely standing.

*I can't die here.*

*...and you won't,* a darker tone of Eve's voice answered. Her darkness took over and flooded her mind, leaving little of what made her mortal intact. A dark aura cloaked her body as her body transformed.

The boar-man squealed in fear as it watched the mortal change. Aelfdene had not mentioned that the mortal was a hybrid; worse, she was an unseelie. It should have noticed the rumors and gossip or at least believed them. Like many others who lived in the Underground, it had been taught that all hybrids had been destroyed. So, when Captain Aelfdene told it there would be distinguished honor for killing the mortal, it took the job immediately. Now, it was staring at a glowing red ball of energy.

Eve smirked as the ball grew in her hands. She nodded slightly at the boar-man and blasted the energy at it. It went through its armor and into its body. It then ignited in bright red flames. It screamed in agony as it burned from the inside out. In its last moment, it fell to its knees and slowly became dust.

Following afterward, Eve grasped her own head and shouted. She fell to her knees as her body weakened, her skin became ordinary, and her breathing labored. Once the transformation to herself was complete, she fell to her side. She had lost control again, and there was this itch at her clavicle. She lowered the neck of her shirt to see that above the left breast, part of her skin was still pale white with inky black branches heading outward from a center point. The transformation was starting to become permanent.

Eve felt her face flush in fear. She was sticky with perspiration, her clothes clinging to her skin. As much as the knight wanted to keep staring, she covered the lasting change and stood up. She had a duty to complete. She grabbed her swords and dagger, ran into the trophy room, and skidded to a stop in front of the casing that had Puck's treasure. She broke the case with the pommel of her sword, the glass shattering around her. She grabbed the dagger blindly, cutting herself on its sharp edge. She hissed, but at least the blood made it easier for her to see the blade better, making it easier to handle.

The now-thief turned to leave, but the High King and Queen came in with their men behind them. Oberon looked at her and the dagger she held. His face turned grim. "Guards, surround her," he barked. With a wave of his hand, the torches on the wall became brighter.

*I am dead.*

#  CHAPTER 20 

KING OBERON CROSSED his arms as he glared at the mortal before him. Behind him, his wife Titania ordered their men to surround the thief that not long ago had hidden in their midst as an ally. There was disappointment and sadness on her face. She raised her hand, catching the attention of the men, and swiftly brought it down. The soldiers immediately rearranged their position and armed themselves. The swordsmen formed the first circle. The archers created the second as they loaded their bows. They aimed slightly above and to the left of the sword fighters in front of them.

Indeed, and with certainty, Eve was going to die. Just when she saw home on the horizon, it was pulled out of her reach by men who wanted to kill her. Damn Aelfdene. she now needed to be intelligent and choose her next words carefully. Unfortunately, as she was contemplating her speech, she said, "It is not what it seems, your highnesses."

She cringed. Her words were obviously, completely, and utterly false. For goodness sake, she was wearing her mask. All around her was shattered glass from the case she had broken. In her hands, she had the proof of her evil deeds in full view. What was in the air that made her blurt nonsense? She usually managed, a majority of the time, to keep her opinions to herself— or at least it had been possible in her realm.

"We were told there had been a fight near this area," a deep, familiar voice called from the doorway.

"Can this night have any more surprises?" Eve muttered to herself as she watched the minotaur master-at-arms push through the circle of her now-enemies with three of his own. The four newcomers took what was left of Eve's empty space, driving her almost to the tips of the swords pointed at her.

The drillmaster's upper lip curled in disgust, and his eyes lusted to see Eve's blood splattered on the ground. "Allow me to give the order to dispose of this mortal," he pleaded to the royal couple. "It would be a privilege to rid our world of this abomination."

"I wish the same, but she needs to be questioned," Oberon informed. The king turned to his wife, giving her charge of the interrogation. The minotaurs backed away from Eve, moving out of the circle she was trapped in.

In a commanding, cold tone, Queen Titania walked forward and asked, "How could you betray us? We gave you a place in our world. Your position is high for an outcast. We taught you our ways and protected you from those who wished you harm. We have been generous."

A tide of guilt flooded Eve's senses. She had the urge to look down in shame. She knew the sin she had committed was grand and a toss of the gifts she had been given, but she had chosen her path, which must be finished— dead or alive. Eve lifted her chin up in defiance. She had already stolen what needed to be stolen and been caught.

"Betraying you was not easy. Yet, it had to be done, and I shall not apologize for my actions," she answered. She tucked in her plunder at her waist and pulled out her swords. "Strike me down if you must. Just know I will kill many of your men before I pass through the gates of hell."

"Silly fool. You jump to your end. Your words place you closer to meeting death. Your demise, I can tell you now, will not be heroic. How can you fear it so little?" Oberon asked with a tiny shake of his head.

"Death," Eve chuckled knowingly," comes for us all. Some of us meet it faster than others." she started to taunt the soldiers. "Who dares fight me first? Come! See how you fare. I will not go down easily."

One of the swordsmen, a fey, walked forward, eyes glittering with arrogance. "Majesties, I shall end this. It will be an honor to take this mortal's challenge. I will show her the superiority of our species." The swordsman looked to Eve with a smirk, saying, "Lest she rescinds her challenge and bows to our powers."

"Fopdoodle. That shall never happen," Eve bit back.

"You say that now, but your words shall change when my blade is at your neck."

"I doubt your blade will even get near any parts of me." The fey glared at her reply, but Eve smirked in response. The swordsman took a step toward her, and the circle widened. The treasured objects were moved from harm's way by a wave of the king's hand. Eve then finally took in her opponent.

The idiotic fey was taller and bulkier than her. He had broad shoulders, and his arms strained in his armor. His blade was wide, long, and extremely sharp. Eve could easily see that the weapon could cleave her in half. However, her adversary had a disadvantage. His attacks would require him to have a large amount of space. The circle gave little movement area. Eve knew that she would have to close the distance between herself and her enemy to have a chance to win.

The swordsman attacked first, and Eve went into defense. She managed to keep herself from tripping when another soldier stuck out their foot, causing her to misstep. They laughed and taunted her as Eve barely defended herself from another incoming attack. She quickly glared at them but nothing more. After observing the moves her opponent favored, Eve ran at him. She then went down to her knees, sliding forward, and sliced the tendons behind the fey's knees. He fell with a cry and a vulnerable space opened between his breastplate and vambrace. Eve thrust her blade into the opening, cutting into flesh and bone, killing the man immediately.

Her victory was short-lived. Angry soldiers grabbed her arms, and she struggled in their grips. She found herself being punched repeatedly in the stomach by another. Winded, Eve used the grips of those holding her to help lift her feet up and kick out. She knocked the soldier who had been beating her to the ground. Sadly, more took his place. Eve's already tattered tunic started drooping down her shoulders with each hit the soldiers dealt. It wasn't long until her dark mark came into view startling the men and women around her. The soldiers dropped and backed away from her. On their faces were disgust and horror. Weak and tired, Eve groaned as she moved to her knees, arms laying heavily at her side, their weight trying to pull her to the ground.

"Ha ha hah haa," a dark male voice laughed. "I see the change is starting. You pushed your magic to the limit. The temptation was too strong for your weak mind. You do belong with this sorry excuse of a family of mine."

"Aelfdene!" Titania admonished.

Aelfdene glared at his mother while leaning casually on the door frame, playing with a small dagger. Afterward, he sneered in satisfaction as half the room gave him the attention he wanted. The other half stayed as they were, keeping their eyes on Eve.

The soldiers who were focused on Eve were Aelfdene's men. They quickly glanced up at him and then back at Eve, awaiting his command. Today was the day for their revenge against the royals who had treated them so badly. They conspicuously watched the captain savor the moment before he would come to power.

"Shut your mouth, Mother. I tire from hearing the tone of a hag," Aelfdene insulted. He smiled cockily as the occupants in the room gasped.

"Apologies," the minotaur master growled, taking a step forward.

"No."

"Insolent boy. I am glad your parents had the sense to remove you from the line of succession. You do not respect nor deserve the world they created. The blackness of your heart shows, and now, your worth is even less than the hybrid mongrel. Apologize or pay the price," the minotaur demanded.

Eve watched weakly as the minotaur walked toward the prince. One of his own followed behind him. Some soldiers stood to watch the possible bloodshed that was unfolding. Others moved further away from the fight. Oberon and Titania did nothing but observe. There was a look of defeat in their eyes as Eve realized they had given up on their son.

The minotaur master's steps were slow, loud with a purpose, eyes focused on Prince Aelfdene, who smirked back at the giant. He was not in the least intimidated by the mammoth man. The nerve under one of his eyes twitched in annoyance. "Apologize."

"I believe I will not," Aelfdene said. "I do not take order from dead men."

The minotaur master's horn was grabbed by another behind him. His head was pulled back, and his neck barred open, vulnerable. A dagger flashed in view. The minotaur master's throat was slit open with a sick accuracy. Aelfdene clapped, laughing at the kill. The murder had occurred quickly; it left most of those in the room in shock.

Eve was the first to find her voice. "Sick bastard," she shrieked.

"Kill the men but leave my parents. They are still needed. Have fun with the hybrid bitch but do not kill her. I would like to enjoy her and have her conscious to feel all of my *tender* skills," Aelfdene ordered as he licked his lips as if he was savoring the juiciest morsel in existence.

The soldiers looked at each other in momentary confusion; half of them had no inkling who Aelfdene was speaking to. It couldn't be the single traitorous minotaur. He was outmanned. There was no way he could kill all of them. Then, in an explosion, fights ensued. It was impossible to tell who was friend or foe. Only those under Aelfdene's command had the advantage because they knew each other. It was easy for them to set their 'friends' against each other.

Eve picked up her weapons, blocking attacks that came at her. Never once did she kill her aggressors as she couldn't tell who her enemies were. She was the thief in the room. Both sides wanted her dead at the moment. The skirmish was different from the ones she had been in before. Usually, only one side wanted to see her deceased, but this fight was untold chaos.

Oberon and Titania fought back to back, working in sync. With their combined magic, they held back the men coming at them. Unfortunately, the royal couple was being slowly cornered and would soon be overtaken by those they believed had been their most loyal men. Obviously, the couple had been surprised and were not fighting logically like they usually did.

Eve knew the king and queen disliked her— probably loathed her at this moment. Yet, she was the closest ally who cared what happened to them. Damn, her idiotic honor to aid others. She shook her head and ran to them but in her weak state, she was intercepted by the minotaur who had killed the swordmaster. He threw her into a wall with one hand, her lower back taking the blunt force.

*Crack.* Eve's eyes opened wide. She felt glass or crystal embedded in her flesh. Her body twitched at the new injury. The dagger she had stolen had broken, and the quest Eve had been entrusted with had failed. Now, she was never going to get home. All was a loss.

*Pop.*

"I am finally— oohhh— well, I was not expecting this. Ello." Puck appeared in a bright blinding flash. At first, he had been jumping up and down, doing some odd dance. Then, he noticed what was happening around him and stopped his prancing. He was dressed in an outfit with large leaves cut into a simple tunic and shorts. His feet were bare. The fighting halted at the newcomer's arrival. "I see you are all teensy weensy busy. I will let myself out. Don't mind me. Continue with the bloodshed."

"Puck," Aelfdene greeted, walking to the banished fey with a sinister smile. "Take my hand, Puck. Join me. Be my right hand, my advisor. I will treat you not as my parents have. Your return has shown me your true worth."

"You have a vein throbbing right here," Puck randomly said, pointing to the right side of his forehead. "It is surprisingly bothering me more than is necessary. Need tea? The English seem to relax with a cup of it. I prefer something stronger— but, alas, none could be found above. Though, about that tea, I do believe it shall not be difficult to find the plant to make the bitter brew."

"Puck," Eve hissed. The fey ignored her and, in favor, began a tirade about the importance of tea to the mortals. Eve glared at the fool, which slowly became one of annoyance. In seconds, she realized her call instead brought the attention of an angry royal family member. Captain Aelfdene quickly narrowed his eyes at her. With nods and a look, two of his men moved to her position and pushed Eve down to her knees, arms pulled back. Still, Puck did not face her. At thoughts of Puck's stupidity and the tense situation she was still in, Eve started to chortle. That chortle soon became hysterical laughter, her chest feeling tight and tears dripping down her face.

"Someone shut her up," Aelfdene ordered. One of the men punched Eve's face, but her laughter continued.

"I believe dear Captain— ," Puck started to say.

"Majesty!" Aelfdene corrected. "I am now the king, Puck."

"Whatever," Puck said with a slight wave of his hand. "I believe the mortal has lost her senses and reasoning based on what is occurring."

*Is this what is happening to me? Have my senses gone?* Eve's quest, she could admit now, was more than she could handle. She was foolish to have listened to Caoimhghin. She should not have attempted to steal this night or any other night. Perhaps, it would have been better to continue her studies and become the royal mage in the Underground. She should have just forgotten home. Too late. The steps she took now led to three paths: death, destruction, or both. She would either die in this fight Eve had no standing in, or she would become death's harbinger. Either way, she was lost as her evil would take over, destroying what was left of her. It was already starting and knowing that the darkness was spreading started another wave of hysteria that dragged Eve closer to despair.

Aelfdene's men stared at her in horror and fear. They watched the mortal woman's eyes open wider than was possible. Her body shook under their hold as her laughter became louder. Her hands tensed unnaturally, almost claw-like. They let go of her, fearing that her insanity could pass on to them. Even free, Eve stayed in placed and continued to laugh, oblivious to nothing else but what she was feeling.

"Stop!" Aelfdene furiously ordered Eve. He moved to stand in front of the young woman and mumbled angrily, "If you don't stop laughing, I will make you." Aelfdene didn't wait long before he pulled out his dagger and grabbed her shoulder, using a solid grip to keep her upright. The king and queen ordered him not to stab the girl. He heeded them not and pulled back his arm to strike. He had all the power now. He was in control of who lived or died. Aelfdene felt pity he would have to kill the hybrid so soon. She was pretty, and he would have loved to have heard her screams as he defiled her, but oh well. Eve was the perfect example to show he was in charge of the Underground.

To everyone's surprise, just as Aelfdene went to stab Eve, Puck jumped on the royal's back. His hands covered the other fey's eyes, who growled in anger. The ex-captain let the dagger go as he struggled to push or pull Puck off him. Aelfdene's men went to assist. He ordered them away. Once free, Aelfdene swore he would kill the fool for humiliating him.

Puck hung on tightly, his arms an iron grip around the neck of the treasonous prince. He looked at Eve, shouting, "I am home. The quest is complete. Get up and fight, girl!"

Puck's cry and push sounded faintly in Eve's mind. It weakly snuck through the constant rhythmic pounding in her head. Her laughter dwindled as she remembered herself. "Puck?" Eve moaned.

"Girl! Your swords! Are you not the White Knight? Your job is to protect. Remember!"

The mortal shook her head. Puck was correct. She was the

White Knight, and a knight never gave up during the darkest hours. A knight protected, and Eve had been a coward for too long. Yet, she still had a problem: she needed a weapon to fight with. "Where did they go?" she whispered to herself.

A nearby minotaur heard her speak and shouted, "Come here!" The minotaur was quick on his lumbering feet. He ran at Eve with arms open wide, torso bent forward, and horns pointed in her direction. At the last second, Eve rolled away, one of the horns grazing her arm. She winced when she felt a new pain and looked to see a long piece of glass embedded in her left shoulder. Eve noted that it would be too dangerous to remove the glass. If she tried, she could bleed to death. In addition, there was no time to take the chance to fix herself up; she was going to be attacked at any moment. That reminded Eve of the minotaur who had attacked her. She turned to see her attacker stuck on the wall due to the force he had rammed into it. The minotaur struggled to get loose and, with a push from a foot, released himself from the wall, breaking one of his horns in the process.

Eve looked at the irritated minotaur, hissing for the poor creature. The impact and the horn breaking must have hurt. "That," Eve started, "is not my fault." She cringed inwardly at the look of death aimed her way. That was conceivably the worst thing she could say. "I apologize. That came out wrong. I meant that perhaps you should not have run at me so. I wasn't that far. Not that there is anything wrong with running, but it would not have ended with losing your— Bugger shit! I shall say no more. Your eyes are making odd and disturbing movements. You should get that...looked...at." Her mouth belonged in hell.

"You will die," the brutish minotaur grunted.

"I am really sorry about your horn."

The minotaur ignored Eve's apology and grabbed the strapped axe on his back. The axe was large. Its blade was wide and sharp, the head the size of Eve's head and the haft half the length of Eve's height. Weaponless, Eve's eyes roved the ground for one but found nothing.

Eve spoke again, "I am unarmed." She opened her arms wide

to show she was vulnerable. "It is dishonorable to attack an unarmed soldier."

"I don't care. You are going to die."

*Hell,* Eve thought. She once more searched the ground desperately for anything she could use as a weapon and shakily grabbed a jagged broken piece of glass. She brandished it threatening. Her opponent smiled and slowly approached her. The young woman stood her ground, feeling helpless and exhausted as she held her demons at bay.

Off in a corner, King Oberon and Queen Titania were surrounded; eyes defiant on those that once, they had believed, been loyal to them. They were ready to unleash their powers to survive but held back. Their abilities could take down the tower and accidentally kill their citizens. This, they did not wish for. Puck was still fighting, holding on to Aelfdene, but not for long. He was tired, and his grip was slowly weakening. His resolve to keep fighting decreased as he looked at the men and women who lay dead or dying on the ground. The fight between the new king and the old was dwindling as one side slowly lost.

"Halt!" Caoimhghin ran into the room, followed by ugly, roughed-skinned creatures in armor behind him, spears in their hands. They had beady red eyes and crooked upper teeth that slightly protruded. "This fight will cease now. Those against my parents will drop their weapons or feel my wrath."

"Brother, nice of you to join us," Aelfdene said as he tossed Puck off him finally. Puck hit the floor and rolled to Eve's feet, unconscious. His chest moved up and down in a constant beat. He must have hit his head when he had been thrown. "And you bring your filth into this castle. The deformed outcast of the elves. They still thoughtless?"

One of Caoimhghin's creatures growled, showing sharp teeth. It went to take a step forward, but with a raised hand, it stayed on its king's order. "My people should not be overlooked. They are stronger than you know. Now, explain yourself!" Caoimhghin demanded.

"What authority do you have over me?" sneered Aelfdene.

"He may have none, but I do." Petal pushed past Caoimghin. "Explain this treachery, as ordered by the next in line, your superior, I."

"My superior," hissed Aelfdene in outrage. He started to laugh, his men joining him nervously, unsure, and worried at the new development in their rebellion. Then, Aelfdene abruptly stopped laughing, the room silencing as his eyes blazed a crimson red. "The throne is mine. Mine! I am the oldest! Not you! It is mine for me to take and take I shall. No one else can have it! If needed, I will kill you, sister!" Spittle flew from his lips.

"You will have me dead, brother?" Petal asked.

"Yes. If it means my rise to power, I will have all of your deaths by my hands."

Oberon and his wife sputtered, wanting to admonish their son but lost for words at his blatant betrayal. Caoimhghin cried out in dismay at his brother's heartless answer. Eve closed her eyes in indifference. Aelfdene's answer was nothing new to her. He was a power-hungry whore, and nothing in his lifetime could fix it. It was greed. It was a sickness that could only end with his death.

Eve's eyes closed, and her mind surged with an understanding. She then opened them. They were black and empty. The rebellion would only end once Aelfdene died.

#  CHAPTER 21 

EVE MADE THE decision to kill Aelfdene. To her surprise, her darkness did not fully agree with her. The myriad of voices fought against one another. One half bid her to leave and run far away. To never look back. The others pleaded for her to shred the revolting being in front and then kill the others. It was either fight or flight. Watching the smug look on the captain's face decided her subsequent movements. Eve's body started to transform and was pulled further into the darkness than she had ever been before. The young woman was proud that she was still conscious, still had control— yet at once, she was in a whirlwind of loss. She had thought she had achieved a certain amount of emergence before, but this was at a higher degree that she had never entered.

Moreover, her body evolved quicker than it had previously, getting her a step closer to becoming a true unseelie. The blackness in her sclera fell back to its natural color. The iris of her eyes altered to a vibrant hue that shimmered between yellow, orange, and red. In addition, heat creeped out from underneath her eyelids, reddening the minute natural cracks on the surrounding black skin. The last metamorphosis change was the upper portion of her ears elongated into a tip, which had an inward curve that flared away from her head.

*Kill him. Tear him apart. Now! Before you can't,* her darkness ordered vehemently.

*He is unarmed,* Eve said to them, remembering Aelfdene's lack of weapons. *We need to give him a sword. It will be wrong to not allow himself the chance to defend himself. Even if armed, we surpass him.*

*You cannot allow him any means to survive. Kill him. That is the only way you can protect these people. Ignore your code. It is just holding you back from doing what must be done.*

"You are not a murderer," a male voice echoed in her mind. The voice of a friend she never had a chance to love.

"Yes, I am. I have killed innocents when ordered to. I have burned villages down to the ground while the houses were still occupied. I have darkness in my soul. I was even born with an evil that stains me now," her voice spat back in self-loathing.

"Say the words. Say the code we followed."

"Always and everywhere be right and good against evil and injustice...there is no use! I am evil."

The ghostly shadow of Eve's love formed in front of her, transparent and fog-like. She knew he was a dead man from an old memory. Nevertheless, he believed in her. If given a chance— if she had told him that she was never a man— he would have taken her from the everyday corruption surrounding her. He would have, or so she hoped, loved her in return. A lost dream that would never come to fruition. He was the one and only good man she had ever had the honor to meet. Sadly, in the end, the pureness of his heart was the reason he died not long after. He had not played the nobles' games, and his life had been the price for his mistake.

Eve internally laughed to herself, thinking fondly of her love. He pushed her to be more. She followed a minority of his code, guilt gnawing on her that she couldn't follow all of them. If he had been alive to see what her life had become...it was easy to imagine the disappointment on his face.

"Say the words," her dead beau pleaded.

*Always and everywhere, be right and good against evil and injustice. Live one's life so that it is worthy of respect and honor.*

"There is potential— great potential in you that I see. You shine with it. You are different and have the chance to change the world. When you are placed in a situation when all you believe is lost...repeat the virtues of the Duke." Eve's flaming eyes moved to make direct contact with the treasonous son. The shadow of the man she wished she had been strong enough to love evanesced. She knew she had to deal with the prince and end the consequences of his madness.

"Temperance," Eve mumbled. Restraint was an arduous action for the young woman. She practiced it many times. The evil man in front of her now made it difficult for her to do so. She knew he would never stop to gain more power, killing whoever got in his way. "Resolution."

"Speak up, hag! What are you saying?" Aelfdene demanded.

*No.* "Truth. Faith. Charity. Justice. Sagacity— "

"Are you a coward?!"

*No.* Eve ignored him. "— Prudence. Liberality. Diligence...and Hope."

"Answer me, you wench!" The ex-captain's spittle flew in the air.

Being moral, being human, did not make one weak. Eve had managed to live long without this curse. It took her death for these abilities to come out and be known. Since then, it had been killing her. Changing her. Eve accepted now that, if needed, she could fight without throwing herself into the black pond of her powers. Just the little she was in at present did enough to heal her to almost perfect health. The young knight pulled her transformation back but left enough for some speed and strength. As her body normalized, she noticed another permanent difference to her ears— although they were slightly tipped, they were no longer elongated.

She spoke to the spoiled prince. "Your life is not for me to decide, and...you are not worth it— boy. But, if you attack, I will not hold myself back from kicking your arse, you slimy wanker."

The prince's teeth clenched; more veins throbbed at the edges of his forehead. His fist closed tightly until the knuckles were white. His eyes flared red again. However, to the shock of the others in the room, the pupils and iris became utterly black.

"What did you do, brother?" Caoimhghin asked in horror.

The captain smiled, and the air morphed, causing Eve's skin to tingle and the objects to reverberate in place. The skin of his hands turned black, and slowly, most of the beings in the room stilled. They became statue-like. Stuck in time. The only ones capable of moving that Eve could see were herself, Caoimhghin, and the queen. The three looked at each other, wondering the same thing: why had they not been affected? Time was present, as evidenced by the wind hitting the window. Sounds of life were audibly outside. Only in this specific room did the sentient beings freeze.

The three took steps forward toward Aelfdene. There was this pull, and they followed. Evil hung heavy on the surface of the mad prince, and the closer they came to him, the aura started to change them. The queen's face became translucent, and the tip of her fingers blackened, nails growing into long, strong blades. Her hair flared out and moved with the strength of her powers. Caoimhghin's skin lightened, and his veins darkened. With a sweep of his hands from his back to the front, he swiftly formed two clear orbs without any glitter flying in the air. One hand tossed the orbs up in the air, which he caught effortlessly. Eve's eyes turned red around her irises. She felt her muscles thicken and twitch at the uncomfortable changes she tried to keep at bay.

Aelfdene chuckled darkly. He cracked his neck and stared back at them. His body grew in length until his head hit the ceiling. His teeth grew, becoming sharp. His muscles became larger where before there had been none or little. The air was no longer thick with the tantalizing overtone, and happily, the three no longer had the urge to get closer to the monstrous fey.

Eve gulped nervously. This was new. She became more shocked when a puff of glitter surrounded her hands, and she found her swords back in her possession. Her eyes looked sideways at the other prince. "You couldn't do this earlier?" she asked sarcastically.

"You are forgetting that my arrival was not that long ago," Caoimhghin answered with a shrug and a cocky grin, daring Eve to reply.

"Children. Another place. Another time," Titania broke in. The two looked at her and nodded in agreement. Then, to her other belligerent son, the queen expressed," What have you done to your father? To the men?"

Aelfdene tutted at her, making his mother angrier. "Didn't you ever wonder about my gifts?"

"You had none," Caoimhghin stated.

"Yes, I did. But why show it to a family who continuously humiliated and put me down? Who, day after day, gave me disappointed and pitiful looks? Though, I should thank you in the end for that. It fueled my anger, sorrow...and hatred. I can stop the movements of any seelie in the vicinity. At first, my abilities were short-term. Thanks to a dear loving mentor who shared my dreams and ambitions, I can hold seelies immobile for eternity if I wish. Additionally, if I die, they die with me."

"Melchior was your mentor," Eve said. She then had an idea how his powers had grown for someone who had received them late. "You followed in his direction. How far have you gone? How much taint have you done to yourself?"

"It can't be. What have you done, boy?" Titania demanded.

"I did what neither you nor father could do. I did what I had to bring order to our world. I made a deal with the king of darkness while Father stationed me near the border those many years ago. I consumed and accepted his gift of the flesh of our people," Aelfdene spoke savagely, saliva spitting out between every other word. His aura grew, and so did its stench. Eve's darkness reared its ugly head out to take the energy offered to them, but she pulled it back in.

"You have become insane with power! You know what consuming flesh will do to you. Additionally, unlike others, such actions affect us worse due to mother's blood," Caoimhghin said. "We love you, brother. You are not far from help. Leave and walk away from this crusade. Place this event behind you, and we shall do the same. We will gladly welcome you back with wide open arms. All is forgiven."

Internally, Eve shook her head. Caoimhghin was a fool. Aelfdene has passed the point of return. Before consuming flesh, it was apparent Aelfdene had been greedy for power for a long time. The years of jealousy of his siblings had turned him into a manic tyrant. There was nothing his family could do now to change his mindset.

"I don't want your open arms," Aelfdene spat to his family.

"We love you," Titania informed her son. "We did not know you felt we were humiliating or causing you harm. Whatever actions or words you were offended by were to make you a stronger leader. All our criticism was to help you grow and prepare you to take our spot as the next ruler." Aelfdene's eyes narrowed into slits. Perhaps his mother had forgotten, but he had been cast aside.

"Your love is useless, Mother. Not once did you take the time to understand me. Not once did your eyes set on me. Your eyes always searched for your favorite child! For the youngest! For Caoimhghin!"

"Brother— "

"Do not dare be brotherly to me when you never have before."

"It was you who stayed away at every hand I gave. I even invited you to stay with me in my kingdom!"

*Sometimes less said is more advantageous,* Eve thought with a slight tiny shake of her head.

As the oldest, Aelfdene probably has assumed to have a small kingdom of his own. Then there was the promise to be the next high king, only to be passed over. His younger sister had replaced the position he once had and had hoped to take soon. Eve's cousin felt the same. As the oldest male heir, her cousin had believed all would have been passed to him. He had been raised to rule the household, and Eve had been taught to fight. Withal, her father had bigger plans than handing the family's wealth to her incompetent cousin.

"Your kingdom," Aelfdene scoffed. The ex-captain turned to his mother. "You gave the family fool, the youngest, a place in our world but left nothing for me. Why? Tell me why I was not deemed worthy to rule any land?!"

"Do not ask. The truth cannot be taken back. You will not like what you will learn. Just let it be."

Aelfdene growled and strode to his frozen father. He grabbed the helpless fey by the throat. He slowly started to dig his nails into him. "Tell me, or I will kill Father."

Eve's hands tightened on the hilt of her blades. The young knight prepared to ram herself into Aelfdene if the situation against Oberon escalated. Only a coward attacked a helpless man.

"No! Unhand your father. Do not blacken your soul with the killing of your blood," Titania begged. "I will give you the answers you seek; remember, this is what you wanted. We did not give you the responsibility you wanted, not because we believed you had no abilities."

"Then why?"

Titania pursed her lips. "When you were just a child, this black cloud hung over you. You were different. Never talked to the others. Played by yourself. We thought it meant that you were special. But then, while you were out with your friends, we came to your room and saw. We saw the hidden room you had created, and curiosity had us know more. We saw the limbs. The wings. The teeth. The multitude of corpses littering the tables and ground. Those small creatures were your citizens and...and we couldn't allow you to rule knowing your potential of cruelty. The barbarity you showed had increased with your attention to our newest arrival."

"I had to know what made those creatures tick," Aelfdene explained. "I needed to know their weaknesses to be stronger than them." He looked at his father and smiled sadly. "I had hoped you would be proud of my work. I had hoped to make you proud of me."

"Liar!" Eve shouted, no longer able to hold her tongue. "You speak only of excuses for your transgressions. Yet, take no responsibility for the harm you have inflicted on others. You are nothing more but a monster."

"You have no right to call me a monster," Aelfdene chuckled darkly. "Your kind are the true monsters. You are parasites that live and destroy the lands. Your people are never happy with what you own. You take and take. Your bellies are never satisfied with the pain caused or the death that follows. Then, most of your people are sheep, mere followers. You kill when ordered to. Kill for money and to see another day while another takes your place to be placed under the soil. You never take a stand when you should. At least I did. I decided not to be a sheep. I am changing my own path. Nevertheless, you call me a monster?"

Aelfdene approached Eve and bent down to be at eye level. His rotting breath caressed and heated her cheeks. "When the future I dream is reality— and it will occur— I will travel to the above and put the mortals under my heel. I will make them submit and place them where they belong. They will beg and bow. I will be their god. For you...I will enjoy putting a collar on that pretty throat of yours. I will keep you alive to watch your kind be enslaved. Then, when that time comes for your death and your mind is finally broken, I will enjoy eating your flesh and consuming your powers." Aelfdene grinned, saliva dripping down his chin and onto the ground.

Eve pointed one of her swords to the captain's face. "You are perhaps correct; my kind are monsters. Yet, there are always the few who give hope that good and love for others exist. You— you are pitiful. You only have this abundance of power by consuming others for it. Without it, you are just a weak fey acting like a child who received love, but it wasn't enough. You are a child having a tantrum due to jealousy."

"You are also a fool. What makes you believe my world will accept you as their god? How fen-sucked are you? My people can't even accept our own deities. Hell, the majority of us despise our rulers. There is always a rebellion. There is always a conqueror changing the rules and the world among them. But for you— for you— they will unite. You going there will be a blessing. My people will no longer be fighting among themselves, though only temporarily. They will all be fighting against you. They may not have your powers, but we have the numbers."

"Then I will kill them all," Aelfdene sneered.

"Then there will be no one to rule upon. No one to kiss your feet and wipe your ass. I doubt your people would be honored to work in such a low position. They, too, will go against you, and more will follow afterward," Eve informed him. "What is more, I doubt the unseelies will follow an abomination like you. You are not even fully one of them. Just a weak imitation. They will kill you after their master has no more use for you. Is that why you are adamant about killing me? Afraid they will toss you aside once they have me?"

"That will never happen. You are hybrid filth!"

"A hybrid unseelie filth. I am part of them. Perhaps more than your mother and brother here. I am a prime specimen of mixed vulnerability and corruption," Eve said cockily. Aelfdene sputtered in indignation, lost for words. Eve saw this as an opportunity to continue. "I am everything you will never be. Were never born to be. You are just a puppet. A blind pet begging and sniffing for a used bone."

Aelfdene sprang forward, hand outstretched to grab Eve by her neck. She side stepped away with a spring. A wide, gleeful smile crossed her face as her eyes swept over Aelfdene. He growled and shouted, "You are wrong! I am the savior!"

"You are a worm," Eve told him. The angry royal stampeded at her, and she swooped under his arm with a simple spin. "I am not even using my powers. Consuming your own seems to not have assisted you in any way."

Aelfdene went to maul Eve's face and missed. His claws came within a hair's breadth from shredding her skin. She didn't flinch, but inside, her heart skipped several beats at being almost harmed. *His speed has increased. He dislikes and can't handle the truth, which feeds into his anger. Let me see if I can push him to make a mistake.*

Aelfdene was beginning to move, which was unnatural for an individual three times taller than was expected. Eve knew she could use his speed against him. If he attacked, she could trip his arse to the floor. He was, at this point, a raging monster. The prince's focus was solely fixated on killing her. "Is that the best you can do?" Eve spun one of her swords playfully. "Where is this great power you speak of, hmmm? It seems to be lacking. Pity. I was hoping for a challenge. The oafs I fought when I arrived fought better than you."

Aelfdene sprang at Eve in a great leap, bellowing as he swung at her with his fists. She barely avoided them. He became quicker, forcing Eve to use her swords to deflect his punches. Her demon roared to assist her so that she may survive. *I can't use you unless you have a way that doesn't end with another's demise. Not this time.*

"I will tear you apart," Aelfdene shouted. He grabbed Eve's shoulder. She stepped back, pulled his arm with her, and used the pommel of her sword to hit the soft tissue under Alfdene's elbow. The well-placed blow forced his arm to bend, his grip loosening. Eve jumped away and created an invisible protection spell around her. She held the urge to breathe rapidly as she was becoming exhausted.

"I doubt it. You can't even catch me properly. Not tired at all, I am not," Eve croaked out with a lopsided and wary grin, wiping the perspiration from her face with her torn sleeve, smudging the blood present. "Do you submit?"

At the edge of Eve's vision, she noticed movement behind Aelfdene. Oberon's fingers had twitched. A leg inched forward, and his eyes blinked. He was moving again. Fantastic. That meant Aelfdene's magic was waning. Eve quickly glanced at Titania to see if she had noticed the positive development. To the young woman's dismay, the queen and her son were no longer in the room. *Bastards.*

"Stop lying. I can see you can no longer fight. Just give in. Let me kill you. Look around; you are alone. Just submit, and I will guarantee your death will be swift."

"Ah, you noticed that did you?" Eve mumbled more to herself than her opponent. That was excellent, she thought to herself. She was alone in the fight until the others were released from Aelfdene's hold. Eve hoped that the fey had yet to be aware that his powers were weakening. It would be nice if his victims broke from his hold faster. Yet, how could she rush them? She had no idea how long it took for magical effects to go away. She needed to give the soldiers more time. What worried her was Aelfdene's men would also come alive. She hoped Oberon and the others would take care of the problem expeditiously. "This isn't me being tired. I am enjoying this game of cat and mouse. I am allowing the mouse to be the victor and become an excrement-wallowing fat cat for once," she said loudly.

"You strumpet!" Aelfdene growled. "I will have this room rained with your blood."

"You can only achieve such a feat if you can capture and hold me for any amount of time," Eve commented.

"Which he will not do as long as our parents rule this kingdom and as long there is air in my lungs," Petal's voice rang out. Her voice was solid and sure.

Eve breathed a loud sigh and let her swords fall, her arms hanging loosely at her sides. She was tired, and her mind couldn't help but contemplate her short experience of the Underground. *Since I have been here, I have been pushed to my limits. If, and when, I see home once more, I will relish and bask in the relative peace of my world. But first, I must survive this constant insanity I have found myself in.*

"My powers are unlimited! How is this possible?" Aefldene screeched.

"You mind that spongy?" Eve breathed out and laughed. "There is no such possibility of unlimited power. That will never come into existence. The God Almighty is the only one capable of wielding such gifts. If an individual had such abilities, it would be the downfall of all creation. You, in all my certainty, do not have that power. I easily managed to distract you enough and move all your focus onto me. Your lack of ability to multitask is a great weakness."

"Your gifts are weak," Petal added. "It is over."

Before Aelfdene could retort, a barn owl flew into the room, followed by a phoenix twice its size. The two creatures were followed into the room by a small army. The room became more crowded with soldiers surrounding the traitors. Just as the betrayers moved, they were pushed to their knees, and a sword brought to their necks. Eve watched in amazement as the phoenix grew and transformed into the queen. Then Caoimhghin emerged from a puff of feathers where once the barn owl had been. The royal family stood together, firm, with an emotionless mask. Inside, they had to be dying for going against one that shared their blood.

"It is over, son. You have lost," Oberon stated.

"I cannot lose."

Annoyed, Eve wondered about the intelligence of Aelfdene. His ideocracy was tiring her. The pigheaded royal had no allies to call upon for aid, and there was no space for the fool to escape. His new physic now made it easier to be captured or cornered.
The young knight magicked her mask away, picked up her swords, and shook her head. "It is over, you dimwit. Can't you see your family is trying to spare your nut-hook life? They love you. Care for you. If this had been my family, I would have been stabbed in the back, disemboweled, cut into pieces, and staked. My body would be in public to show the peasants that there was a change in leadership over their lives." Eve pointed a sword at him, adding, "And this is without betraying them."

Aelfdene growled, "You wouldn't understand. You are just an outsider. You are the reason why I must take the throne."

"Oh, shut your mouth. You planned this rebellion for many moons. Your actions would have happened with or without my presence. Do not dare place blame upon me for your insanity. I will allow your family to be angered with me when I end this travesty."

"How will you manage that?" Aelfdene asked in disbelief.

"I am an unseelie. I am basically a sin-eater by nature. Your power— " Eve's voice lowered and echoed as she transformed, eyes turning black with a single tear dripping down her face, "— smells good." As Eve talked, she debated within herself the magnitude of powers. Melchior had wanted to take her energy and then consume her. Why couldn't she siphon Aelfdene's energy, just the unseelie portion? She allowed her demon to aid and instruct her. They promised her subsequent actions would not kill the prince. Once she consumed all his darkness, he would return to what he was once. *All the same, what will happen to me?*

The wickedness in Eve became silent.

She laughed lightly to herself. It was just her day that her malignity would not speak. She sniffled as worries of different possibilities flitted around her mind as the question she wanted to know remained unanswered. The second worst of them was death—which she hoped for. The outcome she prayed didn't occur was losing her soul and becoming a dark shadow, becoming an unseelie. She rushed Aelfdene. He clumsily went to intercept, and the knight used her powers to move faster at the last moment, catching the prince by surprise. She moved to stand a thumb's distance away from him and pulled her left arm back, surrounded by a blood-red aura. With sickening ease, Eve thrust it into the stomach of the captain. Sounds of shock and cries of fear filled the room.

*Now take it,* Eve's demon cried at once, filling her with a hunger that was not for food or drink. Her unseelie instinctively guided her to look for a thread inside Aelfdene. Her eyes went completely white, and soon Eve could view a thread beaming inside the captain. Her fingers grasped it tight in her fist. There was a painful jolt, and the cord came alive in her hold. It became warm, and she started to draw it into her palm. There was pleasure and pain as she consumed the dark energy. She took it all. Every second that passed, she was corrupting her soul.

"Agh!" Eve shouted as a throbbing pain started at the fingertips of her right arm. It spread very slowly through her hand and further up to her shoulder. Her eyes rolled back, her head flung up, and her teeth gritted. Unknown to the young woman, her right arm was turning black in the same area where she felt the aches.
Lost in the pool of evil, she was unaware that Aelfdene had transformed into his original state. He was lost in an endless spinning hole, his eyes dazed and confused. His hair was plastered to his head from his perspiration. Still, Eve consumed his energy.

"We need to stop her," Caoimhghin urged his parents.

"I am in agreement," Petal said with a nod. The two siblings moved forward and were halted by Oberon. "Father?"

"She must finish," Oberon explained. "Aelfdene may look like himself, but the mortal wouldn't still be feeding if all that made him unseelie was gone."

"Look at her arm," Caoimhghin pointed. "It's black. And it's spreading. We must pull the arm away. We will lose her."

"Somethings are meant to happen," Titania said with an odd look. A look her children didn't recognize. "There are things we can't control. I should know."

"Well, you may do nothing, but I shall," Puck raced forward and dodged the arms, trying to grab him. He reached the two. Being in their vicinity made him feel ill at the pit of his stomach. What was more, there was pressure in Puck's mind. It felt as if somebody had grabbed his brain and was squeezing it. Still, he pressed on through the pain. "White Knight indeed. Black Knight, it should be. Look at me. Where has this bravery come from? I will figure it out and find it later. By doing this, a favor is owned, dear girl."

Puck hesitantly touched Eve, and a shock went through his body. The fey hated his gift, which was being sensitive to others energy when he came into contact with them. During times of battles, before his banishment, Puck's job was to take a look at the injured. He checked if their injuries had become corrupted by the venomous parasitic shadowy ink of an unseelie. "Many debts I will call for."

Puck ignored the feeling of losing his stomach and the evil energy surrounding the girl. He let go and moved his hold to Eve's shoulder. He lurched from the second jolt and clenched his teeth against the pain. Quickly, he started to shake the mortal's shoulder and found her arm would not move at all. It was stuck in place. He released his grasp with a hiss and looked at his hands to see them red. The flesh of his palms had partially burned away. In the cool air, his hand steamed and trembled. He felt foolish and angry with himself. Of course, moving the knight from her prey would take a lot of work.

"There are times when one cannot just watch and wait," Caoimhghin's voice rang out. The young man joined Puck. "I shall assist you." The prince moved behind Eve and signaled Puck to do the same for Aelfdene. Caoimhghin's hands glowed with his powers to keep his hands from burning. He placed them on Eve's shoulder. Puck followed, again hesitant, but was happy to find that when he touched

Aelfdene, there was nothing. Eve had pulled the darkness out of the boy. "At three, we pull," Caoimhghin instructed.

Caoimhghin counted up, and at three, they pulled on Eve and Aelfdene with a yell. Slowly, the two fey separated the mortal and the royal idiot. A sigh of relief came from all in the room. However, no one paid attention to Eve's right-hand light until it became really bright. Afterward, there was the sound of a giant cannon. An explosion occurred, and Eve, Aelfdene, Puck, and Caoimhghin were flung away from each other and to the ground. Puck and Caoimhghin cursed in their native language feeling new aches and forming bruises. Aelfdene lay comatose with his eyes wide open, shaking, and covered in perspiration. Eve fared better than the four physically, but not mentally.

Eve was fully healed, if you didn't count her right arm still being black. Confused, she went to stand but could not feel her legs. So, the woman sat with her legs sticking out in front of her. She attempted to remember what had happened. Her memories, sadly, were jumbled. Confused, she looked at her hands. Her eyes widened to see one of them a different color. She panicked and cried out in horror. She then attacked her skin vehemently, clawing at the black ink. She wanted to tear off the skin that could not be hers. When that action did nothing, she grabbed a fallen dagger nearby. She didn't want her arm and was prepared to slice it off. She went to sever her arm but was stopped by Caoimhghin. Eve wept to her friend to let her go. She didn't care that she would lose her sword arm; it had to go. She didn't want a physical representation of her corruption visible. She already had the spidery-like tattoos, but at least they could be covered by her tunic. Her arm was another matter.

"Shush. It is over. Everything is alright," Caoimhghin whispered in her ear.

"No! Let me be! I must remove it! Please," Eve begged as she tried to remove herself from his hold. Queen Titania was quickly at her side. The queen grabbed the girl's black hand to show she had no issues touching it.

"It is part of you. It will aid you," the queen said.

"Take it! Cut it away! It is the change of my soul that comes to light," Eve pleaded. "Please. Spare me from this humiliation."

"Mother," Caoimhghin asked, eyes wet with unfallen tears. "Is there nothing we can do?"

"Yes, there is." Titania placed two fingers upon Eve's forehead and said," sleep."

Eve fought against the command, but the turmoil and the fight left her defenseless. Her eyes closed, and darkness, screams, and heaviness lay over her shoulders.

#  CHAPTER 22 

EVE WOKE WITH a start, eyes alert, gasping for breath, her back arching up from the bed she had been placed in. She looked around and almost cried at the familiarity of the room. She struggled to sit up and looked around. The healers in the room ignored her as they shuffled about, moving, mixing, and cataloging vials. Eve never thought she would be glad to be in the healer's ward again. It was a vast improvement compared to the dungeon's hospitality. Also, watching the healers glide while doing their tasks gave her a pleasant feeling. She would have to set time aside to ask how they moved like that; it was eerily impressive and intimidating.

She waited for a healer to approach. She wished to know the full extent of her injuries. She also wanted to know how much time she had left before she became an unseelie. She raised her hand to muse her hair and saw her arm wrapped in thick linen. She stared at her covered limb, afraid to touch it and see what lay behind the cloth. *Oh, I had hoped that had been a dream.*

"Staring at it won't return it to its original form," Aine's voice rang out. Eve laughed sadly. "For the few times I have known you, I always wondered— in your world, were you harmed as much as you are here?"

"I cannot really say. These are two vastly different realms. My previous life was without magic, with strict rules that the majority followed. In this lifetime, there is more. So much more. And with it brings dangers I had never thought to dream of. In this majestic world, I feel closer to myself. However, there are more questions about myself I must know. In reality, I know finding my answers will be bleak. I did betray and hide my intentions from the king and queen. Though not as I believed, I conspired to end Puck's banishment. As I can see, my death is imminent."

"Pah. Remember, Caoimhghin and I knew of the plan. We assisted."

"And I thank you," Eve said solemnly. "Though, by my wishes, do not talk of your help to King Oberon. All responsibility shall lay on me and me alone."

"There will be a punishment," Aine informed her.

"Then I believe this shall be my room and pretend I am so ill that death is on the horizon," Eve replied.

"I wouldn't mind your constant company. It does get lonely here," Aine mussed cheerfully. "In earnest, I will try to keep you safe from Oberon. The High King and Queen know this is not and will not be the last for Puck to come and go. That boy lives for mischief. He is bound to get in trouble again."

"What did he do to be banned?"

"I am surprised he never said. He will not get angry," Aine said. "Puck's life revolved around Aelfdene before his banishment. You could say Puck was the boy's caretaker. One day, Puck decided he wanted to make the boy smile. Thus, Puck began, and not for the first time, to use his mischievous ways upon the king. Sadly, the fool he was, his ideas for his antics were fully his own."

"I am guessing Aelfdene had a hand."

Aine nodded. "Indeed. The boy was born with a mean streak. Yet, Puck believed otherwise. He swore Aelfdene had good in him and would show it by making the boy laugh. His thought was laughter healed one's soul that was full of agony. Puck was determined to prove this fact to his friends. When his first attempts at making young Aelfdene laugh or even smile failed, Puck decided to take another approach by going to the source. The dimwit foolishly asked his charge what he wished for. Aelfdene's answer was harmless, even innocent. The boy wanted to witness his father laugh. Not a forced or small laugh. Aelfdene desired a great, carefree laugh from Oberon. Not an easy feat, as the king likes to be always seen as alert and severe.

"Puck's plan was simple. He was going to set up a party with some help from citizens. He would have them dressed silly. There was going to be grand entertainment, fun, games, and drinks. Puck knew Oberon never said no to a celebration. He just needed the king's permission to allow Aelfdene to join the festive.

"This was not enough for the boy. He dared Puck that he couldn't get Oberon to laugh at his antic without others present. Here, I know little as Puck never divulged what his mischief contained. All I knew was the plan consisted of the fool hiding Aefldene in Oberon's chamber. The boy was to witness his father be relaxed and happy even after being pranked," Aine finished.

"I hear no evil doing so far."

Aine tilted her head and lifted up an eyebrow. "Nay. It does not. Yet, this is Puck I speak of. A simple task given to the boy becomes a raging battle of humor and unluck. In this case, the trick was neither. I do not know what occurred behind closed doors, but I will not forget how it ended. Aelfdene had run out screaming. His clothes, his skin...there was so much blood. I checked the boy, and he had no injuries. I ran into the chamber. On the ground lay the king, covered in shards of glass embedded into his body. He was bleeding heavily. Oberon's eyes were blown open in shock and disbelief."

"Where was Puck?"

"Puck was on his knees in the center of the room. His eyes were wide and unseeing. I called his name. I yelled questions. Nothing I did gained any movement from my friend. Then, Aelfdene came in with guards and loudly accused Puck had attempted to kill the king. I noticed something in the boy's eyes as he pointed at his caretaker. I fear to describe it as glee, but decades later, his face was still burned in my mind. I know for sure in his eyes was glee."

"What occurred afterward?"

"Well, no one can call a royal a liar. So, Puck was taken to the dungeons. I was rooted to my spot until Queen Titania's wails reached my ears. I quickly moved and gave Oberon medical aid so that he may live. After the king's life was stable, Titania commanded me to check on the young prince. After cleaning the boy, my first observation was the same, he had no injuries.

"Puck did not fare well. I wouldn't see the poor jokester until weeks later. He was pale and thin. He cried that he was innocent, telling me what I told you but nothing else. After I left, Puck was interrogated. They demanded to know how King Oberon became hurt, but the fey wouldn't say. The queen, in her anguish, sentenced Puck to never return and to be expelled from his home. She then took his powers and placed them into a crystal dagger. Not only did the dagger take away his gifts, but it also kept him from returning. Puck glimpsed young Aelfdene with sorrow when he was taken and transported away. I concluded who the real villain was and why Puck didn't say. Like I, he knew that he could not say. This was the crown prince."

Eve hummed in understanding. So, Aelfdene had been treacherous since he was a child. Was he born a monster? She shook her head. One could not inherit a black soul. They must learn the corruption from someone close to them.

"Now, let us see your arm," Aine requested. Eve groaned but nodded. Her arm was unwrapped, and tears welled in her eyes. She studied it for the first time, not having been given a chance during the fight. She noticed that it was slightly more muscled than before. When she flexed her hand, her movement felt normal. There was a tense and tight feeling when she tightened her hand into a fist. There was also a small amount of inner pain and discomfort. Then, there were her claws. Her nails elongated a bit. She closed her hand tighter and realized her skin must be tougher as her new nails never broke through the skin.

Aine gently grabbed Eve's arm, jerking the young woman forward. The knight watched the old woman move each individual finger. Then, her wrist and elbow joints were turned and bent one way or another. Some movements made Eve wince, but the observation satisfied the healer. Aine placed the hand on Eve's lap and gave it a reassuring and comforting pat.

"Do you have a glove you can lend me that I can wear?" Eve asked. "I would like my hand hidden from gossiping eyes." That was a lie. The glove was not for the others. Eve at this point, did not care about the public's opinion of her image. The coverage was more for herself. She did not wish to look at her hand. It disgusted her. Was this what Caominghin had meant? Not being human anymore. At least with a garment covering her hand, she could pretend all was well. She could at least feel like herself. Aine looked at Eve with calculating eyes. "How soon can your minions get me a glove?"

Aine's eyes narrowed, and she gave a sigh of defeat. She spoke unintelligibly under her breath; from what Eve could hear, her words had no magical purpose. As far as the mortal could tell, the old woman was expressing her displeasure. The older woman couldn't— wouldn't— understand Eve's turmoil. Aine was perhaps accepting of Eve's unlucky plague, but that didn't mean others were. This mayhap in a world filled with oddities at every turn, but even the people present were afraid of what Eve was already. Now, with her transformation, she represented the citizens' fears of a return to the dark deep-rooted evil that lived outside their views. One that, to Eve's keen eye and experience, was almost impossible to destroy unless the opponent was strong or an unseelie themselves.

Eve was the boogeyman the citizens of the Underground feared. She was also the creature the people above told tales about to scare their children from misbehaving. A small laugh escaped her lips. What she once thought did not exist, she was that creature and always had been.

"Oi, what has your mind so far away? Share. What amuses you so?" Aine asked. Eve didn't answer. She heard the healer, but the woman's words did not process in her mind. Seconds later, a sharp slap behind her head, Eve reacted and listened. The young knight turned to lecture the only culprit in the room that was close but, to her confusion, saw a black leather glove floating in the air. The article as clothing slapped her cheek this time, and Eve's eyes narrowed on the object.

Her eyes opened from shock at the force of the hit from the glove. She poked at it angrily. Its attack began anew, flapping at her face in a random bee-like flurry. She fought against it and swore at the offending object, sputtering when her mouth was hit. She growled and snatched the glove. It struggled to escape her grasp. Eve glared at it and quickly stuffed it under her pillow. She felt it squirm around. The hellish object wanted to flee. At least it wasn't smacking her around anymore.

"Neat, yet extremely, annoying trick," Eve commented. "Make it stop.

The healer said nothing.

"I apologize."

"Sincerely?"

"With my soul and being."

"You positive?"

*Sigh.* "Extremely and beyond all I know positive. Please take the word of this lady that I am. I am appalled and sorry for forgetting your kind and helpful presence."

"And?"

"Hmmm?" Eve's eyes widened. What had she forgotten? The glove rattled and withered under her. "And...thank you for this beautiful glove. Though, should it be moving?"

Aine huffed in indignation. "Your attention had been lacking to the reality. Is it that awful where it should be?"

"Yes. Thank you...again. I am grateful, but at the moment, I am injured. As you see, with such observant eyes, I am placing stress upon my body. Doing such work to hold this glove in place might do me more harm. Additionally, I wish not to destroy or ruin such wonderful work."

Aine cocked an eyebrow at Eve. The knight wondered if the

healer was disappointed in her. *Yes, she is.*

Eve gave the healer her best trustworthy smile and made a last plea. "Please."

Aine did a dramatic heavy huff of irritation followed by a graceful hand wave. Eve smiled as the offending glove stopped moving. "I should have tortured you, but I am a healer. Your eyes broke me. You remind me of a pup hound with big doe eyes. How do you manage such a facial expression?"

"How do you walk like you are floating in the air?"

"Ha. That I cannot inform or assist you in. Only the elves can do that. We feys don't float; we just walk."

"Strut like a pompous peacock is more like it," Eve muttered.

"I am getting old. Can you say that louder?" Aine snapped.

"What about the queen and Princess Petal? They walk like the elves."

"They are royalty."

"That isn't an answer." Aine rolled her eyes. Eve smiled smugly, saying, "You have no idea. I can see the frustration of not knowing seeping out from the surface of your skin."

"I would watch your words. I control the glove that is under your pillow."

*Foul! She has me trapped.* Eve's smile faltered, and she fleetly placed a fake one. It was more sizeable than her usual smile, so there was a pain in her cheeks. "You walk beautifully."

"That hurt you, did it not?"

"Absolutely," Eve answered in a false dramatic moan of pain. The two laughed.

Eve pulled the glove out and put it on. It fit perfectly. It stretched comfortably. It did not curl or become too tight as she pushed her tendons, opening and closing her hands. Gleefully, she noticed that her monstrous nails did not even cut into the fabric as she had expected them to. Nay. This glove was impeccable. It was a secondary skin. It would be advantageous during future battles. Just the thought that she would have to fight again made her somber. There was not an *if* she had to fight. It was a *when* she would have to fight once more. She was raised to be a warrior. Not only that, but seeing this world, seeing that what once had been impossible was now possible, confirmed that the old code she had abandoned was returning.

Eve's code of humility would be easy, but the courage to act on it was different. With her future unknown, she needed to earn it back. Getting back that courage would be difficult as it had fled from her tight grasp, even before the war.

There were three future outcomes that Eve could conclude. Suppose it was decided for her to be returned to her world, her magic locked. In that case, she would stand against even her own men and others to protect the innocent stuck between the opposing forces currently fighting for the crown. If she was commanded to stay and never see her birthplace again, she would lay her sword in front of Oberon's feet. She would swear fealty and her life to him without hesitation. Or, if they decided for her execution, which was well deserved for her treachery, she would gladly oblige. There would be fear that she is dying, but she would meet it with her head high. She would take Death's hand and the path he placed in front of her.

Eve needed to stop hypothesizing about the possible moving pieces for or against her. It was depressing as most of it never ended happily. There was little action she could do anyways. "How is my health?" Eve asked to distract her mind from overthinking. "I feel fine, but I may be wrong."

"I had expected that to be your first question upon awakening?"

"Are you going to answer?" Eve cut in.

"Patience. Due to your transformation status, your extreme injuries have healed. Being an unseelie is advantageous, but you are not invisible. You can die, girl; remember that. Nobody lives forever. Your body can only take so many beatings. As you have been informed, the more you use your gifts— "

"The faster I will become an unseelie. Yes, I understand."

Aine's eyes pierced Eve, making her feel guilty. "At the rate you use your magic, that statement must be false."

"Since meeting Puck, there had seemed to be written upon my form that I am looking for trouble and run to me it does."
"That is Puck's magic...trouble," Aine spoke with laughter. She then sniffled, her face becoming serious. "The day next, you will stand in front of the king and— "

*BOOM!*

Cries and shouts ensued. Orders were yelled. Voices outside the window exclaimed that the dungeons had been breached. Footsteps ran and pounded out in the halls. Two sets, heavy and quick, came to the ward and barged in. Eyes wide and wild. Hands at the hilt of their swords.

"We have been breached," the heavier soldier with the face of a boar informed them all. "The unseelie has come!"

#  CHAPTER 23 

THE MOOD WAS a scatter of emotions. Chaos reigned in the room. The soldiers cried and shouted for order, making slow to almost no progress. Seeing their failure, Aine took control. She barked commands that were expeditiously followed. Her voice boomed over the workers, the injured, and the soldiers.

The healers grabbed the needed medicine, putting vials and equipment into handbags with unlimited space. The helpers, or aids to the healers, herded the patients. Using magic, a few of the sick were floating in the air due to their injuries or unconsciousness. The other sick, like Eve, favored a standing position or were still exhausted and unable to move for an extended time.

The soldier with the boar's head mumbled in Aine's ear, eyeing Eve and those who still needed a few more days to heal. He was concerned that the group would be too slow to escape and get to safety due to their injuries. It would be better to place all the injured onto the floating stretchers. The old woman disagreed. She had another idea. With an order, two liquid medicines were handed out in long clear skinny glass tubes. Eve took them without question and gulped them down. One drink, the dark pinkish, took away the pain and the other, a see-through brown, invigorated her. The knight doubted it would last.

Aine did a rapid assessment, checking off imaginary boxes inside her mental journal. When she deemed it appropriate to move, another explosion shook the castle's foundation. Dirt fell from the ceiling to the ground. The floor shook violently, and some of the individuals fell.

The soldiers shouted the immediate need to leave, and Eve agreed. Together the inhabitants of the healer ward left with a majority limping and silent. The boar-headed soldier was in front of the group, walking steps ahead to look for danger. Eve went with him, always behind. He had ordered her to stay with the others, but she didn't. He gave her his dagger when he realized she wouldn't listen. With a strict command, the boar told her not to engage unless she had to. The other soldier, a half-giant fey, was at the back of the group. Aine was with him. She felt it was her duty to ensure no one was left behind.

When the group accessed another hall, the wall behind them blew apart, debris killing half of them. Aine's voice of distress was heard. Eve rushed without thought to the elderly woman. When the knight got to the healer, Eve found her fine with a small cut on her cheek and covered in dirt. Sadly, the same could not be said of a helper nearby who was missing an arm. Eve watched as Aine sealed the wound, cauterizing it close. Then with a flick of her wrist, she lifted the helper in the air. The two noticed another body, this one of a patient who was dead.

"Ready?" Eve asked. Aine nodded, and the group started to move. Eve stayed behind for a few moments and went to follow. After taking two steps, she stopped as darkness clawed in her chest.

*We need to stay,* the darkness cried. *They are here.*

*That little information does not aid me,* Eve thought. She looked back and heard the denizens running and screaming. There was also the smell of death and the tint of blood in the air. Eve raised the dagger, waiting, tense, and ready to engage in battle. A hand grabbed her shoulder, startling the knight. She slashed blindly, but it was blocked. The knight found herself looking at the half-giant soldier covered in bruises. He must have stayed with her, and she had not noticed.

"We need to go."

"Now, why would we do that? All the excitement is here. Stay. We have unfinished business to tend to," a familiar voice echoed in the long hall. Eve squinted her eyes, trying to penetrate the mist of uplifted dirt. Prince Aelfdene emerged like a ghost wearing a simple tunic, pants, and riding boots. He had a sword in his hand. To Eve's horror, she could thus far see it was covered in blood. She noted that he had claimed a life recently as some life source dripped from the weapon's edge and onto the floor.

"How— the dungeons," and then, Eve understood. The unseelie had come for Aelfdene. The explosion must have been from the lower dungeons. Had they given him their powers already? Eve looked at the royal intently from head to toe. She was happy to find he was still a seelie.

"I told you! The unseelie came to my aid. See how important I am. I wrote a note before I battled you. One of my men managed to escape our last fight. Later, he was able to send 'our' friends the message for my freedom." Aelfdene smirked. "Pity he never knew he was part of it. My friends had to feed."

"Monster," Eve shouted. "Nonetheless, they have forsaken you. You are unaccompanied, and this time you will die by my hands. There are so many times a bad dog is forgiven before it must be put down."

"They didn't abandon me; they are with me now." Aelfdene raised his arms. Sinister laughter came behind, and around the fey, bouncing off the walls. The sounds were followed by an unnatural cold that sent a deep shiver down Eve's spine. Suddenly, shadows of multitudes of different creatures covered the ground and became black forms of their previous lives. All had red eyes, sharp teeth, and a wisp of tendrils that weaved around in the air.

Eve's left hand tensed and started to twitch sporadically as a shadow of a giant eagle, a rokh, moved forward. Its beak clicked as its head moved snake-like to observe Eve and the half-giant behind her, who still had a hand on her person. "You. You are one of us," it hissed.

"Nay!"

"*Yes! Do not deny it. I can see it so clearly that it seeps out from your skin.*" After the unseelie spoke, the vines on Eve's chest expanded past her dressing and blouse, transforming into wispy tentacles similar to the shadow monsters before her. Her darkness was overjoyed in meeting its kin. Eve had to close her eyes tight from the feeling of ecstasy that she felt. She squashed the emotion down and pushed her darkness back into its mental cage. The shadowy gas coming from her person went back inside her. She gritted her teeth, fighting the angry darkness that she had confined.

"I am not, will never be you! I will die before I allow myself to become an abomination."

With a gravel voice, the rokh pointed its wing at her and took another path to entice her. "*Join us. We are not abominations; we are gods in our own rights. We do not hide our true selves. We allow it to flourish. You have tasted such joy. Is your hand not a thing of beauty? Is it not strong? Free? Why stay with those who only want to use you as a tool? With us, you can gain power beyond any you have believed possible. You can go back to your world and be a goddess among your kind. Fix all the wrongs and condemn those who have done you injury. Bring peace into a world filled with chaos.*"

Its words reached Eve, the temptation strong. As it had spoken, the horrors and the treatment of those considered low flashed in her mind. The eyes. The tears. The pain. The screams. And the death. The times she had stood and allowed it. She could stop it all. She should not look at her powers as a curse but as a blessing.

Afterward, Eve looked at the soldier with her. There was fear in his eyes, but he had yet to leave. He had stayed. She looked back to the unseelie. It would not be by fear if she were to bring peace to her world. That fear, that power, already existed and she, in her good conscience, could not add to it. "No. I don't need to be a goddess, nor do I want the power."

"*Coward,*" the rokh hissed, displaying its talons at her.

"I am not a coward and you— all of you— will not go any further," Eve told them. She turned to the soldier and said, "You can leave as you wish but what I do next requires me to open myself to my evil. If I turn and you have not run, cut off my head. Do not hesitate."

"How would I know?"

"Probably when I resemble them." The soldier paused in thought and then nodded. He let her go and took steps away but not far enough from his sword's length. Eve breathed out a sigh of relief that the soldier was willing to kill her. She faced the horde and opened her mental floodgates— only for nothing to happen. Aelfdene laughed after a few seconds and was joined by the others. "Come on," Eve mumbled to herself. Nothing. Silence in her head.

"They won't attack. As kin, we control them," another female voice vocalized. Out walked a fey unseelie with her hand open, palm facing Eve, dressed in torn rags that covered little and left little to the imagination. Fear came to Eve as the woman closed her hands. There was pain, and Eve went down to her knees as darkness screamed at her for her weakness. They were pulling her into an obsidian abyss familiar to the first time she had changed. "You are not fully unseelie, and for that, we have power over you. You should have joined us when you had the chance."

Eve felt despair, and her ear rang from a bellow...that was not hers. It was one of battle, masculine, and she swore there was a flash of metal. She saw a blinding bright circle appear from the middle of nowhere. Caoimhghin and his men jumped out of it. His sword was ready, and he was swinging down upon the arm of the fey unseelie who controlled Eve. His blade sliced through it, and the woman let out an awful screech. Eve felt the scream shatter her mind in half. The pain was so consuming that she threw up on the floor. She fell to her side, writhing like a worm pulled from its dirt home.

"Adam— Eve," Puck's voice broke through. Eve felt a hand on her forehead, and a calmness and warmth flooded her. "I have you. Just breathe, girl. We need ya. Are you not the White Knight?"

Eve nodded, breathing deeply to pacify her erratic beating heart. "Then get up. Stand up. Take your sword and fight."

"I don't have a sword," Eve croaked out. Puck laughed and helped her stand, pulling her away from the contents of her stomach. He kept a hand on her as she wavered in place. When he felt it okay to let her go, he unstrapped two swords on his back— her blades.

"I trade ya for that wee dagger you have. These swords are not to me liking," Puck chuckled as Eve wiped her mouth clean and put on her mask. Today, her cover was a comfort and made her feel invincible. Though, this time it did not just appear as it usually did. It formed from the dark wisp of the black shade in her before becoming solid. There was a slight shine to it. "Don' be using your magic when you fight. Just your skills in the sword. You don't need it. Unless— "

"I have no choice," Eve affirmed through gritted teeth. Usually, putting on her mask was a simple transformation. This time, it wanted to be more, and she pushed down the urge to let all her powers out.

"You are already stronger than you were before. Trust what you already have. You don' need anymore."

"I don't," Eve agreed.

Puck nodded in happiness and soon became serious. "I must go. I must stop them. Stay alive, girl." He snapped his fingers and disappeared before Eve could question his meaning.

She wished to have answers, but they would have to wait. She stretched the different joints of her body. She was displeased to find that there was still a dull ache at the back of her head and neck. It did not impede her from joining the fray in the hall. She should not have been surprised but fighting with others was friendly and familiar. Protecting and being protected brought on a feeling of hope and a deep partnership with those around her. She had missed this feeling.

"Down!" a soldier grunted, and Eve went on to one knee. An unseelie troll had almost fallen upon her, but another had saved her. She would thank the man after learning his name. "Get that soft expression off your face and put more life in your steps, or you will be cut in half, you cunt."

*He is a basket-cockle.*

The soldier pulled her up like she weighed nothing. Eve knew he would berate her, but a sword came out from his stomach. A booted foot pushed at his back, and he came off the blade, falling onto his knees. One of his hands went up to keep his lifeblood from leaving his body unsuccessfully. Eve was horrified to see such a giant, a minotaur, be unhanded and surprised. Worse, she knew it was her fault. The knight ran to him and placed him gently on his back. She soothed and told him that he would survive the day and when all was over, she would bestow upon him the most incredible dish she knew how to make. He smiled and grimaced at the pain. Tears welled in her eyes. There wasn't much the knight could do for him but honor him by killing the creature who had impaled him. Her eyes flicked up to the manically grinning Aelfdene.

"I guess I did retire the fool as I had promised all those years ago. Pity he has no heir, as I did have his son killed. You know him as the sword master."

"You bastard!"

"I know who my mother and father are," Aelfdene retorted.

"Why kill, hurt these men, your men? Why not go with your dark creatures and wallow on dead land? Just go and leave these people be!"

"You said it. Dead land. You all are standing in our way of having more. Be more. Just drop your swords and stand down."

"You will kill us all," Eve told him, her chin jutting out in defiance.

Aelfdene bent to her level and grabbed her chin, their noses close to touching and a static tension between them. It was not tension from a possible romance but a deep hatred between two enemies. In their eyes, there was a promise that one day, sooner or later, one would kill the other. Eve hoped it was today. She jumped to her feet, lashing at the prince with one of her swords. He evaded, but not quick enough as the tip of her blade caught his torso, cutting into his tunic and a bit of flesh. He touched the wound with his fingertips and licked the blood off, his smile widening.

"Not all. Just those who don't submit to my rule." Aeflđene pointed at Eve and said, "You...you won't live to see my rule hybrid wench. I would have loved keeping you as my mistress to answer my beck and call, but you can't tame a bitch."

"That shall never pass. As long as people want freedom, they will not stay down. They will fight!" Eve grabbed her other sword and attacked. She and the prince battled. Both evading the other. Both blocking. Neither backing down.

"We do not have the time for this foolhardy captain," a shrill gryphon unseelie screeched.

Eve ducked under Aelfdene's incoming swing, her head almost being separated from her body. She took little time to look at how the fight was going and noticed the unseelies were leaving after killing their opponent. They were heading into another hall opposite the direction the escape group had gone. One by one, they left. The fighting slowly diminished to only a few standing. Aelfdene pulled away from Eve after a thrust, and an unseelie giant took his place to fight. Soon, in the end, there was only Eve and Caoimhghin fighting, standing back-to-back with each other.

"Cease!" a deep voice boomed. All turned to the man who shouted, and what Eve saw almost— almost— had her drop her sword. It was a gigantic fey unseelie. He wore only pants, his torso bare. Tentacles protruding from his back. His arms were identical to Eve's transformed one, albeit more heavily muscled. His eyes were a bright, fiery yellow instead of bleeding red like the others. This creature was a monster, and his powers felt threatening. He was evil incarnate, and Eve's darkness cowed under his aura, freezing her in place.

"Uncle?" Caoimhghin asked, shocked and mouth wide open.

"Let the fallen take them," the demon ordered.

"But Uncle! Let me at least have my joy and cut out this bawd's heart," Aelfdene begged, looking at Eve.

"No! We waste no more time. The bitch's time will come." Aelfdene nodded, though not pleased with the order. The other unseelies swarmed past him, their master, not even daring to glance back to Eve or Caoimhghin.

"No! You can't! Don't do it!" Caoimhghin shouted. He seemed to understand what was going on. "Brother. I beg you, do not do this!"

"Your brother will do as I tell him if he wants the power he seeks," the demon growled, and he floated away after the others. Aelfdene followed.

Before Aelfdene left them alone, he shouted, "I hope you enjoy our gifts."

*Gifts?* The fallen soldiers, dead or injured, rose to stand. Their skins turned black, and a wisp of shadows escaped their lips. They were, and had become, unseelies. "Slap me arse and pinch my cheeks; my eyes must be deceiving me."

# CHAPTER 24

"YOU DID NOT tell me the full scope of the creature's abilities, did you?" Eve accused her friend. "You couldn't take the time just to let me know that an unseelie can transform you into one of them without slithering their way in."

"This is the first time I have witnessed this also," Caoimhghin defended. "At least, when it is our turn to go their side, it will take longer as we are already partially unseelie."

Eve was discontent with Caoimhghin's words. Especially with him saying 'when it is our turn' and 'already partially unseelie.' Had the prince forgotten she was already transforming into the shadowy things that could re-animate life? So, with added worry stacking upon her mind, Eve watched her previous comrades heal with a dazed look. There was no awareness in their eyes of their former identities. She then jumped in fear, when they all hollered an unholy sound. They placed her hands on the sides of their heads. Then they stopped yelling, their limbs dropping to their sides. The dead turned to look at Eve and Caoimhghin. Eve did not like the looks they had on their faces. It was one of hunger and death. "Is this normal behavior?"

"This is different, and even if I knew, would it matter?"

"Of course, it matters. We would be perhaps running. Or, if you were injured to the point of not being able to walk, I would be dragging your heavy arse into a safe area WHERE WE ARE NOT BLOODY SURROUNDED!"

"Touché."

"Touche? That is all you have to say?!" The newly born unseel-ie started to walk closer to them. "In addition, when did you have an uncle?"

"Last my mother told me, he had died in the great war."

"He is not dead!"

"I saw. Surprisingly, you have the same gifts as he."

"Thanks for the observation. It is great. Brilliant. I now have just looked upon my future. I feel much better," Eve sarcastically struck back.

"Wait! You have my uncle's gifts. You can burn them all dead. Turn them into grains of ashes. Why hadn't I thought of it before?"

*The bowl of water test. The scorched marks after my rampage.* "I don't like fire," Eve remarked. "I had always been afraid of it. Still am."

"Why? What is there to fear about it?"

*What wasn't there to fear about fire?* "It called me," Eve admitted, remembering the times she had stared at the flames on different occasions throughout her childhood. She would become easily entranced by the flames' colors. She subconsciously knew that touching it wouldn't harm her the same way it did others. It was her friend. But her teaching of the church kept her from finding out. Fire meant hell. Evil. If she had experimented with the flame and been proven correct, she would have felt obligated to give herself to the church. The knight would have allowed the clergy to act as they believed, even if it meant her death. Thus, Eve feared fire. Today, she could not allow that fear to continue. "What do I do?"

"Your powers never once manifested as a child from your strong emotions?"

"No! I didn't know about my gifts until after I died, and even after, nothing happened with fire."

"You passed over to the great beyond? You never told me."

"How does one tell another they died? Additionally, I believe, good friend, at this moment, this conversation is not proper. What would be appropriate is to tell me how I am to burn these foes without us seeing Death ourselves. Now I ask again, what must I do?"

Caoimhghin nodded, "Yes. Forgive me. What was in your mind when you did the water bowl test?"

"There was anger. Self-loathing. The want to murder Puck." Eve swallowed hard.

"What else?"

"Kill. Kill them all! Burn them." *They all need to die. Make them pay.* "Quiet. Quiet. Quiet!"

Caoimhghin watched Eve's eyes go quickly to red and then black. He produced his glass orb, not yet enchanting it. The mortal's subsequent actions would determine what spell he used.

In a blink, Eve's head swiveled to look at Caoimhghin. "I can't hold this rage for long," her voice echoed. "What do I do next? Hurry!"

"Grab all that rage and place it all on them."

*How dare my kin do this. They pick on the weak. Have honors they do not deserve. They must burn! Burn! BURN! See their shadows.* "Have it."

"Now kill them. Let the rage escape to, and through, your hand! Feel it! You can do this!"

Eve's hands started glowing red as she raised them to her enemies. A ball of fire grew at the center of her palms. She then threw it at her opponents. The force of her energy set the unseelies on fire and tore into their flesh and muscles. Two by two, she killed them. Their screams of death were high-pitched and full of agony.

Caoimhghin collapsed to the ground as his body felt only pain. Eve kneeled down to him, her eyes changing to their natural color. The dark, spidery shade marking stayed at the edges of her mask. She looked over at her friend and saw that he had been stabbed in the side. The prince winced as Eve pushed on his injury to stem the flow of blood.

"We need to stop them," Caoimhghin said. He went to stand but could not. He was too injured and weak. Exhausted. He needed to use what was left of his abilities to heal himself.

"We need to get you help! I know which direction the hag went," Eve told Caoimhghin with a chuckle to lessen the seriousness of the situation. She went to stand, but the prince pulled at the neck of her tunic, bringing her down until they were eye to eye.

"Go after them. They seek to do something horrible."

"But you— "

Caoimhghin pushed her away from him, and she tripped on her own feet, falling on her bottom. She quickly stood up, taking up one of her swords. "Go! Now! Stop them! You will understand when you reach them." Eve nodded and ran. "Hurry!" Caoimhghin's voice boomed, pushing Eve to run faster.

As she ran, all she heard was her beating heart and her feet hitting the hard ground. Eve slid to a halt when the hall split to left and right. She wondered what direction they had taken. Her darkness aided her. *Left. Our kin waits for us! Go!*

She continued in the direction she was told and found herself looking at a stairway that went down into the bowels of the unknown. The young woman had never been to this section of the castle before and was hesitant to keep walking forward. She was worried the unseelie had posted sentries to wait for her, hiding in the darkness. She slowed her breathing and descended the stairway as quietly as she could.

Fortunately, she met no adversaries on her way to the depths of hell the lighting becoming reddish. The lower she walked, the stench of musk and sulfur became stronger. It felt as if the stairs had no end, so, it was a relief when there were no more steps to go down. The young knight walked into another bleak, dark hall filled with freezing air and a sinister atmosphere. Every breath Eve took created a daunting mist. The hall's eerie feeling increased as sounds echoed and crashed upon each other. She could barely make out the growls and glee coming from the unseelies. She ventured on, her heart beating erratically in her chest. A scream of torture rang out, causing her to stop walking. The cry came from a familiar voice that could only belong to Puck. The knight's pace quickened. She had the fool to rescue in addition to stopping the unseelies from their nefarious plan that she didn't know.

The young woman found herself at an entryway. From her spot, she could hear the voices of unseelies. She crept in, staying in the shadows. Eve slinked to the edges, sticking to the walls and evading the wisp of smoke coming from the monsters ahead of her. Across the room, she saw two vertical standing stones connected by a horizontal one. It looked familiar to the stone structures at Salisbury Plain. If Eve squinted her eyes, she could see odd etches of writing carved on its surface filled with a gold coloring.

It took time, but Eve finally found a spot to watch the unseelies. She stood away from them, in a corner, hidden in the umbra, watching most of the room. If the unseelie looked in her direction, they would see similar burning eyes in the dark.

At the center of the room was Puck, injured and bloodied. He was on his knees, beaten. His torso bent down while his head was twisted up by his hair by Aelfdene. Standing in front of Puck was the uncle.

"Why won't the gate open?" Uncle asked, snarling. Puck said nothing. How Uncle expected him to answer, Eve did not know. For a moment, Eve believed Uncle or Aelfdene had killed him. That must be why he had screamed as he had done moments ago. Then, wonderfully, she saw a bubble of blood and saliva form at the edge of Puck's mouth. He was still alive. Due to his physical state, he was incapable of speaking even if he wanted. His lip was bloated and bleeding. His eyes were puffy, swollen, and purple, quickly turning black. It was apparent the unseelies had pummeled the fool close to death.

"We can find another po— " Aelfdene started to say to his relative but stopped talking as Uncle grabbed him by the throat. The prince was held in the air as sharp teeth snapped close to his face. Aelfdene did not kick or try to escape. He stared at his uncle with no emotion. He was either clod-brained, brave, or had an enormous ego that he could not believe he would be killed by a relative that supposedly had died.

"This is the only one that has not been closed. Not tampered with by your parents' foul skills. If you want your kingdom over the mortals, boy, you will shut your mouth." Aelfdene was carelessly dropped, but he quickly landed on his feet. Standing straight, the prince fixed his outfit before he cleared his throat.

"Yes, uncle," he spat, barely holding back his anger.

Uncle went back to Puck and picked up the fey by the neck. "What did you do to the gate? Why won't it open?"

"It... doesn't...like...you," Puck gasped. The fool decided to laugh. Uncle's eyes narrowed, and he shook the fey with a growl of anger. Puck looked like a ragged doll in his weakened state as he was mistreated.

"You have not changed. You love the mortals so much, you are willing to protect them," Uncle stated disappointedly.

Aelfdene stepped in and cautiously spoke, "Perhaps I can give a solution to our problem. I perhaps can counter his spell."

"He magicked the gate so that it will only activate by the hands of a mortal. There has been no mortal in this realm for centuries! The last one is above, probably dead."

*Sard! I need to go. Damn it! I can't leave Puck here. He will indeed be killed. But if I heard correctly, they are trying to go to my home. The world's kings will fall, either by death or begging. I cannot allow this. What should I do? What actions can I take?* Eve watched Puck be thrown to the ground and Uncle's claws elongate. Eve jumped out from her hidden spot as the serrated fingernails came down upon the defenseless Puck. Her eyes were black as she blocked and swung the claws away. To the young woman's surprise, when she had pushed, she had also moved Uncle a few feet back.

"You should be dead," Uncle growled.

"I have been told that many times throughout my life. It has yet to happen."

Uncle sniffed the air. "Why do you smell different."

"Oi! Not something you say to a lady. Not appropriate for our sensitive ears to hear."

"You are...unseelie? Fey?"

"Mortal! She is a mortal. We have the key to open the portal," Aelfdene shouted with a broad smile.

Eve looked at Aelfdene and snapped, "I do not believe the other realms heard you. Perhaps you can shout out my mortality louder."

"You dare talk back at us as if we are equals?" Uncle asked.

"Equals? Wrong. Speak to you lot like you are manure? Yes," Eve grinned.

"You— "

"Ah, mister deadman, before you say an insult that is posed to intimidate me, I will have to inform you I have heard them all, including from miniature you who is trying to sneak behind me. I can see. I am not blind." Without turning, Eve added," Naughty."

"Do you think it wise to aggravate us? You are outnumbered and surrounded," Uncle pointed out.

"I can see that, but I have an advantage that ensures you won't kill me."

"And what do you attain that will protect you from my wrath?"

"Did you not hear? I am mortal. I am the only one who can open your precious gate."

"You are unseelie. Corrupted. Tainted. Magical."

Eve pulled all her abilities into herself, feeling all the aches and pains that had not yet healed. "I am Lady Eve Bonel. I am a mortal and hybrid fey. I am the great bloody White Knight. And...I am the only individual in this room who can open that portal you have risked your lives for."

"Run," a weak Puck groaned.

The knight smirked as she watched Uncle sniff the air to verify her words. Eve wondered how mortals smelled to him. Was the scent irresistible and delicious? It must be because the unseelie master was positively drooling. His attention was all on her. Not only him, though. His horde of minions had their beady eyes on her as well.

Feeling vulnerable but unable to show it, the young warrior

tried to think of a plan. Yet, she had no idea how she would survive, stop whatever evil plan the unseelie were trying to implement, and rescue Puck. At the moment, Eve was relying on faith that help would arrive soon— very soon. Two people would care about absence: Aine and Caoimhghin.

Aine would have hopefully become aware that Eve's presence was no longer present. The woman would then order men back to the path those ill had left from. Then, those soldiers would find Caoimhghin, who would point in the direction he had sent Eve— or so Eve wished was happening.

Uncle approached Eve and demanded, "Open it."

"You have forgotten an important problem."

"And what would that be?" Aelfdene sneered.

"Unless you two gentlemen know how I will do this great feat, we are stuck. I know nothing of opening portals. I am new to this world. Remember? I have no idea how to make...that," she gestured to the stone structure, "work. I apologize." She bowed to them tauntingly. *Even if I knew how to open this door, I wouldn't do it even with one foot over Death's door with Satan standing in front of me.*

Aelfdene went to attack Eve. A simple gesture from his uncle to another unseelie halted any advance he would make. A feminine-looking half-serpent creature pulled Aelfdene away with the tip of her tail. The serpent then wrapped herself around him. The prince struggled in her hold. He cursed at the unseelie in his native fey tongue, but she wrapped herself tighter, almost cutting off his airway.

Eve watched in amusement as the royal prince acted like a child. Her understanding of fey was weak, but she swore he was cursing someone's mother. Yet, she could be mistaken. His tantrum was a welcome distraction from her. Unfortunately, that distraction was temporary. Uncle grabbed Eve at her waist and lifted her. His hot putrid breath had her scrunching up her nose in disgust.

Uncle brought Eve so close their noses were almost touching. "Lucky for you, now that I know what Puck has done to the structure, I know how you can assist me. Trust me. There is not much to it. You just have to put your blood on the surface of the stone. If that does not work, I will tear you apart and splatter all your blood onto it. That would be more enjoyable."

"You positive your knowledge is correct?" Eve asked.

"What?"

"Let us say you splatter my blood all over the surface, and nothing occurs. What then? Perhaps you need me more than for my blood. But, oops, too late. I am dead, and you just killed the only mortal in this realm. Wouldn't that be a shame?"

Uncle mulled over Eve's words and dropped her unexpectedly. He stooped to her level as she lay on the ground, bruised and shocked by his sudden action. "If you want to live, I advise you to open the portal. I will give you a moment to decide, but it will not be long. Your life has a time limit that is starting now. If you are unsuccessful, I will kill you. I will twist and hang your corpse upside down to ensure all your blood is used."

Eve grimaced. The period to wait for help was shortening. The young woman knew that not long ago, she was determined to not open the portal, but she couldn't die. She could perhaps pretend to do what was asked. Fake the task. She nodded as she agreed and rushed to the stone structure. She purposely tripped on her feet, trembling, acting— which was not that difficult— afraid. When she reached one of the pillars, the young woman licked her lips nervously. She stared at the symbols and fisted her hands.

To create time, the young knight examined the writing. The etches she faced were something new. At first glance, Eve believed the drawings to be Egyptian. The symbols were similar to those she had once seen a monk hover over and study. With a blink, she realized the characters she viewed were slightly different.

"What language is this?" Eve asked.

"It is from the Great Beyond," Aelfdene answered. The fey was calm and no longer struggling in the shadow's hold. The unseelie serpent looked at him intently and slowly let him go. The captain stood in place, looking at Eve with an icy stare. "It is not for the kinds of you to learn. Now, the only task you have is cutting that excrement hand of yours and smudging your blood all over this holy rock."

"I will kill you," Eve stated.

Aelfdene cocked his head to the side and gave a smug grin. His movements were smooth and flawless as he pulled out his dagger and proceeded to play with it. He tossed it up in the air, flipping it and catching it. Then, he slowly approached Puck, placing his blade on the unconscious fey's neck. "Be a good girl and put your blood on the stone."

"How do you propose I accomplish this? I do not have a tool to cut myself," Eve happily informed the captain. Her sword was thrown her way, skidding to a stop at her feet. She pouted. *Bollocks.*

The prince narrowed his eyes, waiting for Eve to challenge him or make another excuse. She nodded in acceptance, the corner of her lips twitching. The knight was fighting the urge to not accept the defeat that was happening. The young woman moved sloth-like as she picked up her sword and walked back to the structure. She brought the blade to her right palm, not closing her hand around it. She shook her head. She couldn't do what was being asked. A cough made her look up to see Aelfdene cut into Puck's skin. She glared at him, her lips pursing together angrily. For now, the game she had been playing was lost, but she couldn't lose hope that luck still might be at her side.

Eve wrapped her hand around the sharp edges of the blade and slowly tightened her hand, bitting back a cry of pain. Then, reluctantly, she dragged the knife edge out of her grip. The young knight closed her eyes at the sting. Feeling light-headed, she dropped the weapon. Afterward, she dragged her hand on the rock's surface and watched in awe as the gold etches turned bright, glowing blue. A wind came from nowhere and quickly intensified around the magical doorway. A bright rectangular light grew in the center of the structure until it became a circular door. It was beautiful, but Eve could only think: *SCHITTE!*

All those in the room were distracted by the blinding bright passage and did not notice the smaller portals opening randomly behind them in different locations. Quietly, the castle's soldiers came out and readied for battle. Once all the gateways stopped opening, and no more new ones formed, fighting began between the seelie and unseelie. Eve sprinted to Puck and apologized as she grabbed him from his tunic, dragging him away from the fight. In the present circumstances, neither of them had the ability to assist in the battle.

"No," Puck groaned, waking from his unconscious state. Eve stopped moving and knelled, one ear near his lips. Did she pull on him too hard? Make his injuries worse? She saw his eyes were open through the slits of the brutal beating he had taken. She knew from experience that pushing oneself to see through swollen muscles caused an ache that grew into a headache. She needed to get him to relax, as Puck was causing more physical damage to himself. "No," he said again.

"Puck, all is well. The soldiers are here and will stop the monsters from continuing onward with their nefarious plans." Puck shook his head.

"Portal," he mumbled brokenly. "Take me."

"You want me to take you there? Are you sure?" Eve wanted to confirm. Puck nodded. She looked up and bit her lower lip as she watched the line of the soldiers holding the unseelie back. It was madness to get near the area where all the fighting was. "Why?"

"Sab— o— tage," Puck slurred.

"How?" Puck shakily pointed at himself and then to Eve.

"Ugh! Fine," Eve grumbled. She shook her head and called herself every name one would call a fool. "You better tell me more about your plan without the hand signals and with more than two words."

Eve moved behind Puck and wrapped her arms around his torso. She huffed as she lifted him slightly by the armpits and started to walk back to the ban of her existence. Two soldiers pulled from their formation at her approach. Eve fumbled through the opening they had given her. Unfortunately, the action left the soldiers open. Eve was forced to duck and pull Puck underneath her as an unseelie gryphon attacked. The tips of its wings were sharp knives and slashed into the stomach of one of the soldiers. It screeched in anger for missing the knight and went to strike again. The blade from the other soldier stopped it, killing the evil shadow. The gryphon dropped to the ground and disintegrated.

Eve currently was moving on adrenaline only. She gave a yelp as she heaved Puck back up and continued to move to the portal. A feminine arm grabbed Eve's shoulder just as she made it to the stones. When she saw it was Petal, she could not help but breathe a long sigh of relief.

"What are you doing here?" the princess asked.

"Puck spoke of sabotaging the portal— unless you know a way to cease its current status?"

Petal shook her head, "Once open, it can't be forcibly closed. It will stay open an hour or as long as one keeps a hold of it."

"An hour?" Eve felt hopeless. "What about your parents? Perhaps they know a way to close it."

"Even if they did, they are in the gathering hall with their own men protecting the injured and weak. The unseelie are everywhere in the kingdom. The scouts saw them coming here."

"Your brother?"

"With Aine."

"Sabotage," Puck rasped.

"But how my dear fool?" Petal enquired impatiently. Puck's eyes closed as he fell back to unconsciousness, unable to answer the question. The princess gasped in surprise, and soon, golden energy bloomed at her shoulders to travel down to her palms. She cradled Puck's face gently, and Eve watched in fascination as the swelling in Puck's face decreased. Petal was healing him and continued to do so until he woke again. "Now, tell me how to close the portal?"

"Not close. Not quickly. Scatter. The etches. They keep the path going to the same place at a fixed point in time. Ruin them, and that stability is gone," Puck answered.

*BOOM!* One of the walls exploded inward. Debris of stone, clay, and dirt filled the air and scattered the ground. It became hard to see the enemies and the allies. More unseelie came in, and the battle took a turn for the worse. The soldiers were outnumbered and were dropping one by one to the ground. The unseelies were getting closer to the portal's opening ahead.

"Hurry! Go! Leave me here," Puck gravely ordered.

"I don't understand. By the little of your words, they will still get through," Eve pointed out. "That is my world, yes?"

"Yes. Yet, they will not go together. Better...for them to be... separated than *cough* together," Puck replied.

"Do not worry. We will damage the writing. Hopefully, with the instability, it can be destroyed. May father forgive me," Petal added. She pulled a dagger from the inside of her boots. "Use this. I will use my sword."

Petal went to act, but Eve stopped her with a hand on the royal's arm. "Say we indeed break the writing path; what if it won't close?"

Neither Puck nor Petal could answer. "There is another way. Feeding it your energy. It will kill you, and this option is only in case all else fails," Puck said after much thought.

Eve winced. She couldn't help but prepare herself for that last option. Seeing as her two friends were more important than her own life, the young knight informed Petal she would go alone to close the doorway. Petal gave her a look that her idea wasn't going to happen. Together, the two went to a pillar each. They started to slash their blades into the etches, ruining the writing.

"No!" Uncle shouted as his eyes fell upon the two women. "Defeat our enemies. They stand in our way to victory. We must get through the doorway before it is destroyed!"

Wisps of smoke lashed at the two women from across the room, but they kept attacking the stone. The portal started to flicker intermittently. The more they cut into the words, the portal's instability increased. Then to the women's shock, something kicked at their feet. They fell and lost their blades in the process. Their weapons were then kicked away by the flurry of shadowing tentacles. Afterward, Eve watched the royal get hit by a wing, sending the princess to a wall with great force. Petal fell with her eyes closed and her body limp. Eve was uncertain and could not tell, from where she was positioned, the degree of damage that the royal had sustained. Luckily, the young knight let the worry go as she saw Puck crawl to check on the future queen.

Eve's eyes once more roved the floor, looking for any possible weapon so that she could continue to ruin the writings. Her search was interrupted when a shadowy Kraken came after her, pining her to the ground. Eve slowly started to choke as the monster's smoke of darkness attempted to pour inside her through her eyes, ears, nose, and mouth. Eve fought against the invasion and couldn't breathe. She struggled to escape its grip, but the evil wrapped itself tighter around her. From one eye, Eve glimpsed a few unseelies start jumping into the erratic portal. She then noticed a single Kraken's tentacle inkiness being fed into the portal. Her heart jumped into her throat as the gateway stabilized somewhat.

*No!* Eve released her darkness, and her body flared into a transparent light blue flame which she fed with her strong emotions. The Kraken cried in pain as its tentacles caught fire before being encompassed by the deadly heat. Eve's black eyes watched with pleasure at the death she had caused. Her hand lifted, and the knight consumed the darkness inside her until nothing was left.

Eve struggled to the portal, her feet unsteady. She put her hand on the stone and pushed her energy into it. The stone greedily took her powers, causing an unexpected lurch in her chest. Eve watched the portal vibrate and pulse at the extra energy it had received too quickly. The knight knew it wanted more as she felt her body being pulled forward. She didn't fight it, weak and exhausted. Then, miraculously, an arm wrapped around Eve's waist and kept her from moving into the doorway. A surge of power flowed through the knight to her hands. Electricity started to surround the portal, and soon, it exploded. The explosion threw Eve and her savior across the room. Lying on the floor, she could barely see or hear the chaos around her. Lastly, there was darkness and no more thought.

#  CHAPTER 25 

"INSTEAD OF A SON, I have a daughter," Eve's father scoffed. He was at his desk inking a letter to one of his many noble friends. Eve stood in front of him, her tunic ruffled and torn. There was blood on her face, her cheek was bruised. Her eight-year-old head lowered, shoulders hunched to make herself smaller. "If my *true son* had done what you did, Eve, I would be proud. But...you are not my son. I may have told others you are my son, but you must remember you are not. I need you in pristine condition. No man wants damaged goods. One day *Adam* will be gone, and *Eve* will emerge. When that day comes, you must be in good condition to provide heirs for your future husband."

"It wasn't my fault," Eve squeaked out. "They spat on mother's honor and –"

"Your mother was a whore. It is no secret. She would have died by my hands if not in childbirth. Couldn't even give me a son. Now, get away from me. I wish to no longer look upon your face. Next time you fight, I will break your legs. As long as the rest of you works, that is all that matters."

Eve kept her sniffles in and walked out of the room. She dare not cry. Her father had people checking on her at all times, keeping the wicked man informed of her actions. Her heart grew heavy with hatred for him with every step she took back to her refuge, her room. She wondered if her life would have been different if her mother had survived her birth. All she was, all she knew, was that she was trouble. Why couldn't she have died herself during childbirth? She was no good. She was cursed. Her father didn't even see her as a person.

"Is she healed?" a male voice echoed loudly.

Little Eve stopped walking at the sound. She did not know who had spoken, but it was familiar. The girl looked around and saw nobody in sight. A hand suddenly touched her shoulder. She turned with a shout to look up at one of the many stewards.

"Are you unwell young Master Adam?"

"I thought I heard— "

"Her body is healed, but her mind is lost," an old woman spoke.

"You didn't hear that?" Eve asked the man, who looked at her like she had brought in dirt.

"No," he drawled. "Your instructor has arrived— " Eve ignored the rest as the unknown male voice spoke up again.

"There is nothing you can do?"

"We can bring her out by a linking of minds. There is a big chance she won't remember you."

The steward tapped Eve's head, and she noticed his frowning face. "Are you even paying attention?"

"Do it," the voice ordered.

Eve felt a chill come from a wind behind her, and she turned in its direction. She witnessed a distorted wave form mid-air. It then became an outline. Slowly that outline solidified into the oddest-looking man she had ever seen before. She tugged on the steward's sleeves and pointed to the weird man. "Can you see him?"

The blonde man grinned at her. "Eve! Well, now, aren't you adorable. Big brown eyes and chubby cheeks. It is time to wake up."

Eve glared. "I am awake."

"Who are you speaking to?" the steward asked.

"He can't see me. Only you can," the man explained as he slowly approached Eve. When he reached her, he kneeled so that they were at the same height. "Time to wake up."

"Who are you?"

"Why, White Knight, don't you remember your favorite Caoimhghin?"

"White Knight?" Eve repeated. There was a throbbing pain starting behind her eyes, and not long after, she felt as if her head was on fire. She was burning. Her world tilted and blurred. The pain increased to the point where she almost became unconscious. In a rush, all her memories came in a blur. The young girl was blinded by her world turning bright white as she gasped, "Caoimhghin."

She arched and rose up from the cot, gasping for breath. Hands were already pushing her down, but she resisted. The knight struggled against them; she had to. Eve had no idea where she was or if she was in danger. Many voices tried to soothe her confused mind, but it took two hands grabbing the side of her face and the weathered face of Aine before the knight calmed. Behind the old woman was another familiar but not appreciated being— the elf Luthien who had not long ago, and could still, be a spy for Aelfdene.

"You," Eve growled, and she lunged at the elf, hands ready to grab the woman by her neck and squeeze it. Luthien jumped back with a shriek and took off, running between the standing bodies of the other healers. Eve was grabbed by the shoulder and forcefully held from moving off the cot. With Luthien gone, Eve felt the weariness come upon her. She groaned in pain and slowly looked around seeing that she was in a large tent outside. Fresh green grass covered the floor. Cots were lined up in columns and rows, filled with the injured.

"Are you calm?" Aine asked. Eve nodded. "Good." Aine started prodding Eve, checking for breaks and muscle damage. "Only yesterday did I ask for you not to harm yourself. Yet, you did. I believe you have broken the record for medical help compared to all my patients."

"Trouble-friendly," Eve mumbled to the woman. I do not feel injured. No pain. There are aches. There is also this tiredness that wishes to drown me in the arms of Morpheus."

"Being an elemental has advantages— and disadvantages. You are almost healed. Yet have overused your magic. I do not think your powers will be well in a few weeks. Even if you attempted now, your magic will likely not work."

"Is there an earlier time my magic will be accessible?"

"That is my earliest estimation. Suppose you try to use your powers before the given time limit. In that case, you will inevitably die and be reborn an unseelie. I must press to you that you no longer call your magical abilities. No matter the circumstances."

"Not even for Death?"

Aine chose not to answer but rolled her eyes. "The king and queen request your presence in the Great Hall."

"I do not want to grace them with my presence," Eve commented with a scowl.

"Oh, my parents are not so bad," Caoimhghin said. Eve was surprised to find him in the cot next to her. He looked pale and ill. She should have expected his presence as he was the one to take her away from her past.

"That is because you are their son," Eve retorted.

"Touche."

"As riveting as your conversation is, it matters not your feelings, young one. I find you well enough to go," Aine broke in. The healer waved over the two elf guards on patrol. In their hands, they carried lances. With their empty hand, they helped Eve to stand. She pushed them away, feeling she would be alright. Taking one step forward, the young woman's legs buckled as if they didn't want to follow her commands. Eve found herself as weak as a baby.

She was lucky that one elf had the kindness to stay near her. He caught the young woman on her way down, holding her up. The other elf joined in aiding the mortal. With the two guards at her side, Eve managed to exit the tent with the prince waving goodbye.

Out in the world, out on the castle's grounds, the land had seen its fair fight. The surrounding buildings were charred and incomplete. Some rooves were barely held up by two or a single standing wall, with a beam supporting another corner. On the ground were many pools of blood. Eve stopped before one and bent forward, twisting away from her help. Bile rose from her stomach. The young woman heaved, her contents spilling all over the ground. One elf pulled her hair out of the way while his partner patted her back, pulling her up. The stench of iron, blood, and dead bodies still yet to be picked up irritated Eve's senses.

The rest of the walk to the Great Hall took longer than before. They paused when Eve tired and sometimes took a different path when theirs was blocked. She had taken this route before, but rarely. They entered the Great Hall through the side. The door was of average size. Nothing spectacular as the grand doors Eve had entered through before.

As the three of them entered the room, they saw it was devoid of pews, benches, and chairs. It was almost clean and untouched. Eve was grateful to see no droves of spectators in the room. On the royal dais, Oberon and Titania sat together. A step down and in a smaller chair was Petal. Neither of them appeared to have any visible injuries. At their sides, standing at attention, were their guards. Eve's eyes widened when she noticed a lone figure on their knees with a guard— Puck.

Eve had stopped walking unknowingly when she saw the trickster, the elves almost tripping and pitching all of them forward to the floor. She stared dumbly at Puck until the elves pulled her to stand ahead of the fey. She coughed to gain his attention as she walked past him, but nothing. Eve even looked back at Puck many times; still, he did not look up at her. Her eyes furrowed in worry. A cough on the dais had her looking up, and her eyes widened. Standing not that far away with a sharp axe was the executioner. A stoic angry dwarf who disliked anyone alive— or so Eve heard told by the fancy-dressed twittering birds that roamed the castle.

Oberon clapped his hands and started to speak. "Lady Bonel, since your arrival, events have played in a way not seen before and relatively in a short time." Oberon paused before continuing, "Due to our separation from the mortals and arrogance, we have lost sight and paid little attention to those closest to us. Your presence, unexpected, revealed our errors and a betrayal that was close to home. For this, we thank you."

The young woman shuffled, uncomfortable at the thanks. Her unease was not because she was humble. Nay. Eve was waiting for the dread that had yet to come. Usually, when one started a conversation with appreciation, it ended with some punishment— or so she had learned by experience.

"My appreciation does not mean your wrongs are or can be forgotten. In this very hall, you lied to us and continuously lied to my people since your...arrival. You came to us in false pretense and means. This cannot be overlooked."

"Yes, you had aided us when it was most needed, but as a king, I cannot allow you to not be punished. You have friends and are well-loved by them. Aine and my youngest have spoken for you. So, your punishment, I believe, is unconventional."

Oberon sniffled and stated in an authorial tone, "Your loyalty is in question. Your crime is for speaking falsely and helping a known criminal return after having a lifetime ban. Your punishment and your only— ONLY— chance to show where your soul lies is to take the axe my guard holds and behead Puck. Here. Now. If done, your life is mine. You will be one of my closest guards in the household and, for as long as you live, will have my protection. Do as I command, and there will be only one death this day."

*That doesn't seem fair,* Eve thought. The last crime Eve was accused of was incorrect. Yes, the young woman had lied. She had worked with a man to steal, but she had no idea that breaking the dagger would bring Puck back to his home. He had held back that pertinent information. His unexpected arrival, though, was a blessing. Eve doubted any of the royals and herself would have survived without his return. So, logically, she owned the fey her life. The young woman slowly dropped to her knees with a grimace. "Execute me now. I will not kill this idiot man, nor will I accept the last crime. I accept my fate, though a bit reluctantly."

Eve lowered her head and gulped. She waited to hear the

footstep of the executioner come ever closer and for her head to roll soon on the ground. That did not happen. Instead, after moments of silence, there was clapping. Her head rose to see the royal family with smiles on their faces.

Titania said, "You have passed."

"What?!" Puck and Eve asked simultaneously. The two were pleased to see that they were not the only confused individuals in the room. The guards looked at each other and then at the calm royal members. They also did not know what to do. The dwarf had even dropped his axe, his mouth slipping open.

"Attention!" Petal shouted.

"Puck," Oberon called. "Stand."

The fey slowly stood, apprehensive, waiting for someone to attack him. To his surprise, King Oberon commanded one of the guards to remove his shackles. Eve watched in interest and laughed at the disappointed look on the executioner's face. He angrily threw his axe to the ground and left in a huff, his cheeks puffy.

The guard who had released Puck roughly pushed the fey forward. Puck stood merrily at Eve's side. She nodded at him warmly, and he smiled back at her manically. Unexpectedly, Eve giggled from surprise as Puck hugged her firmly, lifting her up and spinning her in a circle before letting her go. "Thank you! This Puck is indebted to you."

"More than you can imagine," Oberon broke in, his eyes flicking between the two. "Puck is indeed free...but with conditions." Puck's face fell to shock and sadness. Eve could only hope she wasn't damned as she believed she was and that the "conditions" Oberon mentioned had nothing to do with her.

"Before the conditions are given, there is an answer I need to know, Lady Bonel," Oberon said, turning his gaze upon Eve.

*No. Please do not do what I believe you shall do. Oberon would not,* Eve hoped.

"A reward for your loyalty at saving my kingdom must be given. What do you desire? Ask, and I shall do my best to fill your want."

Eve wanted what she had wanted when she had arrived: to embark on one last adventure and then go home. One was now fulfilled, and the other still called for her but for another purpose. "I am grateful for all you have done. I am already content with viewing with my own eyes that few would see. Yet, for so long, my path has been advised and decided by others. To this, I can no longer abide it. So, my wish is to go home and find my mother."

"Has she not expired?" Oberon inquired.

"I was told so, but seeing the strength of your kind, I believe her death is false."

"We cannot allow this," Titania said. By the looks on Oberon and Petal's faces, they were not expecting those words from the queen. Eve's eyes narrowed on the woman as the queen continued, "I understand your *need* to see your mother, to find her, but...if you are unseelie, then she is. Additionally, you know how to reach us. How do we know you will not bring your kind to this world?"

"I don't like them," Eve bluntly answered, causing Puck to snigger at her side.

"And we only have your word," Titania said with a final tone.

Eve went to defend her character, but Petal did it for her. "Lady Bonel has shown that there is hope for the mortals. Yes, we taught them the foundation that helped them rise for them to later go against us. Their minds had not been ready for progression, and we had moved too quickly to teach them our ways. Neither were we ready when the hybrids were born. But this mortal is. So, to soothe your mind of deceit, perhaps there is a compromise. We have a problem and Lady Bonel wants to search for her mother. Both are aboveworld."

"Impossible," Puck commented. "Those *monsters* are spread out through her world and not only by location. They have been spread throughout time itself. It will take years for the girl to find them."

"Time? Years?" Eve squeaked. "What do you mean?— and I am not a girl!"

"Past, present, and future," Puck quickly answered as if time traveling was nothing and not even apologizing for calling her girl.

"I doubt her dear ole' mum stayed in place— or time. What fun would that be?" Petal countered.

"Unseelie cannot travel in such ways. They do not possess such gifts."

"I believe this one does."

"Impossible."

"Lady Bonel has elemental gifts, darkness, and our strengths and weaknesses— "

"She can handle iron," Oberon cut in.

Petal went back to speaking, "That itself shows the uniqueness of such a creature. It posed mortal and married. It had a child. It must be of mother's side to manage such a feat."

"There is no other like me," Titania informed.

"That is not true. Your brother disproved that," Eve snapped back. "He may be all shadow and evil, but who are we to know he can't transform to look like you? He was leading the unseelies with his facilities— his mind— still intact." The edges of Titania's lips tightened in disproval; however, Eve cared not. She only spoke the truth.

"If your mother was— is— such as the man I once considered a brother, can you kill her?" Oberon questioned.

"If she is beyond saving— yes."

"Then we are in accord."

"Pardon?"

# CHAPTER 26

EVE DIDN'T REMEMBER agreeing to any terms. She kept asking what was happening, but Oberon ignored her baffled state. She didn't know what was going on or what the king was thinking. A proposition had not even been made.

The young woman had an inkling though what the agreement was to be. She would like to hear it confirmed by the king and queen that they were of the same mind as what was being asked of her. As far as Eve understood, she would be sent back home to hunt and kill unseelies. At the same time, she would be looking for her mother. How did they expect her to do both and know which location to be at? Then, Puck mentioned time. As far as Eve knew, only God had the capability to travel and see the past, present, and future.

"You will be returning home and Puck with you. You will know what actions and moves to make when the time comes. There are two ways to travel in the means needed for your and our purpose. One method requires a royal family member to accompany you, which is impossible. We have an ancient artifact that works only for descendants of my wife and me.

"The other option is to travel inside an enchanted transportation device. It will suit your needs better," Oberon swiftly informed. "Though I must warn you, this method has some problems."

"I have not agreed with anything," Eve pointed out. She was ignored.

Oberon explained that the transportation did not go where one demanded it to. Sometimes, it would bring the user to places where a critical individual awaited to live or die. That individual was necessary for humanity to change. Eve couldn't help but wonder many things with that given explanation. What if the person was evil? What if the person was good and had to die? Why couldn't one change history? The young woman thought of the countless people that could be saved, that didn't need to pass yet, which was apparently "necessary".

Oberon continued to talk, but Eve didn't pay attention. She was confused, angry and close to bursting into tears. Why would evil be needed to change humanity? It isn't like people ever change. In her short life, people only seem to get worse and smile at the death of others, including the end of those who did nothing wrong. The young woman wondered if this necessity had occurred in her lifetime.

"Rest today. Tomorrow you shall leave," Oberon ended. He stood and left, his family following afterward.

"You two may head to the given rooms and sleep," the elf guard told Puck and Eve.

"I was lost in thought. I missed many things. What rooms? And— I did not agree to anything said," Eve told the guard. He glared at her. The other guards trickled out of the room. "If Oberon expects me to go on this *compromise*, he is wrong."

"You must be joking," Puck said, placing his hands on his hips. "I am stuck with you until it is deemed I have done enough to gain my freedom."

"About that, I believe— no, not believe— know, you did not tell me all."

"I did so!"

"Did not, you fool."

"What did I not tell?"

"Oh! That I am hybrid."

"I wasn't sure that was true," Puck defended.

"Liar," Eve scoffed.

"As far as I knew, hybrids had all been destroyed."

Eve narrowed her eyes, crowing her hands over her chest, leaning to one side. "If you say so. Either way, you did not inform me of the significance of the glass dagger."

Puck smiled sheepishly. "Well, you didn't believe in magic. There was no point telling my whole story."

Eve rushed to wrangle the fool's neck with her hands, a growl escaping her lips and her arms outstretched. The elf guard grabbed her by the waist, holding her tightly. Eve kicked at her captor, but he was firm for a slim frame. Puck stood still in shock, not expecting the attack.

"Stop moving," the elf guard ordered Eve. "You will only strain yourself. Like the fool said, if you did not believe at first, there was no point in telling you the terms of his banishment. Now, if I have to, I will drag and tie you to the bed you are posed to rest in tonight. It is your choice to sleep or not."

Eve stopped her attack and turned to look at the fey behind her. "Rest for what?"

Puck chuckled as the guard groaned. "You really were not paying attention," Puck said.

"Oi! I did. Sort of."

The guard shook his head. He dragged Eve out of the room with Puck walking behind them. Tomorrow, they would leave to hunt down the unseelie who had escaped to the world above. Eve sputtered that she had not agreed to such an adventure. The guard ignored her protests all the way to the room and the same protest she made again when he once more brought her out of the room. Puck came out of the room next to her, bleary-eyed and yawning.

He heard Eve's complaining and commented," They don't care. Can you not be silent? It is too early to argue." The young woman glared at him. She walked beside Puck, silent and fuming.

The group reached the Great Hall. Eve and Puck were

*kindly* pushed forward and surrounded by guards. Eve scoffed. The protection was not needed. She couldn't use any of her *gifts*, and she had no weapons. She was harmless to the royal family who awaited them. She was pleased to see Caoimhghin present, looking better than he had yesterday.

Oberon clapped his hands and merrily started the day with a "Good morning."

The group mumbled the exact phrase back or similar to the king. Eve eyed them with jealousy. Most of the individuals were wide awake and ready to start the day. The knight wanted to sleep and was feeling apprehensive. A disgusting combination. The feeling confused her soul and heart. The apprehension wanted to push her exhausted heart awake and it was beating faster than was healthy. This created an uncomfortable ache in her chest. Eve rubbed her eyes and shook her head to push her body to match the alertness of her heart. Confusingly, she followed the group to a small side door she had never seen before.

The queen waved her hand, and the door opened. Oberon then snapped his fingers, and rows of torches lit inside the room to show a long hall with stairs heading down. He started his descent, and the others followed. Eve noticed the air become colder and more humid. Further on, the walls wept from water staining their surface. Afterward, she heard the lapping of a tide hitting the ground. Her mouth opened in shock as they entered a long cave with a shore and a river stretched out in both directions to an unseen ending.

There was a dock with rows of skiffs tied up that could hold six to eight individuals. They moved up and down with the waves. They looked sturdy as far as Eve could see. Her knowledge of floatation devices was a failing subject on her account. She never needed to ride on one to get from one location to the next. She preferred traveling by land.

Oberon smiled at Puck and Eve. "This boat will aid you. It has been magicked with ancient words. It is Fate and Destiny itself. It will take you where you are needed but not where you want to be. It will be your support. Your ally. Are you prepared to leave?"

"Puck is to be my companion?"

"Puck has been placed in a life debt to you. His powers will be linked to your needs and survival. With this boat, you will travel to yours and possibly back to my world, depending on where Fate deems necessary. During these travels, you will kill the unseelie and find clues about your mother's location. Once the unseelie are dead, at the time, if you had not found your mother, you can come back here or continue your search yourself."

Eve finally accepted that she would carry out these new adventures as nothing she said could change the minds of those in power. Yet, she would not do it without something to defend herself with. "My weapons?" Eve asked. "I will not leave without what I came with." Oberon looked to his daughter and cocked his head to one of the skiffs. Petal snapped her fingers, and Eve watched as her weapons and provisions appeared in the middle of the boat. Eve looked to Puck. "Let us be on our way."

Puck nodded and slowly entered the boat. He was not in a rush to leave home again and wondered how long his departure would last this time. He gave one longing glance to his people before turning away from them. The fey patiently waited for Eve and hoped she would take her time.

She respectfully bowed to the king and thanked Petal. She gave Caoimhghin her goodbye with a long hug. To the queen— Eve did not know how to react. So, she walked to Titania and started to bow but was surprised when the woman pulled her into a hug. Then, the queen whispered in Eve's ear, and the young woman's being was swept with a calming sensation before being let go. Eve pulled away and realized that her clothing had been changed to the ones she had arrived in. A grateful feeling filled her chest at the gesture from the woman. Tears almost came upon her as the queen placed a cloak over her shoulders, keeping the cold at bay. Another cloak was placed in her hands. It was for Puck.

"When you still have not found a home, and if you have not found your mother, remember— " Petal started.

"You are welcomed here," Oberon finished. "If you come

upon problems, Puck should be able to assist you. In case, though, in your provisions, there is a mirror. Call if you need help or advice, and we will appear."

Eve grinned at them and jogged to the boat. She looked at it uneasily. The young woman scolded herself. It has been years since being on a skiff, and perhaps the sickness has eased. Puck helped her enter their transportation after seeing her hesitate to come on board. He grabbed the cloak from her hands before encouraging her inside onto a seat facing him. After making sure Eve was comfortable, Puck put his own cloak on and looked at the broach that held it together. It was a sword with a unity symbol. It was to tell those from the underground, living above, their status of importance to the royal family. Puck felt heat rise to his cheeks to wear the symbol once more upon his form.

Eve was still silent in front of him, and Puck looked at her curiously. He whispered to his companion to untie them from the dock, but she didn't reply. He was surprised to see the young woman so unlike herself and pale. Puck rose a little without ado and unwrapped the rope from the line. Once done, he took a paddle and pushed them away from the wooden platform. The further they moved, a thick mist started to grow. The adventurers were quickly enveloped in it and could only see themselves.

"Farewell once more, sweet home," Puck muttered, his voice loud in the silence. He looked to Eve, thinking he would find her ecstatic and eager. That was not the case. She started perspiring, her pale complexion turning a sickly milky white.

Eve was sick. Her stomach spasmed as the boat hit, what she believed, was a strong wave. In reality, it was a small bump. Her hands clenched tightly. Her heart was beating erratically in fear of the boat tipping over. She dared not look over the edge of the boat unless she wished to be pulled into a deep hole of dizziness.

"You don't look well," Puck observed.

"I don't like boats...or water." He looked at her questioningly. "I learned at an early age that I do not float. I sink."

"You have to be kidding me."

"Make sure I do not fall," Eve blurted before she went to her side to expel bile into the waters.

"You have to be kidding me!" Puck shouted as he rushed to her side and comforted her from her illness. He pulled her back to her seat and watched as she wiped her mouth with her sleeve. "Why did you not say something?"

"*Veni, Vidi, Vici,*" Eve mumbled. "I came. I saw. I conquered. By admitting to my weakness is not what others would see as conquering. If I can't face my fear, I shall not fare well the rest of our journey."

"You fool of a warrior," Puck chortled.

"Indeed," Eve said in agreement before she moved again to vomit into the waters. Feeling her stomach had finally emptied, the knight returned to her seat and attempted to relax. "Now, what happens next?"

"We wait for the boat to take us to our fate," Puck answered.

"Oh, bloody brilliant," Eve sarcastically retorted. Then, oddly, she heard the sound of a horse in the waters but saw nothing. No land. No creature. She squinted her eyes but, still, nothing. "You hear that?"

"Hear what?" Puck inquired. "I heard nothing."

Eve was about to tell Puck about the sound of a horse neighing, but couldn't as the boat hit a rough wave, causing her almost to fall back from her seat. She cursed angrily as nausea dared to rise again. Puck laughed at her anger. "I wish we had at least some captain or someone who knows a thing or two about the water and sailing. Neither of us is a sailor."

"We will do well ourselves," Puck told her with a roll of his eyes.

Then a deep Scottish brood shouted to the east at them. "Who is out there? Do you need help?!"

Eve and Puck looked at each other. Then, up as drops of water fell upon them. Soon it was raining heavily, soaking into their clothes. The wind pushed them from side to side, forcing them to hold on to the edges of their streets. The mist lifted a little. In the distance, there was light.

"What is happening?!" Eve shouted.

"I believe our next adventure!"

# A NOTE TO MY READERS

All artwork/illustrations are done by myself, drawn by hand and digitally colored in. Posters and prints will be available to purchase soon on my website. Please do not hesitate to follow and share my works. I am looking to start a fanbase for a series that is new and unique.

I wish to thank will all of my heart and soul to those who have read my novel. This is my first fiction novel I have self-published. I shall not stop writing and will put forth more of my works for reading to bring new worlds and entertainment to the masses. I hope you enjoy the adventures of my characters and many others that will come later.

# COMPLETED WORKS

*VENI, VIDI, VICI: The Quest* (Book 1)

# EDITING STAGE

*APOPHIS AFTERMATH: Syndicate Rebels* (Book 1)

# DRAFT/WRITING STAGE

*VENI, VIDI, VICI: The Kelpies' Curse* (Book 2)

*VENI, VIDI, VICI: TBA* (Book 3)

*WERID WORLD SERIES: TBA* (Book 1)

*TBA: Horror Anthology*

LORENA C. MONROY

Born and raised in Texas, Lorena Monroy graduated from the University of Texas at El Paso with a Bachelor of Science in Physics. Has taken courses in Mechanical and Aerospace Engineering at New Mexico State University. She has three co-published works in the science community in high-energy astrophysics with binary black holes and magnetic cataclysmic white dwarves. She has always written stories and drawn on the side of her studies and work. Her dreams is to travel into space, become a best-seller, and see her works in the movies or television.

WEBSITE: www.sketch-art.net  @sketchfly  @sketchflygirl

www.ingramcontent.com/pod-product-compliance
Lightning Source LLC
Chambersburg PA
CBHW061948170626
46813CB00006B/2572
* 9 7 9 8 9 8 7 6 2 2 7 2 8 *